SUCCUBUS

Written by Brandon Blake Varnell
Edited by Linda Branam
Illustrated by Lawrence Mann

CONTENT

Chapter 1...1
Chapter 2..27
Chapter 3..43
Chapter 4..57
Chapter 5..69
Chapter 6..79
Chapter 7..99
Chapter 8...111
Chapter 9...119
Chapter 10..131
Chapter 11..139
Chapter 12..151
Chapter 13..157
Chapter 14..167
Chapter 15..175
Chapter 16..187
Chapter 17..197
Chapter 18..209
Chapter 19..215
Chapter 20..221
Chapter 21..225
Chapter 22..235
Chapter 23..243
Chapter 24..251
Chapter 25..259
Chapter 26..271
Chapter 27..293
Chapter 28..299

Chapter 1

It started with a phone call.

Christian glared at the phone on the nightstand, which loudly blared *AC/DC* from its speakers. The noise startled Lilith, who lifted her head to search for the source of the music. Her blond hair swished as she looked around before, like moths being drawn to a flame, her blue eyes landed on the object vibrating its way across the wooden surface.

"Lilith," Christian said, making the girl turn from the cell phone to him. "Would you mind letting me up so I can get that?"

"Oh, sure." Lilith got up slowly, reluctantly. She seemed quite content to remain where she was. Truth be told, so was Christian, but he also knew he had to get that call. Tristin would never let him hear the end of it if he didn't.

Picking up the phone, Christian made his way into the restroom, where he accepted the call and held the mobile device to his ears.

"Tristin."

"Man, is it good to hear from you!" Tristin sounded just as exuberant as always, but Christian couldn't help but feel like there was something forced about it. *"All of us were pretty worried about you, you know? I was biting my nails when I heard you were going toe-to-toe with a No Life King.*

Seriously dude, you really know how to make people wanna shit their pants. Even Samantha has been showing more emotion than I ever expected to see out of her."

"Is there a reason you're calling?" asked Christian. "Or are you just calling to annoy me?"

"A little bit of both, I guess." Christian resisted a sigh. At least the guy was honest. *"It might not seem like much time has passed since the last time we spoke, but it's been a week for me. I've missed bantering with my favorite Executioner."*

"Whatever." Christian smiled in spite of himself. He would never tell Tristin this—or anyone else, for that matter—but he was actually going to miss the annoying intelligence operative after he quit the Executioners. "Please just get to the reason you decided to call me. I really want to get back to sleep."

… Silence.

"Tristin?"

"I'm sorry." Tristin sounded so apologetic that Christian nearly did a double-take.

"Sorry? What are you apologizing for?"

"I have some news, Christian, and you're not going to like it."

"I'll be the judge of that. Now spit it out already."

There was another second of silence. The tension within that small bathroom thickened to the point where Christian could sense it hanging in the air like a plague.

Just as the overbearing pressure was beginning to become intolerable, Tristin said the words that caused Christian's entire world to come crashing down.

"Christian, Lilith is a succubus. You've been ordered to execute her immediately."

This had to be a joke.

"Christian?"

Yes, this was a joke. Just one big joke.

"Christian? Christian!"

Christian stared at the phone in uncomprehending disbelief. Had he heard right? Lilith was a succubus? Impossible. He had spent nearly a full month with the girl and not once had she given any indication of being a succubus, not once had he felt the pull of her allure. What's more, he was still alive. He and Lilith had already slept together, but he wasn't dead. His life hadn't been drained. There was simply no way she could be a succubus…

Right?

"Christian! Answer me! Are you there!?"

Shaking himself out of his stupor, Christian put the phone to his ear again and said, "I'm here."

"Finally!" Tristin exhaled a long breath. *"Look, Christian, I know this is tough for you. Hell, I'm not particularly enamored with the situation myself. I really do hate to be the bearer of bad news. I know how fond you are of Lilith."*

Fond of Lilith? That was putting it very mildly. Christian had been planning to quit the Executioners to be with her.

That was impossible now. Even if, on the off chance, the Church did allow him to go free, they would never allow him to be with Lilith. If she really was a succubus, any hope of attaining that Happily Ever After that he'd read about in books and Japanese light novels would be lost.

"Tristin..." Christian hesitated, afraid. He only continued speaking because he needed to know. "Are you sure Lilith's a succubus? I mean, really sure?"

"Yes." A sigh came from the other end. *"I'm positive. I've compiled a document that contains several incidents where her allure ran out of control. There are, well, there are quite a few, to be perfectly honest. It seems Lilith has an exceptionally powerful allure."*

"But that's impossible. I've been with Lilith for nearly a month now, and I haven't felt her allure even once!"

There was no way he could believe Tristin. If Lilith's Aura of Allure really was that strong, then he would have been affected by it. He would have felt it.

"I don't know what to tell you. There have been documented cases where a man has proven to be immune to a succubus's allure. It's rare. Like, only one in every five-million men have this immunity, but it's not wholly unheard of. You might just be one of those lucky few who are immune."

Immunity? Now that he thought about it, Christian did remember how all the men around Lilith acted like they were possessed. More specifically, he recalled the incident during his and Lilith's first time out, when they had been surrounded by men that had been acting like zombies going after brains. That was not normal behavior. Not even Lilith's unnatural beauty could account for that many males acting like that.

There was also Lilith's beauty to think about. The girl was beyond gorgeous. Everything about her, from her figure to her facial features and hair was perfect. Too perfect. Humans were flawed creatures. Every human in existence had some kind of flaw, something that was inherently wrong with them, physically, mentally, spiritually. There was no such thing as perfection as far as humanity went.

Lilith did not have a single physical flaw. Even her face was perfectly symmetrical.

Succubi were the physical embodiment of lust. It was a prerequisite for them to be shaped in the form of a woman whose beauty was so perfect, they couldn't possibly be human. Lilith met and exceeded that requirement, and yet...

There's no way.

There were other possibilities. It wasn't like attracting men could only be done with a succubus's allure. She could have been cursed. The No Life King could have easily placed a curse on her.

Those were his thoughts, until he remembered Lilith telling him about her teacher in middle school, the one who'd tried to rape her. That happened before she met the No Life King. It wasn't the only incident either. Before that, many boys had shown an unnatural interest in her, hadn't they?

"Christian?"

"I... I understand. Tell Headquarters that I'll... that I'll deal with her." The words tasted like ash in his mouth.

"I'll be sure to inform them. And Christian? I am sorry about this."

As the line went dead, Christian brought the phone back down and looked at it. Huh. He'd never expected to hear such sincerity from Tristin. Perhaps he really was remorseful. Not that it mattered. Remorse wouldn't help him.

Christian walked back into the bedroom. Lilith was still there, sitting on the bed, her legs crossed and her hands in her lap as she leaned against the headboard. She was wearing a nightgown that showed off the gentle swell of her breasts. Blonde hair fell about her face, slightly messy from their lovemaking a few minutes before Tristin had called. Pink lips were slightly bruised from the amount of kissing they had done, but she wore a pleasant smile as she hummed to herself.

The moment her eyes landed on him, her face lit up in a way that put spotlights to shame.

It made his stomach clench unpleasantly.

"You're back. Did your talk go well?"

"I'm... I suppose so." Christian grimaced.

Lilith must have sensed his reticence. "Is there something wrong?"

Yes, something was wrong. Very wrong. He'd been ordered to kill her, to take the life of the girl he'd fallen in love with. This was like a sick, twisted romantic tragedy. That, or God had decided to punish him for falling in love with a succubus.

"Christian?" Lilith climbed out of bed and walked over to him, her bare feet padding along the carpet. She stopped in front of him, hesitated for a second, then reached out and grabbed his hands. "What's wrong?"

Plenty. There were a lot of things wrong about this situation, more than he could even begin to fathom. He'd been given an order to kill Lilith. He'd told Tristin that he would take care of her, but now, standing there with her, Christian didn't know if he could go through with it.

Christian was sure that, should he kill Lilith, he would come to regret it for the rest of his life. Even if he hadn't fallen in love with her, he was positive that he would have forever felt discontent, sickened by it.

Lilith wasn't evil. Despite being a succubus, the girl was as pure and innocent as they came. She'd never done anything wrong. If anything, it was humanity that had wronged her.

She didn't deserve to die, but the consequences of not killing her were extreme. To disregard one's duty as an Executioner was one of the most heinous of crimes a person could commit in the organization, to actively go against the Executioners was the ultimate sin. The repercussions for such a decision was worse than death.

Worse still, if Christian decided not to kill her and run, they would be hunted to the ends of the earth. Lilith was a succubus, and he would be branded a traitor. Traitors were killed with the same mercilessness as abominations.

Members of the Executioners, especially those who were as powerful as him, knew many secrets. These secrets, if they became public knowledge, could easily cause the Catholic Church to crumble from within. That wasn't even going into what the people who were not members of the Church would do. The amount of chaos that could be unleashed from the secrets he possessed was astronomical.

They would go after him with more zeal than they did with any monster, of that he was sure.

"Christian?"

What should he do? He looked at the vision of beauty before him, at the way she stared into his eyes with heart-melting concern, at the tiny frown on her lips, at her hands as they curled around his with such tenderness. Could he kill her? Could he really take her life? Did he have it in him to end her without a second thought now that he knew who she was, what she was like, and that she was not evil?

"Christian?" Blinking several times, he focused back on Lilith. Her eyes, clearer and more vast than the sky, stared at him with worry. "Something's wrong, isn't it? Please tell me. Maybe I can help."

As he stared into those two pools of baby blue, Christian found the answer to his question.

No. He would not, could not, absolutely refused to kill Lilith. Even if it meant living a life on the run, taking her life was something he couldn't do.

"Lilith." Christian stared at her, searching. "Do you trust me?"

"Yes."

Not a moment's hesitation. Christian found himself stunned by how implicitly she seemed to trust him. Had anyone else ever given him that kind of trust? Samantha trusted him, but not to the point where she would share everything with him, not to the point where she would not at least hesitate before stating her faith in him. This girl, whom he had only met around one month ago, already trusted him to the point where she would unhesitatingly state her confidence in him.

Even if he had not fallen in love, Christian would not have been able to kill someone who had such trust in him. He couldn't use a person's trust to kill them like an Assassin did.

"Then get dressed and come with me. We need to leave here."

Lilith's immediate reply of, "Okay," was just another way of showing the trust that she placed in him.

Christian vowed to make sure that her trust was never misplaced.

***

Upon cleaning out his room and placing everything he felt they would need in the case he'd been given by the Executioners, Christian and Lilith walked out of the hotel. On their way out, the hostess bade them a short goodbye, waving at the pair as they left. It wasn't long after they exited the large building that the two found themselves walking along the sidewalk, a large black trunk trailing behind them.

The jean shorts that Lilith wore conformed to her bottom and reveled in showing off her long legs. Her shirt, a sleeveless white T-shirt with an image of Holo the Wisewolf on the front, stretched across her bust. It wasn't something that she normally wore. This just happened to be the only outfit she had on hand.

Because Christian had opted to wear his Executioner clothing; black pants and long-sleeve shirt, combat boots, and a long traveling cloak that reached his ankles, he received a few odd looks from the people passing by. A large number of people were gawking at him, their mouths hanging open and their eyes wide. He did his best to ignore them. Most of his weapons were hidden somewhere on his person. Wearing regular clothes ran the risk of giving others a glimpse of his armory.

The only weapons not currently on his person were his two swords, Michael and Gabrielle. He wished he could have worn them. He felt more comfortable when they were within reach. It was too bad having a couple of large swords strapped across his back would look suspicious.

As they walked through the city, Christian made sure to stick to the most populated areas; the shopping district, the strip mall, and anywhere else he could think of where there would be a large crowd. It was early in the morning, but there was still a decent number of people wandering about. They wandered streets, walked down the sidewalks, some heading to work, while others appeared to be enjoying the morning air.

Lilith stuck close to him the whole time. He knew that she wasn't comfortable being surrounded by so many people, especially when at least half of them were men. She was enduring this for him. That knowledge made his heart beat faster.

In response to her walking so near, Christian slid his free arm around her waist and pulled her closer. It would cause a few problems if he found himself needing to draw his weapons quickly, but with her being so willing to follow him without question, he found that he could do nothing less than make her feel as comfortable and safe as possible.

Besides, the smile she gave him when he put his arm around her waist made it all worthwhile.

This is interesting...

As they passed a group of men who looked to be in their twenties, he noticed something odd. While they did indeed glance at Lilith, most of them were looking at him, not her. Before, whenever Lilith went out, men flocked to her like women flocked to Touma Kamijou.

This doesn't make sense. Isn't she a succubus?

"Christian?"

Christian snapped out of his stupor and glanced at Lilith. "Yes?"

"I was just wondering if I could call Maria and let her know that I'm leaving?"

The words that were on the tip of his tongue stilled before he could give his first response, which was an adamant no. Instead of denying her the right to reassure her friend that she would be leaving, he contemplated the question and, within his mind, listed the pros and cons found within the two responses he could give.

If he allowed Lilith to call her friend, it could put the woman in danger. Maria was a human, however, she had allowed a succubus to live with her. The mere fact that she had befriended an abomination was enough for the Church to take her in for questioning. They wouldn't kill her, but it would still be a traumatizing experience.

Maria was already in enough danger thanks to them. Christian didn't want to add to that danger by allowing Lilith to talk to her as they were making their escape. The less the young woman knew about their situation, the better.

"Not… right now," Christian eventually said. "We'll contact her in a few days, after everything dies down, and you can let her know you're doing well then."

He couldn't deny Lilith's desire to inform her friend that she was safe. At the same time, it would be best if they waited a while, like after the Church had finished questioning Maria. If the Executioners followed standard procedure, the young woman would be one of the first people within Seal Beach to come under scrutiny once they realized that he and Lilith were gone.

"I… yes, that's fine, I guess."

Noticing the downtrodden expression on Lilith's face, Christian leaned down until his lips were practically kissing her ear. "I'm sorry. I normally wouldn't have a problem with you calling your friend, but we're in a precarious situation right now, or we will be soon."

Looking mildly alarmed, Lilith asked, "are we in danger?"

"Not yet, but it's only a matter of time." When he saw the alarmed look that Lilith was giving him, he added, "I'll explain once we're on the train."

Lilith gave him a nod followed by a soft smile. "I understand. I'll wait."

"Thank you."

Once again, Christian marveled at the trust that she was placing in him. Despite the dangers they were facing, or were about to face, he could not help but think that he was one of the luckiest men in the world.

When did I become such a sap?

***

The first order of business was to ditch his cellphone. All Executioner cellphones had tracking devices in them, which meant that it was a moot point to try to escape with one. He ended up slipping it into the jacket pocket of a person who was passing by. That would throw off any pursuers for a while, at least.

His second order of business was gathering funds. It cost money to travel, not just paying for train tickets and whatever other methods of transportation they decided to use, but also food and sleeping arrangements. Despite having traveled many times in the past, Christian was unsure of how much everything was going to cost. He didn't know how long they would be on the run.

Walking up to the nearest bank, Christian and Lilith stood in front of an ATM machine. One of the benefits that came with working for the Catholic Church was that each member of the Executioners had a credit card with a $3,000 limit to fund their expenses while on a mission. While the Church would likely suspend his card once they learned that he had fled with Lilith, they did not know what he was doing right now. The card should still work. Hopefully.

It was a pleasant surprise to Christian when he found out that the card did indeed still work. He proceeded to use the rest of his limit on acquiring cash. Because he had already spent money on food, clothing, and light novels, they only managed to acquire $2,565.89, which wasn't much if he wanted to do a lot of traveling. He hoped it would last them until they were out of the state.

That was Christian's first goal: leave California. He had no idea where they would go after that, but California was where the Headquarters for the entire Western Division of the Executioners was located. Leaving the state was the most logical choice.

As they made their way toward the train station, which was about a half-an-hour's walk, Christian kept a careful eye out for anyone who might be following them. While unlikely because, as far as he was aware, he was currently the only Executioner in Seal Beach, it was not impossible that Samantha had sent someone in secret in case he needed backup. That wasn't standard protocol, but she'd done it before on his first mission after the battle with Abaddon. Given that he'd been up against a No Life King this time, she could have very well done it again.

Yet as he observed his surroundings with keen eyes, he saw no one that triggered warning bells in his head. None of the people surrounding him gave off the dangerous vibe that a member of the Executioners would have. He also didn't spot anyone on the roofs of the buildings.

He was still careful, though. Just because he couldn't see anybody didn't mean they weren't there. If Samantha had sent a member of the Assassins, they could be anywhere and he wouldn't know it. They were masters of stealth, which he was most assuredly not. This was also why he stuck to the crowds. Assassin or not, no one would be able to sneak up on them in a crowd like this.

Paranoid? Maybe, but he would rather be safe than sorry. Constant vigilance and all that.

It amazed Christian that there were still so many people around. Just a few days ago everything had been in lockdown, people had been in a panic, either staying in their homes or trying to leave as soon as possible. They hadn't been able to flee, due to police interference, but he would have expected people to be rushing back to wherever they lived the moment that the city-wide lockdown was lifted.

It just went to show Christian how odd some of humanity's greater traits were. That they could be so frightened one day and not show any signs of having been terrified the next was a phenomena unique to their race.

Humans were a strange breed indeed.

Because Seal Beach was a small city, the train station wasn't large. There were four tracks for trains to come in and go, and the station itself only consisted of several small buildings: a ticket booth, a souvenir shop, and a small strip that had several fast-food restaurants.

It also wasn't crowded at the moment. The crowd had thinned out the closer they got to the station. Christian became even more alert and cautious the nearer they got. If there was someone from the Executioners tailing them, this would be the time they struck.

Most fortunately for Christian and Lilith, there wasn't anybody from the Executioners following them. They weren't attacked, they weren't followed. It seemed his fears were unfounded.

However, there was someone else who spotted them.

"Christian? Lilith? What are you two doing here?"

Turning around, Christian took his arm from Lilith's waist and prepared for possible combat. He moved in front of Lilith, just slightly, to make himself the better target. With Lilith as protected as could be, given the circumstances, he looked at Catherine as she walked down the stairs that led to the boarding platform. He relaxed upon recognizing her.

"Catherine. I didn't expect to see you here."

"And where did you expect to see me? An amusement park? Perhaps the beach?" Catherine sounded amused and curious. Her eyes flickered between Christian and Lilith several times. She looked at them as one might stare at a puzzle. "While most of the SIU has been relocated back to Los Angeles, a few of us were told to remain on standby, just in case."

Christian gave a nod. "Understandable, I guess." He scrutinized the woman. "You seem a bit more relaxed since the last time I saw you."

"I'm off-duty right now," Catherine replied, running a hand through her hair. "I was actually just seeing some of my men off. The LAPD is making us leave in small groups of three and four. Don't know why, but there you go." Now it was her turn to look at them. "I think the real question is: what are you two doing here?"

Christian tried to think up an excuse as to why he and Lilith would be at the train station. Unfortunately, Christian was a terrible liar. Everybody always said so. Tristin had once said that he couldn't tell a lie even if his chastity depended on it. Just what his chastity—former chastity—had to do with lying was something he was still trying to figure out.

It was probably just Tristin being Tristin.

Fortunately for both him and Lilith, while he might be a terrible liar, Lilith was at least able to think up a good excuse on the spot.

"I've decided to go back with Christian," she told Catherine, smiling in that radiant way of hers. "After everything that's happened between us, I couldn't bear to be apart from him."

Christian could have kissed Lilith for coming up with such an excellent excuse. It contained enough truth that Catherine was unlikely to suspect a thing. It was also vague, which could only be a good thing in this instance. Catherine was likely drawing her own conclusions from Lilith's words and wouldn't question them too much. And because no one outside of the Executioners knew anything about the group, the woman couldn't possibly know that relationships were not allowed.

She also didn't know that Lilith was a succubus, which was a plus.

"Ah," Catherine said, smiling. "I suppose I should have expected that. You two care for each other an awful lot. It would only make sense that you wouldn't want to part ways now." She looked off to the left, where a large clock was sitting on a building showing the time: 8:23am. The woman then looked back at Christian and Lilith. "Well, I guess this is it, then. I wish you both the best."

"Yeah." Christian raised a hand in farewell as Lilith waved and smiled. "See you around."

He and Lilith watched as Catherine left. When the woman entered her car, another military-grade ATV, and took off down the road, they breathed a sigh of relief.

"That was too close," Lilith said.

Christian could not help but nod. "Agreed."

***

Lilith sat next to Christian on one of several benches that were evenly spaced across the platform. They had bought their train tickets a while ago. Christian had told her that they would be making their way to Santa Clarica via several trains. Apparently, there was no train that could take them from

Seal Beach straight to Santa Clarica, though he had also mentioned that taking one train the entire way was a terrible idea anyway.

She didn't know where they would be going after that, but she suspected that Christian would tell her once he figured it out. He probably didn't know where their final destination was either.

The train station was much busier now that it was nearing the middle of the day. There were many people standing around as they waited for their train to arrive. A few had gotten the smart idea to follow Christian's and Lilith's lead and were sitting down on one of the benches.

As she looked at him from the corner of her eye, Lilith saw Christian staring at the map he'd placed in his lap, his brow furrowed as he bit his lower lip. The index finger of his left hand traced a path across the map. Sometimes he would stop, his raven hair swaying as he shook his head, mutter something, and then start over again.

He was clearly trying to determine their itinerary.

Equally clear was that he was beginning to get frustrated.

"Why don't you stop looking at that map and relax for a bit?" Lilith suggested, taking the map from his lap and folding it up. Christian looked at her, surprised. It was only after she put the map in the pocket of the jacket he'd given to her that he snapped out of his stupor.

"I was looking at that, you know." There was no heat in his voice, but he did sound somewhat annoyed.

"I know you were. I was watching as you tried to burn it into ash with your eyes." Christian opened his mouth to respond, but any and all words were cut off when Lilith scooted closer to him, close enough that she could grab his arm, wrap it around her, and rest her head on his shoulder. She closed her eyes and took in a deep breath, feeling some of the nervous tension she'd acquired on their way to the station vanish. "Just relax for now. You can figure out where we're going to go next on the train."

After several seconds of silence had passed, Christian tightened his hold on her and allowed his own body to relax. He tilted his head, allowing his cheek to rest on top of her scalp. His messy black hair tickled her forehead.

"Yeah. Yeah, you're right. Sorry. I guess I'm just used to having all my traveling planned out before I actually start traveling."

"It's okay. We left kind of abruptly."

"Yes. Yes, we did."

Another moment of silence descended upon them. Lilith used this time to rest. She hadn't been lying. Their departure had been rather precipitous. Christian had asked her to leave with him without warning. He hadn't even allowed her to go back to her apartment and pack. The act of leaving in such a rush and the anxiety caused by Christian's behavior had left her feeling weary. Once they got on that train, while Christian was finding out their next destination, she would use that time to sleep.

And speaking of Christian, she couldn't help but wonder: just who was he to her? She knew she loved him, and she was positive that he loved her back—he didn't strike her as the type to sleep with someone he didn't have feelings for, but there was still the issue of their relationship. Were they simply boyfriend and girlfriend? That didn't feel right. It was too juvenile, especially after what they'd been through. They weren't engaged, though she certainly wouldn't mind that one day. So then, what were they? How did they define their relationship?

"The one I'm destined to be with," she whispered, giggling at the notion.

"Something funny?" asked Christian.

"No… well, maybe." Lilith paused as her lips twitched into a smile. "I was just remembering something Maria told me the day we started talking about light novels. She mentioned that you were the one I was destined to be with because you don't act strange around me like other men do." Christian's grip tightened for a second before slackening "At the time, I told her that things like true love and destiny were fairy tales made up by Disney to entertain little girls who dream of being swept off their feet. I believed that because of all the trouble I've had with men, I'd never fall in love."

"I sense a 'but' somewhere in there."

Lilith smiled at the somewhat cliched line. With everything that had happened, those words almost made her feel like she was in a movie, one of those romance-laden action movies.

"But now I think she might have actually been onto something," Lilith concluded.

There was another moment of silence. Christian's breathing tickled her hair. It was warm and reassuring. She wished they could stay like that for awhile longer.

"You know something?" Christian said, breaking the solitude with his soft voice. "I think your friend might have been onto something as well." When Lilith took her head off his shoulder and looked up at him, it was to find him giving her a tender smile. "I've never believed in love before—I'm technically not even allowed to fall in love."

"Not allowed to fall in love?" Lilith blinked. "How does that work?"

"I'll explain that on the train as well." Lilith pouted a bit, causing the young man to chuckle before continuing. "Anyway, because I wasn't allowed to love, I never gave the idea of love much thought. There just wasn't any point. And then you came along." When she just tilted her head in confusion, his eyes gained a depth of warmth as he said, "you're the first girl I've ever gotten really close to. I mean, I've spoken with a few girls before, and my boss and I are kinda close too, I guess, but I never got close to any of them like I have with you. From the very moment we met, I found you…" he paused, his eyes searching a bit. "Intriguing."

Lilith stared. "Intriguing?"

"Yes. I thought you were an intriguing individual."

"This isn't a jab at my fear of men, is it? Because if so, I really do get enough of that from Maria, and Stacy never lets me hear the end of it."

"That was part of what made you so interesting at first," he admitted, shrugging. "You have to admit that the idea of a woman as beautiful as you being afraid of men isn't very common. Most women who are pretty and know it use their looks to take advantage of others."

Well, the ones that he knew did that—except for Samantha. She was too straight-laced.

"Now that's just stereotyping."

Christian waved a hand in the air. "I know, and I know there are many women who, much like yourself, aren't like that. But, you can't deny that there are a lot of women who are."

"I wouldn't know. The only girlfriend I have is Maria, and I only know three other women besides her."

"Aunt Kay, Stacy, and the women you work with at the school, right?"

Lilith nodded. "Right." She paused, then added, "and Stacy probably is like that. I can totally see her using her looks to con men into buying her drinks."

"Yeah, I think I can see that, too."

Which was saying something because Christian barely knew her.

"Hey, Lilith?"

"Yes?"

"Why are you so willing to trust me?"

The question caused Lilith to give him an odd look. She stared at him for several seconds, long moments in which time seemed to almost stand still. Christian squirmed, appearing mildly uncomfortable with Lilith's unblinking gaze.

"That is quite possibly the silliest question you've ever asked me," she said at last.

Christian opened his mouth, though whether this was to make a retort, defend himself, or something else entirely would never be known. Lilith kept his mouth from fully opening by pressing a finger against it. Christian's eyes crossed for a moment, but then he looked back at Lilith, who offered him the most tender and loving smile she could.

"The reason that I am willing to trust you so much is because I love you."

***

The train to Sacramento began to move, slowly at first, but picking up speed as it left the Seal Beach station.

Sitting on the train in one of the compartments, Lilith and Christian watched as buildings, cars, and people passed through the window at an ever-increasing rate. Lilith was seated on the edge of the couch, her hands pressed against the window as the city roll by. Christian sat across from her, watching the girl with a slight frown.

"Are you okay?" he asked.

Lilith turned to him. When she saw his expression, she smiled, though it was tinged with sadness. "I'm alright. It's just—" she looked back out the window, her eyes glazing over as she stared into the distance "—I've only lived in Seal Beach for a little over a year, but it was really beginning to feel kind of like home. I had Maria and Aunty Kay and Jannice. Aside from my foster mother, I've never really had a family, but when I think about what it means to have a family, they're the people I think of the most." She paused, grimaced, then added, "and Stacy, too, I guess."

"You and Stacy really don't get along, do you?"

Lilith withheld a snort. "That's putting it mildly. We've been at each other's throats since day one. I don't think there has ever been a time since I started living with her and Maria that Stacy and I haven't fought about something." She frowned. "To her, I'm this perfect little cheerleader who should be, and I quote, 'whoring myself out like every other blonde-haired bimbo with super-sized tits.'"

After blinking several times, Christian slowly nodded. "I can see why you two would fight."

"It doesn't help that Stacy's one of those party girls who loves to get wasted every night she goes out. She calls me a slut because I have blonde hair and blue eyes, but she's had more, erm, well," a blush lit up her cheeks, "she's done *that* way more than I have." The blush became scarlet. "I mean, I've only ever slept with you, so…"

"You don't need to say anymore." Christian could see his own face in the window's reflection, so he knew that he was blushing as well. "I understand what you're saying."

His words were rewarded with a smile. "Yes, I suppose you do."

As Lilith went back to staring at the passing scenery—they were almost out of Seal Beach—Christian once more took to watching Lilith. A lot went through his mind as he observed the girl in question, chief among them being how all of the danger she was now in was because of him.

"I'm sorry."

Lilith looked back at Christian. "Sorry? For what?"

"For this, all this." He gestured vaguely with his hand, indicating the train compartment they were sitting in, the window, and scenery speeding by outside. "I'm sorry for taking you away from your home and your friends, and, well, I'm just sorry that you've gotten involved in this entire situation."

The way Lilith studied him as if he were some kind of puzzle made Christian look away. It was somewhat disconcerting to see such an penetrating stare directed at him, especially when it came from Lilith. She wasn't exactly what he would have called intense. More like shy and demure. Yet the look she directed at him now, one he had only seen on her a handful of times, was easily one of the most potent looks he'd ever seen.

It wasn't on par with Samantha's death stare, thank the Almighty. That woman could melt steel with her glares. Still, it was a close second.

"You have nothing to apologize for," Lilith said after another moment had passed. "I'm actually grateful all of this happened." Christian's incredulity must have been visible on his face, because a second later, her expression became a little bit abashed. "Okay, maybe grateful is too strong a word. But, when I think about it, about what might have been had none of this happened, I realize that I don't regret any of it. Because of what happened these past few weeks, I got to meet you, and I would never in a million years trade all of the bad things that have happened to me if it meant I would have never met you."

"You..." Christian's face became warm. Too warm. He shook his head, trying to rid himself of the feeling, but it didn't work. "I... how could you say something like that so easily?"

He didn't know why her words affected him so much. They had already confessed their love for each other. He'd told her those words before, just as she had. This shouldn't have made him so embarrassed.

But it did. By the Almighty Creator, it did. He felt like a naïve, innocent schoolboy who'd never received his first kiss and had just been confessed to by the girl he'd been crushing on for years but had been too embarrassed to tell her how he felt.

Could his strange feelings of bashfulness be due to a lack of experience? He and Lilith might have had sex, but that didn't mean he was a consummate professional in the art of love and dating. This territory was completely new to him, and somehow, he really doubted that any of the Japanese light novels he'd read would help him with this.

If everyone who read romance novels suddenly became suave and sophisticated gentlemen capable of turning any female into a warm, gooey puddle, there wouldn't have been any single women left in the world.

"I don't really know how I can say these things myself," Lilith admitted. She pressed a hand to her chest, directly over her heart. As she closed her eyes, a small, innocuous smile touched her lips. "Even as far back as two weeks ago, I would have never said something like this. The idea that I would tell someone, a man no less, that I love them was laughable. But now it feels like there's something inside of me that's giving me the confidence to say these words." Her eyes slowly fluttered open, and she looked upon Christian, locking him in place with her enchanting gaze. "Does that make any sense?"

"Not really." He shook his head, trying to ignore his racing heart. "But then again, I don't really think that's something a guy is supposed to understand." A mildly amusing thought entered his mind, causing him to cast Lilith a slight grin. "I heard that most men have the emotional range of a teaspoon, and that our brains are made of seaweed."

Lilith's delightful giggling made his ears turn red. It was soft and sweet, like the gentle tinkling of wind chimes. She looked upon him with mirth, her eyes alight, practically glowing.

"I'm not sure who said those words, but I think they were definitely onto something," she said.

Christian gave her a mock scowl, but after several seconds of listening to Lilith's light laughter, he joined in.

As their laughing fit subsided, he cast her a warm look. "I'm not as eloquent as you are, apparently, but since we're in a confessing mood, I want you to know that I love you as well. Very much."

The smile Lilith gave him was one she had reserved for him and him alone. It was soft yet smoldering. Warm but full of passion. It was a smile that contained equal amounts of love and lust, and it was a smile that caused Christian's body to burn with a need he had only encountered since meeting her.

Her cheeks turned a vibrant pink. For a moment, it looked like she might pounce on Christian, and indeed, the desire was there. Before she could do anything, a wave of dizziness swept over Lilith. She fell forward.

Before she could fall to the floor, Christian was there. He caught her in his arms. With her face buried in his chest, Lilith took several deep breaths.

"Lilith, are you okay?"

"I-I'm not sure," she admitted. "I don't know what's come over me, but I…"

"I…?"

Before Christian could ask her to finish her sentence, Lilith pushed him over, knocking them both to the ground. His back hit the other seat. Lilith straddled his waist with her lovely thighs. Her hair fell over her face, parting like a curtain to reveal flushed cheeks. Half-lidded eyes stared at Christian with a lust that caused his own desire to skyrocket. They were almost at eye-level now, and Lilith tilted her head while putting her hands into his hair and pulling his head to hers.

He didn't resist her.

The kiss started off slow. Christian seized Lilith's lips one at a time and would irregularly switch from one to the other, and then back again. His hands, which had yet to find placement on her body, ended up resting against her hips, with his fingers just inches away from her small, shapely rear. He squeezed lightly, eliciting a beautiful sound from Lilith that caused a shiver to run down his spine.

In response to his ministrations, Lilith's hands began to massage his head. Her nails raked light trails against his scalp. Her fingers threaded through his hair. The actions were slow, languid, but they soon picked up in intensity.

Moaning in satisfaction as Christian's tongue traced the curve of her lips, wordlessly asking for permission to enter, Lilith granted that access, opening her mouth and allowing him to slip inside. The feel of his tongue on hers, the mixing of their saliva as they bumped and rubbed together created an incredible sensation.

More.

Christian's hands slid from her hips all the way to her backside, where they started to grasp, caress, and squeeze, much to the young woman's delight.

I want more.

Wanting to get more of the glorious feeling that being so close to Christian invoked in her, Lilith pressed her entire body against his. Her breasts mashed up against his chest, and her crotch came into contact with the increasingly hard proof of Christian's arousal. Almost as soon as her jean-covered crotch touched the large tent that had been made in his pants, Lilith began to grind herself against him. It was an action that the recipient of her affection had absolutely no issues with, as he also began to move in time to the rhythm she set.

Right there!

"Did you say something?" asked Christian.

"N-no," Lilith moaned as her panties became damp. "W-why?"

"No reason. I just thought I heard your voice."

Christian kissed her again. He moved his hands from her hips to her rear. Lilith had an amazing ass. It was soft yet firm, small and shapely. With his hands caressing her, Christian pulled her hips forward, ensuring that her crotch continued to rub against his dick through their clothes.

Their kiss intensified. Lilith pushed her tongue against his, sliding around his tongue and hooking it with her own. Thus began a small game of tug-o-war. With the increasing amount of saliva their actions generated, it was impossible for either side to win. They would hook their tongues together, then pull, only for them to slide apart seconds later. This did not stop them from trying, however, and both took great joy in the act, moaning and groaning into each other's mouth.

They were eventually forced to stop, Lilith pulling back to take in a deep breath of much-needed oxygen. Yet their hunger was such that neither were willing to truly discontinue with their actions. Even while they were sucking in breath, their eager lips sought each other out in short, intermittent pecks. The last one of those annoyingly unsatisfying kisses was caught by Christian's voracious tongue, ensuring that their session heated up to a degree it had yet to reach.

Yes. This. Right here.

Just because their tongues were occupied didn't mean their bodies were resting idle. Lilith rubbed herself against Christian, squirming in delight as her body's hot center ground against the furnace building in Christian's pants. Her panties and jeans were becoming damp, a stain growing around the area between her legs. It was the feeling of her growing wetness that caused Lilith to realize she still had all of her clothes on, as did her lover.

That would just not do.

Taking her hands from his hair, Lilith reached down and grasped the hem of Christian's shirt. Thankfully, he wasn't wearing his cloak, which he'd hung up on the door after stashing his weapons underneath the couch. Christian lifted his arms, allowing Lilith to pull his shirt off and toss it on the floor.

With his torso now exposed, Lilith did not hesitate to explore the hard angles of his chest and stomach with both her hands and mouth. Her fingers glided along his abdominals, tracing each individual muscle. She pressed her lips against his slightly sweaty skin, taking in the uniquely masculine scent that belonged to him. She soon found the scars on his chest, three in all: one near his collarbone, another just under his right nipple, and the last one almost dead center on his solar plexus. She took the time to place a lingering kiss on each one, dragging her lips across their length. The act caused Christian to shudder underneath her.

Not wanting to be the only one losing his clothes, Christian also made Lilith lift her hands above her head so he could pull her shirt off her body. Inch by glorious inch of Lilith's silken flesh was revealed to his burning eyes. A light pink bra kept her breasts concealed. He longed to take it off, but he kept pulling her shirt up with glacial slowness, as though he was a child trying to savor the unwrapping of a present.

When the shirt was partially covering her face just above her nose, Christian leaned in and captured her lips in another heated kiss. Because her hands were raised and the shirt kept them there, Lilith could do nothing but kiss back. He dipped his tongue into her mouth, pulled back, and then took her lower lip between his teeth and nibbled on it.

Yes!

"Hnnnn!!!" Lilith moaned.

Christian desired to hear more of that sound. He kept her shirt where it was, covering the entire upper half of her face, and placed tiny kisses along her jaw. Lilith squirmed on top of him, her thighs quivering as he continued kissing her, traveling below her jaw to her neck.

Right there!

Christian paused on one particular spot next to Lilith's slender trapezius. He placed his lips against that one spot and kissed her.

Oh, God!!

"Hhnnggg!!"

Lilith's moans spurned him on. He nipped her skin, biting down and sucking on it until he left a mark. Lilith's hands pulled him down. He got the hint and kissed harder.

Christian finally pulled the shirt over her head and threw it away, leaving her in nothing but her jeans and pink bra. With the shirt gone, Christian moved his hands to her back, caressing her flawlessly fair skin. Her shoulder blades twitched as his fingers roamed over them. Her back arched as he slid a hand along her spine. The actions were accompanied by Lilith's moans.

"Lilith…" Christian groaned as she pulled her lips away from his to begin attacking his neck, licking, suckling, and nipping her way along his throat. She was acting much more aggressively than usual, just like their last two times together. Not that he could find it in himself to complain. "Lilith… window…"

It was obvious what he was talking about. The window to their compartment was still open. Anyone could look inside and see what they were doing.

With a moan of complaint, Lilith hastily shut the blinds so she could get back to being with Christian.

When she turned around to jump on him again, she saw that he was lifting the couch.

"Christian?"

"These couches have a pull out bed for long rides," he explained, the muscles in his back moving as his heavy breathing dictated. Lilith made an "ah" sound and let him finish pulling it out. It was a single bed, small, and usually made for only one person. It was perfect for their situation.

It didn't take long before Lilith was laying down on her back, her bra gone, revealing breasts with light pink nipples. Lilith's breasts were not large, but neither were they small. Like two perfectly sized hills, they rose from her chest.

Christian, now wearing nothing more than a pair of briefs, sat on the bed, undoing the buttons and zipper on her jeans. After hooking his fingers into the waistline of both her jeans and panties, he pulled the two articles down her smooth skin. Lilith raised her hips, making them glide across her hips and down her legs much more easily.

The clothing was tossed into the increasingly large pile of discarded fabric. Christian moved directly above her, his hands on either side of her head, his eyes raking across her figure.

"My God, you're so gorgeous," he muttered.

Lilith's body became a blazing inferno. Though his words were filled with lust, there was honest admiration in his eyes and sincerity in his voice. He wasn't saying this because he was overcome like other men would have been, but because he honestly believed his own words.

Rather than using words to respond, Lilith grabbed the back of his head and dragged him into another kiss. Her tongue danced with his. The battle was on once again. It was a battle in which both of them were winners, and they were more than willing to prolong it for as long as their lungs allowed.

As they continued to kiss, Christian kept one hand on the bed, acting as support. The other roamed the contours of her body, gliding along her arm, her shoulders, her neck and collarbone. He eventually reached her chest. As he cupped her left breast, he marveled at how well it fit his hand.

Her nipple became stiff as he touched her. Feeling it poking against his palm, Christian played with it, rubbing it, tweaking it.

Pull it!

"Ahnn!!"

As he lightly pulled on her nipple, Lilith released a loud squeal that reverberated through the train car. Her arms went around his neck, pulling him closer. Christian didn't resist.

She squirmed and moaned underneath Christian as their sweat combined to create a slick, wet coat that lubricated the relentless friction brought about by Lilith's skin rubbing against him. She moved her hands from his neck and roamed the contours of his back, feeling his muscles flex and twitch underneath her touch. They soon moved to his hair as Christian reluctantly pulled himself away from her lips to assault her neck.

Yes!

A knee pressed against her crotch, beginning a coordinated attack on her sensitive flower. Christian's leg was soon coated in her juices, becoming slick and gliding seamlessly along her opening. Each time his leg moved, Lilith would buck her hips, her mouth would open and a keening wail would emit from it.

During their second time together, Christian had discovered something interesting about Lilith. Several things, actually. The first was that she liked to be licked. He didn't know why, but he didn't question it. The second thing was that she was sensitive to his touch. Very sensitive. Sometimes, he almost thought her entire body was one big erogenous zone. There had been many occasions during their last two times where he hadn't been anywhere near standard places of pleasure on a woman, and yet he still caused her to grow crazy simply by letting his tongue trail across her skin.

And that was what he did here. The tip of his tongue trailed along her jaw, traveling up towards her ear, where he gave her lobe a couple of slow flicks before tugging on it with his teeth. As Lilith's moans became cries and her fingers dug trenches into the flesh of his back, he traveled back down her neck. He dipped his tongue over her collarbone, staying long enough to suckle on it and leave a mark before moving on.

As he created a blazing trail with his tongue, a voice spoke to him. It sounded like Lilith, though he knew that was impossible, since she was busy moaning. It told him to stop at certain places, to bite certain parts. Christian didn't know what the voice was, but he heeded its words.

Leaving a glistening trail across Lilith's supple flesh, Christian eventually reached her breasts. While Lilith was sensitive just about everywhere once they got going, it was those two round hills sitting proudly on her chest that were the most hypersensitive spot on her body, or the second most sensitive. He was already assaulting her clit with his leg.

"Oh! Ah! Ahn! Christian!"

The cry came when his lips found her breasts. He traced a circle around her nipple with his tongue. He flicked once, up, and then down, enjoying the beautiful music that Lilith made each time. Lilith's breathing became erratic, her cries a series of staccato bursts.

Her skin had a salty taste as he licked the sweat from her body, but her nipples retained a sweetness. He continued to tease her with his mouth and tongue, switching from one breast to the other. Since his mouth was now occupying her tits, he removed his leg from her pussy and cupped it with his hand.

"You're so wet," Christian said.

Lilith's cheeks suddenly went red. "I-if I am, then it's your fault."

He grinned. "In that case, I should take responsibility for it, shouldn't I?"

The area between her thighs, her legs, it was drenched in her juices. Christian didn't waste time. Her clit was already engorged, so he didn't hesitate. He stimulated it with his thumb, while inserting a finger into her. Her insides were warm, her walls tight around his finger. It made him wonder how he'd been able to fit himself inside of her their last two times.

"OH!!!"

Lilith's hips jerked as he worked her over. The voice inside of his head, the one that sounded like Lilith, continued to give him advice. He listened to it. It wasn't long before Lilith's thighs were shaking as though she were undergoing muscle spasms. The inside of her cunt tightened around his finger, making it difficult to move. Seconds past before, with a loud cry, Lilith's entire body seized up. Several moments later, Lilith's body slumped back onto the bed.

"C-Christian…"

Lilith panted. Her skin was flushed and sweaty. Her chest heaved as she took several deep breaths, causing her breasts to bounce. An intoxicating scent drifted from her, making Christian feel light-headed.

"Christian… I need you… I want you in me…"

"I want to be inside of you as well," he confessed.

The problem was getting himself inside of her without stopping his current actions. He didn't want to stop paying homage to her breasts, but because he refused to look down, he couldn't properly align himself with her entrance. Several times he slid off her, not even close to getting himself inside of her. It was, well, it was embarrassing, to be honest.

In a fit of frustration, Lilith reached down and wrapped her hands around him. He twitched in her grip. She then guided him to her entrance, nearly sighing in relief as he thrust himself inside of her. It was a tight fit. Her walls clung to him, making it hard to push further, but as he became fully sheathed inside of her, something amazing happened.

If asked, neither of them would have been able to truly describe what happened. As they laid there, creating a steady rhythm, the sound of flesh slapping against flesh, Lilith and Christian felt each other. It was as if their minds and spirits had connected and become one. They knew every thought and emotion that passed through the other's head. Lilith knew that Christian was trying to stave off his impending release just so she could experience it with him. Christian knew that she was worrying about what happened in Seal Beach. Christian's feelings of insecurity about his performance in bed, her thoughts on the nature of their relationship, they could feel all of it.

The world soon became a blur. The ardor with which their bodies moved increased. The sound of Christian's hips as he thrust into Lilith, of the grunts, groans, cries, and moans that escaped their mouths, filled the small compartment. Juices started flowing out of Lilith, covering their nether regions and mixing with their sweat. The combination of their perspiration, brought about by their activities and the increasing heat of the room, created a heady, overpowering scent that made both of them feel an overwhelming need for more. It was a need both were willing to satisfy.

Christian moved his hips with fast thrusting motions. Lilith locked her quivering legs around his back, keeping him in place and ensuring he didn't accidentally pull out. Her walls clamped around him with a vice-like tightness, yet still managed to conform to him as he plowed into her. The sound of him plunging into her depths created lewd squelching noises that was overpowered by the sound of their hips smacking together and their grunts and moans.

There was no warning when the end came. One second it was just the two of them caught in the throes of passion. The next, Christian was unable to hold himself back anymore. With one last grunt of exertion, he shot his seed inside of her. As if in trigger to his own orgasm, Lilith followed suit several seconds later, her body shaking as her nails dug into his skin, leaving red welts on his back and causing blood to leak out from between her fingers.

As they came down from their natural high, Lilith looked up at Christian as he leaned over her, his breathing heavy, sweat dripping from his trembling jaw, and his body shaking. The muscles in his arms and shoulders strained, and his back quivered as he tried to keep himself from collapsing on top of her.

He rolled onto his side, pulling out of her with a wet pop. Lilith rolled with him. She lay on her side, facing Christian. Her shoulders heaved along with her chest as she sucked in deep lungfuls of air. She was tired, and a part of her just wanted to go to sleep, yet at the same time, she felt invigorated, as if making love to Christian had given her a second wind. It was just like the first two times they'd had sex.

"I love you."

The words came from her lips before she even realized she was speaking them. She didn't give him a chance to reply as she leaned up and pressed their lips together. While she didn't plunder his mouth like before, she did dip her tongue into and languidly roam his mouth. When she pulled back, it was to give Christian one last smile before tucking her head under his chin and wrapping both her arms and legs around his body.

"I love you, too," he said.

Lilith smiled. She really did love it when he told her that. She loved it because she knew it was true. Mixed in with the lust and desire-fueled passion that burned within him when they were having sex was a love that burned even brighter, which she felt through the strange connection they had when they were one. It was with this knowledge that Lilith closed her eyes and prepared to sleep.

"I just realized something," Christian said.

Eyes still closed, Lilith sighed contently as she asked, "what's that?"

"We're on a train, right? And, well, the walls of a train aren't very thick. I imagine sound must travel through them pretty easily."

Lilith didn't understand what Christian was getting at. Thin walls? What did that have to do anything? And why did it matter if they were on a train?

It was only after putting the words into context with what they had just done that she realized what he was talking about.

Her face began to burn.

"Oh... Oh!" Her face was a combination of hot and cold, as though an icy paleness was trying to compete with her burning shame. "Oh, my God!" She leaned backwards to stare at Christian's face, her eyes wide. "You don't think... do you think our neighbors... did they hear?"

"Uh, I really don't think that's a question you want me to answer."

Lilith looked mortified. "I can't believe we just did that!"

"I can."

His words caused Lilith to give him a scrutinizing look. He looked way too comfortable for someone who'd just had sex in a place where it was highly likely that several people had heard them.

"We just had sex on a train, Christian. Aren't you embarrassed?"

"Hmm." Christian looked truly thoughtful for a second. "I feel like I should be," he admitted. "But for some reason, I just can't find it in me to feel much of anything. Ask me that question tomorrow, and I'll probably have a different answer."

"Ngg!" Lilith pressed a palm against her face. "I can't believe this. How come I'm the only one who feels so... so... ugh, this is mortifying."

Christian snickered in way that was so not Christian it was almost frightening. "You said mortifying."

"Shut up!"

"You should look on the bright side."

A curious look was Lilith's response. "And what exactly is the bright side?"

The expression on Christian's face was very serious. "We just had sex, on a train. I'm sure there are thousands of exhibitionists and nymphomaniacs out there right now who wish they were in our place."

Lilith's response was to bury her burning face against his chest and bite him. "Oh, be quiet."

"Yes, ma'am."

Lilith groaned as Christian snickered. She was never going to live this down.

Chapter 2

Christian lay on the small bed, listening to the sounds of the train as it sped along the tracks. Trains were always noisy, and they tended to shake a lot, making it hard for light sleepers like him to nod off. He was lying on his side, one arm underneath the pillow and the other wrapped around Lilith's waist, his hand resting against the small of her back.

Lilith was also lying on her side, facing him. She had originally been tucked neatly underneath his chin, but he'd shifted back as much as the tiny bed allowed, so that he could watch her while she slept. She looked so peaceful. Locks of blonde hair fell over her back and splayed across her body. Slender shoulders rose and fell with each breath. Her eyes were closed, and her lips were parted ever so slightly. Christian found himself drawn to those light pink lips. He felt a strong urge to kiss them, but he resisted.

As the train jolted a bit, a single strand of hair fell over Lilith's face. Christian unwrapped his arm from around her waist and tucked the strand behind her ear before letting his hand rest on her cheek.

She must have been sleeping lightly because his touch caused her to stir. Baby-blue eyes fluttered open, blinking several times before focusing on him.

"Good morning," Lilith said with a sleepy smile.

Christian chuckled. "It's actually afternoon," he corrected. "We'll be arriving in Lynwood in about, I'd say, maybe one hour."

"Our first destination, right?"

"Yeah," Christian said, hesitating.

Lilith seemed to notice his reticence. "Is something wrong?"

"No." Christian shook his head. "Nothing's wrong. I was just thinking that now would probably be the best time to tell you the truth about myself and why I asked you to leave Seal Beach with me."

Lilith stared into his eyes for a moment, searching, though for what, he didn't know. She eventually seemed to find what she was looking for. She nodded a second later.

The two made themselves comfortable. Christian sat perpendicular to the bed's length, leaning against the cushioned headboard of the couch. Lilith situated herself in between his legs, her back resting against his chest. In return, he had wrapped his arms around her tiny waist, pulling her flush against him. Once they were comfortable, Christian began his tale.

"The first thing you should probably know about me is that I'm a member of the Executioners. We're a secret sect within the Catholic Church whose sole purpose is to slay monsters." He observed Lilith to see her response, but other than the slight tilt of her head, she showed no real shock. "Are you not surprised?"

"Not really." She shook her head, blonde hair swaying with the movement. "After everything that's happened in the past few days, I figured out that you were some kind of monster hunter. I didn't know the Catholic Church was involved, but that explains why you're so religious."

Smart girl.

Christian nodded at her reasoning and continued. "Right, well, the reason I was sent to Seal Beach was because we had received reports about a succubus living in the area. I normally wouldn't have been sent to deal with a succubus, but all the people we sent after her either disappeared or ended up dead."

"A succubus?" Lilith wrinkled her nose in thought. It was unbearably cute. "That's… some kind of demon, right?"

"Right." Christian nodded. "Succubi are female demons who seduce men and drain them of their vitality by sleeping with them."

Lilith's cheeks went pink when he mentioned how succubi slept with men. Even so, she was able to keep the conversation on track. "But you didn't find a succubus, did you? The only monster you fought was Damien, and he was after… me…"

Lilith trailed off. Christian didn't say anything. He could already see in her eyes that she had come to the correct conclusion.

"You were after me," she said at last. "I'm the succubus you were sent to kill."

"Yes." It wasn't a question, but he answered her anyway.

Placing a hand against her face, Lilith revealed her own astonishment via her widened eyes. She took several deep breaths. Her shoulders were shaking.

"I… I had always known that I was somewhat different from everyone else," she confessed. "Men always acted weird around me, but I could never figure out why. I see now. I understand. The reason men act so strange around me is because I'm a monster."

"No." Christian stopped her right there. "You are not a monster."

Lilith looked at him. "But I'm—"

"Whether or not you are a succubus has no bearing on whether or not you are a monster." Christian stared into her eyes as though doing so would help communicate his thoughts and feelings to her. "Succubi kill men by draining their lives through the act of sex, but you haven't done that. Outside of me, you've barely spoken more than two words to a man, much less had sex with them. Those are not the actions of a monster."

Moisture gathered in Lilith's eyes. She turned around until she was pressing her face against his chest and hugged him. Christian hugged back.

"Thank you," she said, her words choked.

"You needn't thank me for something like this," Christian replied. "I'm merely stating the truth."

They remained like that for several minutes before Lilith released him and leaned back. She looked at him, and from her expression, he could infer that she wanted to continue their conversation.

"So, you were sent to kill me?" Lilith asked for clarification.

Christian confirmed her theory with a nod. "Yes."

"That makes sense." Lilith calmed down. "After everything that happened, I thought you were here for Damien, but you were really after me all this time."

Christian studied Lilith, taking notice of her now tranquil demeanor. It was an abrupt change. However, he didn't think she was putting on an act.

"Are you not frightened?" he asked. "Now that you know the truth, aren't you worried about what could happen?"

"No." Lilith shook her head. The smile on her face was like a ray of sunlight streaking through a cloudy sky, "So long as I'm with you, I could never feel frightened. I love you."

Christian felt his breath catch in his throat. "You... you really are an amazing woman, you know that?"

Lilith blushed. "I... I'm not that amazing."

He shook his head as though rebuking her, though he didn't say anything to undermine her words, determined as he was to continue his story. "Anyway, after I ran into you for the first time, I didn't think you were a succubus. Succubi need to sleep with men to survive. A succubus cannot sustain herself without draining men of their lives, which she can only do through sex. The fact that you couldn't even be in the same room as a man made me think our intel was wrong. I asked the Church to confirm whether or not you were really a succubus. I didn't want to have the blood of someone who was innocent of any wrongdoings on my hands."

"Innocent of any wrongdoings?" Lilith repeated, frowning. "You make it sound like being a succubus means I'm no longer innocent."

"I'm sorry," Christian said, abashed. "That came out wrong. It's a force of habit. The Executioners are taught that all nonhuman entities are evil and must be exterminated. I know you're not a bad person, that you don't have an evil bone in your body, but it's hard to break ten years of indoctrination."

"It's alright." Lilith planted a soft kiss on his chest. "I understand. Please continue with your story."

"There isn't much to tell that you don't already know." He shrugged. "While I was waiting for headquarters to confirm your status, I got to know you better and fell in love. That whole incident with the No Life King happened and after the battle, I got a call from the Church saying that you were a succubus and I had been given orders to terminate you."

"Which is why you were in such a hurry to leave," Lilith postulated.

"Yes. Even though you're a succubus, I can't bring myself to kill you. The thought alone is enough to make me sick, but I also knew that if I didn't kill you, someone else would. Not only that, but they would kill me as well for disobeying a direct order and breaking one of the cardinal laws of the Executioners."

Lilith tilted her head, a quizzical expression in play. "Which law?"

Christian smiled down at her. "The one about falling in love. Executioners are not allowed to love. What would happen if the Church ordered someone to do a task that would put the life of their loved one on the line? What if they were asked to do something that took them from the person they loved? Who would they choose? The Church? Or the person they love? Almost ninety percent of the time, they would choose the person they loved over the Church. Hence, Executioners are not allowed to fall in love. The penalties for doing so are severe."

"How severe are we talking?"

"That depends on your rank. Those of the lowest rank, the Casteless, are given a dishonorable discharge and banished from the Executioners. They are allowed to live mostly normal lives, but because they know of our existence, they have a minder who watches over them to ensure they do not reveal our existence."

Christian paused, allowing Lilith to take in and assimilate everything he was telling her.

"For someone like myself, the consequences are much more severe. I know many secrets of the Catholic Church, and I have information on the Executioners that could prove detrimental to them if it was ever leaked. Because I'm a security risk, they would have no choice but to silence me."

"But what if you promised not to reveal that information?" asked Lilith. "You could make them a promise to never say anything and even let them give you a minder. Wouldn't that work?"

"That might have worked if you were human. In fact, I was banking on convincing them to let me go with an honorable discharge due to my my reputation and the loyalty I've displayed up to now, so that I could make a life with you." When Lilith's eyes widened, Christian smiled at her, but the smile soon left as he worried his lower lip and thought about how his plan had been doomed from the very beginning. "I think I might have been able to work something out, but…"

"But you can't because I'm a succubus."

A hesitant nod from Christian was her answer. "Yes. While the Catholic Church may have shown me leniency in light of my service, they won't do that once they learn that I've fallen in love with you, because you're not human."

"I see." Lilith looked away, the light in her eyes dimming and a sad frown touching her lips. "So the reason you're now on the run is because of me."

"No," he said, halting the rest of Lilith's words in their tracks. He was not going to let her get any farther with those thoughts. They were dangerous. "I am on the run because I chose to follow my heart instead of doing my duty. I chose this path, chose to let my love for you dictate my actions, chose to let my desire to create a life with you overrule my desire to uphold my duty." As she stared up at him, Christian cupped her face with his hands. "What's more, I've come to realize that just because someone is not human, it doesn't mean they're evil. Even if I had not fallen in love with you, I think—no, I know that I would have tried to protect you regardless."

Lilith stared up at him, tears gathering in her eyes and a soft, joyous smile lighting up her face. "Christian…"

"The only thing you are to be blamed for," he continued, wiping the tears that leaked from her eyes with his thumbs, "is being so unequivocally irresistible."

Lilith didn't waste a second after he spoke. She lunged at him, her arms winding around his neck as her lips sought out his. Lilith pressed herself against him as though trying to meld their bodies together. She crushed her lips to his, kissing him so hard it felt like she was trying to consume him.

They made love again, with Lilith on top this time. This round of sex was unsatisfyingly short—they only had fifteen minutes before they had to disembark—and neither was satisfied. After disembarking from the train, they decided to take another one where the ride time would be several hours longer. Both of them understood the dangers they were in, and that there was a very real possibility they would be killed, so they wanted to enjoy their time together as much as possible.

When one's life and the life of the one they loved were on the line, people tended to let their passions rule them. In this regard, Christian and Lilith were no different from anyone else.

***

Two days had passed since Tristin conveyed the Church's orders to execute Lilith. Two days since anyone from the Executioners had heard so much as a peep from one of their top Warriors. They tried calling his phone, but he wasn't answering. The tracking chip located within his phone confirmed that he was still in Seal Beach, but they knew nothing else.

Worried that something might have happened to him, Samantha sent in a squad of Executioners to rendezvous with Christian.

Using squads was rare among the Executioners. There were only a few instances where a squadron was needed—two, in fact: when facing a large number of abominations such as a coven of vampires or a werewolf pack, or when faced against one exceptionally strong creature such as a No Life King or one of the more powerful demons like Abaddon the Destroyer. Considering Christian had gone up against a No Life King, it was just another reason that they needed to find him and determine whether or not he needed their help.

As a member of the XIII, one of their top operatives, Christian Crux was invaluable to their cause. His abilities far outstripped those of the average Warrior. He was one of the few members who could take out an entire vampire coven or werewolf pack on his own, not to mention he was the only known person to date who had fought against a greater demon in single combat and won.

It was imperative that they locate him.

Squads among the Executioners always consisted of no less than three members. In most cases, a squad would consist of three members from the same sect, but they could grow larger depending on the task they needed to accomplish. The squadron that Christian had been in when he defeated Abaddon had consisted of thirteen people.

Because the situation they had found themselves in was different from all the others, the squadron that had been sent to Seal Beach was two members larger than normal. It also contained a mix of castes. There was one member of the Warriors, and two Assassins, one male and the other female. With them were two members of the Intelligence Division, another male and female pair.

Tristin had complained when they told him he couldn't go.

"Are you sure this is the right place?" Alice couldn't help but ask again as she looked at the basic two-story house with plaster walls and red roofing.

Her partner was also a member of the Intelligence Division. He had long, black hair and equally black eyes. He was studying a small device in his hands. It was rectangular and thin, sleek, with a large black screen that was currently showing a map of the surrounding area. There were two blips on the map, one that showed their location, and the other which showed the location of Christian's cellphone.

"Yep," he confirmed. "This is definitely the place."

Alice frowned. Running a hand through her dark tresses, she could feel some sweat on her scalp. Her dark skin, plus the sunlight bearing down on them really wasn't doing her any favors. It didn't help that, as a member of the Intelligence Division, she wasn't used to being outside.

"So should we go in? Call for backup?" her partner asked.

It felt odd being out on assignment. Intelligence members rarely performed field work. They weren't physically capable of fighting off monsters of any kind, or even regular humans. It just didn't make sense to send them on a mission when they didn't have any real training besides basic target practice.

But then, this wasn't exactly a normal situation, was it?

"We'll make sure everyone's in place before doing anything." Alice pressed a hand to her ear, her index finger pushing against the communication device stuck in her ear canal. "Report in with your status and location."

"This is David Burnstrode. I'm standing on the roof of a house on your six. I've got you in my sight."

"Kyle Bishop. I'm on the bench behind you and to your left, reading a newspaper."

"Sarah Kale. Two buildings away. East. Out."

"Right. Lex and I will be going in. Remember, one of our best has yet to report in and may be in some kind of danger. Keep your guard up at all times and watch our backs."

Alice received a number of affirmatives over the ear piece. Taking a slow breath to steady her racing nerves, she walked to the front door with her partner and proceeded to ring the doorbell. She took a step back, clasped her hands behind her, and waited for someone to answer the door.

She did not know what to expect when the door cracked open. A monster? A creature beyond her wildest imagination? A being so unfathomable that its very nature struck fear into the hearts of humans? One thing was for sure, whatever she had been anticipating, it was not the person who now stood in the doorway.

"Umm..." Alice stared down at the little girl, who stared up at her with wide eyes. She was a rather cute kid, with shoulder-length red hair and a smattering of freckles on her face. Alice tried to give the girl a smile as she loomed over her. "Hello, little girl? You wouldn't happen to have seen a man with messy black hair and two different colored eyes, have you?"

The girl continued to stare at her, gaping.

"Uh, hey, uh, are you alright, little girl?"

After nearly a full minute of staring, the little girl… began to cry.

Alice panicked. "P-Please don't cry! I just wanted to know if you've seen the person I'm looking for." Unfortunately, her words just caused the little girl to cry even more. The girl's loud, piercing wail echoed across the entire neighborhood.

"Uh, Alice," her partner grabbed her attention. "I think we might want to leave."

Alice looked conflicted. "But we're supposed to find out what happened to Christian…"

"Yeah, well, I don't think that's going to be happening."

"What do you mean? Why?"

In response to Alice's question, her partner pointed at all the people coming out of their houses to find out what the source of all the crying was. When they saw Alice and her partner standing in front of a house, and a crying girl standing in the doorway, they pointed and whispered. Alice didn't need to hear what was being said to know that it was probably not painting them in a favorable light.

"What the hell is going on here?!" a voice shouted from inside.

And just when it seemed as if things couldn't get any worse, a man who could only be the crying girl's father stepped into the doorway. He was a large man, both in height and girth. Alice felt dwarfed by this giant, who looked like he could eat her and her partner and still have room for an entire cow. The man, upon seeing them, narrowed his eyes.

"Who the hell are you two? Why is my little girl crying?"

"Daddy!" The girl hugged her father's leg, attaching herself to him like some kind of limpet. "These scary people keep asking me questions about some man! I don't know anything about a man! They're scaring me!"

"Oh, they are, are they?" A thrill of fear ran down Alice's spine as a dangerous glint entered the man's eyes. This... did not bode well for them. "Sweetie pie, why don't you go upstairs and play with your dolls while I deal with the scary people?"

"Kay." The girl sniffled before rushing back inside, the sound of pounding feet growing softer and softer.

"Now then." The man's eyes hardened as he stared at the duo, causing both of them to gulp. "Why don't you tell me why you thought making my daughter cry was a good idea." It wasn't a question. It was an order.

As Alice stared into the man's eyes, she almost felt like pissing himself. Today, she decided, was not going to be a good day.

***

Samantha was tired. Much as she might wish to deny it, the truth was that she was beginning to feel the stress that came from spending two days filled with worry. There were bags under her eyes, and her normally immaculate hair had several strands out of place. She was running on fumes. Fumes and caffeine.

She looked at the paperwork sitting on her desk. There was a large stack of it. Judging by the size alone, there had to be at least several hundred sheets of paper. A glance at the clock revealed the time to be 3:57pm. Normally, she would have been done with all the paperwork by now, but the stress she felt over Christian's lack of communication made it impossible to think of anything other than worry over the many different kinds of trouble her best operative could have gotten himself into.

Her mind was plaguing her, showing her images of all the different dangerous and potentially fatal situations that Christian could even now be in. She saw him lying on his back, a withered husk after having his essence drained by Lilith. Another terrifying delusion showed him with claw marks raked across his chest, bleeding profusely as the light faded from his eyes.

Many more images bombarded her mind, causing her to worry ceaselessly. These visions even kept her from being able to sleep properly.

A knock at her door caused Samantha to look up. She frowned. "Come in."

The door opened and Tristin walked into the room. His immaculately combed blond hair swished as he walked. Bright blue eyes surveyed her with a casual demeanor that made Samantha frown. He wore a smile that could, and had, seduced many women.

Tristin was her best intelligence operative, but he was also her worst. He was a playboy who had slept with numerous women. The only reason he hadn't been excommunicated or killed was because of his talent at gathering information, and also because he didn't have an established relationship with any of the women he slept with. Sinful though he might have been, he at least knew better than to fall in love. It was just sex.

He stopped several feet in front of her desk and gave her a sloppy salute. "Good afternoon, Commander. You're looking lovely as always."

"Cut the crap, Tristin," Samantha grunted. She knew that he was making fun of her appearance, though she was surprised by how bold he was being. He hadn't toyed with her before. Was he messing with her now because Christian was gone? "Tell me what I want to know. Has Omicron team managed to discover what happened to Christian?"

Tristin hesitated, but only for a second. "... No. No, they haven't. When they went to the location shown on the tracking device, they ended up in a residential district, where they had a nasty run-in with some guy and his four year old daughter."

Samantha gritted her teeth. "What about the succubus' friends? Did they check the apartment belonging to Maria Longfield and Stacy Moon?"

"They did..." Once again, Tristin hesitated, which revealed more to Samantha than the actual answers themselves. "... But much like tracking Christian via the chip implanted in his cellphone, meeting with Maria and Stacy was a dead end as well. Apparently, they don't know anything pertaining to either Christian or Lilith. According to Omicron team, neither Maria nor Stacy have seen those two since before the battle against the No Life King, and all their memories from when they were under the vampire's thrall have disappeared as well."

"So we've got no information regarding either of them?"

"Seems like it." Tristin shrugged.

Samantha narrowed her eyes. "But you've got a theory as to where they might be." It wasn't a question.

"No, well, maybe." A pause. Tristin's brow furrowed. "I don't have any clue where they are right now, but I'm pretty sure they took a train and left Seal Beach."

Samantha looked down at her hands as they rested on the desk. She tightened them into fists. "Are you telling me that Christian has disobeyed a direct order to terminate that succubus and run off with her? Is that what you're telling me?"

"Woah, woah, woah!" Tristin moved backwards several steps and held up his hands in a warding gesture. "Ease up on the dark aura, alright?"

"Tristin, tell me what I want to know. Now."

"Alright, alright! Yeesh!" Sighing, Tristin ran a hand through his hair before pinning Samantha with a look of mild reproach. "Look, I told you before that telling Christian to kill Lilith was asking for too much. He's not an Assassin. He was never trained to kill his emotions. What's more, you know as well as I do that Christian is pretty damn straight-laced. The guy's got the moral compass of a frickin' saint. And that girl, Lilith, she acts nothing like a succubus. Reports received on her from both Christian and outside sources state that she has, or at least had, a serious case of androphobia. She was so afraid of men that one look at Christian caused her to run away in fright."

"She could have been acting," Samantha said.

"Why would she need to? She didn't know we were after her. I don't think even she came into contact with any of the Executioners that were sent to kill her," Tristin fired back. "This isn't confirmed, but I'm about ninety percent certain that the No Life King who was trying to claim her killed all of the Executioners we sent after her before they even reached her. Until that, uh, Domon? Demon? I forgot his name. Anyway, until she was kidnapped by that vampire, I doubt she had any idea that we existed."

Samantha laced her hands together as she eyed the blond man before her. "I fail to see what you're getting at."

Sighing in mild exasperation, Tristin said, "what I am getting at is that until we showed up, Lilith had been living the life of a normal college student. And Christian saw that. He saw that she was just like every other girl out there. It's even worse because he couldn't see that she was a succubus, so he spent nearly a month hanging out with her, getting to know her on a more intimate and personal level. It doesn't help that he fell irrevocably in love with her."

"What?!" Samantha stood up so quickly that the back of her legs hit the chair, hard. The sturdy office chair was sent clattering to the ground. She ignored this and stared at Tristin in shock. "What do you mean he fell in love with her?!"

"Ah, well, when a man and a woman hold a mutual affection for each other—"

"Don't patronize me!" She slammed her hands against the desk and glared. "I know damn well what love is! I don't need you telling me that! And I definitely don't want to hear any condescension out of you!"

"Okay, sorry, sorry. Bad joke." Tristin waved his hands as though warding her off. "Regardless, I don't think you need me to tell why or how Christian fell in love with Lilith. I've been giving you daily reports on their progress, and you've even seen the video footage from security cameras that I hacked. You know how close they've gotten."

Samantha did indeed know about how friendly Lilith and Christian had become. She had seen the footage of the conversation they had at The Crema Cafe—even if she hadn't been able to hear what had been said. She had also witnessed their first time out—and subsequently every other time they went out—as well as a good portion of their first date. So yes, she knew that Christian had been growing fond of the girl. That didn't make the bomb that Tristin dropped on her any easier to swallow.

It was only after he said it that she realized something else.

"You knew this would happen!" She stared at him in shock. "That's why you suggested that we not kill her!"

"Did you think I had another reason for telling you that?" When all Samantha did was stare at him with daggers in her eyes, he sighed. "But, yes, that is why I suggested letting her live. I know Christian better than anyone else here, including you. Why do you think it's so easy for me to get inside his head? Christian is, despite all appearances to the contrary, a hopeless romantic."

Samantha deadpanned. "What?"

"Yep." Crossing his arms over his chest and nodding to himself, Tristin seemed quite proud of the conclusion he'd come to. "Because Executioners aren't allowed to fall in love, Christian has done his best to ignore love in all its forms. He does this by dedicating his life to the protection of others, and it's worked out well so far. I certainly can't deny that. But ever since he met Lilith, that's changed. With nothing to do but wait for us to confirm her status as a succubus, he's had an unparalleled amount of free time and nothing to do with it."

Resisting the urge to rub her forehead, Samantha said, "get to the point please."

"I'm getting there. Don't rush me. Now, where was I? Oh, right. With nothing else to do with his time, it was only a matter of time before he started spending it with Lilith, if only to make killing her easier. Unfortunately, I don't think he really understood what he was getting himself into. He's not the type to willingly kill someone after getting to know them, especially if he gets to know them personally. It's even worse because he and Lilith have a lot of common ground."

Samantha tried to wrap her mind around everything that Tristin was telling her. Unfortunately, that seemed impossible. Her brain felt like it was overloading. Christian, a hopeless romantic? She could see his morals conflicting with his orders to kill someone who he'd gotten to know on a personal level, but to fall in love with that person? That was so far out of left field it wasn't even funny. He wasn't the type to fall in love, or he had at least never shown any interest in love before.

But then, the Executioners weren't allowed to love. Love for another bred disloyalty to the Church. It forced people to choose between their duty and the one they love. When forced to choose between the two, most people wouldn't choose duty over their loved one. That was why all Executioners who fell in love were excommunicated and, depending on their threat level, exterminated with extreme prejudice.

Christian was of the latter. As a member of the XIII, he was considered a AAA-class threat. That was the same threat level as a No Life King or a greater demon such as Abaddon. Only the S-class threats, like the Apostle Ancestors or the Seven Kings of Hell, were considered a greater priority than him.

Thinking about it, could it be that the only reason Christian had never thought of love was because he knew of the consequences? It was plausible, she supposed. But then, why hadn't she seen this coming? Tristin might have known him longer, but she and Christian had grown up being trained by the same instructors. Samantha had been positive that she knew everything there was to know about him.

Could it be that I really don't know him like I thought I did?

The thought depressed her.

After rubbing the bridge of her nose, Samantha shoved aside her inner turmoil and looked at Tristin again. "So, basically, what you're saying is that Christian ran off with Lilith because he loves her and doesn't think she's evil, in spite of knowing what she is?"

"That pretty much sums things up, yes."

Samantha summed up her thoughts in a single word. "Damn."

***

The day was coming to an end. For some people, this meant going home, winding down, and maybe watching some television before going to bed. For Samantha, it meant more stress.

Leaning back in her chair, staring at a point on the ceiling but not really seeing anything, Samantha found herself having a major crisis. Christian Crux, her best and most valuable operative, had run off with a succubus, thereby committing one of the worst crimes among the Executioners. She had sent Tristin off to acquire evidence of this sin, though a part of her fervently hoped they were wrong.

As if responding to her thoughts, the phone sitting on her desk rang. She picked it up and put it to her ear. "What do you have for me, Tristin?"

"Wow. How'd you know it was me?"

A small vein throbbed on Samantha's forehead. "Do you take me for a fool? You're the only person who has any reason to call me at the moment. Now spill it."

"Alright already! You know, you could really stand to lighten up a bit. Maybe after all this is over you and I could—"

"Finish that sentence, and I'll make sure you'll never be able to perform any sort of sexual act again."

"Right. Okay. I got it. No more jokes." A pause. *"You ordered me to find anything I could that would help determine the possible locations of Christian and Lilith. Well, I found out two bits of important info that may help us. The first actually comes from Catherine Siegal of the LAPD. She apparently saw Christian and Lilith at the train station around 0800 hours three days ago. She didn't stay long enough to confirm their destination. From our conversation, I gathered that she assumed Christian was returning to headquarters and Lilith was going with him."*

"Makes sense," Samantha mumbled thoughtfully, her eyes narrowed in concentration. "No one outside of the Catholic Church knows how the Executioners operate. Ms. Siegal couldn't have known that Executioners are not allowed to have relationships." She paused, a contemplative frown marring her face. "Does she know that Lilith isn't human?"

"Doubt it, unless Christian told her, which I also doubt."

"I see. Continue."

"Right, well, after getting confirmation from Catherine that she had seen Christian and Lilith at the train station, I hacked into the security cameras there and managed to find something interesting. At exactly 1230 hours, Christian and Lilith both got on a train heading for Lynwood."

"Lynwood..." Samantha frowned. "That's closer to Los Angeles than Seal Beach."

What was Christian's thinking? Was he willing to risk his and Lilith's life by coming closer to the Executioner HQ, or was that exactly why he was doing it? Perhaps he was trying to throw them off his trail? No, that wasn't it. Something else was going on here. She resisted the urge to rub her forehead. It was times like these that she wished she had the ability to see into the minds of others.

"*It is,*" Tristin confirmed. Samantha blinked. She had almost forgotten that she was on the phone with him. "*Knowing Christian like I do, he's probably going to get off at Lynwood and then do some train hopping to throw us off his trail. Depending on how well he can blend into the crowd and avoid security cameras, he might be able to negate my ability to track him.*"

"Can you figure out where his ultimate destination is?"

"*Out of the state.*"

If Tristin had been delivering this information orally, she would have hit him. "I meant his ultimate destination before that. Where does he hope to go after making escape from California?"

There were four places he could potentially travel to: Mexico, Arizona, Nevada, and Oregon. Mexico was out. Crossing the border was a stupid idea when on the run, since it meant going through the checkpoints and border patrols. That left the three states. What Samantha wanted to know was which state were they going to, and which city were they going to travel through to get there.

"*I don't know. While Christian can be a predictable guy at times, he's also scary smart. He knows that I'll likely be the one looking for him, so he'll know that he can't do things like he normally does.*" There was a poignant pause. "*Or he might do things exactly as I think he will, knowing that I'll suspect he'll not do the things I think he will because it's predictable.*"

"Tristin, you're giving me a headache."

"*Right. Sorry. I'm just saying that it's impossible to predict his destination without tracking his movements for a while.*"

"I understand. Let me know if you find anything else."

"*Talk to ya later, boss lady.*"

Samantha twitched as she hung up the phone. That man, by God did he annoy her. How Christian dealt with him on a daily basis was something she would never be able to understand.

Leaning back in her chair and crossing her arms, Samantha tried to come up with a plan to capture Christian and kill Lilith. While in most cases, the act of treason that Christian had committed would warrant a kill on sight order, his reputation and skill meant they would have to take a more delicate approach to this. Killing him would lower the morale of her men. Worse still, those who she assigned to chase after him would lose what faith they had in the Church.

It was a well-established fact that going against someone of Christian's caliber was a death sentence. He was a member of the XIII. She didn't want to think about how her men would feel if she ordered them to kill someone like that. They'd probably assume she was sending them on a suicide mission.

Pulling out a map from her right hand drawer and spreading it across the table, Samantha let a single index finger land on one of the many cities that dotted California.

"Lynwood, huh?"

Should she send a squad of Executioners there to intercept Christian? Giving the idea a moment's thought, she eventually shook her head. That wouldn't work. Tristin's information was three days old. It was unlikely they were in Lynwood anymore.

She would just have to wait for Tristin to discover where they had gone, or where they were going. Then she could head them off and hopefully bring Christian back into the fold before the bishopric found out. The last thing she wanted was for Bishop Vertrou to discover that Christian had fled Seal Beach with the succubus he was supposed to have killed. If that happened, she would be unable to protect the young man who'd proven himself amongst their ranks time and time again.

Rubbing her face, Samantha let loose a tired groan as she thought about all the trouble Christian was causing her. It was times like this that made Samantha wish she had gone into Cosmetology like her mother.

Chapter 3

The path they had decided to take to reach Sacramento was a winding one, full of stops and changing trains. They had even backtracked several times, going from Pasadena, cutting straight through Los Angeles and into Santa Monica, and then traveling to San Pedro.

It was a confusing route that would have been very hard for anyone to follow simply because there didn't seem to be any rhyme or reason to it. And there wasn't. Christian had determined that if they actually planned their trip out in advance, then the Executioners would be able to predict where they were heading and cut them off. In order to make sure there was no trail to follow, they needed to be so unpredictable that not even they knew where they were going.

They had even taken a cab from Torrance to Inglewood just to add in a new variable.

Paranoia? Not if there really were people out to get you.

They had also been careful not to be seen by too many cameras. The Executioners' Intelligence Division was top notch. They were the best at what they did, better than any standard branch of the military. Intelligence agents could hack into any system regardless of the amount of security surrounding it via a wide range of programs and tools. Not even the US military was safe from being hacked. In fact, the Executioners accessed the databases of numerous countries in search of abominations to destroy every day.

Another thing they had to worry about was being tracked via satellite. As if being spotted on some random security camera wasn't enough, the Executioners could hack into any orbital satellite from any nation and use them to track people in real time.

This was how the Church tracked down monsters. After checking rumors of disappearances under intense scrutiny, the Intelligence Division would hack military and police networks in the area to gain a clearer picture of their targets. They would then utilize a variety of security cameras and real time feeds from orbital satellites to track down and triangulate the position of anybody they suspected of being non-human.

The whole thing was a pretty laborious process, but the Intelligence Division had over one hundred members located at each regional division headquarters, so the whole "hard work" aspect wasn't really an issue.

With so many ways of being discovered, the two had also taken to wearing disguises.

Christian had decided to go with a pair of black jeans and a white T-shirt. Over the shirt was a light gray jacket that wouldn't hamper his movement. He was still wearing his combat boots—because if he had to fight a running battle, then he wanted to be comfortable. To hide his notorious red and green eyes, he wore inexpensive sports sunglasses with metal wire frames and black lenses. He had even dyed his hair a bright, almost obnoxious shade of blond.

Because he had discarded his cloak some time ago, he couldn't wear his swords, which were locked away in his large suitcase. He did have his guns strapped to the underside of his arms using the new accessories the Executioners had given him. The two silver daggers were also hidden inside of his boots. If luck was on their side, the weapons he had on hand would be enough to protect them.

One can always hope.

Much like Christian, Lilith had switched outfits. She was now wearing a full-length, blue jean skirt that went down to her ankles, black leather shoes with slight heels, and a white halter top with a blue jean jacket. While she hadn't dyed her hair, she had taken to wearing it in a messy ponytail.

Christian thought she looked exquisite, and he had told her so. His words had earned him a night of lovemaking... or maybe it hadn't, as they made love almost every night now, but that night had been particularly amazing.

Looking at the map sitting on his lap, Christian tried to find the best route to take in order to reach their next big stop: Sacramento. It was the last big city they would find in California before they could leave the state. If they could reach Sacramento, they would be able to slip out of the state nearly undetected by either hitchhiking or stowing themselves away on a delivery train. At least, that was his goal.

Such a task was easier said than done. If they took a train to Sacramento, there would be no stops. They wouldn't be able to get off, which meant that if the Executioners recognized them as they boarded the train, then it would be a simple matter of sending a couple squads to Sacramento ahead of time and setting up an ambush. If Samantha was feeling particularly crafty, she could have a team infiltrate the train while it was en route to Sacramento. He and Lilith wouldn't have anywhere to go should that happen.

They were in a troubling predicament.

This would be so much easier if we could hop on a plane...

Except planes were even more dangerous. They might escape from California, but security checks were a lot tighter. ID checks. Metal Detectors. Baggage checks. No thanks.

"Mmm..."

Lilith stirred from her slumber as he shifted on the bench. They were currently in a large train station. None of the people walking by paid them any attention.

He looked at the young woman as she raised her head from his shoulder and let out a yawn, her hands stretching above her head and her legs stretching out as far as they could go.

Christian also used this time to surreptitiously take in the prepossessing sight of Lilith as she stretched like a cat. With her chest thrust out, her breasts were pressed tightly into her shirt as the fabric elongated and became taut. Likewise, he could see one lovely leg poking out of the slit on her jean skirt.

As her arms and legs came back in and her posture relaxed, Lilith looked at him with a sleepy smile. "Have you decided on where we should go next?"

"Maybe," Christian answered in a vague manner. "I know where I want to go, but I don't know if getting there via train is the safest route to travel."

"Should we use a cab?"

"No. Too expensive. A pair of train tickets costs about $200.00 each to get from one major city to the next, give or take. A cab would cost twice as much at the very least, and we're running out of funds."

Of the money that Christian had taken from the Executioner account, they now only had about $1,250.00. The cost of multiple train tickets, plus food, wasn't cheap. Christian estimated that they would have enough to leave the state with maybe a little left over if they were conservative, but after that they would need to find a way to earn more money.

Lilith frowned as her brows furrowed. Christian thought she looked cute, but he quickly shook his head immediately after thinking that. Now was not the time for such thoughts.

"What do you think we should do then?" she asked.

"I'm not sure yet. I think we might have to risk it, but…" he trailed off and ran a hand through his hair.

There were just too many variables for him to make this kind of decision and still feel at ease. He knew that they needed to reach Sacramento if they wanted to leave the state. While San Jose and San Francisco were also in that area, they were not as close to the border as Sacramento was, and he did not feel that comfortable in those cities. They were too close to the ocean, which meant he would have less directions to run in should the Executioners come knocking. He couldn't take a ship either, for the same reason he couldn't take a plane.

"In that case, why don't we get a coffee, and you can think on it some more?" Lilith suggested—suggested being an euphemism because it was clear that she had no intention of letting him say no. Before he could even answer she stood up, grabbed him by the hand, pulled him up with her, and then took off in the direction of the nearest coffee stand.

"You've become awfully spirited," Christian commented as Lilith put his arm around her shoulder. "What happened to the shy and demure young woman I first met in Seal Beach?"

"She's taken a temporary leave of absence," Lilith said, smiling at him.

"It certainly seems that way."

Lilith had undergone some startling changes since they started journeying together. It wasn't enough for anyone who didn't know her to notice, but having spent quite a bit of time growing intimately familiar with her, he was able to see the changes easily. She was more sure of herself, less afraid of being in crowds of people, and displayed a confidence that hadn't been present before. Men hardly even caused her to flinch anymore—unless they got too close.

That was the only real change, however, as everything else about the girl was the same. She was still a sweetheart. Wouldn't hurt a fly—unless the fly just so happened to be male.

Another small difference came, not from Lilith, but from the people around her. Christian hadn't spend much time contemplating it before—his thoughts had been elsewhere—but the blonde woman was no longer attracting massive amounts of male attention.

That wasn't to say men *didn't* stare at her, because they did. They just didn't stare at her anymore than they would any other attractive female. It was weird, but Christian couldn't find it in himself to dislike the change. He welcomed it. Now he not only didn't have to worry about cracking the heads of anyone foolish enough to try something with Lilith, he also didn't have to be concerned about her attracting too much attention for her own good.

Sometimes, you had to be thankful for the little things in life.

They stepped up to the booth of a basic coffee shop, where an overweight woman with brown hair, a large nose, and an acne problem stood behind a cash register, waiting to take their orders.

"What can I get for you?" she asked, glaring at Lilith.

Christian shook his head. At least there was one thing that hadn't changed about the people around them. The men might no longer become drooling idiots at the mere sight of her, but the women she bumped into still gave her ugly looks.

Jealousy was a hideous emotion.

"Um, I would like a…" Lilith scanned the list of drinks, her eyes sparkling a second later. A dazzling smile caused her face to light up. "You have coffee milk! I'll take that!"

"Size?"

"Medium."

Christian gave his lovely partner an amused smile. "Excited much?"

"Um!" Lilith nodded. "Coffee milk is the official state drink of Rhode Island. Back when I was a little girl, my mom used to take me to this really small coffee shop where I would always have some."

As Christian gazed at Lilith, he found himself captivated by her eyes. He had always thought her eyes were pretty, even before he'd fallen in love with her. Her blue eyes were clearer than the sky, deeper than the ocean, and sparkled like gemstones. They stole his breath away.

While he admired her, Lilith, too, locked onto his visage. Her eyes flickered a bit, moving from his eyes to his lips. Christian brought his head down as she tilted hers up. Her eyelids slowly fluttered shut as their lips were brought closer together—

"Ahem!" A loud cough knocked the two out of their reverie. Their heads jerked back as if scalded. They looked at the cough's source, the woman behind the register, who was now staring at Lilith as though hoping to burn a hole through her. "And what would you like, sir?"

Christian gave the woman a disapproving frown. Out of the corner of his eye, he saw Lilith giving the lady a frown of her own, though hers was laced with sadness.

The downturn of his lips growing, he said, "I'll also have a coffee milk, large." He looked at Lilith and smiled. "I've never had one before, and since you seem to love it so much, I might as well find out what the hype is about, right?"

His words caused Lilith's frown to turn into a small smile. He got the feeling that she knew what he was trying to do.

She nodded with faux enthusiasm. "Right!"

They moved off to stand near the counter where their drinks would be placed when ready. As they stood there, Christian leaned down until his mouth was right near Lilith's ear and whispered, "don't let that woman get you down too much, alright? She's allowing her perceptions of you to be tainted just because you're beautiful and she's jealous."

"I know." Lilith presented him with a melancholic smile. "It still hurts, though. Back when I was in middle school, all my friends left me because boys paid more attention to me. While I used to play it off and pretend it didn't bother me, it really did." Her shoulders slumped. "Even after I left Rhode Island, changed my name, and tried to start over, nothing changed. Every time I tried to make a couple of really good girlfriends, they would turn their noses up at me. The few girls who didn't outright ignore me on the spot left when their boyfriends tried to take advantage of me. They called me a seductress and claimed that I was just a slut who was only good at spreading her legs."

Some people might have thought that being as alluring as Lilith was a blessing, but Christian was beginning to realize that it was more like a curse than anything. Men ogled you. Women ignored you or, barring that, stared at you with scorn simply because you were prettier than they were. He would've said it was unpleasant, but that didn't seem to adequately describe how horrible her life must have been.

He wondered if that was how all succubi felt, or if it was just Lilith.

Feeling the desire to comfort her, or maybe he just wanted to make himself feel better, Christian moved behind Lilith and wrapped both arms around her stomach. He pulled her close and leaned down so he could set his head on her shoulders.

"I'm sorry," he said.

"Don't be. I did find some good people who weren't bothered by my looks or the amount of attention I attracted." She placed her hands on his forearms and leaned into his embrace. "Maria didn't care. Granted, she's gorgeous, athletic, and gets almost as much attention as I do. I also don't think she cares for guys that much."

"You think she bats for the other team?"

"No. Nothing like that." Lilith laughed. "I just meant that I don't think she really cares about being in a relationship right now. She's really dedicated to her studies and training. Maira is super smart on top of being a star athlete. I think she plans on being an Olympic athlete or a professional cross country runner, or maybe even a professional trainer. She's almost always studying for an exam or exercising for her next big race."

"She sounds dedicated."

"She is. That's why I think she doesn't care that I attract more male attention whenever we go out. She's not looking for a boyfriend, so it doesn't bother her."

"Hn. Makes sense."

"One medium and one large coffee milk!"

Christian and Lilith grabbed their respective drinks and walked back to their bench arm in arm. He was glad to see that no one had attempted to steal their luggage while they were away. Not that they could unless they were a professional bodybuilder. His suitcase weighed at least a hundred pounds.

They sat back down and snuggled together, looking the perfect picture of a young couple in love. No one would have guessed that they were on the run from a secret religious organization. Christian wanted to keep it that way.

"Have you figured out how we're going to travel?" asked Lilith.

"I believe we're going to have to risk taking the train to Sacramento." Christian took a sip of his coffee milk. He blinked. "This is pretty good."

"Isn't it?" Lilith smiled as she drank some of her own beverage. When she removed the—now lidless—cup from her mouth, she set it down near her feet and sighed contently. "I'd forgotten how much I love milk coffee."

"I can see that." Christian was thoroughly amused. "You're enjoying it so much that you've gotten some on your face."

"Really?"

"Yes. Just a little though. Right here." Christian gestured to his upper lip, indicating to Lilith that she had a coffee milk mustache.

"Would you mind cleaning it off for me?" she asked, batting her eyelashes at him.

"It would be my pleasure."

Christian was getting better at reading between the lines, or at least reading Lilith. He knew exactly what she wanted. Leaning his head down, he proceeded to get all of the milk coffee off of her upper lip… eventually.

***

It was done. Sure, it had taken him a long time to accomplish his task, much longer than usual, but that mattered little. He had enjoyed the challenge. Fighting against a worthy adversary was a worthwhile undertaking, and what worthier opponent could there be than his own best friend?

Yes, this game of cat and mouse that they had played was truly enjoyable. He'd had more fun tracking his friend than anything else he'd done in a while. It was too bad they weren't on an even playing field. Maybe if they had time, after all this was over, he could ask Christian for a chess match or something. For someone who thought more with his heart than his head, the raven-haired Warrior was a surprisingly strong contender.

Tristin Baluf leaned back in his chair, a thoroughly satisfied smile on his face. He watched the video playing on the screen. It showed Christian and Lilith getting on a train to Sacramento. They were in disguise—damn good ones, too. He'd almost mistaken them for a pair of random passerby. Only his ability to mentally catalog and match a person's facial structure in mere seconds allowed him to realize that the young man with the obnoxiously colored hair was, in fact, Christian.

He had to give credit where it was due. That was a bold move on his friend's part. Tristin would have never suspected his friend of dying his hair and using sunglasses to hide his eyes, even to lose potential pursuers. Truly, it was an inspired idea.

"Bravo, my friend." Tristin grinned. "You made a good play, but you've clearly underestimated me. You should know that no one can get the best of Tristin Baluf! Bwahahahahaha!"

Tristin threw his head back in his seat and laughed. While he did his best impression of a stereotypical villain from a B-budget movie, several other intelligence agents took one look at him, and then decided they needed be somewhere else. He noticed them leave, but he wasn't bothered. None of these people could understand how awesome he was.

As he settled down, Tristin breathed in a deep, satisfied sigh, and then tried to figure out what he should do with this information. Should he give it to Samantha? Delete it? Or something else? There were a number of options, but he just couldn't tell which was the best one. He had no intention of letting his friend die. Aside from Christian being his best friend, he was also Tristin's greatest source of entertainment. It would be a right shame if he were killed.

And his friend's pretty little succubus, too. You just don't kill a beauty like that—too bad she was with Christian, and a succubus. Tristin doubted that he and she would get along when they met. It came with the territory.

Sometimes it was a curse being him. Why were all the most beautiful women succubi?

"I suppose I could give this information to Samantha," he spoke out loud. There was no one around to hear him, so it didn't matter. "She doesn't want him dead. Then again, shit sometimes happens on missions like this, and I doubt Christian is going to just go with whoever she sends without a fight. And heaven forbid something happens to Lilith. Christian would be devastated. He might even go on a rampage."

He pondered some more. Damn, this was a tough one. What a predicament he was in. To tell or not to tell? That was the question. Or was it the answer?

"Really, it would depend on who Samantha sends, I guess."

She would probably send a squadron at first. It would be a small one most likely. Trains were not conducive to large battles with a lot of people, so a group of no more than six Executioners; three to travel from the back and three from the front. Yes, that sounded about right.

"Hmm… hmm…"

Still thinking, Tristin spun around in his chair. He really liked how these chairs could spin in one direction or the other without end.

"I think I'll tell Samantha," he decided, nodding his head. "It would be for the best."

He would just have to find some way to inform Christian of any sneak attack or ambush an hour or two before it happened. His friend could handle the rest.

Cackling away, Tristin began hacking into the security cameras located on the train that Christian and Lilith had taken to Sacramento.

Never let it be said that Tristin Baluf didn't look after his friends.

***

Samantha was waiting for Tristin's report. He'd been hard at work for three days—at least, she was pretty sure he was hard at work. She hoped he was, for his sake, because if she caught him slacking off, there would be hell to pay.

Having never been part of the Intelligence Division—she had no talent with computers—she didn't know how long it would take to track Christian down, but she did hope it would happen soon. If anyone could find her wayward Executioner, it would be Tristin. He knew Christian the best.

That said, having Tristin be the one to determine Christian's location, or his next destination, may prove to be a double-edged sword. Just as Tristin knew everything, or almost everything, that there was to know about the raven-haired Executioner, so, too, did Christian know nearly all there was to know about Tristin. It was the very definition of the unstoppable force versus the immovable object scenario.

She was still confident that they would find Christian before he left California. Where Christian was working mostly on his own, with just that succubus to help him, Tristin had the entire Executioner network at his disposal. With the ability to hack into any system, anywhere, at any time, there was simply no way Christian could remain invisible. The question wasn't a matter of *if* they would find him, but *when* and how long it would take.

Hopefully, not too long.

While she waited for Tristin to come through for her, Samantha had taken to wiling the time away by doing paperwork. It was the bane of her existence. She was almost positive that Satan was the one who devised paperwork as a form of mental torture. There was simply no way that the merciful Almightly would ever fabricate such a horrid practice.

It was during this time, as she was about halfway through her stack, that someone knocked on her door. Thinking it was Tristin to deliver a report in person, she bade them to enter. "Come in."

The door opened. Samantha had to refrain from scowling.

In walked an old man who could stand to lose a pound or twenty. Sitting on his bald head was a large ceremonial hat, white and gold intermixed, with embroidery running along the gold trim in the form of crucifixes. As he walked into her room, shutting the door behind him, his stately robes, the white and gold robes of a bishop, swished.

"Bishop Vertrou," she greeted as cordially as possible. "I'm surprised to see you here."

"Really?" The old bishop seemed amused. The smile on his face indicated enough. He walked further into her office and sat down before she could even make the offer. "You shouldn't be. You should have known that I would come here eventually."

"Do tell?" Samantha feigned ignorance.

"Christian Crux." When she stiffened in her seat, the aging bishop chuckled. "Don't act so surprised, my dear. You should have known that I would find out about this eventually." He leaned back in his seat, a twinkle in his eye. "So, our dear Quatra has become a turncoat. I'm not surprised."

Quatra was the nickname given to Christian after he defeated Abaddon. It signified how he used two swords and two guns to dispatch his enemies.

"Christian is one of my best operatives," Samantha bit out, just short of snapping at him. She was having a hard time controlling her anger. She disliked it when people insulted her subordinates, especially when that subordinate's name was Christian. "He has completed every mission with distinction, going above and beyond the call of duty every time."

"Until now, you mean," the bishop couldn't help but snipe.

"That mission was a hoax from the start and you know it!" Samantha slammed her hands on the desk, generating a loud boom from the action. "You sent him on a mission that no male should have even attempted! That he was strangely unaffected by that succubi's allure is a miracle in and of itself! Never mind the fact that he ended up in combat with a werewolf we had no information on *and* a No Life King! I would say he's done a far better job of doing his duty than anyone else here!"

Samantha truly hated this man. Bishop Vertrou was a blight upon the Catholic Church. Never before had she met such a repugnant person. She would have liked to know how he even managed to become a Bishop, because there was simply no way someone who was so unsympathetic and condescending could ever earn such a high position on his own merit.

"Sit down, Samantha," Bishop Vertrou said, sending her a stern look. Samantha sent him a glare of her own, though she did acquiesce to his request. She hadn't even known that she'd stood up. "Are you calm now? Good, because I suggest you listen to me. Christian Crux is a menace. Oh, I don't deny his skill. I don't even deny his dedication. But, let's be realistic here, Christian is a stain upon our organization. He is something that should not exist, a danger to all that our holy community has worked towards."

"What are you talking about?"

"Oh, you mean you don't know?" Bishop Vertrou feigned surprise, right before he gave her a condescending smile. "Well, far be it for me to spoil the surprise. Just know that Christian is something that should not have been born into this world."

"What are you doing here?" Samantha finally bit out. "Or are you just here to insult my subordinate?"

"You mean former subordinate." Samantha's glare intensified. Bishop Vertrou maintained his condescending attitude. "Don't be so angry. I am speaking nothing but the truth."

"Why are you here?" she asked.

"I am merely here to see how your search is progressing."

"You don't need to worry about it. Christian will be found soon enough."

"That's good. I am most pleased to hear that. Now then, I do believe I'll take my leave. It's getting a bit stifling in here."

He was probably referring to the heated glare that Samantha was sending him. She had been trying to see if it was possible to burn a hole through someone with her eyes.

The old, overweight bishop made for the door. He paused upon reaching it, however, and turned his attention back to Samantha, who was glowering at him from where she sat. "I'll give you a chance to clean up this mess you've made. But, if you can't succeed, then I shall have someone more capable deal with it," he said.

Then he was gone.

Samantha growled, a guttural sound that bubbled from deep within her throat. Her nostrils flared as she breathed out of them, eyes glaring at the door as though willing it to combust. Her body shivered once, her rage barely suppressed. She took a deep breath, and then let it go, slumping into her chair. Much as she wanted to rage at the bishop's words, she couldn't. Not because she agreed with him, but because it would be unprofessional.

As she calmed her seething mind, Samantha pondered over the old bishop's words. What did he mean when he called Christian 'a danger to their community'? How could that be? She knew that Christian was not well-liked amongst some of the Clergy despite his faith, but she couldn't comprehend why anyone would think of him as a danger.

She shook her head. Vertrou was probably just trying to throw her off. That man loved his mind games.

The ringing of her phone snapped Samantha from her reverie. Picking it up and holding it to her ear, she snapped out a quick, "What?!"

"Oh, dear. Someone is in a foul mood. Is this a bad time?"

"Tristin." Samantha was almost relieved to hear from him—almost because she really didn't want to listen to his patronizing voice. "Do you have something for me?"

"What's this? No friendly banter? No 'hi, how are you?' for your friendly neighborhood intelligence agent? No—"

"Tristin!"

"Fine. You're just like Christian. Always ruining my fun." The man on the other end sighed. Samantha wished she could stick her hands through the phone line so she could wrap them around his neck and strangle him. *"I have the information you want."*

"You mean you know where Christian and the succubus are and where they are headed?"

"Yep."

"Then tell me everything I want to know," Samantha said, immediately forgetting that she was supposed to be annoyed with him. This was too important to let something like annoyance get to her.

It was time to bring her wayward Executioner home.

Chapter 4

There were various types of trains and each one was used for a particular purpose, from delivering goods and supplies to taking passengers. They could be used to travel throughout a single city, an entire state, or even nationally. There were also trains in Europe that traveled internationally, moving from one country to another.

The term high-speed rail was coined in 1964 when the first system of its design, known as the bullet-train, began operations in Japan. Conceived with the idea of high-speed travel at around 250 kmh, or 155 mph, high-speed rails like the bullet-train were especially created for the purpose of delivering passengers to and from their destination with as little travel time as possible. Some people had, at one point, called them the transportation of the future, as most were designed with sleek, streamlined appearances.

The train that Christian and Lilith had boarded was one such locomotive.

Sitting in their own compartment, the young couple cuddled together underneath a blanket as rain splattered against the window at near-inconceivable speeds. Night had long since fallen. Even without the rain outside, it would have been impossible to actually see their surroundings.

Not that it would have mattered at the speed they were traveling.

For once, they were not having sex. They were even dressed. At the very least, Christian was wearing a pair of pants while Lilith was clad in a small white nightgown and panties. They also weren't reading a light novel, which was another pastime they often did together despite being on the run, though Christian was still reading something.

Christian scrolled to the next page of his digital bible, smiling as he began reading the verse: *'If we confess our sins, he is faithful and just and will forgive us our sins and purify us from all unrighteousness.'* John 1:9 was his favorite verse from the bible, and it was one that made him think. All men were sinners. Humans were sinful creatures. The wrongful acts they could commit upon each other were as numerous as they were disturbing. Murder. Rape. Abuse. Desecration. Destruction of property. Unfaithfulness. Theft. There were an innumerable amount of atrocities that human beings committed upon each other on a daily basis.

So then, why is it that humans are creatures worthy of being saved and those who are not human aren't?

It was a question that had been turning in his mind for some time, ever since he had found out that Lilith was a succubus, actually. She was purer than many humans he had met. There were many people within the Executioners who were more sinful and loathsome than her. Why were they worthy of being saved when she was not? What made them deserving of salvation and Lilith damnation?

He did not have the answer, not yet, but Christian suspected that he would find it sometime during this new journey.

There were many other verses that he liked, proverbs that made him think: John 3:16, Romans 12:2, among others. Each one made him think that maybe, just maybe, the path that the Catholic Church—and the Executioners in particular—were taking was wrong.

"It's been a long time since I've read a bible." Christian stopped reading to look at Lilith, who was staring at the words on the screen with a strange kind of fascination, like they were an alien language or hieroglyphs from a long dead civilization. "I haven't even touched one since my mom died."

"Was she Catholic?"

"Christian."

"Ah. And what about you?"

"I was Christian too, I think. Sometimes I wonder if I just went to church because my mom did. I never really believed in Christ." She looked up at Christian, a self-conscious expression on her face. "Does that bother you?"

He sighed. "I would be lying if I said it didn't." His words made her flinch, but he just smiled and kissed her temple. "But it's not like I'm going to hold it against you either. There are many Executioners who do not follow the bible, or have even picked up the book. I think, of the fifty-six or so members in my caste that live in the barracks with me, only about one or two were devout followers of the faith. The rest are simply there because we needed strong people to fill our ranks."

At his words, Lilith relaxed into his embrace. She rested her head on his shoulders. Christian returned her gesture by tightening his hold around her.

"Why do you believe in God?" she asked in a soft voice.

Christian pondered her words before answering. "Because I find it impossible to believe that this world could have been created by anything other than an all-powerful being that transcends humanity's ability to understand. And to be quite frank, I find the idea that the universe and everything in it was created from an explosion to be even more ridiculous than there being a single creator who did the same thing. An explosion is the release of accumulated energy. If nothing existed before the Big Bang, then there would be no energy for the explosion that created the universe."

"I don't know if I can ever believe in God," Lilith admitted after a moment of silent contemplation. "So many bad things happen in this world. All the boys in my class acted like pigs around me, my own teacher tried to rape me, my mother was murdered before my eyes by a vampire, and that very same vampire tried to claim me as his property. And that's only what happened to me. You look on the news and all you hear about are collisions with drunk drivers, children being killed in school shootings, rape, murder, war. If there is a God, how could he let this happen to us?"

"That's a question I think a lot of people who don't believe ask." Christian paused, shook his head, and then amended his statement. "No, even people who do believe in God ask that question. I have."

"And what do you think? Do you know why God allows these horrible things to happen to us?"

"I have my guesses." Christian furrowed his brow. "I think the reason these horrible things happen is because God gave humans free will, and because he gave us free will, it means we are free to make mistakes, as only a race that is imperfect can."

Another moment of silence passed. The only sounds were the rattling of the train as it moved across the tracks and the rain hitting their window.

"Do you think God made a mistake when he created everything?" she asked.

"I don't know. I suppose that would depend on what God's plan for us is." Christian shrugged.

"And what is God's plan?"

Christian chuckled, the sound reverberating in his chest. "That is the question that I think all of us would like to know."

***

After he finished answering nature's call, Christian walked back to their compartment. To his right were several windows, evenly spaced apart by a couple of inches, showing a view of the darkness and rain. His left side consisted of doors with a number on them, each one leading to a compartment. His compartment number was 104.

The hallway was small, and as he walked along the off-white carpet, his booted feet made dull thudding noises to accompany the sound of water hitting glass. A flatscreen television hanging on the wall showed the latest news. Apparently, someone had attempted to rob a bank in Los Angeles. No surprise there. That city was rampant with crime.

He was just about to turn away from the TV when the screen went blank with startling suddenness. It flickered with white nose, and then came back on again. Yet what it showed was not the news but a message: *"They are infiltrating the train tonight at 9:00pm. Be ready."*

Christian froze. His eyes widened and his muscles became stiff. Reflexes soon kicked in, and he whirled around, his eyes searching for any sign of something in his vicinity that should not be there. It was only after a second of searching that he noticed it, not something off or wrong, but something that he hadn't paid attention to because his disguise had given him a false sense of security.

There was a security camera located in the corner of the hall near the bathroom.

"Tristin," he muttered, glaring silently at the camera. It had to be him. There was no other explanation. Was that man watching him even now? How had he seen through his disguise? After searching the area and finding nothing there, he looked up at the television again.

It now displayed a timer. *Ten minutes left*, it read.

Cursing to himself, Christian quickened his pace and rushed into his compartment. His haste startled Lilith, who nearly jumped off the seat when he opened the door too quickly and caused it to slam against the adjacent wall.

"Christian! You scared me!" She held a hand to her chest, shoulders heaving as she took in several calming breaths of air.

"Sorry," Christian murmured, rushing over to the couch that Lilith was sitting on and dropping to his knees. "We've got a situation. Get dressed. Hurry."

Without preamble, he pulled out the trunk from underneath the seat with a slight grunt. Laying it on its side, he flipped through the code, causing the hatch to unlatch, and opened it up. His swords and the sniper rifle rested inside.

"Why? Is something wrong?" asked Lilith, even as she snatched her clothes from where they were folded on the other couch.

"Yes. The Executioners will be infiltrating this train in less than ten minutes."

"W-what?" Lilith's eyes widened. "How?"

Christian grabbed the straps connected to his sheaths. Gabriel and Phanuel were already sheathed. He strapped them across his back and adjusted them for easy access. As he worked on getting himself ready for action, he said, "If they follow standard procedure for infiltrating a moving train, then they'll come in through the roof. From there, they'll split up into two teams. One will come in from the front. The other will come from the back. It's a standard tactic."

He knelt back down and looked over the rest of his weapons. There was a good deal of ammo left over, normal bullets mostly. He frowned. The squadron was probably going to be wearing bulletproof vests.

"I'm not sure how many they'll send after us," Christian added as he grabbed several magazines and attached them to the front of his sword straps. He also took the liberty of clipping several to the specially-designed ammo holders on his thighs. "But there will be no more than six coming in at the start. It's too cramped in these trains for any more people than that to fight efficiently." His eyes narrowed in thought. "I wouldn't be surprised if they have more waiting in case backup is needed."

"W-what should we do?" asked Lilith.

Upon hearing the tremor in her voice, Christian stopped what he was doing and stood up. He placed his hands on Lilith's shivering shoulders. Her eyes had grown wide, pupils dilated. She was frightened.

"You trust me, right?" he asked. Lilith nodded. "Then trust me when I say that I will not let anything happen to you. No matter what happens, I will protect you."

The shivering stopped. Lilith stared up at him. She then took a deep breath, visibly calming down.

"Okay," she said, nodding.

Christian smiled at her before kneeling down once more. This time, he picked up the as of yet unused sniper rifle and began putting it together with the skills of an expert. He had spent so many hours training to use this that he could put it together with his eyes closed. It was too bad that he was still a terrible shot.

He never would have imagined that this thing would help save his life one day.

That Sebastian guy must have been psychic or something.

***

Several meters above the train, hovering and keeping pace with the high-speed vehicle as it moved along the tracks, was a peregrine-class dropship, a heavy troop carrier used for carrying infantry to and from the battlefield. Designed after the very bird for which they derived their names, peregrine dropships were one of the newest inventions created by the Executioners' Science Division. It was one of the few truly useful things they had created.

Much like the name suggested, it was shaped in the semblance of a Peregrine Falcon. Sleek and sturdy, the dropship was painted a dark blue so as to better blend in with the night and mask its presence from anyone who might have been looking at it.

Like most things the Science Division was known for making, peregrine-class dropships, while not necessarily meant to be used for battle, were more than capable of causing serious amounts of property damage and destruction via explosions. With one 70mm rotary cannon, two ANVIL-II ASM missile pods, and a rear-mounted AIE-468H HMG, the flying armory had quite the payload. And that wasn't including the ten troops each peregrine was capable of carrying.

Following standard operating procedures, the Peregrine came in close to the train, hovering six yards above its surface. With a hiss of hydraulics, the bottom hatch cracked open. Six people stepped up to the lip of the vehicle. Each one was clad in black, wore lightly armored clothing, had a sword strapped across their backs and a gun strapped to their thighs. Night-vision goggles covered their faces, though they looked more like visors than goggles.

Several lines were launched out of the Peregrine. There were three in total. They struck the roof and remained connected, the metal ropes snapping taut.

Six members slid down the ropes one at a time, until all of them were standing on the train's roof. The wind tore at them, causing their clothes to whip about. The roof was slippery from the rain. Two of the strike team almost lost their balance when they slid across the metal surface.

The leader, a man who had slightly different, more streamlined armor and shoulder pads, made several hand gestures. Two of the other five came up to him, while the others went in the opposite direction. More hand gestures followed, and the two with him began following him as he made his way to the front of the train.

When they reached the second to first car, they stopped. There they knelt down. The leader gestured to the team member with ropes strapped securely to her belt, then to the roof in front of the nearest window. The woman nodded and knelt next to the spot indicated.

She took out the rope, unlatched it from her belt, and then attached the magnetized end to the train. After pulling on it a few times to make sure the rope was secure, she nodded at her leader and took several steps back. The man tossed the length of the rope off the train, letting it hang down. He then grabbed it with both hands, attached a small device on his belt to it, and then slid down its length, until he was standing vertically in front of a window.

He reached into his pouch and pulled out a small device that looked a lot like a metal twig with really long arms and a suction cup. Sticking the device to the window, he pressed a small button on its top and watched as it went to work. The arms extended until they reached the ends of the glass panel. They began emitting intense, red lasers that cut through the glass by super-heating the material. When it was done, the arms retracted and the man grabbed the device and pushed.

The glass fell inwards, but it did not fall to the ground, which would have no doubt alerted passengers to their presence. He moved forward, slipping inside head-first while simultaneously unhooking himself from the rope. Now inside, he took a quick look around. Once he had confirmed that no one had seen him, or was even in the hall, he stuck a hand outside and gestured for the other two to come in.

Seconds later, they were all inside.

Another gesture and their weapons came out. The woman unsheathed a pair of knives strapped to her thighs. The other male in the group pulled a standard 9mm pistol with a silencer from its holster, and the leader unsheathed his sword. Together, they slowly made their way through the car.

They reached the car with the compartment that housed the traitor and the succubus inside at the same time as the other group. The two parties looked at each other from across the room, silently communicating. Apparently, the team that had started from the back hadn't run across the two either.

Did that mean the famed Quatra didn't know they were there? What luck.

Still, just because he was unaware of their presence didn't mean they could be reckless. This was still the man who had defeated a greater demon on his own. Trickery, guile, and stealth were needed if they wanted to succeed.

The one in charge slowly gestured towards the other group, telling them to move with caution. He received a nod and both groups stalked forward.

They had just gotten within two meters of the door when, without warning, the door and the walls exploded in a violent spray of fire and a powerful release of energy. Everyone near the door was blown back and bombarded with large chunks of metal, plastic, and wood. The large pieces of debris impacted their bodies as they were thrown about with impunity. Several particularly hot pieces of shrapnel managed to penetrate the group's armor, digging into their flesh and unleashing white hot fire in their veins. And then, just as the energy pushed away all of the super-heated air, the lack of oxygen near the explosion caused all of the air to reverse course and try to fill the space left by the blast, causing more debris to smack against them. When everything was said and done, there was a large chunk of the railway car missing, looking almost like something with several rows of massive teeth had taken a bite out of it.

The six groaning Executioners laid on the floor in a daze.

***

The restroom was obviously not meant for two people. This was a given. Restrooms within trains, or any moving vehicle large enough to have a restroom, weren't designed with comfort in mind. They were made with the idea of conserving as much space as possible. That said, Christian couldn't find it in himself to complain, despite the perilous situation.

He and Lilith were standing in a bathroom, their bodies pressed tightly together. They weren't kissing, which was kind of a shame, but given the situation, it couldn't be helped. Christian needed to be alert for what was going to happen next. He couldn't remain aware if he was busy sucking face.

When did my thoughts get so lecherous?

Shaking his head, he closed his eyes and strained his ears, listening. He could hear Lilith's soft breathing. It was a little shaky. She was obviously still scared. He couldn't blame her. He could also hear the wind howling outside, the rain as it splattered against the roof and walls, and the wheels as they ground against the tracks.

He could even hear the footsteps and light breathing of exactly three people walking past the bathroom.

Seconds later, an ear-splitting explosion ripped through the air. Lilith didn't scream, but she did clench her eyes shut and bury her face in Christian's chest. He held onto her as the thundering, concussive noise burst in their eardrums, deafening them. The world seemed to shake as the train bounced. Christian's back hit a wall, but he didn't react and merely wrapped his arms tighter around Lilith. When the sound and shaking died down, Christian unlatched himself from Lilith, grabbed her hand, and opened the door.

Outside the restroom was a mess. Some people might have said it looked like a hurricane had blown through. Christian would have said that the science department had, once again, done their job too well. Their compartment was gone. Not destroyed, just gone. Where there had once been a room, there was now a gaping hole in which he could see nothing but darkness and rain.

There were also several people lying on the ground.

Christian pulled Lilith to the door at their end of the car, opened it, and ran through, closing it shut behind them. He dragged her along, forcing her to keep up as he hurried forward. A sound from outside made his ears twitch.

He recognized the low-pitched whine of high-propulsion engines. The Executioners had definitely gone all out in capturing him if there was a Peregrine involved. He just hoped they didn't have a member of the XIII on board.

The plan that Christian had come up with to escape was simple. Part one was activating the detonation device on the sniper rifle and setting it to explode when it detected a heat source exactly two meters away. Taking into account the density of the wall, the blast radius of the explosion, and the amount of force it would have generated, Christian determined that the eruption of energy would be enough to, if not knock the Executioners after them unconscious, then at least daze and confuse them without killing them.

Even if he was no longer an Executioner, he still refused to kill a human unless he had to.

He and Lilith would then make their way from their compartment toward the back, where they would eventually disembark via one of the emergency hatches. It wasn't the best plan he'd ever crafted. Some would even say it was downright insane. It probably was.

It also happened to be the only plan they had.

Checking out the window, Christian could see a small amount of light flashing by overhead. That would be the Peregrine. It would likely search up and down the train using infrared technology to see if they could find any suspicious movement. Then it would drop the last four Executioners right on top of him.

At least he didn't have to worry about it opening fire.

Acting quickly before it could reach them, Christian pressed Lilith against the wall, earning a startled yelp. "Sorry," he breathed as he pressed himself against her and crashed his lips into hers. Lilith's eyes went wide for all of one second, right before they shut closed and she began kissing back just as hard.

While he made out with Lilith, Christian tried to keep his ears open. With luck, the Peregrine's pilot would assume the mass of heat that composed of him and Lilith was just a young couple making out in the hall. The whine was getting louder now. The keening hum of propulsion engines soon reached a crescendo, yet it didn't stop and kept on moving. Relief swept over him as the sound disappeared.

He released his hold over Lilith's mouth with a gasp.

"Christian," Lilith moaned almost petulantly at the loss. She looked, well, hot and bothered. Her face was flushed, her breathing heavy, and a small trickle of sweat ran down her neck, glistening in the light.

"Sorry," he apologized. "We can pick up where we left off once we're out of danger."

Lilith did not look pleased. She also didn't complain.

With the Peregrine gone, Christian ran toward the nearest emergency exit. He unsealed the hatch before kicking the door open. As the large metal object descended into darkness, he closed his green eye and looked into the night.

Something he had discovered about himself after he'd defeated Abaddon was that his red eye had a form of night vision. When he focused, his red eye gained the same qualities found in most nocturnal animals. If he focused really hard, he could even give himself a basic form of 360 degree vision. It was a boon in battle, and also a great help when he was fighting against multiple opponents.

"Christian..."

"Hmm?"

"Your eye..."

"What about my eye?" asked Christian as he peered outside.

"I... no." Lilith shook her head. "Never mind."

Christian frowned, but he decided not to let her hesitation bother him. He needed to concentrate on getting them out of there alive.

They were passing over a river. Judging by how long they had been traveling, he would hazard a guess and say it was the Stanislaus River. Not exactly as far as he'd been hoping for, but better than could be expected, considering they'd been attacked by the Executioners. After staring into the river, he concluded that there was a thirty meter drop from where they stood. It would be painful—for him—but survivable.

He looked back at Lilith. "Ready?" A hesitant nod was his answer. "Then grab onto me and don't let go no matter what."

Lilith did exactly that, latching onto him with near bone-crushing force, her fear and the adrenaline pumping through her veins fueling her strength. He didn't let that bother him. He hugged her back just as tightly.

"Okay." He breathed in, steadied himself, and then breathed out. "Here we go."

With those words, Christian threw them both out of the emergency exit.

Chapter 5

In Newtonian Physics, free-fall is described as any motion of a body where its weight is the only force acting upon it.

Christian not only had his own weight acting upon him, but he also had Lilith's.

Figuratively speaking, this could still be considered free-fall, just not in the technical sense because both his and Lilith's weight were affecting his descent.

The act of free-falling was a very unusual feeling. You don't actually feel like you're falling, but rather, like you're floating. The wind whips fiercely around you, howling in your ears. A part of you knows that you're moving at an incredibly high speed, but you can barely tell save for the way the air pushes against you as you plummet to the earth.

Christian had undergone this action many times in his life, usually from really high buildings in order to get the drop on his targets, sometimes even as high up as ten stories. He'd become something of an expert at it and not breaking every bone in his body. Most people thought he was crazy because the only way to learn how to fall properly was to practice, which involved breaking a lot of bones before getting it right. But so what? What were a few broken bones over learning a valuable skill?

Dropping thirty meters from a train into a river with a screaming girl gripping him for dear life was nothing at all like the kind of fall he was used to. Aside from the wind whipping around them being freezing cold and the rain flying against his face, smacking him with a harshness not normally found in small drops of water, there was also the girl in his arms to account for.

All these thoughts felt strangely slow yet they passed through his head in a matter of seconds.

A glance down with his single open eye showed that they were getting much closer to the river. Six meters. Preparing to hit the water's surface, which was sure to leave bruises come the marrow, Christian did his best to relax every muscle in his body with the exception of his arms and hands. He needed those to keep hold of Lilith. Three meters. He breathed in as slowly as he could. Two meters. Lilith continued screaming in his ear, making the act of calming down much harder than it should have been. One meter.

They hit the water.

Pain slammed against him, a stinging pain in his chest and a more spread out agony in his back. Christian could feel his ribs snap. At least two of them were broken. Fire spread through his body, like molten lava filling his organs. One of his ribs must have pierced his insides.

Fortunately, the pain didn't last long. Barely a minute passed. After which, an icy chill swept through his body. It covered him, numbing the pain and allowing him to focus. Water, he realized. That's what was keeping the pain at bay, freezing cold, rushing water.

Lilith was still holding him tightly. She wasn't screaming anymore, but now she was shivering. Pushing himself to work, Christian kicked his legs as hard as he could. He released a few bubbles from his mouth to make sure he was moving up instead of down. He was, thank God, and the two of them eventually breached the surface.

A heavy gasp came from both him and Lilith. The girl clutching his body like a life-saver looked around wildly, her hair flinging about—and also smacking him in the face with a series of wet slaps—and her body shivering from the cold.

Christian, realizing the girl was on the verge of panicking, shouted, "kick your feet!"

She promptly did so. What else could she do?

As Lilith helped keep them both afloat, Christian took stock of their situation. The river was moving quickly. Very quickly. The current tried to drag them down. It was a chore to keep their heads above the water's surface. If they didn't do something soon, they would drown.

He closed his left eye. His enhanced vision picked up the edge of the river several yards away. He kicked his feet, propelling him and Lilith forward.

His breath came out in heavy gasps. Water splashed into his mouth, making him choke. His legs quickly turned to lead. He needed to reach the edge of the lake. Lilith would die if he didn't. Faster. Harder. Kick. Kick!

With one last surge of effort, Christian made it to the edge. There was a tree root sticking out of the dirt wall. He kept one arm around Lilith and latched onto it with his other hand.

"Lilith!" he shouted over the sounds of rushing water. "Grab onto the root!"

She reached out and grabbed the root—tried to anyway. It kept slipping from her hands. Christian gritted his teeth as the girl panicked. He gave one more surge of effort to enable another attempt, but he failed as the dirt wall crumbled. He and Lilith were once more sucked into the turbulent depths of the river.

Unprepared and already in mid-gasp, Christian ended up inhaling a massive amount of water.

He tried to cough. It didn't help. He only ended up sucking in more water.

This couldn't be the end. He had to at least save Lilith. He needed to… needed to… needed…

***

Lilith didn't know what to do. She and Christian were being dragged along a river. She couldn't breathe. She could hardly think. She was cold and tired and at a complete loss.

I need to do something! I have to save Christian! What should I do?

Christian wasn't responding to her. His body was limp in her arms. She held onto him as tightly as she could. She didn't want to get separated from him by the current.

I need to find a way out of this river! I need to do something!

She kicked her legs. It was one of the last things Christian had told her to do before he blacked out, so that's what she did. She kicked and kicked and kicked and kicked. Yet no amount of kicking seemed to be helping her. Why wasn't anything happening? Why were they no closer to shore?

Oh, God, please don't let us die here! Don't let Christian die here! Please!

It was a little late to be praying to God. Lilith hadn't prayed since the last time her mom made her go to church, but she did so anyway. She had nothing left to lose.

Please! Please, God! Please help me save Christian! Help!

She was losing oxygen. She could feel it. Her lungs were burning.

Is this how we're going to die? she asked. Was this their end? Drowning in a river? *God, please, if you don't want to save me, then at least save Christian! Please!*

Lilith begged, pleaded for a miracle. If nothing else, she wanted to at least save the person she loved, the one who meant the world to her.

Please!

The world was becoming unfocused, beginning to blur, growing fuzzy. Her vision was fading. Her lungs begged for oxygen. If only she had a vine to grab. If only a vine could grab her and haul them out of this river.

Just as her world was about to become consumed by the blackness that seeped at the edges of her vision, something grabbed her hand. No. It didn't just grab her hand; it wrapped around her hand. It slithered up her arm and wrapped around that, too. There was a hard jerk. Lilith felt her arm get pulled out of its socket, snapping her back from the brink of unconsciousness. It didn't hurt, strangely enough, but it did cause her to lose her hold on Christian as they were both flung out of the river and tumbled through the air.

Lilith landed on her back, hitting hard ground. She gasped, her face scrunching up and tears leaking from her eyes. Her lungs heaved for several deep breaths as she looked around wildly, trying to see what had saved her. Had someone pulled her out of the river? Who was it?

There was no one. Nothing. Just a bunch of trees.

Lilith stumbled to her feet, wincing as her nerves flared up. Her legs hurt, a lot, but she tried to ignore that. She had to find Christian.

"Christian!" She called out, holding her useless right arm as she staggered blindly through the murky shades of dark silhouettes. "Christian!" Her foot hit a root, causing her to trip and smack her face against hard soil, making her nose throb. She could feel blood leaking from it, but she ignored that in favor of her search. "Christian! Answer me! Please!"

She eventually did find Christian. He was lying facedown on the ground. She had almost missed him. It was only because she had tripped over his leg that she'd managed to find him at all.

"Christian!" She dropped to her knees in a blind panic. "Please be alright! Please!"

She pushed him onto his back, his arms and legs flopping like sopping wet ramen noodles. He was pale. Even in the darkness of the night, she could see how pale his skin was, so white that it seemed translucent. His eyes were closed. He felt cold to the touch. She placed her head over his chest, pressing an ear to his shirt.

There was no heartbeat. He wasn't breathing.

"No… No! No! No!"

He isn't breathing! Why isn't he breathing?!

Lilith struggled to remember what to do in this situation. His lungs. She needed to send oxygen into his lungs. CPR. Mouth to Mouth. But what was the first step? What was it?! Oh! Right!

She knelt next to his chest, her right arm flopping uselessly beside her. Grabbing it, Lilith cracked it back in place in one swift, brutal motion. Her body underwent agony as her nerves flared up. Molten fire dripped through her arm. She gritted her teeth. She couldn't let the pain overwhelm her. Christian needed her.

She placed her formerly useless hand on his chest and placed the other hand over the first, waited for one second, and then pushed down, putting all of her weight into the act. One. Two. Three. She pinched his nose shut, placed her lips against his, and breathed. She then placed an ear to his mouth.

Nothing.

She repeated the process. Again. Again. Again. There was no way for Lilith to know how long she sat there, trying to resuscitate Christian. Seconds. Minutes. Hours. They meant nothing to her. The only thing that mattered was reviving her love.

One. Two. Three. Breath. Repeat.

It's not working!

Tears streamed from her eyes as she tried to breathe life into him again. One. Two. Three. Breath. Repeat.

Why isn't it working?!

Crystal liquid flowed down her cheeks and chin before dropping onto Christian's face. She tried again. And again. And again. And again.

"No! Come on, Christian!" Her pushes turned into violent shoves. Christian's arms jerked as she compressed his chest. "You're not dying on me! I won't let you! Now!" One. "Get!" Two. "Up!" Three. "Please!"

Just when Lilith was about to lose all hope, Christian coughed. Several different kinds of fluids erupted from his mouth, including a large gob of dark, crimson liquid. His eyes flew open. He coughed some more, then sucked in a deep breath. He looked around, eyes wide and panicked, and then his eyes landed on her.

"L-Lilith…"

"Christian!" Lilith cried, collapsing on top of him. Her body shook uncontrollably as emotions too numerous to name ran rampant through her body. Her heart rate spiked, beating almost painfully fast in her chest. That was when she began to cry in earnest. A torrent of salty water poured from her eyes and onto his already soaking wet shirt. "You're alive! I can't believe it! You're really... I was so worried!"

"L-Lilith, w-what... where..."

"We jumped into the river. You tried to make me grab a root, but I couldn't and we slipped and then you were knocked out and I didn't know what to do and I—"

Her fast-paced, frantic talking was stopped when a hand came to rest on her head.

"It's alright," Christian muttered, running his hand over her wet hair. "I'm alive. We're alive. Just take a deep breath and tell me what happened after I blacked out."

Lilith did exactly as told. She took several deep breaths. They didn't calm her down much. She was still jittery, but they did help, at least a little. Only when she was sufficiently calm did she begin speaking.

"After you blacked out, I didn't know what to do. You were unconscious, and my kicking was getting us nowhere. I don't... I can't understand what happened next. One minute I was certain we were going to die. The next something was wrapping around my arm and threw us out. I don't know what it was, but it felt weird, like it wasn't all there." She frowned, as did Christian. "And then I remember, I landed on the ground and found you. You weren't breathing, so I had to use CPR, and then... and then..."

"It's alright," Christian reassured her. "I'm right here. I'm alive, thanks to you. You saved me."

Lilith sniffled, but managed to smile. "I guess I did, didn't I?"

"Yes, you did." Christian tried to sit up. He didn't get far before a grunt of pain escaped his mouth and he fell back down. "Lilith?"

Responding to his call, she placed a hand on his back and helped him sit up. Once he was sitting, he tried to stand. He didn't make it very far before falling back down.

"C-Christian, take it easy!" Lilith tried to scold him. It wasn't very effective because of the worry in her voice. "You almost died. You shouldn't be moving right now. Get some rest. We can leave after that."

"Can't rest," Christian grunted, struggling to stand again. He failed. "The Executioners are bound to notice that we're no longer on board the train. When that happens, they'll send out a search party, and this is the most likely area they'll search because of the river. We need to be as far away from here as possible before that happens. Lilith, help me up, please?"

Hesitating for but a moment, Lilith eventually complied. She slung his arm over her shoulder and put her arm around his waist. Letting him lean on her for support, she helped him climb to his feet, grunting as she realized just how heavy he was.

"How much do you weigh, Christian?"

"145 pounds," he said as they began to walk at a snail's pace. The buckles of his straps clinked together, the noise accompanied by the sound of their wet slogging. "But with my swords, guns, the ammunition, and combat boots, I probably weigh somewhere around 260."

"Ugh." For some reason, Christian felt heavier now that she knew. "Maybe you shouldn't have told me that."

"Then you probably shouldn't have asked."

"Good point."

They walked in silence for some time, stumbling and tripping. Neither were sure which way they were traveling. It was dark and gloomy, and the only thing they could make out was the inky shapes of trees. Christian tried to use his eye, but he was too tired to focus properly.

"Christian, do you think that maybe we can drop some of your weapons?"

"No. We're going to need those at some point. I doubt this will be the last time we run into the Executioners. They'll come back, and when they do, we're going to need every bit of ammunition we have available."

"What about those grenades in your pocket?"

"Explosions make good distractions."

"I think you just like creating explosions," Lilith countered, remembering how he'd turned that long gun into an explosive and the damage it had done to the train.

"I'm not a member of the Science Division," Christian muttered like a petulant child.

"What?"

"… Never mind."

***

Neither of them knew how far they had traveled. It felt like they had been walking for miles, but given how slowly they were moving, it was probably closer to yards. Eventually, after who knew how long, they reached civilization. Trees became houses. Grass turned into pavement.

Light posts illuminated the way for them, allowing them to see the deserted streets.

Christian began shivering.

"We need to get you inside," Lilith determined.

Christian grunted, too pained to speak anymore, his shivers growing in intensity, and his breath coming out in quick, harsh pants. Lilith didn't know what was wrong, but she imagined that his injuries combined with the chill that was no doubt seeping into his bones was the source of his problems. She couldn't do anything about his injuries. All she could do was find a place to warm him up.

Lilith half-dragged Christian along the street. She scanned their surroundings. They were in a mostly suburban area. On either side of the street were houses, all lined up in rows. All of them had the same general shape and size, differing only in the color of their roof, the paint used on their walls, and the number of stories in height. None of the lights were on. The homeowners were most likely asleep.

For half a second, Lilith thought about knocking on a door to ask for help. She dismissed the idea seconds later when she thought about how someone would respond to their presence. If someone were to come up to her house dragging a half-dead man with swords, guns, and a lot of ammunition strapped to him, she'd probably call the police.

She would have to find somewhere else where they could spend the night.

Lilith walked on. Her feet ached. She was cold. A deep chill had entered her bones. Her legs felt like lead as she struggled to keep moving, step after step, dragging Christian's nearly dead weight.

After what felt like ages of walking, she eventually came across a school. Large, rectangular buildings made from concrete and painted a light tan were spread out in a decently sized space in front of a parking lot. The largest building, perhaps the main office, had big, bold lettering painted on the front in red and gold. It read Calico Middle School.

Below the letters was the painting of a bird. She couldn't tell what type of bird it was because it looked partly human, possessing a human-like face with a beak. It didn't really look like a bird at all. She could only tell what it was because of the wings.

"Come on," she said, grunting as she was forced to carry more of Christian's weight. He was losing strength fast. "It's just a little further. Once we get inside, we can find a nurse's office and warm ourselves up."

Christian didn't even bother to grunt. His head was lolling from side to side, and his eyes were flickering between half-lidded and closed. He was barely clinging to consciousness.

By the time she reached the door, Christian was almost dead weight. Lilith, with strength unknown to her, somehow managed to drag him all the way to the entrance. She was breathing heavily as she stared at the door that led into what appeared to be the main building. There was a greeting room, complete with a counter and several chairs lined up for people to sit on while they waited. All schools had a similar layout to each other. If this was the main office, then the nurse's office should be attached to it.

The door was locked. That was expected, though disappointing. Lilith reached into Christian's holster, feeling the cold weight of the gun, and pulled it out.

She had never used a gun before, but she did now, not by firing the gun, because she was afraid the noise would attract attention. Instead of shooting off a round or two, which she had no confidence that she would be able to do without blowing off her own foot, she used the butt of the gun to break the glass around the handle. When there was a wide enough hole, she stuck her hand through and unlocked the door.

Much like she had expected, the inside was indeed a reception room of some kind. Near the counter that the receptionist would sit behind was a hallway.

She lugged Christian in that direction.

After passing several doors labeled principal's office, vice-principal's office, and several other titles that she didn't bother remembering, Lilith found the nurse's office at the end of the hall.

Like most nurse's offices, this one sported a white tiled floor. There were three chairs backed up against the wall for students to sit in while they waited. Next to the chairs was a heating unit. It was old-fashioned, but some places still had them. A small cubicle-like office sat in the corner. She could see a desk, a swivel chair, and a computer inside. Over to her left was a cabinet filled with vials, containers, and boxes; it was most likely a medical cabinet. On her left was another room with a bed. That was what she'd been looking for.

Of course, it wasn't really a bed. It was more like an examination table that was cushioned so students sitting on it wouldn't be uncomfortable. It was good enough for her purposes, though, and that was all that mattered.

After setting Christian on the bed, she began to strip off his clothes. It was hard. His clothes were wet and stuck to his skin. It didn't help that Christian was no longer conscious. She tried not to panic when she realized this. He was breathing. If he was breathing, then it meant he was still alive. So she stripped him of his clothes, all of them. She also took off his ammo, grenades, guns, swords, sheaths, and anything else that she could find. The weapons she put under the medical bed. The clothes were spread out near the heating unit after she turned the dial as high as she could.

She then went in search of a blanket. Even with the heating unit on, they would need something to keep warm. She wasn't as bad off as Christian, but even she was longer able to ignore the chill seeping into her bones. Her shivering was getting worse.

Good fortune must have finally been with her because she found one in a chest in the small cubicle with the swivel chair and computer. It was large and quilted. It would do a perfect job of keeping them both warm.

Lilith laid the blanket on top of Christian. His body was shaking worse than before, and his skin had somehow become even more pale. She didn't think he was going into shock or hypothermia or something, but she didn't want to take any risks. After putting the blanket over him, she stripped herself bare, laid out her own clothes near his, then went back into the room where Christian slept.

Lifting up the blanket and crawling underneath it, Lilith cuddled so close to Christian that a slip of paper couldn't fit between them. She shivered horribly as her already cold skin came into contact with his freezing skin, but she ignored her own discomfort in favor of trying to help him generate body heat. After they had fought against a No Life King, tried to escape the state on a train, caused an explosion on said train, and jumped off that very same train into a freezing lake below and almost dying, she had no intention of losing him to something as inane as hypothermia.

As she waited, Lilith's eyes drooped. She tried to stay awake, but she eventually became so exhausted that her eyes closed on their own. Her breathing evened. Her body relaxed.

Lilith fell asleep clutching the young man underneath her like a lifeline.

Chapter 6

Christian woke up feeling warm. Warm and secure. His eyes were still closed, but his body felt like it was enveloped in a thick blanket. It wasn't until several seconds of laying there, trying to regain his bearings, that he realized that the reason he felt like he was wrapped up in a blanket was because he actually *was* wrapped up in a blanket.

He also wasn't alone underneath the large blanket either; Lilith was with him. They were both nude. He could feel her body as she lay on top of him, her breasts pressing into his chest, her nipples rubbing against him as she breathed in and out at a slow, steady rate. Her hands rested on his pectorals, while her legs were tangled with his own.

He raised his arms, the movements slow and a little spastic—he was more than a little sore. His arms felt like they had lead weights on them. With a grimace, he slowly moved until his hands rested on her back.

For a moment, Christian let them rest there. Lilith's back was warm and soft. Her supple muscles shifted beneath his touch. Soon, simply letting them remain there wasn't enough.

He moved his hands up and down, luxuriating in the feel of Lilith's soft skin, nothing at all like his own rough flesh. Lilith shifted, stirring just a bit. She mumbled in her sleep.

"No… Holo… don't eat so many apples… you'll get a stomachache…"

He snorted.

Finally opening his eyes, Christian found himself staring at a paneled ceiling. A tilt of his head revealed that he was in a small room with only one door that led into a larger room, which looked a lot like a very basic medical room. He could see his and Lilith's clothes lying on the floor next to a heating unit, and beyond that were chairs and a cabinet filled with medical supplies.

How did I get here?

His memory of the night before was more than just a little fuzzy. There were huge gaps in his memory in which he could not recall a single thing. He remembered their escape from the train, the detonation made by the sniper rifle turned explosive, jumping off the train with Lilith and then… ah, yes, that's right. They had fallen into a river. He couldn't recall much after that. All he remembered was trying to swim to safety and then a lot of walking.

What else had happened? How did they get here? And just where was here?

Lilith's breathing picked up and became heavier. Christian was worried at first, but then he realized that the reason her breathing was heavier than it had been a few seconds ago was because one of his hands was fondling her rear. When did that happen? He didn't remember moving his hand to her butt.

The girl stirred again, shifting on top of him and rubbing her body against his. Her breasts pushed further into his chest; her stiff nipples raked across his skin. Christian could feel the hairless beginning of her mound as it pressed down on his growing erection. It was a bit too much stimulation. Way too much.

As his hands continued to fondle her as though they had minds of their own, Lilith's breathing shifted, going from a soft hitch to a deep pant. Her fingers twitched against his chest. A second later, a low, soft moan escaped her parted lips, causing a strange, tingling sensation to travel down his spine.

Lilith stirred some more, then sat up, pushing herself off his chest with her hands and straddling his waist with those lovely thighs of hers. The cold air hit his chest, causing it to prickle and form goosebumps. He ignored the slightly chilly air in favor of the girl on top of him.

"Lilith."

She looked down at him, her sleepy eyes blinking several times. Even though her nose was bruised from what looked like a blunt force injury, and her eyes were rimmed with red, he still thought she was the most gorgeous woman that he'd ever seen.

"Christian?" She didn't seem to be awake yet. She was just sitting there, staring at him with those tired, half-lidded eyes, as if she wasn't quite sure what to make of him. After another second or two of this, her eyes widened fractionally as her mind rebooted. "You're awake! How are you feeling?"

"Fine," Christian said, taking a second or two to run a basic mental scan of his body. Having become intimately familiar with his own physical conditioning and limitations, he could easily tell what kind of damage he'd suffered from yesterday's events. "My back's a little sore, and there's a dull ache in my chest. Nothing seems broken, though, so that's good."

Strange, too. He couldn't remember much after falling into the icy cold lake, but he was pretty sure at least two of his ribs had snapped. Christian remembered the dull ache of them breaking as he hit the water's surface.

Tears formed in Lilith's eyes. "I'm so glad you're alright."

Without a second's hesitation, Lilith leaned down and pressed her lips to his in a kiss that seemed to convey all the worry and longing she'd felt the night before. Christian did not hesitate to respond, kissing her back, closing his eyes and allowing his mouth to move in sync with hers. He enjoyed the sensation of her soft-as-velvet lips as they glided over his. Few things in this world could compare to the delight that was kissing Lilith.

It was only several minutes after they started kissing that Christian realized Lilith was crying. Tiny droplets of water splashed against his face and traveled down his cheek. When he opened his eyes, it was to find tears streaming from between Lilith's thick eyelashes and creating a wet trail down her face.

"Hey," Christian whispered against her lips. He removed his hands from her back and cupped her face, brushing his thumbs over her cheeks, gently wiping away the tears. "What's wrong?"

"I thought I'd lost you," she hiccuped, sniffling as the tears continued to flow. "I was so afraid that I was going to lose you. I don't know what I'd do if you died."

"I'm sorry." A perturbing feeling settled in the pit of his stomach. Guilt. Lilith was crying because of him, because he'd done something stupid and nearly gotten himself killed. He felt like an insensitive jerk. "I didn't mean to worry you."

Lilith shook her head. "No. I'm sorry. The only reason we're in this mess is because of me."

"That's not true. I'm the one who dragged us all the way here. The decision to get on that train was mine, not yours."

"But if I wasn't a succubus, we wouldn't be in this mess to begin with."

"Don't say that like being born a succubus is a sin. You can't change who you are, or what you are." Christian gave her a stern look. "Just like some people are born with brown hair instead of blond, or blue eyes instead of green, you were born a succubus. That's not something you should feel ashamed about."

Ever since he'd realized how much Lilith meant to him, Christian had been starting to question the words of the Catholic Church on supernatural matters. They claimed that creatures like Lilith were evil incarnate, that they were the physical representation of sin, and that it was imperative that they be cleansed from this world.

And yet, for all the Church's talk of how these supernatural beings were evil born of sin, they never spoke of how human beings were also sinful creatures. Humans were not perfect. They were far from it, in fact. More than ninety percent of the world's crimes were not committed by werewolves, vampires, mermaids, succubi, or any other supernatural creature. They were committed by humans. Humanity committed more crimes, more atrocities, against each other than supernatural beings like Lilith committed against humanity. That was an indisputable fact that even the Church couldn't outright ignore.

Christian was beginning to think it wasn't *what* you were that mattered, but rather, *who* you were and what you did with the life you were given that truly made the difference.

"If you hadn't been born a succubus, then you and I would have never met." Christian smiled up at the girl, whose blonde hair, despite being frazzled and messy, somehow still looked utterly bewitching. Her long locks were draped over her shoulders. It pooled around them like a curtain. There was very little light in the room, but each strand seemed to shimmer with an otherworldly sparkle. "I don't regret anything that's happened up to now because doing so would mean I regret meeting you. I'll never regret meeting you, so you shouldn't either."

Lilith stared down at Christian with unblinking eyes. It was often said that the eyes were the windows to the soul. It was a cliched line, but there was some truth to those words. People could be trained to keep their face blank, devoid of all emotion, but it was almost impossible to completely mask the emotion in their eyes.

Christian could almost see the thoughts flashing through Lilith's mind by staring into her irises. They were light and clear, like a combination of the azure sky and the deep blue ocean. Her eyes made her seem vulnerable.

They stared at each other for an indefinite amount of time. Neither of them blinked, neither looked away. Finally, like rays of light parting the clouds, Lilith smiled, and Christian discovered the most beautiful thing in the world.

"Thank you," she said.

He grinned. "There's nothing to thank. I was only being honest."

"It's because you're being honest that I'm thanking you."

"Hm… in that case, I suppose you're welcome."

Still smiling, Lilith leaned back down, her lips seeking him out. Their kiss was delicate, ephemeral, nothing more than a light grazing of flesh—at first.

Her lips soon pressed down harder. Christian kissed back with equal vigor, taking her lower lip in his mouth and nibbling. Beautiful noises emerged from the back of Lilith's throat. They served to spur him on, pushing him forward and bringing out his desire, his need, for the girl on top of him.

His hands slid down the smoothness of her cheeks and neck. They glided over her shoulders and down her back. A single finger grazed a gentle trail across her spine, making her shiver under his touch. Upon reaching her lower back, Christian rubbed against the indent in the small of her back, causing her spine to arc as a delicate moan escaped her lips.

With her back arching and her head thrown back, her throat was exposed. Christian leaned up and began a gentle assault on her lovely neck. He suckled on her skin, finding her pulse points and grazing them with his teeth. Small gasps escaped from Lilith and her breathing hitched as her heart sped up.

Yes… right there. Bite it.

The voice returned. It echoed around inside of his mind. This voice, which sounded so much like Lilith it was startling, made Christian wonder whether or not it was Lilith.

Was this another power that succubi had? Was this an ability that the Church had not discovered? No one who slept with a succubus had lived to tell about the experience. What the Church knew about succubi had been painstakingly researched by sending numerous men to their deaths, but since everyone had died during their first night, all they knew was a succubi's basic abilities: Aura of Allure, and the ability to drain men of their lives through sex.

Christian pushed himself up until he was sitting instead of lying on his back. With one hand wrapped around her back and the other set behind him like a pillar, he continued his coordinated assault on her neck. After leaving several red marks on her smooth skin, he soon traveled south from her neck to her collarbone. He nipped and licked at the soft, fair flesh, feeling the way her body shuddered and writhed on top of him.

Her hips moved involuntarily, bucking and grinding against him, the feel of her skin rubbing against his creating a delicious friction that made him twitch. Juices flowed from her, covering his crotch and thighs in a slick, wet coat. The wetness flowing from between her legs created a natural lubrication that allowed them to rub against each other much more easily. The sensations created from their actions, the constant rubbing and grinding, caused shivers to run up and down their spines. Soft moans, low groans, and heavy panting accompanied the sound of their bodies moving together in ceaseless continuity.

Lilith grabbed his head with both hands. She pried him off her collarbone before pulling his face to hers and crushing their lips together. He did not mind. Groaning in approval, Christian kissed her back, his mouth opening and his tongue coming out to meet hers. They shared a sloppy kiss, their tongues dancing around each other, twirling and hooking and grinding and pushing.

Sweat coated their bodies as their activities grew in potency. The scent of their slick, wet bodies grew heady. It pervaded the room and spurned them ever onward.

Not breaking their kiss, Lilith pushed him back down onto the bed, sliding her hands along his chest and abs before reaching out and grabbing a hold of him. Soft, delicate digits curled around him, touching him in ways that no one aside from Lilith had ever touched him before, not even himself. He pulsed underneath her fingers, twitching eagerly as she used her hand to guide him inside of her.

Lilith's walls stretched around him, conforming to him in a way that made him think they were made for each other. They were a perfect fit. He was neither too large to fit inside of her, and she wasn't too tight for him to move inside of.

Lilith pulled her mouth off of his, placed her hands on his chest, and pushed herself back into a sitting position. She smiled down at him, causing him to smile back.

Then she began to move.

He hadn't noticed it the first time they made love, and he had only felt an inkling of it the second time. It wasn't until the third time they'd done the deed that Christian had felt the connection between them. When they were combined like this, it felt as if he and Lilith had become one. In some ways, this connection was frightening. In others, it was his greatest joy. When they were connected like this, it was nearly impossible for him to tell where he ended and Lilith began.

With their bodies becoming one, so too did their mind and soul. It was an unusual phenomenon. Everything she felt, he could feel. Every thought that entered her mind, he knew. When he did something that she liked, the reaction of her mind and body guided him and allowed him to repeat it for her enjoyment. When she felt a thrill of pleasure, he felt it as well, a continuous loop that heightened their shared experience.

Their bodies moved in synchronization, a perfectly choreographed dance of mind, body, and soul. There was no Christian. No Lilith. It was just two people whose very being had merged to form a single entity.

Then the end came. Something coiled inside of Christian's lower abdominal. He tried to say something to let Lilith know, but the overwhelming sensation of her wrapped around him, of the continuous pleasure that shot through his mind from their bond, left him speechless. It didn't matter anyway. She already knew.

He climaxed, filling Lilith with his essence. Seconds later, as if in response to Christian's ending, Lilith cried out and she clamped down around him. Within his mind, he could feel her pleasure spike, causing his body to react and shoot inside of her again.

Lilith fell forward, collapsing into Christian's arms. Her lips met his once again, the last of their passions ebbing away as they came down from their natural high. Their bodies remained connected, neither wanting to let their link to fade. If possible, they probably would have stayed like that.

Fate had other plans for them.

"Why the hell are you two fucking in a school nurse's office?" a demanding voice asked.

Freezing in shock, and more than a little fear, Christian and Lilith turned to find someone very familiar staring them down. It was not all that long ago that she had helped them fight against the No Life King. With her hands on her hips, which were cocked at an angle, and her brown eyes narrowed, Catherine Siegal glared at them with an expression that epitomized the word 'displeased'.

"Uh…" Christian's mind worked at a million miles per second to come up with something to say. "I guess you're wondering what we're doing here. It's a funny story, really."

"Oh, good. I love funny stories." Catherine's dry voice felt like sandpaper against their ears. "Why don't you get dressed and tell me all about it while we're in the car? Who knows, maybe if I find your tale entertaining enough, I'll think about not tossing you two in jail for having sex on public property."

Christian and Lilith gulped.

This was so not good.

***

A red Jeep Cherokee drove down one of the many streets in the residential district near Calico Middle School. It was the only vehicle currently on the road, and the deep thrum of the engine was the only sound in the vicinity. It was still far too early in the morning for most people to be awake.

The sun had already begun its rise over the horizon, which was painted with the colors of early morning. All around, sitting in the driveways of lots of houses, were cars of various types and makes; jeeps, mini-vans, sports cars. There were even a few really expensive vehicles like a Lamborghini painted to look like a bumblebee.

Sitting in the driver's seat, looking straight ahead and steering the car was Catherine. Unlike the last time they had all been together, she was not wearing a business suit, but instead sported a pair of jeans, a basic black t-shirt, and sneakers. She was also frowning. Out of the corner of her eye, she saw Christian and Lilith. They were sharing the front seat, Lilith on Christian's lap, in complete violation of the law.

Her frown deepened.

"There's something you're not telling me," Catherine said at last. She ignored their lawbreaking for now. It was a minor violation anyway, and there were more important things to worry about. "Your story has a lot of holes in it, enough to let me know that you're not being entirely honest with me."

They had shared the tale of how they'd managed to wind up all the way in Riverbank, but she could tell that there was something off about their story. She didn't think they were necessarily lying about how they got there. There was no wavering in Christian's voice when he spoke to her. At the same time, there was just so much that seemed to be missing that nothing added up.

Christian, dressed in his now dry clothes, sighed. "You're correct. We are keeping things from you, but trust me when I say that you're better off not knowing. This is for your protection as much as it is ours. The less you know, the more you can claim ignorance."

"Plausible dependability is all well and good—" Catherine snorted. As if she believed that. "—but I think you're forgetting that I'm also a cop and the deputy of the Special Investigations Unit. Ignorance is something I can't afford. So why don't you just come out and give me the whole story?"

"You don't need to worry about that," Christian said. Lilith remained silent. "We've not committed any crime, so you shouldn't worry about the specifics."

"Do you honestly expect me to let this go just like that? I'm not the type of person to let myself remain blissfully unaware of a situation after finding two people who should be living somewhere in Los Angeles all the way out here, naked, and having sex in a middle school. I also find your words about not committing any crime laughable. You broke into a middle school. That's a crime right there."

Both Christian and Lilith had the decency to look abashed. Their faces turned red with shame. Neither of them could so much as look at her after that.

"It's not like we meant to have sex," Lilith muttered, even as she buried her burning face into Christian's shoulder. Her voice was muffled as she added, "It just… happened."

"A lot of things just happen," Catherine retorted. "And I don't really care about what sort of shenanigans you two get up to. What concerns me is that you both look like you just fought against a rampaging giant, and I don't know why."

"There was no giant involved, so don't worry," Christian said.

Her eyebrow twitched. "It was a figure of speech."

"I know." Christian sighed. His eyes hardened as he looked at her. "Look, Catherine, I respect you and your position as a member of the LAPD. That being said, I can't tell you anymore than I already have. If this is going to be a problem, then you can let us off right here."

"What makes you think I'd do that?" Catherine narrowed her eyes. "After what you two did, you'll be lucky if I don't throw you behind bars."

"You and I both know I would never let you do that."

"You say that like you have a choice."

"There's always a choice."

Catherine spared a glance at Christian. She took in his straight-backed posture and the dangerous gleam of his eyes. She also noticed the tip of a barrel poking out from between him and Lilith, pointed right at her.

She looked back at the road. "You're a real troublemaker, you know that?"

Christian shrugged. "I've been called that before, though usually it's for a different reason than this."

"I'm going to get you back for this."

"I imagine you'll at least try."

“Tch!”

***

Catherine, it appeared, lived not too far from the middle school, about four miles or so. Her house was a nice, if plain, two-story house with purple roofing and white plaster walls. It had a chimney and two of the windows on the second floor were open, allowing the cool morning air to enter the house. They pulled into the driveway. Christian noticed the well-maintained garden in front of the house behind a small metal fence as Catherine parked the jeep.

“I’m surprised you live this far out of Los Angeles,” he commented as they disembarked from the vehicle.

“Because I’m part of the SIU, they only call me in for operations that involve the supernatural,” Catherine said, walking to the front door. “I don’t need to be on standby all the time since very little happens that you Executioners haven’t already dealt with. It’s allowed me to buy a place out here, away from any big cities.”

“Must be nice, not having to live in a city like Los Angeles,” he commented.

“It is,” Catherine agreed. “Though when I do get a call to come in, I have to travel for several hours just to get there. It’s a tradeoff, but it’s well worth it in my mind.”

“This place reminds me of Seal Beach,” Lilith said, smiling as she looked around. “Only without the beach. It’s very peaceful.”

“That’s because not much happens this far out of the city. We’re a small community. There’s only a couple thousand of us living here.”

“Oh…”

Catherine unlocked the door, opened it, and stepped inside. She turned to Christian and Lilith just as they entered her abode as well.

“Take your shoes off. I don’t want you tracking mud on my floor.” While they did as told, not wanting to upset the woman who was inviting them into her house despite her suspicions, Catherine walked down the hall. “When you’re done, come into the kitchen. It’s down this hall on your left.”

Looking at each other, the two hurriedly removed their mud-covered shoes and followed Catherine.

The kitchen was a spacious room. It had a floor made of white granite tiles and an island sitting in the center. Black marble counter tops covered every surface and pantry cabinets hug overhead. The stove/oven was a top-class gas stove made from stainless steel. A refrigerator situated against the eastern wall sat between the pantry and counter with a cutting board. As

Christian and Lilith walked in, they could see that it was an open kitchen connected to the dining room.

"Pull up a chair you two," Catherine instructed as she opened the pantry door and began looking inside. "I imagine you're hungry." As she said this, Christian's and Lilith's stomachs rumbled, making the older woman chuckle a bit while they flushed red. "We don't have a whole lot, but you can at least have some cereal or something. Do you like Frosted Flakes?"

"Uh, yes," Lilith said.

Christian shook his head. "Never had them."

"Then this will be a new experience for you because that's what you're having."

Christian snorted a bit, amused by Catherine's blunt way of speaking.

Breakfast was a quiet affair. After the heavy conversation they had in the car, none of them were keen on talking much. Christian had a lot on his mind anyway.

He and Lilith had failed to reach Sacramento, though they were much closer now. If they could convince Catherine to take them to the nearest train station, they could easily reach the city within an hour or two. The problem was that he couldn't be sure if continuing there was the right course of action. Would the Executioners be waiting for them? Would they get caught before then? Now that the Executioners had discovered them once, it would be much easier for them to locate him and Lilian again, especially if they kept on the same course.

After finishing her own breakfast, Catherine moved into the living room, connected by a flapping door. There was a moment of silence, and then the sounds of the television came from the room. It sounded like the news.

The woman came back in a second later and looked at them both. "You two can stay here for a while to get your bearings. After that, I'll be willing to drive you anywhere you want that is within reason. I suggest you use this time to think about where you want to go."

She's being awfully accommodating now.

Christian withheld his frown, not letting her know that he felt a bit suspicious of her offer. She'd been so adamant on making them tell her what was really happening. Catherine didn't seem like the type who changed her mind easily, and she also wasn't the type to be swayed by threats. At the same time, he didn't want to offend her.

"We understand," Christian spoke for both of them. Lilith nodded her head. "Thank you."

"You're welcome, I guess." Catherine released a deep, gusty breath, as she pressed a hand against her face and pushed her bangs away. "Sometimes I think I'm too damn nice for my own good."

Christian and Lilith shared a look.

"Mommy, who are these people?" a voice asked.

Three heads turned at the sound of the new voice. Standing in the entryway to the kitchen was a little girl no older than six or seven. She had auburn hair and blue eyes that looked almost purple when the light hit them. Her skin was light, and a few freckles dotted her small nose. She was wearing pink pajama bottoms, a white T-shirt with a pink hem, and a pair of pink toe socks.

"Elle," Catherine smiled at the young girl, her eyes becoming warm in a way that looked completely out of place on the tough as nails cop image she often presented. Christian was surprised by the sudden change in demeanor. Lilith smiled at the sight. "What are you doing up so early?"

"I wanted to sleep with you, but you weren't there." Elle yawned, rubbing her eyes in that adorable way only children could do. "I heard the TV and thought you'd be down here."

"Ah. Well, mommy's pretty much awake now, and I don't think I'll be going back to bed." Catherine knelt down next to her child and lifted the little girl up. "However, you, young lady, should be going back to sleep. It's far too early for you to be awake, and a princess needs her beauty sleep, you know."

"M'kay." The girl yawned again. She set her head on Catherine's shoulder, her eyes closing, her breathing becoming deep and even.

"Why don't you two head into the living room while I put Elle back to bed?" Catherine didn't wait for them to reply before walking out of the kitchen.

Looking at each other, he and Lilith decided to do what Catherine said and made their way into the living room. The news was indeed what their host had turned on, and the pair sat down on one of the two chairs, cuddling together as they waited for Catherine to put her kid back to bed.

"What should we do now?" Lilith asked into the silence.

With the noise from the TV, we should be able to talk without Catherine overhearing us.

"I don't know," he admitted, wishing he had an answer. "We can't stay here, though. Standard procedure for search parties is to start where someone disappeared and expand their parameter in a net. If we don't want them to catch us, we need to leave before they show up."

"Where will we go?"

Christian hesitated. "I… I'm not sure. I don't think we should go to Sacramento anymore. They'll probably be waiting for us. We could try for San Francisco. It's farther from the border, but they have trains that leave the state there. Though, again, there is also the possibility of there being an entire battalion of Executioners waiting for us."

Lilith frowned, her nose wrinkling and her eyes narrowing in thought. Christian could almost see the cogs turning as she tried to think of a solution.

"Could we take a plane?" she asked.

"Not possible." He shook his head in the negative. "Airport security is too tight. We can get past train station security easily enough, even like this, but without a modified case lined with Orichalcum to fool the x-rays, there's no way I can bring my weapons on board, and we lost our case on the train. What's more, they require an ID. The Executioners will be able to track us if either of us use our IDs for anything."

"What if we sneak on board where they store the luggage?" Lilith suggested as she began playing with his hair.

"That… that could work." Christian bit his lower lip, thinking. "We might be able to do that, but it would involve disguising ourselves as workers and sneaking in when no one is looking." He opened his mouth, but the sound of footsteps approaching caused Christian to stop. "We'll talk about this later," he said just as Catherine entered the room.

Catherine stared at them as she walked over to the other chair and sat down. The two forced themselves not to squirm in discomfort as her gaze pierced them. She wasn't even blinking.

"You two should be more careful when you're talking, otherwise someone might overhear you," she said at last. Christian's and Lilith's eyes widened as Catherine held up a small device. She pressed a button and the device replayed their entire conversation back to them.

Christian blinked. "How did you—"

"At the nurse's office," she interrupted, grinning at them with a sort of victorious viciousness. "Before I gave you both your clothes to get dressed."

Christian swore as he began checking his clothes. He soon found the listening device in the left breast pocket of his jacket. It was tiny, just a small, round sphere that looked like a wireless speaker someone might find on a bluetooth headset. No wonder he had missed it.

Lilith didn't have one, which made sense. It would have been too hard to hide one on her since she didn't have pockets.

At least now I know why she turned on the TV. She was luring us into a false sense of security.

He had seriously underestimated this woman, to the point where he wanted to bang his head against a wall. It was obvious that Catherine wouldn't give up. Christian should have realized that from the start.

"So, then…" Catherine crossed her left leg over her right one. She put her left hand, the one with the recording device, on her thigh, while holding a gun in her right hand, which was pointed at them. "Care to tell me why you're being chased by your own people?"

Behind Catherine, the newscaster continued reporting.

"And just last night, a high-speed train came into Sacramento with a large hole blown into one of the cars. Forensics suggests that the damage was due to a bomb that had been planted inside the train. Fortunately, there was no one inside the car at the time and nobody was injured. Police are still investigating. In other news…"

Catherine, Christian, and Lilith all stared at the newscaster as he spoke. Two of them looked like they had been betrayed. The other was resisting the urge to strangle someone.

"You're also going to be explaining that," Catherine added, the gun now shaking in her grip. "Because I just know you two had something to do with it."

Christian and Lilith gulped for the second time that day.

***

"I see," Catherine said as Christian and Lilith finished telling their tale, the full story and not the half-baked crap they'd been trying to shove down her throat on the way home. "So, Lilith is a succubus and the Church ordered you to kill her. You refused, and now you two are on the run."

It was a very basic, downgraded version of their story, but that seemed to be the gist of it.

"More or less." Christian shrugged. He didn't look too comfortable about having to reveal the reasons he and Lilith had turned up in Riverbank.

"There's a lot more to it than that," Lilith added her own input, "but that's basically how it happened."

"So, I'm not necessarily sure I understand," Catherine said at last. Placing her forearms on the table that the three found themselves sitting around, she fixed Christian with a look. "Why did they order you to kill Lilith?"

"Because she's a succubus." Christian looked at Catherine oddly for a moment. Catherine continued to stare at him. He blinked, shook his head, and then elaborated. "The Executioners of the Catholic Church were created for one purpose and one purpose only: the slaying of monsters. Demons, vampires, werewolves, succubi, mermaids, anything that is sentient and not human is indiscriminately targeted and killed regardless of age, gender, or whether or not they've actually done something wrong."

"And you're a part of this group?" Catherine asked, looking absolutely disgusted. Her face was scrunched up in a way that made her look sort of like a combination of wrinkled baby and pug. It wasn't a very pleasant face, but then, what they were talking about was decidedly unpleasant.

"Was," Christian corrected, "I was a part of that group. Don't forget, I'm on the run now because I refuse to kill Lilith." He paused, then looked at her with a curious expression. "It sounds like you don't approve of what the Executioners do."

"Of course I don't approve." Catherine scowled as if his words were an insult of the highest caliber. "The SIU's job isn't to kill monsters. One of the women in my unit, someone you actually fought alongside during the battle against the No Life King, is a Gorgon. And I have another man in my group, who was also there at Seal Beach, that's a werewolf. We do not discriminate against monsters. We merely stop the ones who cause trouble."

"Really?" Catherine nodded, causing Christian to lean back in his seat and look at the woman in shock. "Oh, wow. I didn't know that."

"We don't go around shouting it out loud, but there are several supernatural beings in the SIU. We wouldn't be half as effective at what we do if we were just comprised of humans."

Christian had to admit that she had a point. What better way to defeat someone supernatural than have them fight someone else who was supernatural?

It really gave the term "fight fire with fire" a whole new meaning.

"So the police don't ascribe to the belief that all ab—non-humans need to be killed." He rubbed his jaw.

"We'd never believe in something so stupid. We don't care who or what you are." Leaning back, Catherine crossed her arms under her bust, a humorless expression in play. "The only thing we care about is that you follow the law. If you can do that, and not cause any trouble, then I don't see why you should be judged based on your species."

It seemed to Christian that he wasn't the only one who had come to the belief that it wasn't what you were that made you good or evil, but who you were. Apparently, he wasn't even the first person to think this way. Who knew there were other people, cops even, who not only thought exactly like he was starting to, but had been doing so for at least a couple of years now?

It really made him wonder, what else was he missing?

"Then do you think you could help us?" Lilith asked before Christian could say anything.

Catherine frowned. "I suppose I could. It's not like we're going to be allied with the Executioners much longer after this."

That caught Christian's attention. "Why not?"

"Are you kidding me?" Catherine looked at him like he'd grown a second head and sprouted a tail out of his hindquarters. "You just admitted that the Executioners kill indiscriminately, regardless of whether the beings in question have actually committed a crime or not. That's *not* how we operate. Chances are good that once I bring this to Commissioner Fletcher, we'll cut all communications with the Church. I doubt we'll actually go against them," she added upon seeing the expressions on Christian's and Lilith's faces, "but we won't aid them either."

"If that's the case you'll want to be careful," Christian told her. When all Catherine did was raise an eyebrow, he continued. "The Church has spies everywhere, in every country, in their military's, in the police departments, everywhere. I know for a fact that there is at least one spy within the LAPD, though I have no idea who."

"I see." Catherine narrowed her eyes. "That does complicate things." She paused, contemplating everything that had been said thus far. "I have to take my daughter to a daycare before I run some errands. You two can come with us, and I'll take you to the nearest train station. I can't help you anymore than that, and I would suggest against doing something illegal, like trying to stow away on board an aircraft. If you did, then you'd have not only the Executioners on you, but the LAPD as well."

Christian and Lilith looked at each other, silently communicating in a way that only couples could do. When they looked back at Catherine, Christian gave her an affirmative nod. "We understand."

"Thanks for the help," Lilith added.

"It's fine." Catherine stood up from her seat. "Now, if you'll excuse me, I have to wake up my daughter."

Their conversation had lasted well over two hours, and it was now 9:00 am. Given everything that had been said, however, it was understandable that so much time had passed.

She walked over to the open entryway, about to leave, but she paused and turned to look at them.

"Oh, and I would recommend fixing your hair dye as soon as possible. It looks like your time in the river took most of it out."

With that she walked upstairs, leaving the two alone.

"She's right," Lilith added, staring at his hair, which was now a combination of black and faded out blond. "Your hair looks awful."

Christian sighed.

There was just no pleasing some people.

***

This day could not possibly get any worse. News had just come in last night that Christian and the succubus had gotten away. While the reports were sketchy, the leader of the mission, one Adam Jackson, believed the two had jumped out of the train while it was moving and into a lake. One of the emergency exits had been opened, seemingly confirming his report.

Of course, Jackson also couldn't be sure of his own theory because he'd been knocked unconscious without ever seeing the two.

If that wasn't bad enough, the pair seemed to have known they were coming. A bomb had been planted in the train, one that had gone off, rendering most of her men unconscious when it exploded and knocking the rest into a daze. No one had been killed, fortunately, but the fact that both of their targets had escaped left a bitter taste in her mouth.

Samantha was none too pleased by this turn of events.

She had sent a search party out last night around midnight. They had reported back this morning, claiming to have found footsteps. According to the team she sent, there had been two sets, confirming that at least two people had been there at around the same time the train passed by the river. This helped confirm Jackson's report. What it hadn't done was help them find the two they were looking for. Samantha could only hope they would expand their search net soon, or the trail might end up going cold.

A knock came at the door. Samantha, thinking it might be someone delivering a report—she had the Intelligence Division scrambling to find all the information they could on Christian and the succubus's possible whereabouts—bade them to enter. It was in the moment that the door opened and someone walked in that she realized something.

Her day, which she had feared could not get any worse, just got worse.

"Bishop Vertrou." Samantha busied herself with her work. So long as she wasn't looking at him, she could control the urge to throttle him. It also gave her an excuse to get this man out of her hair as quickly as possible. "Please state your business quickly. I have a lot of work to do, in case you couldn't tell."

The aging bishop merely chuckled, as if amused by her dismissive tone. The reasons became clear a second later. "Very well, if that's how you want it. I've come to inform you that you are being taken off the search for the traitor and the succubus."

Samantha's head snapped back up. Shock coursed through her as she stared at the old bishop. "I'm sorry, would you care to repeat that? I don't think I heard you right."

"Your antics are amusing, but unneeded. You heard exactly what I said."

"Christian is my subordinate." A threatening look came to her eyes. "When one of them goes astray, it's my job to bring them back into the fold."

"And that is exactly why the Church has decided you are ill-suited to the task," Bishop Vertrou said, smiling. The twisted man looked like he was taking great pleasure in her boiling emotions. His face held the kind of expression most people had when enjoying a fine wine. "You're simply too… involved, too emotional, too attached to properly deal with him."

"Properly deal with him?" Samantha practically hissed, her eyes narrowing. She knew exactly what the old bishop meant by those words. "You mean you're going to kill him!"

"Of course. You know the rules. Anyone who betrays the Executioners is to be exterminated with extreme prejudice. Christian has betrayed us, fleeing from his duty with the very monster he was supposed to kill. There can be no recourse for him. Death is the only option left."

While the old bishop sounded remorseful, she knew the truth. He was the one who sent Christian on that mission to begin with!

"I won't allow it!" Samantha slammed a fist down on the table. "Christian is *my* operative, therefore he is *my* responsibility! I'm not going to let you kill him just because he rankles on your nerves!"

"I'm afraid you don't have a choice," Bishop Vertrou said in a mild tone of voice. "And I would watch how you speak to me. Do not forget that while you may be the head of the Executioners for the entire Western hemisphere here in North America, I still hold seniority over you as the United State's Bishop." Samantha gritted her teeth. "Besides, this is an order from the pope himself."

"What?!"

Almost grinning, Bishop Vertrou pulled out a scroll from within his robes. He unrolled the scroll and set it on the desk in front of Samantha so she that could look at the contents. And Samantha did look at. She scrolled down the entire sheet of parchment, reading every last word, and upon finishing, her face twisted into a rictus of fury.

She was not happy.

"Now you see?" asked Vertrou, smiling in that way that made her skin crawl. "The pope has decided to take you off this task and focus your efforts elsewhere." Samantha could do nothing more than glare at the older man.

"Now, now, don't give me that look. You knew this would happen. From now on, I am charge of dealing with Christian." He chuckled. "But don't worry, I will make sure his death is quick and painless in respect for his past services to our cause."

***

Samantha glared at the door that Vertrou had departed through. Who did that man think he was? Demanding that she hand over the responsibility of dealing with Christian to him? He might have been a high ranking clergyman, but by the Almighty, she was the one who had been placed in charge of the Executioners!

She looked down at the scroll on her table again. It was an official scroll complete with the seal of approval and the new pope's signature. The contents detailed how the responsibility of eliminating Christian and the succubus were now being handed over to Bishop Vertrou due to negligence and failure to fulfill her duty on Samantha's part, though just how he planned on dealing with one of the thirteen most powerful Executioners in the world was beyond her. The bishop had left the scroll in her possession. She knew he had done so as a means of adding insult to injury.

A knock soon came at the door.

That had better be Tristin.

"Come in!"

The door opened and Tristin walked in. There was a cheery smile on his face, same as usual, but the moment he glanced at her and saw the stormy expression she possessed, he spun about and made to leave.

"Get back in here now!" she snapped.

Tristin sighed, turned around, and walked back into the room with the resigned air of a man who was on death's doorstep.

"You called?" he asked.

"The pope has decided that I'm too unreliable and has taken the responsibility of dealing with Christian and the succubus from me and given the task to Bishop Vertrou," she explained.

"Really?" Tristin looked surprised. "That's an awfully unorthodox move. The bishop might hold a higher rank than you, technically, but he's not an Executioner." Everyone knew that Executioner matters were always handled by Executioners. The pope could technically do this; he had the power, but it was a highly unusual move. "How does he plan on dealing with them?"

"I don't know, but it doesn't matter." Tristin raised an eyebrow, but Samantha was no longer paying attention to him. She was a woman on a new mission. "I want you to find out anything and everything you can on Bishop Vertrou. I don't care what you have to do to get it. So long as you can get that information into my hands, I'll overlook any laws or regulations you break."

Tristin stared at the woman for several seconds, his eyes slightly blank. When he did speak, it was slow and deliberate, like he was carefully choosing each word before actually saying them. "Are you telling me that I have free reign to spy on one of the most powerful men in the Catholic Church?"

The look he was giving her made Samantha grimace. She got the feeling that she might very well come to regret doing this, but it was too late to turn back now. "Yes."

Tristin gave her a grin so wide that it caused his normally pretty boy good looks to appear almost sinister. "You can count on me! I'll get that information to you pronto!" He rubbed his hands together in barely masked glee. "Ooh, this is going to be so much fun!"

Yes, Samantha thought to herself, putting her face in her hands and quietly groaning as Tristin began to cackle like a madman from a cheesy cartoon, *I'm definitely going to regret this.*

Chapter 7

San Francisco was the only consolidated city-county in the state of California. Encompassing about 46.9 square miles on the northern end of the San Francisco Peninsula, it was the most densely settled city in the entire Western hemisphere, and the second-most densely populated city in the United States after New York City.

As one of the densest cities in California, San Francisco was a mass of towering skyscrapers intermixed with smaller buildings that were still larger than the average structure found in most cities. A major city in California, and the centerpiece of the Bay Area, San Francisco was well-known for its liberal community, hilly terrain, Victorian architecture, scenic beauty, summer fog, in addition to its great ethnic and cultural diversity. It was a city that had a lot of offer and was one of the most widely traveled to cities in the United States as the perfect tourist destination.

Looking at himself in the reflection of a mirror attached to the back seat of the chair that he was behind, Christian decided that he didn't like having two green eyes. He absently pressed a finger against his right eye, which had a green contact lens in it, frowning. Sitting beside him on the train, Lilith pressed her face against the glass window, staring out at the city they had entered just fifteen minutes ago.

"Wow," she breathed, her eyes sparkling. There was a large, open-mouthed smile on her face as she tried to take in all the sights. "It's so beautiful and big. I've never been to such a big city before."

Christian looked at his companion and grinned. She looked so excited that it was hard not to let her enthusiasm affect him. Her expression reminded him of a teenager buying their first light novel.

"San Francisco is a nice city," he agreed. "It's also better maintained than Los Angeles." He scooted closer to Lilith until he was pressing into her side, so that he could also look out the window. "And yes, it's really big, too. There are a lot of people here. San Francisco has a dense population, which means it'll be easier for us to get lost in the crowd."

That was why he'd decided on San Francisco instead of Sacramento. If Samantha was smart, she would station Executioners at both cities and wait for him to show up. At least in this city, he and Lilith could disappear into the crowd if they needed to.

Lilith leaned into him. Her intoxicating scent invaded his nose. It was difficult to resist the temptation to kiss her silly, but he did resist. They couldn't do anything in their current situation anyway.

"Do you think we can do some sightseeing while we're here?" she asked, turning in her seat, her large, baby blue eyes pleading with him. "I know we're sort of on the run and everything, but this is the first time I've ever been here. I've wanted to come here for a while now, but…"

"You had a problem with crowds."

"Yeah." Lilith nodded.

That was the entire reason she had moved to Seal Beach instead of Fullerton, despite how the college she went to was located in the much larger city. There were fewer people, which meant less men who might attack her and fewer women who would glare at her.

She didn't have a problem with crowds anymore, though, Christian had noticed. As more and more time passed, Lilith's fear of being in large crowds had slowly disappeared. These days, even when she was in a train full of people—and men—she seemed perfectly comfortable.

The train ride to San Francisco was the perfect example of her newfound courage. Because they didn't have much money left, Christian had been forced to downgrade their travel arrangements and get tickets for economy class. Despite being forced into enclosed quarters with a couple dozen people, all packed tightly together on a series of bench-like seats, Lilith didn't seem the least bit concerned. Indeed, she looked perfectly comfortable being surrounded by people.

He wondered where this new confidence was coming from. It couldn't be natural, could it?

Not wanting to look a gift horse in the mouth, Christian thought about her request. Part of him wanted to say no, that it was too dangerous for them to be walking around in broad daylight. Another part of him recognized that while, yes, they were on the run, Lilith was still a young woman and needed some way to release the stress she was likely feeling. While making love helped with that, this would probably help as well. And perhaps acting like a young couple touring the city would allow them blend in better. It was worth a shot.

Christian didn't admit that he also wanted to tour San Francisco.

"I don't see why not," Christian said, shrugging. "We're probably going to be staying here for a while anyway."

He needed to plan their next move. Should they take the train to another city? Should they try and leave the state from San Francisco? Or should they find a different method of transportation? There were a lot of options, and he needed to find the one with the best chance of securing them passage out of California.

"Really?" Lilith looked at him with bright eyes and an even brighter smile that reminded him of the sun on a clear day.

"Really." He flashed her a warm smile.

Lilith turned around in her seat, leaned up, and placed a chaste, lingering kiss on his lips. She then pulled back, beaming. "Thank you."

"You're welcome." He wasn't sure why she felt the need to thank him, but he didn't argue. There were more important things to talk about, like ground rules that needed to be laid down to ensure their safety. "Now, even though we can tour the city, we'll need to be careful not to draw attention to ourselves. Our disguises will be enough that someone giving a passing glance probably won't pay us any heed, but anyone searching for us will likely recognize who we are right away."

"Right." Lilith nodded.

"We also can't afford to spend too much money. We only have about $1,000.00 left."

"Okay."

"And we're going to want to avoid anything that will require us to hand out personal information."

"Christian."

"We should also think about finding a hotel while we go sightseeing. Since we don't have much money, we'll have to book a cheap hotel."

"Christian."

"We might want to also think about getting a travel brochure or something. I don't know how much it will help, but—"

"Christian!" Lilith interrupted. Christian's mouth snapped closed with an audible click. Blinking, he looked at his beautiful companion. Lilith shook her head at him, smiling in a way that implied she was amused. "Try not to worry so much. You're not going to be doing yourself any favors if you keep pushing yourself like this."

"Right." He took in a deep, calming breath, then released it. "Sorry, I guess I'm just a little high-strung. While the Executioners' presence is small in San Francisco, I do know that there is a small operation center somewhere in the city."

The last thing he needed was for the group stationed there to discover him and Lilith. If that happened it would be a running battle to escape the city, and he wasn't sure if he could fight while trying to escape and protect Lilith all at the same time.

"I understand." Lilith's gaze softened. She rubbed her thumbs against the backs of his hands in soothing circles. The action served to calm him down. "You have a lot resting on your shoulders right now. Our safety is dependent on you." She grimaced. "I wish I could do something to help, but I don't know how to fight, and I don't know a whole lot about traveling. The only time I traveled was when I used the money my mom left me to travel from Rhode Island to Seal Beach."

That had been a dark time for Lilith, Christian knew. After the death of her foster mother, she had managed to just barely get her high school diploma by going to another school on Rhode Island before she was forced to flee the state thanks to Damien. She had then changed her name and bought a one-way plane ticket to California immediately after, hoping that by running to the other side of the United States, the No Life King would lose her trail and give up.

Things hadn't worked out quite as planned, but thankfully, the powerful vampire had met his end at Christian's hands. It was just too bad that another danger had presented itself. Still, Christian would do everything he could to protect her, even if it meant sacrificing himself.

No pressure, right?

***

Having never been to such a large city, Lilith was in awe of San Francisco. All of the buildings towered over her like enormous monoliths of brick and steel. There wasn't a single piece of architecture that was less than three stories tall, and most of them were much larger than that. All of the buildings were also packed closely together, each one spaced so close to the other that there was little room in between, and each one held a vastly different appearance from each other, presenting a strong dichotomy that, rather than clash horribly, produced a beautiful blend of asymmetry and color.

Her inner graphic designer loved this city.

She and Christian were walking hand in hand down one of the many sidewalks. Christian was holding a travel brochure in one hand, though he hadn't looked at it yet. Strapped across his back was a large guitar case that, surprisingly enough, didn't look all that out of pace on him. It must have been the clothes. His black jeans and white T-shirt with a dark jacket combo made him look a little like a musician. His messy, rock star hair probably helped sell the image as well.

Of course, there was no guitar inside of that case, but a miniature armory instead.

There were hundreds of other people walking alongside them. Most appeared to be tourists. She could tell because they were in large groups, were holding cameras, and were taking pictures of just about everything in sight. The gaping expressions on their faces also helped, just a little.

I wonder if I look like that.

Tourists weren't the only people out, of course, as she could also see businessmen and women as they walked to work, passersby who didn't spare a single glance toward their surroundings as they moved with a purpose, and a large number of young people who were dressed in unusual clothes that would have stood out anywhere else, but seemed natural in this city.

The streets were surprisingly hilly for a city. Lilith would have thought most large cities would be flat, but San Francisco appeared to be made entirely of hills. All of the various roadways that she could see at crosswalks sloped up and down, the surface rising into a large swell that made seeing further into the city impossible.

It made her wonder how many car accidents this place had to deal with each year. Probably a lot.

"Lilith?" Christian gently tugged on her hand. "Let's stop there for a minute." He pointed toward a small coffee house called Fivebarel Coffee. It was a small shop set into a building made of dark blue steel girders and glass. The transparent surface had a reflective quality that shone brightly in the light, making it difficult to see inside from where they stood. "We can grab a drink and figure out what we should do next."

"Okay," Lilith agreed easily enough. She didn't have a problem with stopping to get a drink, and Christian made a valid point. Just wandering around wouldn't do them any good, especially if they got lost.

The two entered the coffee shop, which was much larger on the inside than it looked on the outside. The reason being was because the outside only showed the width. This shop was a lot longer than it was wide.

There were a good number of people already sitting at the tables. There was even a musician sitting at a booth with a violin case at his feet. There seemed to be no end to the variety of people enjoying a drink.

Lilith followed Christian as they walked along the polished floor, which looked like some kind of red rock. They walked up to the cash register, where a young teen who was tall, skinny, and looked like a stiff breeze would blow him into the stratosphere, stood. There were a number of freckles and acne on his long face, which made Lilith think of a cucumber.

"Good morning." He stared at Lilith, blatantly. "How can I help you today?"

While she had gotten used to crowds, that didn't mean she enjoyed being ogled like a piece of meat. Men no longer made any moves on her for some reason. Even so, they still stared at her, and it was still disconcerting.

She tightened her hold on Christian's hand.

"You can start by not staring at my girlfriend," Christian said in a dry tone. The teen turned his head to look at him, and then froze when his eyes met Christian's. A shudder traveled down the boy, going from the crown of his head all the way to his toes.

Lilith looked at her companion from her peripheral vision. She remembered seeing him do this exact same thing to the nerdy kid who manned the specialty comic shop back in Seal Beach.

"R-right," the boy stuttered, sweat dripping down his face. His eyes flickered to the door behind them, as if he was contemplating whether or not he could flee before Christian killed him. "M-my bad. You've got a really pretty girlfriend."

"I do," Christian agreed, nodding in a mild manner. "And you're just digging your grave deeper."

"A-ah, um, s-sorry!" The teen squeaked. "So, uh, what can I, um, get for you two?"

Christian looked at her. "Lilith?"

"I want an almond latte and the sugar brioche tarte with summer berries and vanilla cream," Lilith said.

"And I'll just have a dark roast coffee," Christian added.

"O-okay. Y-your t-t-total co-comes t-to $12.65."

Christian opened his water-sealed wallet—the only reason his money didn't get destroyed when they jumped into the river—and pulled out the necessary cash.

"Y-your order will… will be up in just a second," the barrista said. "Just, uh, f-find someplace to sit, and your, ah, your o-order will b-be right up."

"We'll do that. Thank you."

Christian took Lilith over to one of the comfy-looking cushioned chairs. There were several of them, all arranged around a long, rectangular glass table with numerous magazines on top. After setting the guitar case down, Christian plopped himself into a seat and made room for Lilith as she squeezed in beside him. Because the chair wasn't that big, they had to sit so close that their bodies were practically melded together.

She didn't mind.

"Thank you for doing that," Lilith said. "You really didn't need to, though."

"I know, but I didn't like the way he was looking at you." Christian wrapped an arm around Lilith's shoulder. "It was disrespectful."

Lilith smiled and leaned over to kiss Christian on the cheek. "You're sweet, but we're going to have to get used to it eventually. We might as well start now. Plus, didn't you say we shouldn't do anything to stand out?"

"I guess I did say that, didn't I?" Christian ran a hand through his hair, sighed, and then looked at her with a gleam of admiration in his eyes. "That's a really mature way to look at it. Are you sure, though? I know how uncomfortable you get when guys stare at you."

"Yes, I'm sure," Lilith said. "To be honest, it doesn't really bother me anymore." She beamed at him. "I think it just doesn't matter if other people stare at me because I have you now."

"You really have come a long way, haven't you?" Christian said after a while. "When we first met, you could hardly stand to be in the same room as a guy. Now look at you. Being near a man doesn't even phase you anymore."

"I wouldn't say it doesn't bother me. It's just—" she paused, her face scrunching up as she tried to find the right word. A second or two later, she gave a helpless shrug. "—I don't really care anymore, I guess."

"Hn."

There was probably more to it than that, and they both knew it. A month ago, Lilith had been absolutely terrified of men. She literally couldn't be within ten feet of a member of the opposite sex and not run away screaming. Now she practically ignored the way men ogled her, though a part of that may have had something to do with how none of the guys they crossed paths with recently had become a drooling mass of hormones. Either way, both of them knew that something strange was going on; they just didn't know what.

"What's our plan for today?" Lilith smoothly changed the subject.

"The brochure has recommended two options for touring the city," Christian said, grabbing the pamphlet and opening it up to show Lilith what he had discovered. "We can take a guided tour on a double-decker bus. They have hop-on, hop-off stations where we can get off and tour the area on foot before getting back on. Or we could take a bike tour. We won't be able to see as much on a bike, but it'll be less expensive to rent a bike for two or three hours than it would be to take the bus."

Lilith eyed the brochure, looking at the images presented therein. Most of them were of the bus. It was probably the more attractive option for most tourists, who didn't want to spend any effort getting from point A to point B.

"Which one would you like to go on?" she asked.

"It doesn't matter to me," Christian said. "The only thing I care about is that you're happy with whatever we pick."

Melting. That's what Lilith felt like she was doing. Could Christian be anymore perfect?

Granted, he wasn't exactly perfect. He tried to plan for too much, he could be rough at times—like when he was manhandling her on the train, though she could forgive him since they had been in a life-threatening situation—and he was reckless when it came to himself. There were times where Christian would throw himself into a situation with little regard for his own life. That bothered her a lot. She still wanted to scold him for how reckless he had been during his fight against Damien. Just remembering the number of times he'd nearly died in that battle gave her nightmares.

Still, his good qualities often outweighed the bad. Most of the time. Besides, if Christian didn't have those negative attributes, then he wouldn't have been the person she loved.

***

Through unanimous vote, which basically meant Lilith had made the decision, the two decided to rent a bike and tour the city. They could have taken a bus, but the idea of being on a bus with a bunch of tourists didn't appeal to Lilith. She might not be as bad about crowds as she used to be, but that didn't mean she wanted to be stuck in the middle of a cesspool of filthy, sweaty bodies. She'd heard horror stories from Maria about unwashed, unhygienic people who took those tours and stunk up the entire bus. No thanks.

They rented out a two-seater bike for five hours at a shop called Fire Crotch Bikes. Lilith thought the name was funny. Christian had just rolled his eyes.

The pair rode through as much as the city as they could. Because they were on a bike, they weren't able to cover a lot of ground in the time given, but it was more than enough to see some of the more popular attractions.

They traveled through Golden Gate Park. Built to, in some ways, mimic Central Park of New York City, Golden Gate Park was created out of unpromising sand and shore dunes known as the outside lands. Though ostensibly conceived for recreation, the underlying purpose of Golden Gate Park was housing development and the western expansion of the city.

Large, powerful-looking trees that felt almost as if they could withstand the test of time dotted the landscape. Grassy fields spread across much of the terrain. Numerous people were using these areas as picnic grounds. Children played around while parents sat on top of unfolded blankets, basking in the sun's rays. A number of artificial streams, small rivers, and lakes gave the park a natural beauty that complimented the many different types of flora and fauna. There were paths for them to bike through, small roadways that had a wide array of flowers. It was a truly wondrous sight, especially for Lilith.

"Isn't that the Japanese tea garden?" Lilith asked Christian from her place in the back seat, pointing over his shoulder toward a large oriental-style building.

"It is," Christian said. "It's also the oldest Japanese garden in the United States."

The Japanese tea garden was built with a series of paths for people to walk through, ponds, and a teahouse. Among the many sights were a number of buildings built in traditional Japanese architecture, lanterns, bronze buddha statues, pagodas, and multiple bridges. They even had a zen garden and several different types of Japanese fauna, including Sakura trees, whose pink petals added wonderfully contrasting colors to the peaceful scenery.

As they pedaled down another road, Lilith admired the wide variety of flowers that could be found in the different gardens.

"Those flowers are so beautiful!"

"I guess."

"What a typical guy answer."

"Hn."

Golden Gate Park wasn't the only place they visited during their bike tour. They rode up and down many different streets, looking at the map in their pamphlet to determine where they were. There was a lot to see in San

Francisco and very little time to see it. That didn't stop them from enjoying themselves. The pair saw as much as they could before deciding to end their tour by taking the Battery East Trail to the most famous sight of the city: The Golden Gate Bridge.

"Amazing," Lilith whispered in a hushed tone of awe. She looked through the disposable camera they'd bought for the tour, snapping photos of the Golden Gate Bridge as she and Christian stood on the sands of a nearby beach. "I've seen the pictures of this in history books, but those really didn't do it justice."

"They certainly didn't," Christian agreed. "Maybe one day, we'll be able to actually drive over it, or maybe ride a bike over it."

Lilith stopped looking through her camera long enough to shoot him a smile. "I'd like that."

After ending their tour, Christian and Lilith returned the bike to the shop and walked to the nearest hotel.

The Hotel Monaco was a large, seven-story building made of brick. At the top of the building was an ornately decorated entablature. Each level had a number of windows all spaced several meters apart. Some of the lights were on, indicating people were inside. The entire structure was beautifully crafted, like most of the buildings in San Francisco, and it definitely lived up to the city it was situated in.

Christian hoped that didn't mean this place would be expensive.

After entering through the double doors, they were greeted to the sight of a large room with light patterned carpet. Arrayed around the room were a number of comfortable-looking armchairs surrounding a round glass table. Adding some color to the interior were several potted plants, including a couple of small palm trees, and there was a large fireplace with flickering flames burning inside.

They walked up to the front counter where an attendant, a young woman with dark hair and a friendly smile, greeted them. "Good evening, you two. How can I be of service?"

"We'd like to rent a room for the night," Christian answered for them.

"I see. Do you have a reservation?"

"… No."

"I'm sorry." The woman gave an apologetic smile. "Because there are a lot of people calling in to get a room with us, we only allow people who have made reservations to get one. If you want, I can talk to my manager to see if we can help you, but you might be better off trying to find another hotel."

Christian blew out a deep sigh. "I understand. Thank you."

The two moved out of the way to allow a group of people, tourists, to stroll up to the counter.

"What should we do?" asked Lilith. "Try to find another hotel?"

"We're gonna have to," Christian said, giving a contemplative frown. "It's not like we can spend the night outside. Well, we probably could, but the police patrol the streets and parks to make sure no one's trying to sleep on public benches or something." He clicked his teeth. "I was hoping we'd be able to stay here. The brochure said they had decent, if a little pricy, rates, and they aren't as dingy as some of the other hotels I saw for the same price."

"How about the next time we come here, we plan ahead and make reservations?" Lilith joked.

Christian smiled at her, uplifted by the fact that she could remain so upbeat. "Yeah. Next time we'll definitely do that."

They both knew there was a possibility that there might not be a next time, but neither of them said it out loud.

"Excuse me," a voice said.

The two turned to see the attendant standing in front of them.

"Oh, sorry. Did you want us to leave?" asked Lilith.

"No." The attendant shook her head. "I actually wanted to ask: are you two Christian Crux and Lilith Vie?"

Christian and Lilith shared looks of alarm. They hadn't given out their names, so how had she known who they were? Was this a trap?

Trying to play off his sudden anxiety—and ignoring the way adrenaline began pumping through his veins—Christian looked at the woman. He thought about lying, but if this really was a trap, it would be better to spring it now rather than later when he might not be as prepared.

"We are," he replied.

"Oh, good." The attendant breathed a sigh of relief. "We actually got a call saying that you two would be coming by sometime today, and that your friend, a Mr. Baluf, has made reservations for you to have the Monte Carlo Suite. If you'd like, I can get your card keys and have someone show you to your room?"

Green eyes met blue as Christian and Lilith shared a silent conversation. Both were thinking the same thing. This was most likely a trap. The only question was: what kind?

"That would be nice," Lilith said at last. "Thank you."

Chapter 8

"Here is your room," said the young man that the attendant had convened to show them where they would be staying. He slid the card in his hand through a small slot near the door. A light on the handle turned green, prompting him to open the door for them. As Christian and Lilith stepped inside, the bellhop handed Christian two card keys. "Here are your keys. If you have any questions or would like some room service, just press the button that says 'service' on the phone on your desk."

"Thank you," Lilith said, smiling. The young man blushed, stuttered a bit, and quickly scrambled out of the room. Lilith frowned. "Huh, that's never happened before."

"There's a first time for everything, I suppose." Christian was just grateful the kid hadn't tried anything. He would not have taken kindly to the bellhop if the boy had made a pass at Lilith.

The room was definitely one of luxury. Spacious, too. The living room was separated from the bedroom by a sliding door. In the middle of the living room was a modern square table with a vase full of flowers on top. Pressed against one of the walls was a desk made of varnished wood, its surface gleaming in the light, while a flatscreen TV sat on top of it. Several couches were arrayed around the living room, along with a couple of chairs for the table and a queen-sized sleeper sofa. The curtains were drawn, allowing bright sunlight to filter in and provide the room with a natural luminescence.

Much like the living room, the bedroom was one that seemed to speak of opulence and wealth. The king-sized bed sat against the wall in the center of the room, covered in white linen sheets, and a large, blue blanket with ringlet patterns lay folded on the end. A cushioned bench sat in front of the bed, and an ornately fashioned nightstand with a lamp and a vase of lilies could be found on either side. There was a large dresser on the wall opposite the bed and right next to the door, with another door to their left that led to what was probably the bathroom.

Painted in contrasting colors of blue, white, and red with pink and yellow accents, the walls presented a very modern art feel. The several paintings that hung neatly on the walls complimented this room's sense of contemporary aesthetics.

Lilith was in love with the room already.

"If this is a trap, your friend has picked a very nice place to set up an ambush," she said as they walked further into the room. "He's got good taste."

"I don't think the room itself is the trap," Christian said, warily scanning the interior for any sign that someone else had been there. "Most likely, the trap will be a midnight assassination. They'll want to kill us as quietly as possible, especially since we're in a densely populated city. There's also the possibility that they'll attempt to poison us with the food here."

Lilith paled. "They can do that?"

"If they have an agent in place, yes. The Executioners have intelligence operatives in many different industries, including hotels, restaurants, auto shops, gun stores, government jobs, the military... you name it, the Executioners probably have someone on the inside."

Not seeing anything that could be considered remotely threatening, Christian walked over to the TV. There was a note attached to it.

Turn on the TV.

Christian frowned. This note had Tristin written all over it. Had he been in this room, knowing they would come by? Implausible. It was more likely that Tristin had been following them via camera ever since they stepped foot in San Francisco and made different plans depending on which hotel they went into. Did that mean there was an intelligence operative in this hotel? Maybe. He could have also paid someone off.

I wish I had more information.

"Something wrong?" asked Lilith, no doubt sensing his turbulent emotions. She'd been getting much better at reading him these days, to the point where she could tell when he was feeling distressed.

"It seems someone left us a note." He handed the note to her. "What do you think? Should we do as it says?"

Lilith hesitated. "Do you think the TV could be a bomb?"

He shook his head. "No, they wouldn't risk setting off a bomb in a place like this. Too many civilians."

"Then I don't see the harm in doing as the note suggests."

Christian concurred. Finding the remote lying right beside the television, he grabbed it and pushed the "on" button. The screen flashed for a moment, then went back to black, before an image popped up. It was Tristin, at least from the shoulders up.

"Yo, Christian!" The far-too-cheerful response made Christian's right eye twitch. This man never could read the mood. "It's been way too long since we've last spoken, and while I would love to catch up, now isn't really the best time."

Christian's left eye soon joined the right in twitching. Of course now wasn't a good time. Tristin was a member of the Executioners, and Christian was a traitor who fled because he refused to kill his target. It was highly unlikely there ever would be a good time for them to catch up. Assuming that Christian even wanted to, which he didn't.

"To start things off, I would like to congratulate you on finding yourself a girl. You don't know how proud I am that you've finally discovered the joys of sex." Tristin wiped an imaginary tear from his eye. To go along with his words, he even added some fake sniffling. "Finding out that you've been doing the horizontal mambo was one of the happiest moment of my life."

"Who's this?" asked Lilith, flushing at the blunt way Tristin mentioned hers and Christian's sex life.

Christian sighed and pressed a palm to his face, mostly in an effort to hide his own blush. "That's Tristin. He works as a member of the Executioners' Intelligence Division."

"Oh." Lilith studied the blond-haired man on the television. "He's kind of funny, isn't he?"

"Annoying is more like it."

"A lot's been happening over here on my end, too much to really tell you about," Tristin continued. "I can only give you the basics: Samantha has been forcibly laid off the search for you by orders of the pope. Bishop Vertrou is officially in charge of finding you and your lovely succubus friend. Unfortunately, I do not know how he intends to accomplish this.

Even more unfortunate is that your life is now in jeopardy. Samantha's intent was always your capture. Bishop Vertrou is out for blood, so you'd best be on guard."

Christian frowned. He wasn't sure what this knowledge meant for him and Lilith exactly, but it couldn't mean anything good.

"One more thing before I go. I've set up a bank account for you. Don't worry, it's not linked to the Executioners' network at all. Now, I know what you're going to say, 'Tristin, this is too much! How ever could I repay you?' or something like that, right?"

Christian snorted. "More like question what you're getting out of all this."

"Don't worry about repayment. You're my best friend, and best friends always look out for each other."

"You've got a really good friend," Lilith said with a smile. Christian coughed into his hand and looked away.

Tristin continued. "You can access this account by filling in a deposit check at your local Ameribank. Here's the bank number, and you'd better write this down somewhere so you don't forget."

"Lilith?"

"Got it."

Lilith quickly secured a pen and a piece of paper from a drawer underneath the desk.

"It's 66500023. Remember that, okay? It would totally suck if all that effort I put into helping you went to waste." Tristin looked off to the left side of the screen, frowning. He then looked back and grinned. "Well, it looks like this is all the time we have today. Thank you for playing 'Who Wants to Piss Off the Pope!' We hope to see you again soon!"

The screen went black.

Christian and Lilith stared at the now blank screen, then turned to each other.

"So..." Lilith looked completely unsure of herself, "what do you think?"

Frowning as he rubbed his cheek, Christian replied, "honestly, I'm not really sure what to think, but I do know that Tristin isn't the type of person to go through all this trouble just to set up an ambush. And while he enjoys screwing with people—" especially if their name was Christian "—he's not the kind of guy to put in this much effort to play a practical joke." Sitting down on the sofa, Christian stared at the wall, his eyes narrowed in deliberation. "He's also never been particularly devoted to the Executioners or their cause." After another moment of silence, he nodded. "I think we can trust him."

"Are you sure it isn't just because he's your best friend?" asked Lilith, sitting down next to him and gracing him with a somewhat amused smile.

"Best friend? Yeah, right. Try personal pest."

Lilith giggled as she leaned her head on his shoulder and placed an arm around his waist. "It's okay to just admit that you think of him as a friend. No one's here but me, you know. I won't judge."

"Tch!"

Christian couldn't think of anything to say that would make her see the truth, so he just looked away.

***

Bishop Vertrou smiled a pleasant, amiable smile as he walked along the halls of the church. He greeted the people he passed with the kind of modesty and compassion one would expect to find in a man of the cloth.

"Ah, Clergyman Typhon. How are you this afternoon?" he greeted a man walking past his door. The clergyman, a giant of a man with a balding head and a nose that made one think he'd told one too many lies as a child, greeted him with a smile.

"I am doing well, Bishop." Typhon's voice boomed in a deep, bass rumble. "And yourself? I heard you had a meeting with those *Executioners*," he spat out the name like it was something vile.

"Come now, Typhon, the Executioners are necessary." Bishop Vertrou's smile widened just a fraction. "They do good work and keep the people safe. We cannot ask for much more than that."

"I suppose."

"In either event, could you please inform everyone that I am going to be in an important phone conference with the other Bishopric and must remain undisturbed?"

"Of course."

"Thank you."

"God Bless You."

"And you as well."

His smile and personality lasted until Bishop Vertrou reached his office, where it immediately dropped. The humility was gone. The affability was gone. Where there had once stood a man that no one would have hesitated to say was a man of God, there was now only an expression of avarice.

Reaching his desk, the aging bishop slid open one of the drawers, reached in, and flicked a small switch located on the underside. The wall behind him shifted, a section moving inwards and then to the left, revealing a well-lit passageway. He entered the passage and pressed a button that closed the path behind him.

He walked to the end of the path, his feet tapping a light rhythm on the white tiles. The hallway was a bit barren for his tastes, but since he was the only person who used it, he had decided not to waste good art decorating it. Upon reaching the door at the other end, he slid a keycard through the slot on the left. The door slid open as he put the card back into his robes and proceeded inside.

The room was cylindrical. It wasn't very large. Just enough to fit a round table with eight chairs and still have room to walk around.

Another person was already sitting at the table.

Toothpick-thin, the middle-aged man with his feet propped on the table in a lazy manner looked more than a little weedy. His scraggly brown hair hung in large clumps down his head, some of it covering his face, and the five o'clock shadow that he was sporting only served to give the impression of a homeless person. Of course, the stately white robes that he wore and the knife that he was playing with contradicted the hobo-esque appearance.

"Vertrou," the man greeted, grinning a slashers grin. "I was wondering when you would call me."

"Where are the others?" asked Vertrou.

"Not here," the man stated the obvious as the bishop sat down. It was, much to the man's clear amusement, the seat farthest from him. "They're off doing other tasks. I'll be enough to handle one measly Executioner."

It was bothersome that only this one had come. However, Bishop Vertrou couldn't say anything. The other six were probably preparing the seals necessary for the first stage of their plan, getting ready to pave the way for their legions.

"Don't underestimate this one," Bishop Vertrou warned. "This isn't just any Executioner. Much as I am loathe to admit it, the man I am sending you after is powerful. He is—was—a member of the XIII."

The man stopped playing with his knife and focused his attention more fully on the bishop. "A member of the XIII, eh? Heh, this might actually be fun then."

"Try not to go overboard, *Nicholas,*" Bishop Vertrou said without humor, spitting out the name with a great deal of sarcasm. "I don't want to have to pick up after you again."

"I'll try not to go all out." Nicholas chuckled. "So who's my target?"

Bishop Vertrou pulled out a pair of photos and slid them across the table. "Your target is Christian Crux and the young woman he is with, a succubus by the name of Lilith."

"A succubus? Sounds like a treat." He looked at the first photo, which had a young man with dark hair and two different colored eyes, and then flipped to the next one. He whistled. "Well, hot damn. I've had many succubi in my time, but this is a mighty fine piece of ass. Oh, yeah." He licked his lips. "She's definitely someone I could see myself having a good time with."

Bishop Vertrou shook his head in disgust as he heard the lust in Nicholas' voice. He didn't know why anyone would want to be intimate with a succubus. Then again, birds of a feather and all that.

"You can do what you want with the succubus, just make sure to capture the one called Christian alive. You don't know how difficult it was to arrange his downfall. I'd hate for all that effort to go to waste."

"Hey, this is me we're talking about." Nicholas wore an ugly smirk as he gestured to himself. His eyes flashed with barely restrained bloodlust. "You know that I never fail to capture my mark."

"As you say," Bishop Vertrou said, unwilling to argue.

He did not care for this person, or the other six, but to get what he wanted, he had promised to work with them. Soon, their plan would commence. Only after their goal had succeeded would Bishop Vertrou gain everything he wanted in life.

He just needed to be patient.

Chapter 9

For a single night, Christian and Lilith spent their time in that ritzy hotel. They enjoyed the delights of the posh interior, taking advantage of every amenity the room had to offer. Lilith was particularly enamored with the jacuzzi-tub, and after convincing him to join her—it took very little convincing—Christian was, too.

One night. For that single, glorious night, all of their worries vanished. The Executioners were nothing more than a minor inconvenience, the knowledge that Bishop Vertrou was now hunting them down didn't even show up as a blip on their radar, and the fact that there was a very real possibility that all of this would end in the most violent and brutal manner possible meant next to nothing. For that night, there was only one thing that mattered: enjoying their time together.

The next morning, it was business as usual. They left the hotel, slipping out as the first rays of light were rising over the horizon and lighting up the cityscape in a warm glow, and traveled to the nearest Ameribank.

Ameribank was the most unusual bank to be found anywhere. It was open twenty-four hours a day, seven days a week. The reason for this was because everything was automated. There were no humans at Ameribank. Only machines.

Of course, calling it a bank might have been a little misleading. It was only a bank insomuch as it did all the things that banks were supposed to do; it created accounts for customers, held money in their name, allowed them to deposit and withdraw money from their account, etc. Unlike most normal banks, however, Ameribank was just a bunch of ATM machines located throughout the United States. As far as Christian knew, they didn't even have their own Headquarters.

It was almost enough to make him wonder how they managed to stay in business.

He was also curious to know how people received checks, debit cards, and credit cards, since they obviously didn't get them at the bank.

When they reached the nearest Ameribank, Christian wrote a deposit check using the free slips that the ATM spat out. He was both surprised and not to find out that the bank account was, in fact, genuine. Tristin wasn't the type to lie, shockingly enough, but the fact that he'd gone through all this trouble, for reasons that Christian simply couldn't decipher, was a shock.

This didn't mean that Christian was not going to take advantage of this opportunity. He was an upstanding young man with a hard moral fiber, but he wasn't a saint, and someone was offering him free money. He really did need the money.

The fact that Tristin was the one who gave it to him probably helped.

"How much did you put on the check?" asked Lilith, shivering as she stood next to Christian.

It was a cold morning—mornings in cities near the ocean were always chilly, but there was also a biting wind that caused the frosty air to seep into their bones. It was a good thing there wasn't any fog, Christian concluded. Lilith would have been much colder otherwise.

"Ten-thousand dollars," Christian answered, absently watching as the ATM made all kinds of obnoxious noises. He really did hate ATMs, or anything mechanical that dealt with important matters that should have been left to humans.

It wasn't that he didn't trust machines, because he used mechanical devices all the time, but for something like this, he would have preferred dealing with a human. There were so many things that could go wrong, and by the Almighty, he really did need that money, so the possibility of something going wrong was not desirable in the least.

How would he and Lilith survive without money?

While waiting for the machine to cough up his cash—it was taking a terribly long time—he chanced a glance at his partner. Her fair skin shone with a brilliant glimmer in the morning glow of the sun. Her long, shimmering blond hair looked like each strand contained a piece of yellow fire. Even the way her clothes conformed to her body, the pale T-shirt flowing across her chest and narrowing at her waist, and her long jean skirt as it sloped over the gentle curve of her hips, conveyed a sense of perfection that couldn't have been considered human.

Succubi really are something.

"You're cold," he noted the way Lilith shivered. "Come here."

Lilith did not hesitate to do as instructed. She moved directly in front of him, allowing him to wrap her up in a warm embrace. Leaning back, Lilith snuggled against him, taking in as much warmth as she could.

"You're always so warm," she murmured softly, her sleepy, half-lidded eyes staring at the ATM as it processed their transaction.

Christian was also staring at it. Why the heck was it taking so dang long?

"That's because my body temperature is higher than most people." It was just another oddity about him, one that had been noticed by Anastasia Adams when she first became his personal physician. She'd told him that it wasn't anything to worry about, so he'd never let it bother him. "My normal body temperature is one-hundred and one degrees."

"Hmm…" A soft sigh. "I rather like that, especially since it means you can warm me up like this."

It could also cause a lot of problems, like when his temperature had plummeted during the incident where they'd almost drowned. His body couldn't afford to drop below a certain temperature or it ran the risk of shutting down.

"I'm sure." Christian stiffened a chuckle.

Seconds later, the machine spat his deposit check back out. Glaring, Christian read the screen on the ATM saying that it couldn't complete the transaction because his check requested too much money. This was why he would have preferred dealing with people. They wouldn't have denied the transaction for such an inane reason.

"So, what are we gonna do now?" asked Lilith.

Christian grunted as he reached for the screen. "Try again, with less money this time. What else can we do?"

The day had just started and he was already annoyed.

***

In spite of his argument with the Ameribank ATM machine, he did eventually manage to get his money. He'd done so by taking money out in smaller increments. Apparently, the ATM machine could only spit out a certain amount of cash at any given time and couldn't exceed $2,000.00. Who knew?

"How much money were you able to get?" asked Lilith, watching as Christian flicked through all of the bills in his hand, counting them up. Most of them consisted of $100s and $50s, but there seemed to be a good deal of $10s and $20s, and a large number of $5s and $1s as well. The machine had obviously run out of large bills at some point.

It was just another reason to hate ATM machines.

"It looks like I was able to get fifteen-thousand dollars before the ATM ran out of money," Christian replied, eyes focused on counting the cash instead of where he was walking. It was a good thing that Lilith had a firm grip on his arm, because if she didn't, he would have been nothing more than a red stain of splattered blood and liquified brain matter after nearly getting run over by a truck. "It really makes me wonder how much Tristin has in that account of his. I'm beginning to suspect there might be even more than this, though I don't think we'll need it."

"Probably not. Fifteen-thousand is enough to buy a new car. It's too bad we can't travel that way," Lilith said. Getting a car at a dealership required handing out personal information, something they could ill-afford to do if they wanted to keep as far off the radar as possible. "Then we wouldn't have to worry about constantly taking trains."

Of course, if they could find someone who was willing to sell them a car for cash, without them needing their ID and other personal information on hand, they would be in luck, but what were the chances of that happening?

"Agreed," Christian said.

They soon arrived at the train station and proceeded to the nearest ticket booth.

Much like the ATM, tickets were sold via machine rather than a person. You selected the destination you wanted, paid for by inserting cash or a credit card, and then went on your way. The procedure was simple, and even Christian couldn't deny its effectiveness. Certainly, it was more effective than Ameribank's attempt at relegating a task that should have been left to humans to a machine.

There weren't any trains stationed out of San Francisco that went to what he planned on being his and Lilith's final destination, but there were at least several options to get them out of the state. He selected the city that would take them closest to where he wanted to go: Las Vegas, Nevada. It wasn't where he'd been hoping they would go—Las Vegas was not a place he'd visit willingly—but it was the closest to his goal. Unfortunately, that wasn't saying much since it was still very far from where he planned on their final destination being.

The train was set to leave at 6:45am. It was 6:30am right now.

While they waited, the two ordered drinks from a small cafe. By now, Christian had enough of a handhold on Lilith's tastes that he was able to order what she wanted without needing to ask. When their orders were ready, they grabbed their drinks and walked hand in hand to their train's platform.

"It's too bad they didn't have any coffee milk," Lilith said after she finished taking a sip of her chai latte. "But this is pretty good, too."

"You're a big fan of sweet drinks." Christian took a sip from his own beverage, a black coffee. Unlike Lilith, who loved drinks that were sugary and sweet, he preferred drinks that were neither sweet nor bitter. Regular coffee was good enough for him.

A bright smile appeared on Lilith's face. "You know me too well."

While on their way to the platform, someone bumped into Lilith, causing her to spill her chai latte all over her shirt.

"Oh, crap! I'm sorry about that, miss," the person who jostled her said. "Here, let me help you clean it off."

"Ah! No, no! It's fine!" Lilith said, backing away slightly, looking just a little wary. "You really don't need to worry. It's just a latte. I can clean it off in the restroom."

"No, no. I insist. Let me help you," the person persisted.

The figure who had bumped into them was a man—a very thin man who looked like he was a former holocaust victim. Thick, scraggly brown hair sat atop his head, creating a startling contrast to his gaunt face. Much of that face was covered by several days' worth of beard. His thin body was covered in a tan duster that looked like it had seen better days, a filthy white T-shirt, blue jeans with a number of holes in them, and a pair of cowboy boots that not even a good shining would help fix. Beyond his off-putting appearance, his eyes held a look of faux cheer and congeniality, like there was something hidden within those depths that others couldn't see.

Christian narrowed his eyes.

"Thanks for the offer of assistance," Christian said, putting himself between Lilith and the man who was trying to clean the spill off her shirt with a dirty rag. "However, you don't need to worry. I can help clean her shirt."

"Hmm..." The man eyed him up and down for a second. "You're going to help her, eh? You her boyfriend or something?"

"Or something."

Their relationship couldn't be defined as a mere boyfriend and girlfriend. Those were terms the juvenile used when they wanted to describe someone who was more than friends but less than family. Christian didn't want to define what he and Lilith were by such childish words.

The man chuckled. "Well, alright. I guess I'll let you deal with the mess. Good luck to ya."

As the man walked off, Christian scowled. He glared into the crowd, watching as the man disappeared within the mass of people.

"Christian?" Lilith looked at him in concern. "Is something wrong?"

"No," he answered, though he continued to glare in the direction the man had left. For some reason, he didn't like the look in that man's eyes. It was hard to spot, but he'd seen the lust hidden behind that cheery facade. "I'm fine. Come on, let's get that cleaned up."

***

There were few things that he loved more than an orgy of violence. These things could be counted on a single hand and still have three fingers left over: having himself a good time with a gorgeous gal, and listening to her agonized screams as he brought himself to orgasm and her to death. There was nothing quite like that final release as a beautiful woman's agonized gasps of pain reached their crescendo. Oh, how he loved it when he could reach that moment of ecstasy just as his partner breathed her last.

It was a hobby that never grew old.

Ah... to be in the human world once again.

Looking at Lilith as she entered the restroom, Christian right outside and leaning against the wall with his arms crossed, the one that Bishop Vertrou called Nicholas just knew that this was going to be his greatest conquest yet.

"Oh, yeah." He licked his lips. Just thinking about the coming sensual sadism that he would commit, gratifying all of his carnal desires on that perfect body, was giving him a pleasant tingle. "I'm gonna have me a real good time with her."

***

Lilith frowned as she scrubbed at her shirt with several sheets of wet paper. Very little of the chai tea latte was coming out. It was going to leave a stain, and this was her only shirt.

Several more seconds of scrubbing at her T-shirt proved futile, so she stopped. There wasn't much point if it wasn't getting clean, especially since it was also making her shirt soaking wet.

When she walked out of the restroom, Christian took one look at her and, uncrossing his arms as he pushed off the wall. "I guess we're going to need to do some clothes shopping before we head onto the train. I saw a small souvenir shop just a little ways back that sold T-shirts. We can get a pair, if you want?"

Beaming at him, Lilith accepted the offer. "I'd like that."

Walking over to the small souvenir shop, the two eventually ended up getting a set. Christian's was a white T-shirt that had an image of the Golden Gate Bridge with the words San Francisco below it on the front. Lilith had gone with a formfitting black shirt that almost looked a size too small. On the front was a line drawing of the city from an overhead view. Christian thought it looked really looked good on her, and he didn't hesitate to tell her so. His words earned him a bright smile and a kiss.

By the time they finished buying their new articles of clothing, the train set to take them to Las Vegas had arrived, and they both got on board.

Having been given enough money that they wouldn't need to worry about how much they spent for a while, they had bought a sleeper car. Taking off their shoes after they arrived, they let their feet touch down on the slightly rough, tan carpeting, as they flopped onto their backs.

Christian stretched his arms over his head, staring up at the beige ceiling as he thought about everything that had happened. So much had gone on in such a short period of time. It was almost unbelievable to think about. In less than a month, he'd gone from being one of the thirteen most powerful individuals within an organization created by the Catholic Church to slay monsters, to being on the run from that same organization because he'd fallen in love with a girl who was one of those monsters.

How was that for ironic?

"Hey, Christian," Lilith's soft voice reached his ears. He turned his head to find her looking at him, her baby-blue eyes inquiring. "What should we do after we reach Las Vegas?"

"Las Vegas isn't a place I want to stay in for too long," Christian said. "Much like Los Angeles, the city has a large Executioner base."

It wasn't as big as the one in Los Angeles, because it wasn't the HQ for the entire Western Division, but it still had over thirty Executioners. He was confident in his skills, but not confident enough that he was willing to fight thirty people trained in combat and pumped up on super-roids.

But then, Tristin had said that Samantha had been taken off the case. Did that mean that the Executioners were no longer a threat? Bishop Vertrou was not an Executioner, so he held no authority over them. Would they still go after him? Or had the bishop been given special permission to expropriate their aid?

All these questions were giving him a headache.

"What about that Vertrou guy?" asked Lilith, twirling a strand of hair between her fingers as she stared at him. "What are we gonna do about him?"

"I don't think there's much we can do."

Christian looked back at the ceiling. Aside from Lilith, there really wasn't much to stare at in this room. Plain walls, plain ceiling, plain floor. Even the bed was basic, with white sheets and white pillows. Compared to the luxurious suite that he and Lilith had stayed in last night, this room was austere, unadorned, bare, and basic. Christian was beginning to miss the suite.

"Why do you say that?" she asked.

"Because Vertrou is a bishop," Christian stated, furrowing his brow. "As a bishop, he is nearly untouchable. Much like Samantha heads the Western hemisphere of North American for the Executioners, Vertrou is the bishop for the entire United States. His job is to oversee all aspects of religion here in the states, and he has almost unlimited authority over everything that happens here. You can be sure that, even if we find out where he is, he'll be too well protected for us to do anything to him."

"I didn't mean we should attack him or anything," Lilith chided. "I was asking about what we should do when he comes after us."

"Oh." Christian felt embarrassed. Just a little. "Well, I doubt he'll come after us in person, and unfortunately, I don't know how he plans on going after us. He might find some way to use the Executioners to do his bidding, but then, he might also have a way that no one else is aware of. I really couldn't say."

"So, we should just be prepared for anything, then?"

"Yes, we should." Christian closed his eyes, feeling tired. All this talk of "what ifs" and "should we" was exhausting. "Preparing for the worst case scenario is about the only thing we can do."

***

Lilith woke up to the sounds of a steady heartbeat, light breathing, and the train as it ran along the tracks.

She glanced at the clock situated on the wall by the door. 9:54pm.

Lifting her head from the chest she was resting against, she looked down at Christian's sleeping face. His breathing was deep and even, eyes closed; he looked so peaceful at rest. It was a stark contrast to when he was awake. He always looked so worried when conscious, burdened even, like he was carrying a large weight on his shoulders. Seeing him like this, calm, tranquil, untroubled by the world and all of its problems, was nice. Lilith wished she could find a way to make him look like that all the time. She wanted to take away his worries so that he would never act as if he was bearing the weight of an entire world on his shoulders.

Maybe some day, she would be able to do just that. If she lived long enough.

As she shifted on the bed, her bladder let her know that she had to use the restroom. It was probably from all those latte and coffee-based drinks she'd been having. With a reluctant sigh, she lifted the covers and climbed out of bed.

The semi-cool air caressed her naked body, causing her to shiver as goosebumps danced on her flesh. She began the task of picking up her clothes, which were strewn about the compartment without rhyme or reason. Her panties were the hardest to find, as it looked like they'd been caught by the small luggage rack overhead, which she had only noticed when she looked up by chance. How they got there she didn't know. Lilith had to stand on the bed to get them, which caused Christian to stir.

"Lilith…" Christian's mumbled voice had her looking down. The young man was blinking up at her with lidded eyes. He wasn't wearing the green contact right now, so she could see both red and green underneath his eyelids. That pleased her. She rather liked his unique red eye. It contrasted well with the green.

"Sorry," she apologized. "I didn't mean to wake you."

"S'okay," Christian mumbled, still blinking. "Why are you up? Come back to bed."

Smiling at the appealing suggestion, Lilith knelt down, straddling his waist, and planted a soft kiss on his lips. Despite being half asleep and likely having the reflexes of a sloth, Christian returned the kiss as best he could.

"I would absolutely love to join you again," she assured him. "However, I need to use the facilities." She kissed him again. "Don't worry, though. I'll come back once I'm done." Another kiss soon followed. She gently stroked his cheek with the backs of her fingers. "Go back to sleep. You need the rest."

Christian looked like he wanted to argue, at least for the few more seconds he remained awake. Before he could get a word in, his eyelids slowly fluttered closed and his body relaxed. Lilith stared at him for a moment, then planted one last, lingering kiss on his lips, before getting off the bed.

Putting on panties always felt weird after having sex. The cloth stuck to her skin, making her feel uncomfortable as it unpleasantly rubbed against her. It didn't help that there was some white, sticky fluid leaking from between her legs that had yet to fully dry. She did her best to ignore the feeling and focused on getting dressed. The sooner she was dressed, the sooner she could take a leak, and the sooner she could get out of her clothes and back in bed where Christian's warmth awaited her.

After sliding the panties up her legs and buttoning up her skirt, she put on her bra, t-shirt, and sandals before stumbling down the hall. Going to the bathroom in this train was a bit of a bother. The car they were in didn't have a restroom installed for whatever reason, so she was forced to traverse through the train toward the back, where the coach seats were.

Blinking as she walked down the mostly silent hall, Lilith looked out the windows as she passed. Night had fallen some time ago; she didn't know when, but sometime between the time she and Christian had fallen into slumber, the sun had finished moving beyond the horizon and the moon had come out to grace them with its presence. The moon and stars created a vivid luster that fell upon the land. She could see the trees, slopes, and cliffs outside of the windows. It looked like they were passing through a mountain.

Entering the next car and walking forward, Lilith felt her lips twitching into a frown. She looked around, glancing to her left and then her right. Her frown deepened. The car was empty. Where had everybody gone?

She kept moving, passing one empty seat after another. A chill ran up her back. The place reminded her of a ghost town, or a ghost train. There should have been a lot more people on board. She had seen at least several hundred passengers getting on with her and Christian. It couldn't be possible for there to be a car that was completely empty, could it?

A strange sensation welled up within her. The hairs on the back of her neck stood on end, prickling precariously and making her shudder. There was a feeling in the pit of her stomach, like a tightly packed ball of suppressed nerves that were flailing about wildly. Each step she took pounded loudly in her ears, or maybe that was just the heavy beating of her heart, which felt like it was threatening to burst from her chest. This silence was disquieting. It felt wrong somehow.

She shook her head. There was no reason to feel so discomfited, was there? No. Of course not. They probably just didn't have many passengers and decided to consolidate them all into the cars that had more. Yes. That must be it. There wasn't anything wrong going on. Nothing at all unusual...

Or so she thought, until she came into the next car.

The first thing that hit her was the stench. It was a scent that reminded her of ripened fruit that had been left out in the sun for too long. Mixed in with it was a metallic scent, coppery, and with a poignant sweetness that made Lilith's stomach churn. Blood. That's what she was smelling. The scent of blood was thick and cloying and repugnant, and she was forced to cover her nose lest she wanted to regurgitate all of the food she'd eaten for dinner.

It was only after the overwhelming stench finished invading her nose that she saw why the smell of blood was so thick. The car was covered in it. Like a mad painter had just decided to take buckets of red paint and splashed them across the interior of their shop, it was everywhere, splattered along the floor and trailing patterns that looked like the blood had been shot out of a hose. The walls appeared to have been doused by a fire hydrant that spewed out red. Dripping from the ceiling like glistening droplets of carnelian fluids, blood coalesced into small raindrops that fell to the floor below.

Mixed in with the blood were large, meaty chunks reminiscent of beef. Some were large, others small. A few were even recognizable as having once belonged to a human, albeit, barely. There were several that looked almost like a leg, arm, or hands. There was even the remains of a torso that had been cut in half.

Standing in the center of this carnage was a man. It was the same man who had bumped into her. He stood there, his back to her, his head turned so she could see his profile. There was a smile on his face. The smile was actually very pleasant, like he was incredibly pleased by his surroundings, which only made it that much more terrifying.

Lilith's already queasy stomach rebelled against her. What else could it do in the face of something so horrifying? She dropped to her knees, the food she'd eaten that evening forcing its way out of her stomach. The bits of regurgitated food and liquid splashed on the ground by her feet, congealing with the blood to create a sickening, murky brown color.

"Ho?" The man turned around, his eyes opening to reveal sharp, cat-like irises. He stared down at Lilith as she dry heaved. "I was wondering when we would meet again. I haven't been able to get you out of my mind ever since I first saw you, you know?"

Lilith's shoulders began to shake. Her heartbeat accelerated. She tried to breathe, but all that came out were quickened pants as her mind tried and failed to come to terms with the image before her.

A boot hit the floor. She looked up. He was there. The man. He was walking towards her, a large grin spreading across his gaunt face, splitting it in half. Each step he took caused her breathing to come out faster. She was beginning to feel light-headed.

"You don't know how pleased I am to see you," the man continued to speak as he walked inexorably forward. One of his booted feet landed in a pool of blood, creating a loud, squelching sound as crimson droplets flew into the air. "From the moment I saw you, I knew that I had to have you. That body, oh that body, it calls to me! I need it! I need you! I need to hear you scream!"

He was standing right in front of her now. Lilith's eye were wide. Her irises quaked. She couldn't breathe. Her vision was filled with a nightmarish visage of the man, of his grin filled with a lust for blood and gore and death. She could see nothing but his crinkled eyes as they stared at her with flecks of insanity and a perverse, twisted longing.

He knelt down in front of her, bringing them face to face. The flash of light glinted off the knife he brought up and gently rubbed against her face, smearing the blood that was on it all over her skin.

Lilith lost control of her bladder.

"So please..." The man's grin couldn't have gotten any wider if he'd tried. "Scream for me."

Chapter 10

Lilith tried to scream. She wanted to scream, to let a piercing wail tear from her throat. She wanted to call for Christian, to cry out to him so that he might come to her rescue. She wanted to do all that, but she couldn't. Her throat had closed up. It was constricted with fear. Her body refused to move, save for the way it quivered underneath the terrifying gaze of the man before her.

"What? No scream?" He seemed disappointed, as if he had expected a more exciting reaction from her. "How discouraging. And here I was hoping my introduction would have inspired terror and instilled a sense of dread and panic in you. Clearly, I've lost my touch. To be fair, it has been five hundred years, but still…"

The man looked at her curiously, as if she were a commodity he'd never seen before. His eyes roved up and down her body, making Lilith feel like someone was taking the razor edge of a knife and scraping it against her skin. Even this man's gaze felt dangerous. The way he looked at her made Lilith feel like she was on a precipice, and down below was a pit filled with sharp, jagged rocks that could easily pierce her body and leave her a bleeding, broken shell.

This man would probably push her off for his own amusement.

"Perhaps I should try something else? Maybe something with a little more panache. What do you think?" When Lilith didn't answer, the man frowned. "Oi, oi, oi! I asked you a question! What do you think?" Still no answer. "Dammit, bitch! Listen to me when I'm talking to you!"

He backhanded her with the hand holding the knife. Lilith cried out as she fell to the floor, her skirt staining red as it soaked up blood from the ground. She held a hand to her face, feeling the searing pain in her cheek, along with the carnelian liquid running down it from where the knife had cut her.

"Hmm." Now calm again, the man stared down as he loomed over her. Soon, a smile came back to his face. "You look rather fetching in red. I wonder, if I were to put more of that lovely color on you, how much better would you look?" Lilith circled her arms around her torso. A protective gesture to try and mitigate her own fear. Useless. "I know! Why don't we find out?"

"N-no!" Lilith choked, finally speaking for the first time since entering the car. She backed up, her legs pushing her body as she scraped along the floor, her clothes soaking up more blood and chunks of meat as she tried to get away from this man. "S-s-stay back! Get away from me!"

"Oh ho! So now she speaks? I've been wondering when you would finally say something to me. Still..." He pouted at her. "Those are some hurtful words you're speaking. I've wanted to be with you ever since I first saw you, yet here you are, telling me to stay away?" He shook his head. "Sorry, honey, but that's not how I roll."

He advanced on her. Lilith scrambled farther backwards until her back hit the wall. Even then, she still tried to keep moving. Her legs pushed and pushed and pushed as the man continued his walk toward her with ponderous, lumbering steps that echoed loudly enough to ring within Lilith's mind.

He's going to kill me!

He was here to kill her. He was going to kill her, and there was nothing she could do about it.

The man continued his advance.

Christian... please... help...

She wished Christian were here. He would have protected her. But he wasn't here. He was still sleeping in their compartment several cars up.

The man stopped in front of her.

Oh, God... is this how I'm going to die?

Was she going to die here, alone, with no one but this psycho to know of her passing? She didn't want that. She still had too much to live for. She wanted to find a place where she and Christian could settle down. She wanted to start a family with Christian, to watch her children grow up, to live a long, happy life beside the person she loved. Was that too much to ask for?

"So I've been thinking," the man's voice reached her ears. "You've got way too many clothes on you. We're gonna have to do something about that."

He was standing in front of her again, towering over her like a giant looming over an ant. His eyes, those godforsaken eyes that made her feel like a thousand knives were cutting into her flesh, penetrating her right down to her soul, stared at her with ardor. He craved her. He wanted to torture her, to mutilate her body and violate her until she was nothing but a broken doll. Only then, when he had satisfied his deranged fantasy with her, would he let her die. This, she knew.

N-no...

She prayed as the knife came up and sliced the front of her shirt. The fabric tore, the sound several decibels louder than it should have been. He then cut the front of her bra, nicking her skin enough to draw blood and leaving her breasts to bounce free.

Please...

She prayed as the man grabbed her what was left of her shirt and ripped it from her body, exposing her torso to his hungry eyes. He licked his lips. "It's even better than I imagined. Yes. Oh, yes. I am going to enjoy you like nothing else."

Please help me...

She felt the knife slice into her skin, a shallow cut that traveled across her breasts. Blood leaked from the wound, traveling down her body and creating a stark contrast with her skin.

I don't want to die...

Like fire the knife cut into her flesh, biting and sharp as it made several incisions on her skin, leaving small cuts along her body.

I want to live...

More and more red liquid leaked out from the multitude of gashes, pouring out of the so far shallow wounds and leaving winding trails down her flesh.

I want to live!

The man made to cut into her again. His sick, twisted grin spoke of all the things he wanted to do to her. The expression on his face showed his desire, blatant and clear as day. It revealed the brutal savagery contained within his mind. He moved the knife forward. This time, he would dig it in a little deeper.

I WANT TO LIVE!

***

CHRISTIAN!

Christian jerked up in bed. He looked around. No one was there.

Jumping out of bed, Christian grabbed his pants, jerked them on, grabbed Phanuel and Gabriel from where they lay, and then ran out of the compartment.

He didn't know how. He didn't know why. However, somehow, someway he knew.

Lilith was in danger.

***

Just as he was about to pierce the flesh of Lilith's stomach, the blond-haired woman with baby blue eyes disappeared. Vanished. The man blinked. He stared at the empty spot in front of him, his eyes blank.

The splashing sound of shoes hitting a puddle resounded behind him. He turned his head, slowly, mechanically. Lilith was behind him. She was running toward the door at other end of the car. He watched as she reached the door and exited with frantic haste, nearly stumbling in her desire to flee from him.

He stood up.

"Ho?" He smiled. "It looks like things are finally beginning to get a little more exciting."

Chuckling, he brought his knife up to his mouth and licked the blade clean. He'd never tasted the blood of a succubus before. It was sweet. Was it love? That must have been it. Her blood was sweet because of love. That meant it would be even sweeter when he took that love away.

With a large grin appearing on his face, he moved toward the door that Lilith had disappeared behind.

He did so love it when his prey tried to run.

***

Lilith's shirt flew about her, smacking against her with loud, wet slaps. Blood flew off with every jerky movement. She ran as hard as she could down the hall. Her breathing was ragged, more due to fear and adrenaline than exhaustion, and she stumbled often, tripping over her own two feet in her haste to escape from that frightening man. Nothing else mattered right now. Nothing mattered except escaping from the monster that caused her heart to quake in terror.

The walls on the cars she flew through were stained with blood and chunks of muscle, meat, and skin. She tried to ignore the red, viscous liquid that splattered across the interior. She tried to ignore the chunky bits of flesh that had once been human. She did her best to ignore the stench, the repugnant odor of blood that pervaded her, violating her nose in ways she had never imagined possible.

Her mind raced as her body flew across the floor. She and Christian were near the very front of the train, which would explain why they never heard the screaming from the other passengers, if they had even been given the chance to scream, that is.

Car after car flew past Lilith in her attempt to get away from the madman out to claim her life. She ran as far as she could, until she could run no more, until the train ended, and she had nowhere left to go.

She stared out of the window in the back of the train. It was covered in crimson, but she could still see a bit of the landscape outside. The darkness of night intermingled with the vibrant color splashed across the window's surface.

The sound of a door opening made her spin around. The man that she'd been running from had entered the car with her. As he closed the door behind him, he flashed her a grin.

"Thought you could run from me, eh? You didn't honestly think you could escape, did ya?" He spread his arms in a wide, all-encompassing gesture. "Where could you possibly escape to? There's nowhere to go. Now...." he walked toward her like a rabid beast that had just seen its prey, "I believe it's time you and me have some real fun."

Tears ran down Lilith's face as the man stalked forward. She was trapped, cornered, with no way out except through him. The only way for her to escape was through the same way they had both come in, and she was on the wrong side.

Despite this dangerous dilemma, her brain worked as fast as it could to come up with a way of getting out of this situation. Unfortunately, there was nothing. She couldn't even begin thinking up a plan to escape. Every time she tried to think of something, she came up blank. It was maddening and frustrating and she wished there was something she could do. Only there wasn't. It seemed luck, fate, or maybe even God, had decided that she was going to die here.

Christian... I'm sorry...

Lilith closed her eyes. The sound of booted feet hitting the bloody floor with squelching slaps bounced all around her as the man kept walking. She didn't want to see her death, didn't want to look into her killer's eyes as he toyed with her, breaking her in both mind and body. The act was sure to be painful enough without seeing the ways he planned on violating her.

Because she had closed her eyes, Lilith missed the face appearing in the glass window behind the man.

She did not, however, miss the sound of gunfire going off.

Her eyes snapping open, Lilith witnessed several holes appearing in the metal doorway near the handle. The door was then blasted off its hinges as though someone on the other side had taken a plastic explosive and blown it open. The metal door, dented and beaten in, smacked against the ground, nearly hitting her tormentor in the process as it bounced once, twice, three times, and then rumbled to a stop.

Hope rose within her as Christian stood in the doorway, dressed in combat boots and black pants. He wasn't wearing a shirt, making it clear that he hadn't bothered putting one on in his rush to get here. In one hand was one of his guns, the silver one; in the other hand was a sword, the black one.

His breathing was heavy, his eyes narrowed into a tempestuous glare that was so intense it made her think of a natural disaster. There was a storm brewing within his eyes. All that anger, all that rage, all that hate, was being directed at the man standing between them.

"Tch! I'd been hoping you'd sleep a little while longer," the man said, turning around to face Christian. "You've ruined my fun." He tilted his head, contemplating something, and then grinned. "But then again, maybe it would be even more fun to string you up and have you watch while I enjoy breaking your little succubus girlfriend. Yes." He nodded several times, satisfied with his idea. "I think that'll be a good punishment for you."

"I don't know who you are." Christian's voice came out in a guttural growl. "But you are going to die."

His body was shivering, and it took a moment, but Lilith soon realized that Christian was enraged, though that word seemed to undermine just his fury. He was, most assuredly, incensed beyond anything she had ever seen. While Lilith couldn't be sure it wasn't just a trick of the light, she could have sworn that his red eye was glowing, as in, literally glowing and not the metaphorical glow of anger.

Christian lifted his hand holding the gun, pointing it directly at the man.

"You think you can kill me?" The man snorted. "Boy, I've been around for a long time, and I can tell you right now; you're a hundred years too soon to beat someone of my caliber."

Christian frowned, but he did not respond to the man. Instead he looked at Lilith, worry clear in his eyes. "Are you alright?"

"I—"

Lilith opened her mouth, about to tell him that she was fine, when she paused. Her throat closed and compressed, the words refusing to escape, because the truth was that she was not alright. She was frightened, tired, and sick to her stomach. Her body was shaking, and her mind felt seconds away from cracking like the fragile shell of an egg. She felt flimsy. Vulnerable. Weak.

She shook her head, tears blurring her vision.

Christian's grip on his weapons tightened. "I see."

His eyes flickered back to Nicholas, the barely restrained tempest within them undulating violently as it threatened to break free.

Despite his obvious outrage, his voice was calm as he said, "I've always tried to follow the Ten Commandments; I've never placed another god before the one true God. I've never worshiped something other than God. I've never taken the lord's name in vain. I always remember the sabbath. I try to honor my mother and father to the best of my abilities. I've never committed adultery." He paused here, thinking for a moment, and then nodded to himself. "I've never stolen, or born false witnesses against my neighbors, or coveted anything they possess."

"I noticed that you didn't say anything about killing." The man appeared amused by his speech. "You know that's an important commandment, right?"

"I wish I could say I've never killed, but that would be a lie." Christian shrugged. "I've killed a lot in my time. The number of creatures whose lives have been ended by my hands are too numerous to count. I won't even make the excuse that I only did it because it was commanded of me. The choice to kill them was mine." He narrowed his eyes. "However, I have never taken any joy in the act. I've never found myself with a craving to kill more. The idea of killing is not one that I enjoy. That being said…" Christian bent his knees and adopted a stance that reminded Lilith of a tiger getting ready to pounce, "I am going to take great pleasure in ripping you apart."

"Come on then!" Nicholas gave Christian a "come here" gesture with the hand that held the knife. "Let's see if you can back those words up with action!"

Chapter 11

Nicholas's words were all the invitation Christian needed. Without preamble, he rushed forward, hurtling toward Nicholas, blood splashing around him in his wake. The man was grinning at him as he closed the distance within seconds.

There was a flash of sparks as Christian's sword struck Nicholas's knife. The two pushed against each other, each vying to overpower the other. For someone so skinny, Nicholas was surprisingly strong. He barely budged despite Christian putting all of his weight behind his sword.

Deciding to break their stalemate, Christian pointed his gun at Nicholas's head, pulling the trigger and firing off a round. The other man tilted his head. The bullet flew past him and struck the ceiling in a shower of sparks.

Two steps back took Nicholas out of Christian's range. The sword that had been grinding against his knife flew past his shoulder, nearly but not quite grazing his clothes. With the blade now past him, he moved back in and tried to shove the sharp end of his knife into Christian's right eye. The attack was redirected when the barrel of a gun smacked it away. Christian pointed that same gun at Nicholas's face. There was a flash and a thunderclap as the gun went off. Once again, it was dodged when the gaunt-faced figure tilted his head.

Strikes were traded at lightning speeds. It would have been impossible for most human eyes to follow. Nicholas swiped at Christian's face. It was blocked. Christian tried to bisect Nicholas from hip to shoulder. A loud *clang!* echoed as it, too, was blocked. Sparks flew and steel clashed. Attack met parry. The sound of gunfire filled the air, accompanying the noise that their bladed weapons made when they struck each other.

A horizontal swipe with Raphael had the other man swaying backwards, his scraggly brown hair bouncing along with him. Nicholas came back in with a swift, decisive jab aimed at Christian's stomach. The former Executioner avoided impalement by sidestepping to the right whilst bringing Raphael up and letting the blade glide along the knife's edge. As sparks emitted from the grinding steel, he pushed the weapon wide, opening a hole in Nicholas's defense. Christian did not hesitate to exploit it.

It was too bad his opponent had no intention of letting Christian gut him. Nicholas dodged the thrust that came sailing at him by moving to the left and tucking into a shoulder roll. He curved around Christian, kipped back up to his feet, and lashed out with a series of quick slashes at Christian's unprotected back. With his teeth grit and his heterochromatic eyes narrowed, Christian parried most of the attacks coming at him by making minor adjustments to the angle and position of his sword.

A loud clang rang out each time Raphael was struck by the knife being wielded by Nicholas. Despite managing to block the attacks coming at him, Christian still found himself being pressed back. Step by step he inched backwards, his body just barely able to keep up with the fast-paced onslaught. His muscles shook. His arms strained. It was only after taking his last step that his sense of danger flared to life, warning him of impending doom.

He stopped just as something began cutting into his back. It was a wire, he realized. A thin, microfiber wire that was so small he hadn't even noticed it glinting in the light. As blood ran down his back, Christian thought up a plan. He moved forward, into the guard of Nicholas just as the other man attempted to slit his throat. The attack missed when Christian tilted his body to the left. He used the momentum of his tilt to swerve further left, at the same time opening up into a 360 degree spin. Raphael came up, slicing the microfilament in two. The fibrous metal wire remained for a split second before giving in to the blade's bite.

Christian sensed danger. Reflexes kicked in just a second before his life was taken, allowing him to survive by ducking low to the ground. Several strands of hair was sliced off his head as something passed over him. A light glint revealed another thin microfiber. It cleaved through the walls of the train with ease, slicing a long, thin line through both sides of the train. As Christian came back up, he made a quick, vertical slash that cut the wire before it could do more damage.

Spinning around, Christian brought Gabriel up and fired a salvo of bullets at Nicholas. The man's wide grin stayed on his face as he swayed back and forth, his body blurring in a way that Christian had never seen a human do before, as he dodged the hail of bullets with ease. The gun clicked empty. Wearing a wide grin, the duster-wearing psycho launched himself at Christian with a loud, deranged laugh.

Coming in at a near-sprint, Nicholas made a diagonal slash through the air with his dagger, trying to slice Christian's face apart from right eye to left jaw. In retaliation, Christian tried to remove the hand holding the knife with a swipe to the wrist. It didn't work. The attack was blocked when Nicholas shifted his knife from a normal grip to a reverse grip. Raphael clanged off the knife as Nicholas pushed the sword away.

The scent of blood hung heavy in the air. Christian remained calm as sweat dripped from his brown, leaving a trail down his face. His eyes were narrowed as he tried to think of a method to dispose of this man. Everyone had a weakness. He just needed to find Nicholas's.

A flash of insight was all Christian had to let him know that something was wrong. The warning came a little late. While Christian was preparing to launch a combination attack, his instincts screamed at him. He spun to the side as Nicholas made a yanking motion with his knife hand. A sharp, stinging pain struck his cheek. Small flecks of blood flew from the clean slice in his skin. Another flash in his vision let him know that the object that had cut him was another one of those thin micro-wires.

A lull entered the battle. Christian and Nicholas jumped away from each other. Nicholas was smiling. Christian had a frown. He wiped at his cheek, and then looked at his hand. There was blood on it but only a bit.

"Ho?" Nicholas looked at him curiously, his eyes squinting. "Your bleeding has already stopped. My cut must not have been as deep as usual. I wonder if that means I'm losing my touch?"

Christian's narrowed eyes gained a contemplative quality. "I see now. Your main weapon isn't that knife, but those wires." He looked at the knife again, finally noticing that the bottom appeared to have a small hole from which a long wire was coming out. "You lure people into thinking that your knife is what they need to worry about, when what they should really be focusing on are the wires."

"Heh, the wrinkly old man was right. You are good. But, let's see if that knowledge of yours can save you from me!"

Nicholas charged forward, his form seeming to blur as he sped across the floor. His attack came at Christian, reckless and fast. The man with the scraggly hair and beard lashed out with an aggressive offensive. The knife came in from all sides, at all angles, slashing and stabbing and swinging. However, it wasn't the knife that Christian had to worry about. That was just a distraction.

Christian brought Gabriel up to block the knife strike that came for his head. The attack was blocked, but Christian suddenly found his gun wrapped up in a wires. He tried to pull the wires apart, but it was impossible. Whatever they were made of, they were too strong for anything other than a sharp weapon made of Orichalcum to cut.

Making several leaps back to put some distance between them, Nicholas gave his knife a yank. Because Christian's weapon was made from Orichalcum, it did not fall apart as the wire bit into it. Instead the weapon was yanked from Christian's hand, leaving him with just a sword.

"Haha! Looks like knowing how I fight isn't helping you much, is it?"

Snarling, Christian tried to move in close. Without having both of his swords, using the *Fake Opening Style* was out of the question. He simply didn't have the speed to react to any attack when he only had a single weapon. That meant bringing the fight to Nicholas.

As Christian tried to mow down the distance between them, Nicholas grinned and pulled on his knife again. Several lines of wire that had previously lain unseen on the ground sprung up to try and cut Christian into large chunks of oozing meat. He was able to avoid this fate, but only just. Using his quick reactionary time and incredible reflexes, Christian brought up his blade, slicing the wires apart before they went straight through his skin. Fortunately, the wires were set up in a crisscrossing pattern that made cutting them easier.

Unfortunately, Nicholas had hidden several more wire strands that came up the moment Christian sliced the others apart. Six different strands of wire bit into his flesh. He avoided the worst of it by throwing himself backwards, but his right arm, both legs, chest, left shoulder, and the inside of his right torso had all received several nasty cuts.

"Christian!" Lilith screamed in horror at seeing the man she loved bleeding from multiple deep wounds.

By now, Christian's pants were all but shredded from dozens of near misses. The cuts on his skin bleed profusely, pouring down his body. It stung. His body felt like it was on fire.

"Hahaha! Worried about your boyfriend?" Nicholas grinned as he turned his head to look back at the young woman. Lilith flinched. "Don't be. You'll be next after I finish with him."

"You won't touch her!" Christian's face became a rictus of fury. He snarled at Nicholas and rushed forward. Several wires sprang up to stop him, but this time he was ready. His sword flashed out once, twice, thrice, slicing through six different wires in half as many cuts.

"Ho ho! It seems I made the kid angry!" Nicholas laughed as he yanked on his knife and more wires sprang up around him. "Alright then, let's see how you deal with this!"

He manipulated his knife, causing the wires to undulate wildly. Christian only had enough time to realize the danger before he found himself surrounded. He was soon forced to dodged the many thin metal wires coming his way. Yet even someone with reflexes like his could only do so much. For every wire he avoided, two more scored a cut on him. When he sliced one apart with his sword, another three would take its place.

While he tried to stay at least one step ahead of Nicholas's wires, he searched wildly around the car. There wasn't much to look at; there were a couple of demolished chairs that had been sliced apart by the wires, him, Lilith, and Nicholas. Not to mention the wires themselves.

As he studied the layout of the wires, he noticed that they appeared to be wrapped almost gently around several poles and the trunk compartment overhead. He pondered this. How could something that easily cut through flesh and metal not destroy the poles they were around? It was almost like his opponent... but no, that was impossible, wasn't it? No one could have the concentration necessary to change whether or not a weapon could cut through something. Could they?

"Come on! Come on, come on, come on!" Nicholas shouted, his eyes wide with glee as Christian wove through several wires. "Bleed for me! Bleed! I need to see your blood! I want it! I want all the pretty red colors to ooze out of your body! That's it! That's it! More! Give me more!"

Christian grimaced as the man began ranting while trying to kill him. This Nicholas character was clearly not all there. He supposed it was to be expected. Very few people who were in the business of killing managed to stay sane. Most eventually cracked under the pressure. Christian had only lasted as long as he had because of his strict moral fiber and strong faith.

"Yes! That's it! Bleed! Oh, so good! You're so good to me! But I need more! I'm almost there! Hurry! Bleed faster!"

After trying to come up with several possible solutions, Christian realized that there was really only one option that presented itself. If he wanted to avoid getting diced apart by these wires, he would need to take out the one controlling them. Cut off the head and the body would fall.

Too bad that seemed to be an impossible task.

"Christian!"

Lilith made to move toward Christian in an effort to help him, though just what she planned on doing, he didn't know. Before she could take more than a few steps, his voice stopped her cold. "Stay back! I don't want you getting involved in this battle! It's too dangerous!"

***

"Yeah, yeah! Stay back! Your time will come soon enough! Hahahaha!" Nicholas cackled as he waved his knife around like a madman. Wires from all around the room came to life and tried to attack Christian. They glinted in the light.

Christian did his best to dodge, but even Lilith could see that he was having a hard time. Blood appeared on his skin. Every second that passed, a new wound opened up. He wouldn't last for long.

Lilith dithered. Should she listen to Christian? Could she? What would happen if she didn't? He was currently on the ropes. Only by stint of his superior reflexes and excellent physical shape had he managed to avoid death thus far. How long would his luck last? Lilith couldn't bear the thought of Christian dying.

But, still, it wasn't like she could actually do anything, could she? She wasn't a fighter. She had no talent for combat. What's more, she lacked the mentality necessary for people who lived a life of battle and bloodshed. Yet even so, she still wanted to help.

She looked around, trying to find some way that she could be of use to Christian. The young man that she'd fallen in love with was fighting for his life, his hair whipping about him in a frenetic frenzy as he moved, danced, and twirled about the small cage of wires that he was trapped in. Blood gushed from a wound on his forehead, streaming into his left eye and forcing it closed. His sword flashed out, brilliant and gleaming. It cut through several wires, but more of the fibrous strands rose up to take their place, glinting in the light of the lamps overhead. Christian was being pushed to the brink. His back was against the wall.

Standing several feet away from Christian was Nicholas. The twig-thin man was laughing with the kind of psychotic laughter one would normally only hear from cartoon villains like the Joker. He was manipulating the strings via his knife, shaking it left and right while making minute twitches at the same time. He wasn't paying attention to her right now, busy as he was taunting Christian.

She still wouldn't risk going near him. If he was half as good at sensing approaching enemies as Christian was, he would notice her long before she had a chance to do anything. What should she do? What could she do?

Taking one last frantic survey of the area in the hopes of finding something, anything, that she could use to rescue Christian, Lilith froze. Just a few feet away from her was Christian's gun. It gleamed silver in the light, a sharp polarity among the bloodstained carpet. Lilith looked at Christian and Nicholas. Then the gun. Then Christian and Nicholas again. The gun again. Her eyes narrowed.

Lilith pressed her back against the wall and slowly moved toward the gun. She remained cautious, watching Nicholas for any sign that he knew what she was up to. He did not, fortunately, or if he did, then he was very good at hiding it.

She soon reached the gun and picked it up. It felt heavy in her hands, heavier than when she had used it to break open the door to that middle school office. There was a strange weight to it, and Lilith couldn't help but think it weighed far more than it should have.

Shaking these thoughts off, Lilith gripped the handle tightly and took aim. She tried to line up her shot, but her hands were shaking. They didn't want to cooperate with her. They trembled as she held the weapon in the same way she'd seen police officers do in those movies that Maria liked to watch. It felt awkward, or perhaps that was just the jerky twitches she was making. She couldn't get a clear shot at Nicholas because every time it looked like he was in the gun's sights, her hand would spasm violently and throw it off course.

Gritting her teeth and closing one eye, Lilith did her best to take aim, and then she pulled the trigger.

Nothing happened. There was a soft click, but that was all. She pulled the trigger again. Still nothing.

It was only after trying to fire the gun several more times that she remembered something. It was out of ammo.

"Trying to fire at me behind my back?" Lilith looked up, her eyes wide. Nicholas had turned his head, his left eye staring at her. "That's a very naughty thing to do. I'm going to have to punish you for that. But first…"

He turned back to Christian. The young man had tried to use his distracted state to move through the tangled mass of wires and close the distance between them. However, in doing so, he had left himself wide open.

A long wire shot up from the ground. It twisted around Christian's legs, tying them together and causing him to fall face-first to the ground.

Before the young man could rise, the wire wrapped around him further, pinning his arms to his sides, encircling his entire body.

Nicholas pulled on his knife some more, tightening the wire. Christian groaned as the small metal fibers cut through his pants and dug into his flesh. A long, spiral-shaped laceration manifested on his skin as the wire sliced into him. It started from the shoulder and moved down his body, his arms, his torso, his legs. Dark red liquid oozed from the long wound, seeping out of his body and pooling along the floor.

"Oh, God! Christian!" Lilith screamed in horror at seeing the young man caught. She dropped the gun, letting it fall to the ground with a loud thump. She stood up and tried to run over to him, but she was intercepted by a backhand.

"Lilith!"

Seeing the young woman struck caused a surge of hatred to well up inside of Christian's soul. His struggling grew, his body shaking, jerking, and straining against the wires holding him in place. More blood gushed out of the wound. Even so, he continued to struggle, to fight. Lilith couldn't even imagine how much pain he was in, nor how strong he must have been to ignore it.

"That's right, you two! Struggle! I want to see you fight with everything you've got! Breaking you won't be nearly as fun if you're not giving it your all to defy me!"

Nicholas laughed, his bloodcurdling cackles sending shivers down both Christian's and Lilith's spines. The scraggly man then focused his attention on Lilith, who felt her body freeze in terror. She only had a moment to recognize the danger that she was in before a long strand of wire wrapped around her body. She cried out as the wire cut lightly into her flesh as it twisted about her.

"I wouldn't suggest trying to struggle," Nicholas told her. "While those wires aren't made from Orichalcum, they're still sharper than most bladed weapons." He chortled when Lilith froze. "Ah, but don't worry. I'm very good at controlling this wire. Lots of practice, you see. Right now, they're only tied tightly enough to keep you in place, provided you don't squirm too much."

He walked over to her and knelt down. A stomach-churning grin marred his face, repulsive and horrifying at the same time. Underneath the man's lustful stare, combined with that terror-inducing smile, Lilith felt petrified and helpless.

"Lilith! Lilith!" Christian shouted.

Nicholas turned his head to look at Christian. The young man's struggling had grown even fiercer. He shook and jerked and squirmed, his body straining with an extreme amount of force. His muscles were visibly flexing, veins bulging in his arms and neck, as he seemingly ignored the way the wires were digging into his flesh.

"I like that look in your eye, kid. Keep struggling. Struggle and watch as I break your pretty little girlfriend. Let your despair and helplessness consume you as I violate her in every way imaginable." He turned back to Lilith, his eyes lighting up in euphoria. He shivered as though he'd just orgasmed, licking his lips in anticipation. "I am going to enjoy this so much. You have no idea how much pleasure I'm going to take from playing with you."

His knife went to her back, the cold steel making her body shudder and her spine stiffen. Nicholas then slowly shoved the knife into her pliant flesh, causing Lilith to cry out and struggle against her bindings, which only served to make the wires cut even deeper furrows in her skin.

"Lilith!" Christian continued struggling and fighting as Lilith began to cry. He glared at Nicholas with a burning, all-consuming hatred. "You sick fuck! I'm going to kill you!"

Nicholas just laughed. "Such foul language. That's very unbecoming of you. I thought you were a man of God?"

***

Christian snarled as he continued to fight against his bindings. The wounds were growing deeper, the wires now cutting into his muscles. He ignored the pain, however, as his pain meant nothing to him. Lilith. Lilith was suffering right in front of him. She was in pain. She was hurting. He had to do something. He refused to let this man break the woman he'd grown to love.

But what could he do? He was helpless, trapped, caught in the web of a spider. The more he struggled, the harder it became to break free.

I need power.

He looked at Lilith, her body covered in lacerations, blood staining her skin.

I need more power.

He saw Nicholas kneeling over the woman he loved, taking pleasure in causing her pain.

I need more power!

Something inside of him broke, like the snapping of a chain. He heard a strange shattering sound within his mind, and his left eye began to burn, a searing sensation, as if a hot poker was being shoved into his iris. Liquid welled up in his eye, viscous and thick. Not water. Blood. It traveled down his cheek, dripped off his chin, and splashed onto the floor.

Power.

His muscles throbbed. He could feel the wires being pushed out of his skin. His flesh began stitching itself together, a strange, stinging pain that irritated his skin and reminded him of the times he'd had to get stitches.

Adrenaline coursed through his body, invigorating and powerful, giving him a strength that he didn't know he had. His body straining against his bindings, Christian put every ounce of willpower he possessed into breaking the wires that held him. There were several snaps as the fibers holding him broke.

Christian surged to his feet, his fierce, determined eyes blazing with the ferocity of a firestorm. Putting on a burst of speed, his raven hair thrashing about him in wild abandon, Christian allowed the adrenaline pumping through his veins to decrease the time it took to get from point A to point B.

Point B was Nicholas.

The older man only had a moment to look up before Christian was there, swinging Raphael at him. Nicholas tried to block, but Christian, his hatred fueling him, moved far too fast for the man to react in time. The blade came up, and the hand that had been holding the knife flew off in a spray of gore.

Nicholas stared at his missing hand in shock. "Well, that sucks."

Nicholas looked up just as Christian swung his blade again. Raphael appeared as nothing more than a brilliant glint of light before it disappeared. There was a short pause. Seconds later, the skin peeled apart, along with the tendons and muscles as Nicholas's head fell backwards, off his body, and rolled along the floor.

Nicholas's body remained upright for a few seconds more. There was surprisingly little blood flowing from the stump of a neck, just a few spurts, like a broken fountain that could no longer shoot out water properly. Then the body fell back, crumpling to the floor with a dull thud. It twitched several times before going still.

Christian did not bother looking at the body as he knelt next to Lilith and used Raphael to cut the wire holding her apart. Despite being free, the girl did not move. She seemed petrified.

"Lilith?"

Lilith twitched, but she did not respond otherwise. He called her name a few times, but Lilith didn't seem to hear him. It was only then that Christian understood. Her mind was lost in limbo, having shut down lest it be forced to endure the pain and terror as Nicholas tortured her.

"Dammit!" Christian was unable to keep himself from cursing. Lilith wasn't responding to him. He looked into her eyes and noticed their glazed, dead appearance. It was like she wasn't even there. "Dammit!"

Scooping Lilith into his arms, he rushed back toward the compartment that they shared. The girl hung limply in his grasp. Her head lolled against his shoulder. She blinked once or twice, but other than that, her eyes remained dead.

Chapter 12

Upon reaching their compartment, Christian gently set Lilith on the bed. He made sure that she was sitting up. Lilith, whose body appeared to have shut down, fell forward, but he caught her and pushed the young woman back until she was leaning against the bed's headboard.

After making sure she was sitting up, he pulled out his guitar case. Setting the case on its side, he opened it up, and began rifling around inside. The case contained his sword, Michael, his gun, Phanuel, some ammunition, various types of grenades, and a good deal of supplies. They were mostly basic utilities. He had soap, shampoo, shaving cream, and razors. Among the stockpile of basic provisions was a box that contained body-cleansing pads, which he and Lilith used to clean their bodies with when they were unable to take a shower during their travels.

He opened the package and pulled out one of the wipes before turning to Lilith, who was staring listlessly at the bed. Her head was tilted downward, and her eyes remained sightless. Just looking at her made his heart ache.

"Lilith," he said, getting her attention and making her look up. She blinked at him, her dull eyes staring into his with a sense of apathy. Christian grimaced and, once more, began to curse Nicholas. He considered himself a decent person, and he'd never condoned torture or prolonging another's suffering, but that man had gotten off far too lightly.

"Christian?" Her voice came out slowly, eyes flickering. It was almost as if she couldn't quite see him, or maybe she could, but her mind just wasn't all there.

"It's me." Christian tried to smile, but it didn't come out right. He could tell. His face felt pinched. Lilith didn't seem to notice, if her blank stare was any indication. "Listen, I'm going to clean you up. Is that alright?"

He normally wouldn't have asked such a question, mainly because he and Lilith had gotten close enough to the point where they often helped clean each other. He wouldn't do that now. After what she had just gone through—he still didn't know everything that Nicholas had done to her, but he knew that it must have been horrifying—Christian didn't want to take any of the liberties that he normally would have.

Lilith stared at him for a long while. Christian met her gaze, trying not to let out any of the emotions he felt at seeing her toneless eyes. There were many emotions boiling just underneath the surface, too many to count, and he was afraid that if he let them out now, he'd explode into a bloody rage. He didn't want that, as it might frighten Lilith.

She eventually nodded, not saying anything, just bobbing her head up and down once. Christian took this as his cue. He knelt in front of her and caressed her face, using the wipes to tenderly clean away the grime. He took note of the cut on her left cheek. It wasn't deep, and it was no longer bleeding. Much like the other small cuts that littered her body, this one would probably heal sometime within the next day. As long as he disinfected and cleaned it properly, it shouldn't leave a scar.

"Lilith?" Christian got her attention again. When he was sure that she was focusing on him, he said, "I'm going to clean off your body now. Is that okay?"

Lilith looked at him, her head tilting in what would have been an inquisitive gesture were it not for the detached look in her eyes. She nodded after several moments of silently staring. Christian took a deep, slow breath, and looked down at her chest.

There were several cuts marring her skin. One was from where Nicholas's wires had cut into her, but several must have been made before Christian found her. There wasn't much blood. That was good. It meant her wounds were shallow.

He got to work, wiping down the rest of her body and taking extra care when he cleaned the lacerations. He moved his hand over her skin, cleaning off the sweat, dirt, and blood. He wiped the blood off her breasts, but he didn't linger any longer than was absolutely necessary. With how she was acting, he didn't know what her reaction would be to being touched in such an intimate place. Fortunately, she didn't seem to mind, or even notice.

He paid extra attention to where the wire had wound around her skin. The wound was light but long, traveling from her shoulders all the way to her legs. It looked worse than it was, thankfully. Christian cleaned the wound, then used a cloth covered in disinfectant to sterilize it. Lilith twitched as the antiseptic stung her skin. He then opened a bottle of ointment, which would help heal the wound without leaving any scar tissue, and lightly applied it to her skin before rubbing it in.

After he finished with her upper body, he moved on to the bottom. He asked her to stand up, which she did, and then carefully removed her torn skirt, letting it slide down her hips and legs, leaving her in nothing more than her panties. Lilith shivered a bit, but she didn't react much otherwise.

Christian cleaned her hips and legs the same way he had her upper body. When he finished, Christian searched through his case and pulled out a shirt. He turned back toward her and said, "lift your arms, please."

Lilith lifted her arms above her head. Bunching up the shirt, he raised it over her and put her arms through the arm slots, then brought it down. Her head appeared through the neck of the shirt, and Christian had her lower her arms and sit back down.

With Lilith now taken care of, Christian decided to focus on himself and the grime that he'd accumulated from the battle. As he cleansed his body with the small bath wipes, he took stock of his own injuries. They'd all healed up, miraculously enough, and were now nothing more than small lines of light pink skin. Even a few of the shallower cuts had disappeared entirely.

Huh...

This confused him. Those nanomachines inside of the topical cream that Anastasia Adams, his former personal physician within the Executioners, had rubbed on him should have disappeared a long time ago. Why was he still healing so quickly? He supposed this was just another mystery that wouldn't be solved for a long while, maybe never. It wasn't like he could ask Anastasia.

Shaking his head, he refocused on getting himself cleaned up as quickly as possible. When he was done, he put his shirt back on, and then helped Lilith to her feet. He placed his hands on her shoulders, regarding her carefully. She stared back at him. However, her gaze revealed nothing.

"Are you alright?" he asked.

As if his words had triggered something inside of her, a flicker of emotion finally appeared in Lilith's eyes. She began to nod, only to quickly change it into a negative head shake. Her body started to tremble and her eyes to tear.

A second later, she threw herself at Christian, grabbing fistfuls of his shirt. Powerful sobs wracked her body, shaking her frame as she let out all of the emotions that had been boiling inside of her. The salty liquid pouring from her eyes stained Christian's shirt and soaked into his skin. In spite of having not expected such a strong response due to how she'd been acting, Christian still entwined his arms around Lilith in a tight, loving embrace, as if doing so would somehow shield her from the horrors she'd just faced.

"It was horrible! That man was—he killed everyone! I went into the car, and they were all dead! And everything was covered in blood and body parts! And he kept saying that he wanted me! That he was going to make me scream! And he ruined my shirt with his knife and kept cutting me and cutting me! And it hurt! It really, really hurt! And I was so frightened! I didn't know what to do! I couldn't… couldn't…"

"Ssh," Christian hushed the young woman as she dissolved into indecipherable gibbering. He raised his left hand and ran it through her hair, the tips of his fingers grazing her scalp in soft, serene motions. Meanwhile, he placed his right hand on her waist, rubbing circles in the small of her back as he pulled her closer. "It's okay. Everything's going to be okay now. He's gone."

"Christian," Lilith hiccuped, "how much longer are we going to have to keep running?" She looked up at him, her eyes red and her cheeks stained with tears.

"I don't know." Christian wanted to look away. Seeing her like this, so weak and vulnerable, made his chest hurt worse than if he had been stabbed. "I wish I could tell you more, but I just don't know."

He cursed his inability to help Lilith by giving her a definite answer. She was suffering, and he was unable to do a single thing to help her. It made him feel weak, incapable. If he couldn't even help the one person that he loved the most in this world, then what good was he?

"I don't know how much more of this I can take," she admitted.

Christian didn't want to admit that the wetness in his eyes was due to tears. Lilith, despite her non-human origins and dark past, was still just a normal person. She wasn't used to dealing with such unmitigated and savage violence. She didn't have the hardened heart that came from years of battle and bloodshed. Her mind had not been desensitized to the horrors that were out there. Even after everything that Damien had done to her, the young woman's heart remained unbelievably pure.

If Christian had his way, that heart would never be tainted by the kinds of strife and conflict that had destroyed his.

Of course, I've already failed at this. A humorless smile threatened to appear on his lips.

"Lilith, I have no clue when this will end. I don't even know if it will ever end. However…" Christian cupped Lilith's face with his hands, wiping away a few stray tears with his thumbs. "I promise you that no matter what happens, no matter who or what comes after you, I will protect you."

Lilith sniffled. "Promise?"

"I promise."

Even though he'd promised, Christian had no idea how he was going to keep it. With the forces that were arrayed against them, an unknown threat in the form of a bishop with vast powers over the Catholic Church, and who knew how many other hardships that were waiting for them out there, making this kind of promise could very well lead to tragedy. And yet he still promised her because he refused to let himself believe that it was impossible. He would protect Lilith, even if he had to take on the entire Catholic Church to do it.

Where there was a will, there was a way, as the old saying went, and Christian had more than enough will.

Chapter 13

The train coming from San Francisco, California arrived in Las Vegas, Nevada at 8:37am. It drove into the train station near Audrie Street and East Flamingo Road, slowing down with a squeal of metal wheels on tracks. It pulled up to a platform, where one-hundred or more people were gathered.

Everybody knew that something was wrong the minute the train arrived. The windows that would generally offer a view of the interior were covered in red, splatters of something dark and thick. Whatever the stuff was, it had quite obviously been there for a long while, as it was beginning to dry.

Those waiting on the boarding platform took a step back in unease, their faces, body language, and general demeanors shifting. It was like a herd of antelopes who'd sensed a pride of lions nearby. No one was sure what to expect, but everyone had a bad feeling settle in the pits of their stomachs as they stared at the darkened windows.

Then the doors opened.

That was when the stench hit them.

A pudgy young woman who had round cheeks, a strange-looking updo, wore far too much makeup, and was wearing a dark blue business suit with a skirt, was the first to scream out in terror as everyone there was given a glimpse of the train's interior.

Others soon followed as they, too, saw the massacre that had occurred inside; the blood decorating the entire train car, the meaty chunks of human body parts that looked like they'd been tossed around the train, and the repugnant sweetness of rotting flesh. It was too much for them. Most people never even got to see a dead body, except at maybe a science exhibit that showed well-preserved cadavers. To see such a brutal and horrifying scene was more than the average citizen could handle.

Those who did not immediately lose their breakfast ran about in a panic, screaming, crying, and causing a large scene. Within the chaotic cacophony of symphonic voices crying out in terror, it was very easy for two people to slip out of the back of the train and stealthily move down the tracks completely unnoticed.

***

Christian, one arm wrapped around Lilith while the other held onto the guitar case carrying his weapons, moved swiftly along the tracks. He wanted to get as far away from the scene they'd left behind as fast as humanly possible. If anyone saw them there, looking like they did, they would have undoubtedly been arrested and brought in for questioning. At the very least, they would have drawn a lot of suspicion upon themselves.

They managed to sneak past most of the people on the platform via the train tracks. They soon found a set of stairs that could take them down to street level. This particular station was surprisingly small for a train station in Las Vegas, consisting of only two railways for trains to travel on, and two platforms for people getting on and off from. The trains themselves moved along a track that was raised several yards above ground level by a series of archway-like bridges, and the station itself was built like a simple one room building painted a light green with a sloped roof and several sets of stairs. Christian and Lilith made it to the stairs before any of the panicking civilians noticed their presence.

As they walked, Christian chanced a glance at Lilith. She was wearing one of the spare shirts he'd gotten for emergency purposes. It was a large, plain white T-shirt that looked several sizes too big on her. Perhaps it was because she was a succubus, but in spite of the unflattering shirt, she still looked incredible, even if her face was practically devoid of all emotion.

The young woman had been silent ever since her breakdown after the battle with Nicholas. Aside from the occasional sniffle that had escaped during the rest of the ride to Las Vegas, she'd not shown any sort of emotion, almost like she had become dead inside. Her eyes were withdrawn and haunted, red-rimmed from crying, and possessing the far off look that Christian had seen in some members of the Executioners who suffered from Post Traumatic Stress Disorder.

He really, really hoped that Lilith hadn't developed PTSD, as people who had it often underwent a number of psychological developments that never ended well. The last person he knew who suffered from PTSD ended up going insane and had to be put down after killing nearly five other members of the Executioners. He couldn't kill Lilith. He wouldn't. Therefore, his only hope was to pray that she wasn't suffering from such an affliction.

"Hey," he whispered to her. "How are you holding up?"

"Fine," Lilith murmured, the first words spoken since her breakdown. She was clearly not fine, just as it was clear that she didn't want to worry him. It was too bad that seeing her so listless and emotionally detached only served to worry him more.

"Look, Lilith, once we find a place to stay for the night, if you want, we can… we can talk."

"Talk?" Lilith tilted her head, looking at him with blank, unblinking eyes. It was a disconcerting gaze. Those light, baby blue eyes were normally so full of life, so vibrant. Seeing them like this, lifeless and lackluster, caused a cold, ironclad fist to grip his heart.

"Yeah, talk. You know, about… about what happened… back there, I mean." Christian tried not to squirm in discomfort as Lilith blinked several times as though contemplating his suggestion. After a moment, a small hint of emotion flickered in her eyes as she looked away.

"I… don't want to talk about it."

Christian thought about pushing the issue. She was obviously bottling her feelings. Keeping a lid on one's emotions like she was apparently trying to do was never a good way to get over one's problems. More often than not, keeping someone's emotions locked down tight only exacerbated the issue.

He didn't say anything right then, though, and not just because it was neither the time nor the place. They were attracting a crowd. As Christian looked around, he noticed that several dozen people were congregating near them. A number of those people had pulled out their cameras and tried to snap photos, causing Christian to turn his head and pull Lilith close enough to him that her face was blocked by his body. The last thing they needed was people who could give the police their photos. It would make disappearing within the city that much harder.

Several people who'd gotten out their cellphones began texting or calling. Christian really hoped they weren't contacting the cops. That would be almost as bad as having their photos taken by a bunch of random passerby. The only thing that would have been worse was if they posted those photos on a social media network for everyone to see. He could only imagine the kind of disaster that would ensue because of it.

With some deft maneuvering and careful positioning, Christian was able to hurry away from the crowd, Lilith wrapped in his protective embrace. He was sure he'd managed to avoid giving people a clear shot of either of their faces. At least, he hoped he was.

When they got past the crowd, he directed them into the nearest parking garage. It was the closest structure in the area and likely the least crowded as well. The first few floors had a large number of cars of different shapes, sizes, makes, and brands. Almost every parking space was filled up. Christian didn't want to deal with anybody who might walk up to their car while they were present, so he moved up to the next few levels until he found one that didn't have a lot of cars.

The fourth floor was practically empty. From where he stood, Christian could only count three cars in total; there was a white minivan, a large red Ford truck, and a small mini-cooper painted to look like the British flag. The rest of the large, open spaced lot was empty. Good.

"Come on," Christian said softly, directing Lilith over to a support pillar. He bade her to sit down, which she did, sitting with her legs straight and her back leaning against the pillar.

Now that they were alone and had a second to themselves, Christian tried to think of what they should do. Obviously, they needed to find a place to stay. They also needed to craft some disguises. Even if no one had managed to get a clear picture of them, they would still know what he and Lilith looked like. That meant new clothes, dying their hair, and maybe even getting new colored contacts. There had to be a store in Las Vegas that sold those.

Directing his gaze back to Lilith, Christian bit his lip. The girl's head was tilted down, staring at the cement, or maybe her feet. Her blonde hair fell about her like a curtain, casting shadows over her face, hiding her from view. He couldn't even see her eyes, but he knew they would be as desolate as her demeanor suggested.

Moving over until he was directly in front of her, Christian knelt down and cupped her cheeks with a tenderness that no one but Lilith would ever see from him.

"Lilith," he whispered, eliciting a single blink before Lilith focused on him. His heart ached when he saw her emotionless gaze, but he tried to be strong. He was not the one who had suffered. "Do you think you can follow me? We have to get moving before any cops come by to search for us."

Lilith nodded her head once, slowly, as if she was in a daze. He knew this was all a part of her shutting off the connection between herself and her emotions. It tore him apart to see her like this, but there was little that he could do about that. For now, at least, he could only hope that she would hold herself together until they found a place to take shelter for the night.

Avoiding the crowds by taking backstreets and alleys, Christian made his way through the city of Las Vegas with Lilith in tow. He kept a firm grip on her hand, afraid that if he loosened it even a bit, he would lose her. It might have been an irrational fear, but then again, it might not. He didn't want to take a chance.

While they were walking, Christian thought about their next move. First things first, they needed new clothes. Not only had their only other pair been ruined during the train battle, but the ones they had on weren't going to cut it. People had seen them, taken pictures of them, and now knew what they looked like. There was no doubt in his mind that the cops would become involved with this, and there was an even stronger possibility that the bishop would learn about what happened here, and that he and Lilith were in Nevada. If that happened, they would have even more trouble on their hands.

During their journey, Christian came across a small clothing shop called Maddison's Clothing Boutique. It was a tiny little boutique made of red brick, steel window frames, and large glass windows. The store displayed several mannequins with different sets of clothes just inside on a small, raised platform. From looking at the mannequins, he could see that the establishment sold both men's and women's clothing. The shop was set in between a porn shop and a church. Thankfully, it wasn't part of the Catholic Church, just one of the many cathedrals where people who went to Las Vegas to elope often got married in.

Christian shook his head at the sight of a church next to a porn shop, and then proceeded inside. His feet made light clacks against the polished, dark gray cement. A number of stands and racks filled much of the interior, and shelves lined the walls. The store was divided into two sections, one for men and one for women. Standing in front of a cash register, with her chin set on the butt of her left hand, was a bored-looking woman who was far too thin to be healthy.

"Come on," Christian said.

Keeping a careful hold on Lilith's hand, Christian led her to the women's section. There, he found everything from skirts, dresses, T-shirts, and shorts to hosiery, lingerie, bras, and panties. The many different types of clothing, with their multitudes of color and sizes and styles bombarded him, overwhelming him just a bit. He wasn't much for clothes shopping. This was only the second time he'd gone shopping for Lilith. Both times Lilith had made all the decisions regarding her attire.

She wouldn't be doing that this time.

Looking over the selection, Christian thought about what he knew of Lilith. Most of what she wore seemed fairly normal, at least as far as he could see. She usually wore full-length dresses and sundresses, with a few accessories such as jackets and the like. She had a couple skirts that, like her dresses, were also full-length, traveling all the way down to her ankles. She didn't wear many jeans and she had no shorts to speak of, yet she did have a number of shirts in various styles.

Maybe he should just go with something simple? Yeah, that would probably be best.

After looking over the wide selection of articles, Christian eventually chose several simple pieces of clothing that he hoped Lilith would like. He also made sure they were functional and wouldn't hamper her movement should she need to run. With one handful of clothes and the other occupied by Lilith's hand, Christian walked over to the dressing room in the back.

Still standing behind the counter, the woman manning the register watched them, still looking slightly bored, but now appearing somewhat interested in her two customers.

"Here." After reaching the dressing room, Christian turned around and placed all of the clothes in Lilith's arms. She looked at the clothing in what almost appeared to be confusion. A small frown marred her pretty face, and her brows were just a little furrowed. She looked up at Christian, a question seemingly in her eyes. He said, "try those on and see what you think. I'll wait out here for you."

Lilith shook her head. One hand left the small pile in her arms and grabbed hold of his shirt sleeve.

"Lilith?" Christian asked. Lilith shook her head again, her fingers gripping his clothes tighter.

"Don't leave…" It was a soft whisper, a pale shadow of a once vibrant and beautiful song. Lilith's voice was nothing but an imitation of the generous and lilting tones she once had. "I don't… don't go…"

Christian withheld a frown. This was not Lilith. He didn't know what happened to her when that man had first attacked, but it was hard to fathom that this was the same woman who'd dared to stab a No Life King in the back with a sword.

"Hey, now." Christian gently undid the fingers latched onto his arm. He took her hand in both of his. "I'm not going anywhere. I'll be right here, waiting for you to get out."

Lilith dithered. "Promise?"

Christian brought her hand up to his lips and placed a kiss on it. "Promise."

Another moment passed. Lilith nodded and went inside the dressing room, closing the door behind her. Christian turned around and leaned against the wall. With his arms crossed over his chest, he surveyed the room. Only one other person, a woman, had entered the shop since he and Lilith had come in. That person was currently over in the men's department. Maybe she was buying some clothes for her husband.

The sound of the door behind him opening made Christian turn his head. Lilith walked out. She was wearing a pair of basic blue jeans. The shirt that she had on was short-sleeved, white, and had a brand logo on the front.

He was surprised by her choice in clothing. He had given her several choices, but he'd only grabbed one pair of jeans because she never wore them. Most of them had been skirts and dresses that went down to her ankles.

"You chose the jeans," he said.

Lilith looked down at herself, then back up at him. "Jeans are easier to run in."

Her answer made sense. At the same time, it was shocking. If she was thinking about practicality like this, then it meant she was doing better than he had initially thought.

She's strong...

Any other civilian who'd gone through what she had would have broken by now, but even though Lilith had withdrawn into herself, she hadn't been defeated. She was hurt. She was lost. She was frightened. However, that was not the same thing as being beaten.

I need to find some way to help bring her back.

Christian asked Lilith to try on several more outfits, mostly jeans and t-shirts since she had decided on being practical, but he had also handed her one or two sundresses, just because he knew she liked them. After they had what he felt was a good amount of clothing, he went over to the men's section. Lilith followed close behind him.

Christian was not one for clothes shopping. Never had been. Part of that was just because he never needed to shop until he'd met Lilith. The

Executioners had provided everything he needed: clothes, food, utilities, weapons, everything. Really, the only thing he'd ever had that wasn't something they bought for him was the KLReader, which he'd been forced to abandon during the train ride to Sacramento.

While he was studying two different pairs of jeans, one black and one blue, with the kind of intent that one would never expect to see on someone shopping for clothes, Lilith walked up to him. He turned to her. She had set the clothes they'd picked out for her on one of the racks and was now holding a sweatshirt, a hoodie, Christian recognized. It was a dark, burnt orange color.

"You think I should get that?" asked Christian, blinking as he studied the article.

Lilith gave him a slow nod. "In case you need to hide your face from cameras."

It was a great idea, and one that he hadn't thought of. Christian marveled at Lilith for a moment. He didn't know how, but at that moment, he made a promise to help her out, to bring back her vibrant personality. Rather, he felt his desire to help bring her out of the shell that she had withdrawn into become stronger.

"Okay. We'll get this, too." Lilith's eyes became just a bit more vibrant. That was a good sign. Maybe he should get her talking some more. He held up the two jeans, one in each hand, and asked, "what about these? Which one do you think I should get?"

Blue eyes flickered back and forth between the two pairs of jeans. After another second, she pointed at the black pair. "The black jeans will go better with the sweater."

"Good choice." Christian looked at the black pair. "I like black better anyway."

It didn't take long to find clothes for Christian, and they soon found themselves standing in front of the cash register. From up close, it was clear that the woman who rang up their orders had some kind of eating disorder. Christian thought she was skinny from far away, but up close, her body looked like it was made of twigs. She wasn't *just* skinny. She was so unreasonably thin that there was excess skin hanging off her arms. The black dress that she wore looked tiny—it would have fit Lilith perfectly—but it was still about three or four sizes too large for her.

Dark brown eyes peered at him and Lilith from behind ridiculously large and obviously fake eyelashes. The thick lashes clashed horribly with her pale face, which seemed to be the result of someone using far too much powder. Christian couldn't see her skin, and he was sure that, should he take a finger and run it across her face like a drill sergeant inspecting a room, he'd come away with at least several centimeters worth of make up.

"Your total comes up to $353.76." The woman rang up their order, putting the folded clothes into two separate bags, one for Christian's and another for Lilith's. After pulling out his wallet and handing over the necessary funds, Christian accepted the two bags and the receipt. "Have a good day, you two."

"Yeah, you as well," Christian said.

He grabbed the bags in one hand, took Lilith's hand in the other, and walked out of the store.

Chapter 14

The night was late. The sun had gone down long ago. The stars and moon were out, creating a twinkling spread across the velvet sky. Not that anyone in Los Angeles could see the stars, least of all Tristin.

Sitting in front of his console, typing away at blazing speeds, Tristin was doing his best to hack into a network that was so secure that even he was left baffled. He had just managed to find himself in the Catholic Church's database. It wasn't the one that belonged to the Executioners, but rather, the one that belonged to the Church itself. The network was fairly new, but despite that, the security they had was top-notch. Whoever wrote the code for these security programs really knew what they were doing.

Tristin had already run a basic scan of the network's security. This had almost resulted in him getting caught when the system detected his presence and attacked him as though it was a virus, only one that aided the network instead of destroyed it. He'd managed to avoid having his own network fried, and he even managed to escape detection, but it was a near thing.

Even after he'd managed a basic scan, actually getting into the network was a laborious task that he was beginning to think might be impossible—he'd been running on caffeine pills and energy drinks for the past two days, and he hadn't been able to have sex! His energy reserves were running low. If he didn't get some soon, he might die.

My girls are going to have their work cut out for them.

The network's security was damn near impenetrable. There were multiple firewalls with constantly shifting algorithms that changed at what appeared to be random intervals or when the unsystematic security sweeps detected intrusion. Fifteen times he'd been forced to log out just because a security sweep had nearly caught him. The first time it happened, the sweep *had* caught him. It had been a sweat-inducing task trying to lose it, so that it couldn't follow him through the many backdoors and proxy servers he'd gone through to reach the network.

When he finally managed to breach one firewall and proceed further into the network, the thing would shut behind him! And it changed algorithms again! So not only did he have to proceed through each firewall with twice as much caution, but he had to constantly break the other firewalls he'd already breached just so he could leave in case another sweep detected him. It was maddening!

"Dammit!" Tristin swore as he was forced to divert at least half of his attention to the closing firewall, doing everything he could to keep it from shutting behind him and leaving him trapped. He'd already tried burrowing a small tunnel through it so he would have a way to escape, but that hadn't worked out too well. Case in point, he'd been forced to run when the firewall closed and one of the other security algorithms detected the hole. "If I ever found out who made this security system, I'm going to shake their hand, and then I'm gonna murder them! This is really beginning to piss me off!"

He had to give credit where credit was due, though. This security system was amazing. In all his years of working with the Executioners, he'd never seen a security system so complex and hard to crack—and he hacked the fucking Pentagon on a near daily basis!

More information began popping up on the screen. Another algorithm. It looked like a DES, the encryption algorithm that the US government defined and endorsed as the official standard. This one was a triple, or 3DES, which was more secure than the basic DES, but it was still nothing he couldn't destroy within seconds. That was exactly why he didn't break it down. It was too simple, too easy. There had to be a trick to it. Tristin narrowed his eyes. Perhaps it was a more complex encryption disguised as a basic algorithm. It could also be a trapdoor, something he would break down and go through, only to find himself caught on the other side with no way out. A false firewall? Perhaps. Damn, this was tricky.

"Alright." Tristin got ready to start typing some more. His eyes were narrowed in a fierce expression, and there was a rather prominent grin spread across his face. In spite of, or perhaps because of, the difficulties he was facing, Tristin was really enjoying himself. "Let's try—wait, what!? Oh, shit!"

Tristin's eyes widened as another sweep passed through. It was a localized sweep, aimed at a specific part in their network, rather than an area-wide sweep. And, naturally, the sweep was aimed right at him.

"Dammit! Shit! Fuck!"

Tristin's fingers sped across the keyboard like never before. This was bad! This was so bad it wasn't even funny, though Tristin was sure he'd have a laugh later, like, when he managed to escape from this. Damn those tricky motherfuckers. They'd set this trap in advance in case someone managed to make it this far. It was probably some kind of algorithm that could detect when negative space was being filled, which basically meant if he wanted to not trigger another sweep like that, he'd have to keep moving forward, regardless of whether he was walking into a trap.

He managed to clear the three firewalls he'd already hacked and log out before any of the virus traps could latch onto him. Tristin shut down his program, leaned back in his seat, and wiped the sweat from his forehead.

"Phew! That was way too close for comfort." He stared at his monitor, which had gone to the standard screensaver mode. Samantha would be so upset if she knew that he was using a picture of his harem as a screensaver. "Ugh, looks like I'm gonna have to try again. Samantha is not going to be happy with me."

He rubbed his eyes. By the Almighty Creator's left nutsack were they sore. He'd definitely been staring at that computer screen for way too long.

"I think I'm gonna take a shower." He glanced at the clock. 9:35pm. "And get some shuteye. My brain is fried, and I don't think any amount of caffeine is going to help me now."

Tristin thought about sneaking out of HQ to visit his girls, but he quickly discarded the idea. He'd been really good about not letting anyone know about his relationships. It would be a shame if someone were to discover them now.

The last thing he needed was for Samantha to have an inkling that Tristin wasn't quite who she thought he was.

***

The No Tell Motel was, to put it bluntly, the dirtiest, dingiest, piece of crap hotel a person was ever likely to come across. The walls, stained beyond belief with God-only-knew what, looked unstable and wobbly, like simply pushing on them would cause the entire wall to collapse in on itself. There were exactly four windows on the entire building, and each one was covered in thick, oozing grime that had hardened in between the cracks, sealing the windows shut and leaving them unable to be opened. The entrance, much like the walls and windows, was covered in a thick, black gunk. As Christian opened the door, the hinges squealed, a loud, grating, grinding sound that caused his teeth to rattle.

The inside wasn't much better than the outside. Christian's booted feet crunched into the carpet as he walked forward. At least, he thought it was carpet. Covering it were a number of stains that he hoped were made from coffee and soft drinks. It wasn't like he could really see the stains that well. They not only covered nearly the entire floor, but the lights from the overhead fan were dark and kept flickering on and off with the low buzzing of static electricity.

In the far back of the room sat a long desk that looked like it belonged in the kind of dingy bars that he expected to find in a detective film. There was a man standing behind the bar, his features indeterminate in the dark lighting. He was leaning against the table, casual and nonchalant, though his eyes, piercing and sickly green, seemed to glow as they stared at him and Lilith with a disconcerting sharpness.

Among the interior was a rundown, beat-up old couch. It was stuck against the back wall, next to the door. In front of it was an equally dingy table that didn't appear to have been cleaned off for several years, maybe even several decades. There were a couple of magazines on the table, all out of date by at least sixty years. To the left was a hallway that led further into the building, presumably where the rooms were.

Christian took in a deep breath, gathering up his courage. He wasn't afraid of much these days, and he certainly wasn't scared of this room—put off maybe, but not frightened by any means of the word. He was, however, very nervous.

He'd been to many places and seen many things. He'd fought beings that could destroy cities and battled against enemies that would make other people piss themselves in fear. Yet in all of the years he had been in service to the Executioners, he'd never gone to a place like this, a place that made the back of his neck stand on end, where he would not be the least bit surprised if someone tried to slit his and Lilith's throats in their sleep.

It was only ten seconds after they had stepped inside, and he already didn't like this place.

"Stay close to me," Christian whispered.

Lilith didn't need to be told twice. She was already as close to him as physically possible without being attached at the hip. As they walked up to the table, she hid behind him. The man, whose glowing eyes couldn't have been human, stared at the two of them with what could only have been considered undisguised interest.

Christian moved in front of Lilith when the man's eyes stayed on her longer than either of them were comfortable with, forcing those green irises to look at him. From up close, he was able to see that the man was quite deformed. He wasn't leaning over because he wanted to, but because he had a large hunch in his back. Much of his figure was covered by dark pants and a long-sleeve shirt, but Christian could see that he was possessing of dark skin that was cracked and dry, like old parchment that had been wrinkled into a ball and then laid flat. His face looked hollow, not necessarily gaunt, but more like there was simply nothing inside. Long, thin, bony fingers with sharp, claw-like nails tapped a staccato rhythm against the table.

"I'd like to rent out a room," Christian said.

The man looked him over, eyes traveling up, then down, giving him a once-over in a way that made Christian feel vulnerable, more so than he had ever felt before in his life. The man then looked into his eyes, and he felt his body grow stiff. The hair on the back of his neck prickled, his sense of danger blared within him, warning him that this man, this *thing* before him, was dangerous, incredibly so.

Then the man smiled, revealing putrid, yellow teeth that had mold or fungus growing on the gums.

"We've got a couple of empty rooms," a wheezing, crackly sound emerged from his mouth, "but I don't know if I should be renting 'em out to you… Executioner."

Like greased lightning, Christian dropped the bags in his right hand, reached beneath his jacket to grip the hilt of a gun, and whipped out Gabriel. The gun gleamed in the low lighting, its silver form appearing ominous as he pointed the business end at the man's face.

"That's former Executioner." Christian narrowed his eyes.

How did this man know that he had been an Executioner? That wasn't common knowledge. He might have been a member of the XIII, and while they were pretty well-known in certain circles, their identities had always been a carefully guarded secret. There was no way this man could have known about his former identity.

"He he he he," the man cackled, a coughing, raspy sound that was like sandpaper on Christian's ears. Lilith's too, it seemed, from the way she was trying to bury her face in his back. "You won't be wantin' to kill me, boy."

"And why is that?"

"Because even if you did kill me, it wouldn't do you any good. I'll just come back in a few years. Besides, this little motel would disappear along with it. You wouldn't be wantin' that now, would ya? If I ain't mistaken, you can't afford to go anywhere else."

"Tch! Poltergeist."

Poltergeists were the souls of people who'd committed a sin so atrocious that even after their bodies died, their souls remained anchored to the place of their sin, unable to move on. They were, in a sense, damned souls that were confined to a single location for the rest of eternity.

Most were only able to manifest as an invisible entity capable of making a minor disturbance, moving an object, locking the doors, turning on the TV, that type of thing. The exception to this rule were poltergeists with wills so strong that they had regained their physical form. They still couldn't leave the place they were bound to, but they could interact with everything inside of that area.

In some ways, they were one of the most dangerous beings alive. It was impossible to permanently kill them, and if someone entered their territory, they could easily kill that person. Everything within the place they were tied to was controlled by them.

Which meant if this thing decided to attack, he and Lilith were screwed. He wasn't an exorcist, which was a branch of the Catholic Church not related to the Executioners. Executioners only dealt with physical beings: cyclops, demons, gorgons, naga, succubi and incubi, undines, vampires, werewolves, anything that was composed of a physical body that could be harmed via weaponry. Spirits and spiritual entities like ghosts, poltergeists, and elementals were always dealt with by the exorcists.

"I suppose I could let you have a room here," once more, the poltergeist wheezed as he spoke. "If you can offer me something to make it worth my while."

The way the poltergeist's eyes seemed to almost peer through Christian made the young man realize what he was talking about.

A snarl crossed his lips. "How about you give us a room and I won't impale you with my swords! You may be a poltergeist, and I might not be able to get rid of you permanently, but I know that Orichalcum hurts spirits like yourself just as much as it does everything else."

He might die before he could manage it, though, which would leave Lilith at its tender mercies, but Christian was confident in his skills. If nothing else, he was sure that he could force it to disperse before it managed to kill him.

"Orichalcum, you say?" The poltergeist took a closer look at the gun in Christian's hand. "Ah, yes. I see now. I hadn't realized you were one of the XII as well." It seemed to ponder this, untroubled by the gun pointed at its head. "I guess I'll let you stay, provided you keep things interesting while you're in the city. I haven't had any good entertainment for a while, and you look like the kind of person that trouble follows worse than a bad curse."

Christian, his gun still pointed at the poltergeist, pondered what do. He didn't really want to stay in this dump of a motel. At the same time, he couldn't afford to stay at a place with security cameras. Most unfortunately for him, every other hotel he'd run across had hundreds of them. Almost all of the hotels in Las Vegas doubled as a casino. Due to the need for extra security, to make sure people weren't trying to rob them blind or cheat at their games, the security was extra tight. They didn't just have cameras, but guards and bouncers, too. Staying at a place like that was too high a risk.

It was also late. He was tired. Lilith was beyond exhausted. Neither of them had gotten any sleep since ten last night, and it was now nearing midnight. They didn't have the energy left to search.

"How much is it going to cost?" he asked at last.

The poltergeist tilted his head. "Hmm. How 'bout $25 a night?"

Christian thought about the price for a moment. "It seems reasonable." He turned to look at Lilith. She still seemed quite petrified of the poltergeist, but when he placed a hand on her cheek, she looked up at him and relaxed. "What do you think?"

Lilith blinked several times to let him know that she was thinking. He eyes flickered slightly, a bit of life returning before they dulled again. A moment later, she nodded. "Okay."

Christian gently caressed her face with his thumb. He then turned back to see the poltergeist grinning at him. "What?"

"Nothin'." The poltergeist laughed. "Just never expected to see an Executioner, former or not, being so kind to a succubus."

Christian rolled his eyes. "Yeah, well, things change."

"Seems so."

Upon paying for a single room, Christian was given a set of keys and told their room would be the first door on the right. After that, they left for the room. Neither of them wanted to be near that poltergeist any longer than necessary.

Much like the rest of the motel, the room was a cesspool of filth. The floors were stained and crunchy, making Christian think he was stepping on a thousand tiny bones instead of carpet. Red splatters tainted the walls. Blood, Christian realized. Blood from a long time ago, probably back when the poltergeist was alive. It might even be from his victim. The ceiling fan was broken, and the air was musty and smelled putrid, like something had died in there years ago and was just left to rot. It wouldn't have surprised him.

The bed was, surprisingly, not quite as dirty as he thought it would be, which wasn't saying much. The bed was still a mess. Broken frame. Broken springs. No legs on the bed post. At least the quilt was clean.

"I'm sorry we have to stay in a place like this," Christian apologized to Lilith.

She shook her head. "It's okay."

It wasn't okay. It really wasn't. He knew that. She knew that. He was sure she knew that he knew that. However, for the sake of not arguing, he didn't pursue that line of conversation.

"Hopefully, we'll only have to stay here for tonight," Christian added as he inspected the bed. It didn't look like any of the springs had broken the surface, which was good. He didn't feel like being stabbed by a bed. That would have been a humiliating end to his life. "Tomorrow, we'll try looking for another hotel. There has to be at least one that doesn't double as a casino." When Lilith didn't answer he looked up. "Lilith?"

Lilith blinked, her eyes tired and with bags underneath them. Christian understood. She hadn't slept for at least twenty hours, and she had experienced an incredibly traumatizing event that he knew she still hadn't come to terms with. She needed rest before they could do anything else.

"Come on." Christian climbed onto the bed and took off his boots. He didn't fancy stepping on the floor, even if his feet were covered by socks. "Let's get some rest."

Lilith climbed on to the bed and removed her sandals. She crawled over to Christian, snuggling into his side, her body curling slightly, legs tangling and hooking with his while her arms went around his waist. She placed her head on his shoulder, taking several long, deep breaths.

Christian watched Lilith as she jerked several times, as though she wanted to sleep but didn't at the same time. She blinked once, twice, and then her eyes drooped. Lilith soon closed her eyes, falling asleep in his arms. He waited for a second longer before closing his eyes as well.

He could only hope that the next day would be better than this one.

Chapter 15

He was there again. He stood over me as I lay on the ground. My body shook and my mind froze. I couldn't move, I couldn't breathe, I didn't dare even think for fear that he would hear my thoughts. Surrounded by a sea of gore and violence perpetuated by the very man standing before me, the only thing I knew was fear.

The man knelt in front of me, his gaunt, sunken face seeping with amusement at my plight. His eyes held a glint that spoke of lust and a desire to cause pain. And his grin, my God his grin! Insanity did not begin to cover it! Madness. Dementia. Lunacy. These words didn't even begin to describe the terror-inducing psychosis this man exuded from his every pore, causing my heart to quiver in my chest so fast I felt like it might explode.

I could feel myself losing control of my bodily functions. Urine ran down my legs, the acrid smell nothing compared to the poignant stench of raw meat or the coppery, metallic tang of blood. I barely even noticed it save for the stickiness that soon covered my thighs.

My eyes were focused only on those brown orbs that shone with a kind of hunger that I had never seen before. It wasn't the same look that men and boys used to give me as I walked down the street. This was different. It spoke of a different kind of hunger. In his eyes I could see his desire to break me, to destroy everything that I am and ever would be, until I was nothing but an empty shell of my former self, a broken doll whose sole purpose was to be used and tossed aside.

"I want to have fun, so, please." The man's grin couldn't have gotten any wider if he'd tried. It stretched across his face, malicious and filled with depraved intentions toward me. "Scream for me."

I began to cry as my clothes were slashed to ribbons. I screamed as his knife bit into my flesh. I prayed as blood welled up, tiny trails of crimson making paths across my body as dozens of lacerations marred my skin. I called out for Christian as the man's actions grew in violence, as my wounds became deeper, as my ichor flowed freely.

When he grabbed my legs and spread them apart, preparing to violate me in the most invasive and demeaning way possible, my body began to convulse. I started to feel sick. I couldn't stand the thought of this man, this thing, this monster, this incomprehensible nightmare made flesh, assaulting my body and defiling me in a way that not even Damien had done. This man was not my Christian. He wasn't the one I loved. The thought of him taking me, of even touching me, made me nauseous.

"Why are you crying?" The man laughed as he positioned himself near my entrance. I could feel him poking me, and my already violent convulsions grew in severity. "You should be happy! After all, a good hard fucking is all your species is good for!"

As I felt his head begin to push into me, tearing me apart and making me lose what was left of my dinner, I struggled more. I kicked. I screamed. I fought. I struggled. All the while, all I could hear was his laughter.

"Lil... ith..."

Why was this happening to me?

"Lilith..."

Where was Christian?

"Lilith...!"

Why wasn't he here to save me?

"Lilith!"

Why?

***

"LILITH!"

Lilith's eyes snapped open as a scream tore its way out of her throat. Something was grabbing her! Someone was grabbing her!

She bucked wildly, kicking out her legs and flailing her arms. Her fist hit something solid. There was a loud grunt, followed by an even louder thump. The feeling of hands on her wrists disappeared.

For that single, solitary moment, she thought she was free. It was only for a second, however, as the hands latched back onto her again. Lilith fought back with all her strength, but it was no use. Whoever had grabbed her was much stronger than she was.

"Lilith! Stop it!"

Oh, God! It must be *him!* He was still trying to violate her! To penetrate her body, to toy with her, to break her. Why? Why, why, why! Why couldn't he just leave her alone!? Why couldn't she break free!?

"Calm down!"

Everything was getting blurry. She couldn't breathe. Why couldn't she breathe? Why was… and where… she couldn't… couldn't…

"Lilith! Lilith, it's me! It's Christian!"

Christian.

The name penetrated her brain, striking a chord within her mind. It traveled through the rest of her body, suffusing her with warmth and feelings of security. She knew that name. It was a name that she had become intimately familiar with, a name that brought with it happy memories and feelings of love. Her body relaxed.

"Christian?" she asked.

Now that she was no longer panicking, her eyes were beginning to regain focus. The blurry, fuzzy images started to sharpen. What was once a blob of black, white, green, and red, soon became a crystal clear image. It was Christian's face.

"Christian…"

"Hey." Christian's gaze was soft and warm, containing all the worry he felt for her. He stared at her, a single hand going to her cheek as tears began leaking out of her eyes and running down her face. "Are you okay?"

Lilith continued to stare at him, not saying anything for all of one second. When the second expired, a great, heaving sob wracked her body before she sprang up and lunged forward, tackling Christian. She buried her face in his chest as her arms went around his torso. The young man, his red and green eyes staring down at her as she began to stain his shirt with tears, returned the hug. One hand went to her hair, running gentle fingers through it. The other rubbed up and down her back in slow, soothing motions.

"It's okay," he said. "Just let it all out. I'm right here."

She did not know how long she stayed like that, holding Christian like a lifeline, crying until her eyes turned red and puffy as she ran out of tears. Yet as she began to calm down, something else started to take its place.

Lilith took a deep breath, Christian's scent tickling her nose. He smelled of metal, mostly, probably from his swords and guns, but mixed in with the metallic scent was a smell unique to him. This scent, and the feel of his hard muscles as his arms engulfed her, was unlike anything else. All thoughts on her nightmare, the visions it brought to her mind didn't necessarily go away, but a bright, warm light seemed to pierce straight through it, carrying with it the potential to wipe all of the terrifying visions from her mind.

She knew what she needed to do. In order to rid herself of that experience, she needed the person she loved. She needed to replace the memory of that man with something better, something stronger.

She needed Christian.

Heat welled up within her. A strange tingle started from below her abdominal muscles. It then spread to the rest of her body, making her feel like she was sitting in a sauna. Along with that heat came a desire, a deep-seated need that was rooted so far into her psyche that Lilith hadn't even known of its existence until that very moment. It overwhelmed her, this craving, this hunger, this yearning. She needed someone to quench the fire burning in her, to help her get rid of the remnants of that nightmare, to make her feel wanted, loved, and safe.

There was only one person in the whole world who could do that.

What had started as her burying her face into Christian's chest to cry soon turned into her lips seeking out his naked flesh. They had gone to bed wearing their clothes—neither had wanted to sleep on the bed when it looked like someone might have died in it—so Lilith raised her head and found the exposed flesh of his collarbone. There, she began to kiss, lick, and suckle on his somewhat pale skin.

"L-Lilith?" Christian shuddered as her hands slid under his shirt and pressed against the hard, corded muscles of his abs. She felt his body twitch as her fingers moved across his skin, mapping out the sharp angles of his body. "Wha-what are you doing?"

"Christian…"

It wasn't a word. It was a moan. Christian's entire body went stock still, and his eyes widened to the point where they looked almost inhuman.

Lilith slid her body along his, pushing herself into him. She straddled his legs close to his hips. She could feel him grow underneath her. Something hard poked her. She shuddered as he grazed her crotch. The thought of being with him was making her wet. Her juices were already beginning to stain her panties.

She moved her hands from his abs to his shoulders, where she pushed him onto his back. Christian didn't resist. Lilith lay atop of him, pressing her body against his as her lips found his neck and worked him over.

It wasn't until she reached his nipples and pinched them that Christian finally gathered enough wits to react. He pushed her away, his hands on her arms as she sat on him, staring at her in shock. "Lilith, what's wrong with you? Why are you acting like this?"

"I don't know what you mean." A moan tore from Lilith's throat at the same time that Christian groaned. She rubbed herself against him again, the feeling of his shaft running along her cameltoe making her shudder. "I'm not acting any differently."

"Y-yes, you are." Christian's breathing was heavy, his eyes hooded. He desired her, she knew. Yet he was still resisting for some reason. "This isn't like you. You've never been this… this…" He shook his head as though trying to deny something, or perhaps trying to resist something. "There's something wrong. I know there is. After what happened the other day, on the train, you—"

"Don't. Please don't bring that up," Lilith pleaded with him, desperate. She didn't want to be reminded of that nightmare. That was the whole point of her actions. She needed to replace the memories with something else, something she could cherish. "Please." Lilith slid her hands back under his shirt, lifting it up to reveal inch after inch of powerfully built abdominals. "I need you. Please. Please don't turn me away. If you turn me away now, I… I'll…"

Christian looked like he was about to continue resisting. He appeared quite ready to tell her that he couldn't be with her when she was like this, but he didn't, or maybe he couldn't. His mouth, which had been opened, snapped closed as something wet splashed against his now naked chest. His eyes went wide as he stared at Lilith while she cried at the thought that he might not want her, that he might deny her.

"Why are you resisting me?" she asked as more salty, crystalline droplets ran down her cheeks. "Do you find me repulsive now?"

"No!" Christian shouted. "Of course I don't find you repulsive! You know that! I love you!"

"Then why won't you make love to me? Don't you want me?"

"Look," Christian began. He tried to look away, eyes flickering to the side, but they always came back to her. "I… it's not that I don't want you. It's just… I don't want you to feel like I'm just using you or something, especially after…" he trailed off, something that Lilith was grateful for. She didn't want anything having to do with *that* being brought up.

"You wouldn't be using me." She laid down, her head on his chest, arms rubbing against his torso. She could hear his heartbeat. It was fast, almost frantic. Was it because of her? "I want this. I need this." She lifted her head and looked into his eyes. "Please, make love to me. Let me know that you love me. Let me feel your love inside of me."

The look on Christian's face was one of conflict. His morals were conflicting with his desire to do what she asked of him. He was closing to breaking. She just needed to give him one more push.

"I want to forget about… that night." There was no need to elaborate. He knew what she was talking about. "I want to move on. Please." Her eyes were imploring and desperate. "Help me get over what happened."

There was only a second's pause before Christian gave his answer. His body slowly relaxed, and he nodded his head. "Okay. If it will help you, I'll do it."

Lilith smiled at him. "Thank you."

She leaned up and kissed him on the lips. He didn't resist. Christian kissed her back, matching her tenderness and care. His warm hands landed on her back. Perhaps it was because of how sensitive she was, but her entire body felt like it was burning as he touched her.

The kiss picked up in intensity when Lilith pinched his nipple, causing him to yelp. Her tongue slipped between his lips and teeth. She pushed against his tongue, ran over his teeth, his cheeks, the roof of his mouth. Christian did his best to keep up, but Lilith had the clear advantage over him.

The inside of his mouth soon filled with saliva, which they stirred around without care as their tongues danced around each other. Noises reverberated through the air, the steady sound of lips smacking and the sloppy, slurping noises from their exchange.

Breathing was eventually required. Lilith pried her face off of his, her lungs heaving for breath. Christian tried to do the same, but almost choked on all the excess spit, which went down the wrong passage.

Ignoring this, Lilith kissed her way down his body. Her lips touched his chin, his jaw, they grazed along his earlobe, which she also took between her teeth and gave a swift yank. Christian gasped. She then traveled down to his neck, suckling on several pulse points and leaving shiny red love bites. The same happened to his collar and chest before her tongue left a wet, glistening trail along his stomach.

She unbuttoned and unzipped his pants. Then she hooked her fingers around the hem of both pants and briefs, pulling them down his legs. Christian, unable to really think properly, helped her out by lifting his hips off the bed. Instinct. That was all Lilith was running on. She threw the two articles of clothing away, not caring where they landed.

Lilith found herself staring at the object in front of her, the very appendage that made Christian a male. Having never seen another man before, she couldn't really judge his size. She thought he was of a decent size, but it didn't really matter. As far as she was concerned, he was perfect.

She leaned down and breathed in his scent. She then moved down further and proceeded to lick him. Christian's hips bucked wildly, his hands gripping the quilt they'd slept over. Several deep gasps and low groans erupted from his mouth as she coated him in saliva. Lilith stuck out her tongue and, starting from the base, dragged her tongue all the way up to his head. She did this several times, then took him in her mouth.

"Oh, shit!"

It was the first curse word she'd ever heard from Christian while they were in bed, and one of only a handful she'd heard from him period. She knew it was because she was making him feel good. Perhaps it was the succubus in her, but knowing that made her feel quite proud of herself.

Resisting the urge to shake her head, Lilith took more of him in. She couldn't even get him halfway into her mouth before it was too much. Lilith gagged. Her head jerked back as she coughed and sputtered. This was her first time doing something like this.

"Li-Lilith?" Christian lifted his head to give her a concerned glance. "Are you okay?"

"I'm fine." Lilith coughed several more times. "I just wasn't prepared, that's all."

Christian didn't look convinced, but he didn't get a chance to say anything as she went back down on him. He merely threw his head back and let out a low groan.

This time, Lilith didn't try to take in nearly as much. She stopped just before it became uncomfortable. She bobbed her head up and down, using her tongue to lick him as she moved.

What parts of Christian that her mouth couldn't reach, her hands did. She wrapped her hands around him and slid them up and down, the thick coating of saliva acting as a lubricant to allow her hands to glide across his pulsating flesh more easily.

She could feel his hips spasming as he tried not to buck them. Christian was on the edge, his head thrown back, fingers scrabbling to find some kind of purchase on the bedsheets, and his body seizing up as the pleasure from her actions overwhelmed him.

There was no real warning when it came. The pulsing in her mouth increased for a second, then several shots of white, sticky fluid spurted out of Christian and into her mouth. Lilith was so unprepared that she nearly choked. She had to let go of him, gagging several times as she was forced to swallow his seed.

She frowned as the flavor hit her tongue. It tasted odd, not at all like what she had expected. Having heard stories from both Maria and Stacey, she had expected it to taste bitter and disgusting, and it was a little bitter, but it wasn't as bad as she had been anticipating. It was kind of salty. At the same time, there was hint of sweetness to it. Lilith quickly determined that it didn't taste terrible. In fact, she thought she could come to like it. Christian's taste.

Looking down at her clothes, Lilith saw that what she hadn't been able to swallow had gotten all over her pants and shirt. Frowning, she divested herself of her clothing, her shirt first, then she struggled with her pants before ridding herself of her bra and panties.

Lilith threw her clothing onto the floor and moved up Christian's body until she was rubbing against him again. He'd only deflated slightly, and when her hot center came into contact with him, he twitched and quickly rose to the occasion again. It must have been that Executioner stamina working for him.

She panned across his physique. He was covered in a layer of sweat, the slick coat making his body shine in the low light of the room. The defined pectorals of his chest moved up and down as he took in a number of deep breaths. She could see the definition in his arms, the U of his triceps flexing as he clenched and unclenched his hands. His eyes were glazed over, and he was gazing at nothing.

That look, that expression, it made her want him even more.

She placed her hands on his stomach, palms flat, fingers spread. His abs twitched, and emotions flickered across his eyes. Christian lifted his head to look her way, only to throw it back again, hitting the slightly stiff, old pillow, as she rubbed her drooling lips against him. The stifled noise that escaped his mouth sounded almost like a growl.

Pushing herself up, Lilith positioned her body over him until she could feel him knocking against her entrance. She wobbled, but Christian grabbed her hips to keep her steady. After taking in a deep breath, Lilith slowly lowered herself onto him with some aid from Christian. She felt him penetrate her, felt her walls widen to accommodate his size and girth, felt him as he rubbed against her in ways no one else had ever done or ever would. Then the connection was complete.

This was always the best part. This strange connection. There were many things about the act of sex that she liked. It felt good. When Christian kissed her, when he touched her, when he licked her or bit her, all of it felt incredible. It caused her body to become flush with pleasure, her mind became hazy with ecstasy, all thoughts fled except for the incredible sensations that permeated her body and excited her nerves.

All of that paled in comparison to The Connection.

She could feel the love he had for her. It wasn't a physical thing, but more of a metaphysical perception, an awareness that caused all other sensations to become enhanced. When they were connected in this way, neither one could hide their thoughts or feelings from the other. Knowing that he loved her, being able to feel it this way, it warmed her heart.

How many people could say they had ever felt this before? How many people could say with one-hundred percent certainty that their significant other loved them? There was almost always that niggling doubt in the back of their mind, wondering, questioning.

Lilith did not need to question because she knew. Every time they became one, she could feel it, the way his heart yearned for her, his desire to protect her, how he cherished her, and how he wanted to stay by her side forever. His hopes. His dreams. His fears. Everything that made Christian who he was flowed into her, just as she flowed into him. For those few, glorious minutes they were connected; they were one.

As she felt him and he felt her, she also felt her fears, the ones she had gained from that night on the train, beginning to disappear. They dissolved into nothingness as Christian's love for her overpowered the terror those unwanted memories caused.

They were still there. An unfortunate fact of life was that people could never forget their past, no matter how much they might have wanted to. But her memories didn't seem as bad as before, they didn't feel as horrifying, didn't inspire the terror they did when she thought about them. She imagined now that, should she close her eyes, she wouldn't see that man's gaunt face leering down at her with a wicked gleam in his eyes, but the handsome features of the young man underneath her.

She and Christian moved. Being on top, Lilith had to work harder than she normally did. She wasn't on top often because she preferred being on bottom… or doggy style. She liked that too. With her hands on his chest, she moved her hips up and down. Christian helped. He held her hips and lifted her up. He also timed his thrusts to match hers.

It was glorious, indescribable, this feeling. Lilith's body was on fire.

Lilith leaned over and kissed Christian, her tongue seeking entrance into his mouth. He granted it. Lilith moaned as she swirled her tongue around his. The volume of her voice rose when Christian's hands settled on her ass. He helped her move in this new position. Her insides were churning as he filled her. She wished this moment could last forever.

The ending came too soon. She didn't want it to, but there was no stopping it either. It started as a coiling deep within her stomach, like a knot that was about to come undone. More juices flowed out of her, the clear liquid running down her thighs and covering Christian. Her shoulders and chest heaved as she moved faster. Christian, too, picked up the intensity of his movements, timing his thrusts with hers in a way that they could only do because their minds and bodies had become synchronized.

Then it happened. Her body convulsed. Her thighs quivered. Her toes curled. She could feel her walls tightening around Christian's cock as her insides became increasingly wet. Christian came barely a second later, filling her with his warmth and love.

She fell forward, her body spent. Lilith landed on Christian's sweaty chest, breathing in with long, deep breaths as she slowly came down from her post-orgasmic high.

The two lay there in bed for several long, silent minutes. Only their breathing and the distant hum of the city outside could be heard. Lilith sighed, content, rubbing a single hand over Christian's body, heedless of the sweat layering him. She felt a pair of arms wrap around her and pull her closer to the warm figure beneath her. There was no resisting. She wouldn't have been able to even if she wanted to, and she didn't want to.

"Lilith…" Christian's soft, whispered voice washed over her. He sounded just as spent as she was, maybe even more so.

Lilith looked up, eyes glittering and a smile splayed across her lips. With her hands around his neck, she pulled herself toward Christian and kissed him, soft and loving, then leaned back and said, "I love you."

Christian paused. His was the look of someone who had been about to say something, but was now thinking better of it.

"I know," he said at last. "I love you, too."

Lilith's smile widened. He returned her smile with one of his own, right before a frown crossed his face. Christian gave her a serious look.

"Lilith?"

"Yes?"

"I think we should burn those clothes."

Lilith had no idea how to respond. What a random statement. Clothes? Burn them? Which clothes was he talking about? And why should they be burned?

Seeing her obvious confusion, Christian gestured to the floor, where she'd thrown both his and her clothing. She took one look at the articles, lying there on the disgusting, stain-coated floor. Her nose scrunched up as she realized what he was getting at.

She looked back at Christian. A single, affirmative nod was given. "Agreed."

Chapter 16

Something odd was going on. Ever since Catherine received a call claiming there was an emergency and that she had to come out to the Los Angeles police department ASAP, she knew that something was wrong. She could feel it in her gut.

Like all mornings in Los Angeles, the air was foggy. The sun had yet to dry up the condensation that hung in the air and created the thick, white clouds of precipitation that covered the freeways and kept her from seeing more than several feet in front of her, even with the fog lights turned on. She frowned, wiping some of the moisture that had coalesced on her forehead. The dark green business suit she had taken to wearing that day was clinging to her skin most uncomfortably, and despite having the air conditioner turned up to full, she still felt as if her body was seeping with a thin layer of sweat.

Catherine had never liked mornings in Los Angeles, or anywhere that had a large amount of fog. Aside from the disagreeable sticky feeling that came from all of the moisture that gathered from the bay at night, there was also the fact that the thick fog permeating the city conceived a very warm atmosphere, despite them being right next to the ocean. It made her sometimes wish that she had never moved to this state.

She really should have stayed in Michigan.

The building that housed the LAPD was a large, towering structure of steel, glass, and brick. While not as large as some of the skyscrapers surrounding it, the edifice was much more immense than most other police departments in other states. It was also a lot more pristine and well-maintained than some of the other departments that she had worked in.

She entered the building through the front. The room before her was a wide, spread out interior with very little in the way of amenities. There were a few chairs, a table, and a desk where a wide-eyed young man with freckles and red hair sat. A waiting room. Several people were already sitting in the chairs; a crying woman was being comforted by a husband, a young man was holding his head in his palms—nursing an obvious hangover—and another youth was wearing black clothes, lipstick, and far too much eye liner.

"Morning, Scott," Catherine greeted the young man behind the desk as she walked by.

Scott was a boy who dreamed of becoming a member of the LAPD. Unfortunately for him, it just wasn't happening. He lacked the gumption and the physical prowess to make the cut. His arms and legs were skinny, lacking any kind of muscle, and he had a gut, not a big one, but big enough on his thin frame that people took notice. He had no talent for firearms and was more than likely to shoot himself in the foot than an enemy. Not to mention he was clumsier than most people who'd been out on an all-night drinking binge.

Some people just weren't cut out for police work. He was one of them.

"Ah, hello, um, Ms. Catherine," the boy greeted, blushing as she passed.

Catherine snorted. Scott had been crushing on her hard since he began working at the police department. It never amounted to anything because even if she had been interested, which she wasn't—young boys who acted like schoolchildren with a crush didn't do it for her—he couldn't even speak to her without growing red in the face and stuttering.

No relationship could be built on embarrassment. It just didn't work that way.

The LAPD police department was a ten-story building with two basements. Each level held something different. The top floors were for the commissioner and his deputy. The ninth was where the SIU were stationed. Levels eight and seven possessed standard offices, cubicles for regular officers. The sixth was forensics. The fifth held all the files of every case the LAPD had ever been involved in. Levels four through two were meeting rooms for when people were working on a case. The first was the waiting room, and the two basements contained the shooting range and the exercise room respectively.

Catherine went to the top floor. Just as she expected, the commissioner was in his office, sitting down behind a large desk with dozens of sheets of paper and various files thrown haphazardly on top of it. Commissioner Fletcher had never been the most organized of individuals.

The heels of her shoes clicked as she walked along the gray carpet, until she was standing in front of the desk. Because they were so high up and the sun was now out, there was no fog, allowing sunlight to shine through the window. The natural lighting made visible the large shelf on the right, filled not with books, but with various awards and trophies. She could see two Best Shot of the Year awards from the years before she had joined the force.

"You called, sir," Catherine greeted her boss.

Commissioner Fletcher was a tank of a man. He wasn't very tall—she was taller—but his stout body was packed with the kind of muscles that people expected to see on a professional bodybuilder. The long-sleeved blue shirt filled out completely, stretching against his barrel of a chest and straining not to tear around his thick, vein-covered arms. Despite spending most of his time behind a desk these days, the commissioner kept himself in excellent shape.

"Catherine." Commissioner Fletcher looked up at her, hard, brown eyes glinting like diamonds underneath a head of graying hair. His clean-shaven, square face was set in a frown as he gestured toward one of the chairs in front of his desk. "Have a seat."

Catherine did as told.

"There's been a disturbing report coming out of Las Vegas that we've been asked to look into," Commander Fletcher continued.

Reading between the lines, she realized that he wasn't talking about the LAPD, but the SIU. Did that mean something outside of the police's ability to comprehend in a logical and forthright manner had happened? Of course it did.

Commissioner Fletcher lifted a file from the desk and handed it to her. "This file contains all the information that the Las Vegas police force has been able to acquire. However, the basics are this: a train stationed out of San Francisco left at exactly 6:45am two days ago. When it arrived at the station in Las Vegas the next morning at approximately 8:30am, all of the passengers were found dead, their bodies literally ripped apart."

Listening with half an ear, Catherine studied the files in the folder. She turned green when some of the pictures came to her. The kind of violence perpetuated in the photo was positively nauseating, even for a woman like her, who had seen numerous gruesome murders. Who could do such a thing? She did her best to ignore her queasy stomach, which was threatening to make her throw up that morning's breakfast, and instead tried to see if there was anything in the rest of the file that would help her.

There was. Just one small discrepancy within the photos. Most people would have missed it, what, with the gore and all, but Catherine was not just anyone.

"There's a whole body in this one." She pointed a single, manicured finger at one of the photos. "All the other bodies were in pieces, but this one is whole, except for the head."

"Yes. That's one of the confusing things about this case," the commissioner said. "The Las Vegas police department hasn't been able to make heads or tails of it, and they don't have their own Special Investigations Unit. That's why they've asked for aid."

"So you're sending me to Las Vegas?" she asked.

"You and three others," Commissioner Fletcher confirmed. "We can't afford to send anymore than that, since Sin City is technically outside our jurisdiction. Make sure to pick the people you think are best for the job. You're set to leave some time today. We want you on this case before the trail grows any colder."

So she wasn't getting much time to actually get ready? That was just great. And this looked like it was going to be a tough case, too. Catherine wasn't even sure where to start. Had the train been cleaned out? Had the Las Vegas police department gathered all the evidence? Did they even know what to look for? If they screwed up before she even got there, the chances of her discovering anything were slim to none. She was good at what she did, but she was no miracle worker.

Not letting any of the doubts that plagued her show on her face, Catherine stood up and saluted the commissioner. "Understood. If that's all, sir, I would like to begin getting my team together. We'll need to gather some equipment before we leave as well. I doubt the Las Vegas police department has an energy emission scanning device that can pick up the energy signatures of supernatural creatures on them."

"Probably not," the commissioner agreed, saluting back. "Very well, Sergeant Catherine Siegal, you are dismissed."

"Sir!"

***

Christian was worried. He didn't want to say anything for fear that verbally expressing his fears would cause them to become reality, but he really was concerned.

After this morning, in which he'd woken Lilith up from a nightmare and subsequently had sex with her, the young woman in question had been acting rather cheerful. She was a little too cheerful, if you asked him, especially when he took how she had been acting previously into consideration. Now she was acting the exact opposite of how she had been after the train battle. It was almost like someone had flipped a switch inside of her.

He stared at Lilith as she walked alongside him, her blonde hair swaying with each step, her blue eyes alight and alive in a way he had been afraid he'd never see again. There was a smile on her face, brilliant and enchanting enough to lure any man to their doom. She was humming a soft tune to herself, one that he didn't recognize, though he could not deny that it was a beautiful melody that soothed the soul. All the while, both of her arms were wrapped around his right arm, holding it close.

"Lilith…" Christian hesitated, but only for a moment. "Are you sure you're okay?"

"Of course!" Lilith turned her head to him and smiled that dazzling smile of hers. "Why do you ask?"

"Well…" Should he mention the train? Part of him thought that doing so might not be the wisest idea. What if it caused her to revert back to that quiet, emotionless, doll-like persona? He didn't want that. So, yes, mentioning the train battle was definitely out of the question. "No reason, I guess. I was just worried because yesterday you were acting, well, you weren't yourself."

They stopped. Lilith moved to stand in front of him, keeping him from moving forward. She peered into his eyes, a sad smile touching her lips. Lilith reached out and grabbed one of his hands, bringing it to her chest.

"I'm sorry I worried you. It wasn't my intention. I just—" she took a breath, then shuddered "—what happened back then with Nicholas, I don't think I was prepared to deal with that kind of… violence." She paused, her head tilting slightly to the side. "Damien, for all his faults, never actually harmed me in any way, and never acted with that kind of savagery, at least not in front of me. He was always very careful about what he let his 'Queen' witness." She frowned, her eyebrows furrowed just a little. "When… when Nicholas… assaulted me, it was different. He physically attacked me in a way that's never happened before, but he also brought up bad memories. You know he's not the first person to attack me, right?"

Christian gave her an affirmative nod. "I know. I remember you telling me about how some of the boys in your high school and college tried to attack you. You also told me about how your middle school teacher tried to rape you."

"They did, and some of them even came close to succeeding, though not as close as Nicholas had gotten. Still…" A shiver ran down her spine. "What happened on that train brought back all of those horrible memories, and then magnified them, made them seem even worse than they already were. I don't think… I just wasn't prepared to deal with all that. And then there was the blood, and the body parts, and…"

"I understand." Christian forestalled any further attempts at an explanation, raising a free hand in the air. When, after several seconds passed, he was sure that he had Lilith's attention, he asked, "You're really feeling alright, then?"

"Yes." Lilith grabbed the hand he'd raised and brought it back down. She took a step forward, her head tilting up to stare into his eyes. "Thanks to you. It's… hard to explain, but when you and I—what I mean is, when we were together, it just made everything better. Like, like…" she scrunched up her face. "It was like being with you caused all of the bad memories and negative emotions to just not seem as bad, I guess. Like I said, it's hard to explain."

Christian had to agree with her. Whatever she was trying to tell him must have been exceedingly difficult to put into words. He couldn't even begin to understand what she was talking about, though he did wonder: did it have something to do with the connection they had with each other during intercourse? Maybe. Possibly. It was hard to say for sure. He wasn't an expert on love or sex, and he was even less of an expert on what they experienced when together.

Clearly, Lilith was much the same.

"Well, so long as you're alright, I guess," he sighed. Nothing mattered to him except for her happiness, so if she really was okay, then he wouldn't speak of this anymore.

Giving him a smile that seeped with gratitude, Lilith leaned up on her toes and pressed her lips to his. Christian returned the kiss. When she stepped back, the smile was still there. She reached out with her hand. Fingers delicately ran through his hair before a strand was taken by two fingers and absently twirled about.

"I think I like you better with black hair," Lilith decided.

In response to her words, Christian stared at his reflection in the nearest glass window. His once raven hair was now a muddy brown, and his eyes were colored much the same. He was wearing a set of clothes they had bought yesterday, black jeans, a white shirt, and the dark orange hoodie. They fit him well. Hopefully, it would be enough that no one would recognize him.

Lilith had also changed quite a bit. Her hair was now dyed a light auburn color, with an almost orange tint to it, and it was tied into a ponytail at the back. Dark green eyes peered out from beneath a set of slightly longer than average bangs. Her outfit consisted of a bleached yellow sundress, strap on sandals, and a black jacket. The jacket was unzipped.

Something compelled Christian to return Lilith's gesture. He raised his left hand, brushing a few bangs from her eyes. A small grin appeared on his face. "I have to admit, I also like you much better with blonde hair and blue eyes. You just don't look the same."

She grinned. "It's too bad we had to dye our hair like this."

"Mmm. Yeah. But, you know why we had to do this, right?"

"I know."

They both turned their heads to look into the window of a small store that sold electronics. There were a number of televisions on display in front of the window. All of them were on, and all of them were turned to the news.

"And in other breaking news, an entire train of people traveling from San Francisco, California to Las Vegas, Nevada were massacred around two days ago. All of the train stations are currently in lockdown and no one is being allowed to leave the city. While there are no reports of the police having any leads, several civilians in the area saw two people who were leaving the train station around the same time that the train pulled in."

Two images suddenly appeared on the screen. They were drawings, and decently accurate ones, too, of Christian and Lilith.

"The two images were drawn by police sketch artist, Henry McDoile. The male is said to be a man of about 5'10" in height, with black hair and two different colored eyes. The woman has blond hair, blue eyes, and is supposedly around 5'6". The man is also said to be carrying a large guitar case. If any of you see either of these people, please be sure to call the police as soon as possible."

Early yesterday morning, they had both learned from the poltergeist that the police were looking for them. Apparently, the late night news had made the same report. It even gave the same detailed description of him and Lilith.

Knowing that people were going to be looking for two individuals matching their descriptions, they had quickly gone to a convenience store and bought some hair dye from a young man who didn't seem to have watched the news. The contacts, fortunately, had been some of the few they hadn't used up from when they were in California.

"We'll need to be a bit more careful from now on. With the police on our tails, it can only mean more trouble," Christian said.

Lilith nodded. "Yeah."

They continued on their way. Few people paid them any attention as they walked by. It was a relief to know that their disguises worked. They really weren't much, but most people only looked at the eyes and hair anyway. So long as no one took a closer look at them, they should be fine.

If only disguising ourselves was as simple as putting on a pair of glasses, things would be so much easier.

Their mission that day was simple. They were looking for another hotel—one that didn't have a casino attached to it or, at the very least, lacked any real type of security through which the police could track them. Thus far they had been unsuccessful. What hotels were available appeared to mostly consist of large, ritzy casinos with thousands of people filing in and out at all times. The only thing that appeared to be in more abundance than the very kind of hotel they *weren't* looking for were churches for people who wanted to elope—and porn shops. Those were popular, too.

It seemed to Christian that the Las Vegas Strip had been given that name for a very good reason.

"Hey, Christian. Do you know why Las Vegas has so many porn shops?"

"Not really, but Las Vegas has been known as Sin City for a long time now, due to their red-light district. There's always been a lot of prostitution going on in the area, and adult entertainment is pretty big here because most of the tourists are adults looking for a good time." He paused. "I think it might have something to do with how sex is becoming more and more acceptable in American culture… maybe. Samantha once complained about how all of her favorite TV shows were being taken over by reality shows that starred sexed-out floozies whose only reason for being popular was because they slutted themselves up for the camera."

Having never watched television, except during rare circumstances when he needed to see the recent news for a mission, Christian knew very little about the United States' recent glamorizing of sex and sexual relations. Heck, if it wasn't for Tristin's complaints about people not knowing that plug A wasn't supposed to enter slot C, he wouldn't have even been aware of the gay rights movement.

There was a reason that he preferred reading to watching television.

He missed his KLReader.

After walking through the city some more, the pair eventually, finally, found a hotel that didn't look like a five-star resort for adults. Built within a part of the strip that had a number of casinos but didn't appear to be a casino itself was a tall building painted white. Judging by the number of windows, it stood at seven stories in height. A large, tacky, neon sign sat on top of it, the name *Fermont Hotel* shown across it in glowing yellow lights.

"What do you think?" asked Lilith as she, too, looked up at the large sign situated on the roof in mild distaste. "That thing, it really clashes with the white of the building, doesn't it? What were those people thinking when they put that up? It's atrocious! It's neither complementary nor contrasting. It's just gaudy and hideous. Whoever put up that sign should be sued."

That was probably the graphic designer speaking. Even though she wasn't going to college anymore—being on the run made that kind of difficult—she still had a sense of aesthetics. How to properly utilize color and negative space to create a visually pleasing presentation was in her blood.

"I guess." Christian shrugged. He wasn't a graphic designer, so the sign just looked tacky to him. "It looks pretty gaudy if nothing else. Still, this might be the only place that won't have security cameras at every junction."

"Then it looks like we've got no choice." Lilith began dragging him behind her as she walked toward the hotel. "Come on, let's go inside and at least take a look around."

As they entered the hotel, Christian found himself smiling in spite of the ever present danger. Sure, things might look bad right now, but if nothing else, at least Lilith was no longer suffering from what happened on the train.

Now he just needed to wait for everyone else to forget about what happened on the train. Then everything would be kosher.

Fat chance of that happening.

Chapter 17

The airport. It was normally a place filled with crowds of people, boarding or disembarking from airplanes. Now it was a deserted series of buildings that were connected via several walkways. The many stands, shops, and restaurants were devoid of life. The security checkpoint, which often had a line nearly a mile long, had no one standing in it. The entire place had literally become a ghost town.

There were only a few people hanging around the airport. Their blue, long-sleeved shirts and slacks of the same color, with small golden badges pinned to their chests and more badges stitched to their shoulders, identified them as members of the Las Vegas police department.

Much like the railways and train stations, all of the airports in Las Vegas had been locked down. While there had been a number of complaints, including a few from high ranking and politically important individuals, the police weren't taking any chances with a possible psychotic killer on the loose. Better to have a bunch of people angry and dissatisfied than dead.

Coming in for a landing at the airport was a plane, a standard airliner with a bulbous nose and a long body that tapered off at the end to make its shape aerodynamically smooth. The landing gears extended as the plane began its descent. It bounced once, twice, thrice, as it hit the ground, and then it ran along the black pavement, a sort of shrieking sound emitting from the rubber wheels as they were worn down against the landing stretch.

Slowing down substantially within as little as thirty seconds, the plane made its way into the airport. It stopped in front of a boarding hall. A ramp extended from the hallway and connected to the plane's exit hatch.

Sitting on the plane with three other people—not including the pilot and co-pilot—was Catherine. She stared out of the window near her seat, observing the terminal and stretches of land that led to the city beyond. From where she sat, she could see the distant rise of tall buildings on the horizon. Sin City. What a dreadful place.

"Now this brings back memories," a deep, booming voice said in her ear. "It's been a long time since I've been back to Las Vegas. Doesn't look like it's changed much."

Turning her head, Catherine found herself staring at a man who appeared to be in his mid-forties—appeared because she knew he was far older than that. His hair was wild and untamable. The dark brown cascaded down his head in unruly locks like a lion's mane. Incandescent yellowish eyes held a ferocious quality to them. Those eyes were sharp, focused, and dangerous. Every so often they would flicker, the small pupils sharpening into feline-like slits as he focused on the distant horizon. His five o'clock shadow hid a strong, square jaw.

Wolverine had nothing on this guy.

"That's right. You used to live here, didn't you, Andy?" she asked.

Andrew James Fortis was a beast of a man, both in a figurative and literal sense. He was tall, towering over everyone who knew him and packing hard muscles that made him look like a pro-wrestler. Unlike most cops, he preferred wearing all black clothing similar to SWAT members, though he didn't wear the bulletproof vests. *It cramps my style.* His words. Not theirs.

"Heh, that's right." Andy grinned, revealing incredibly sharp teeth that looked like they could easily rend flesh from bone. He crossed his arms over his chest, his shirt straining as his muscles bulged. "I used to work for the Las Vegas police, I think it was, fifteen? No, sixteen years ago. Man, that brings back memories, not all of them good."

"Sounds like we're gonna be hearing another one of your old man war stories again," the comment came from a somewhat nasally voice. Nerdy was what Catherine would have called it. The voice sounded like a stereotypical nerd who spent his every waking hour in front of a computer.

Both turned to see a lanky young man with brown eyes hidden behind square spectacles. He was wearing the standard police uniform; blue shirt, blue pants, a black belt with a gun holster attached to it. The clothes didn't fit him despite being small, and much of the fabric hung from his body with a good deal left in excess.

"Tch, you'd better be careful, kid. This old man can kick your ass six ways to Sunday," Andy said.

Kyler Benson didn't have any real outstanding features that would have made him a good cop. In a purely physical sense, he lacked everything that the LAPD looked for in a police officer. However, what he lacked in physical prowess, he more than made up for with his cognitive abilities and extraordinary intellect. Not only was he a computer whiz capable of hacking into most secured databases, he also had an IQ of over 200.

"Ugh, you men and your pissing contests," a female voice complained.

The last member of their group was a woman that reminded Catherine of Olympic Gymnasts. Wearing police clothes that did nothing to flatter her lithe figure or muscular legs, the young woman with her dark brown, almost black, hair done up in a severe bun was a study in austerity. She was attractive, to be sure, but due to the clothes she wore, most people would never have noticed her.

Because of her harsh brown eyes, which were sharp and held within them a vicious quality, and her caustic attitude, men were always turned off by her. The fact that she could lay a beatdown on just about any male courageous enough to touch her certainly didn't help.

Kreya Fraja stared at the two men with eyes like claymores. "Why don't you two wait until after we get off the plane and I'm well away from you before you start playing 'my cock is bigger than yours', hm?"

"Oh, man. You're harsh as always, Kreya," Benson said.

Kreya merely crossed her arms under her bust and glared.

"Alright, you three. That's enough arguing for now." Catherine stood up and opened the compartment overhead. There were a number of cases and bags inside. She began grabbing them and taking them down. "We've got work to do, and I want to get started as soon as possible."

"Haha!" Andy's barking laugh rang out as he, too, began helping take down the bags. "You've always been the consummate professional, Catherine." Being the strongest of the group, he grabbed all of the larger cases, the ones that weighed over fifty pounds each. "I would love to see you loosen up for a change."

"I do loosen up. When I'm not on the job."

"Psh! That's not what I'm talking about and you know it. You're too serious all the time whenever you're at work. That can't be good for your health. You should try smiling more often."

As Catherine rolled her eyes, Benson, who was pulling down a small, sleek silver case, couldn't help but comment. "This coming from the guy who's always smiling like he's the lowest common denominator. At least Catherine's got her priorities straight. If it weren't for your freakish strength and unique… genetic traits, you wouldn't have even made it on to the police force."

Andy clicked his tongue. "And if it weren't for that freaky dinky brain of yours, you would have never even been considered for the police."

"Would you two shut up!" Kreya snapped. "God, I've been listening to you playing 'who's got the bigger dick' ever since this plane ride started. Turn off the fucking testosterone already."

"Hmph! Someone's in a bad mood," Andy mumbled under his breath.

"You say something, Fortis?!"

"Not a thing."

After they had all gotten their bags, the group of four made their way out of the airplane and into the terminal. There, they were met with several members of the Las Vegas Police force. One of those people stood at the helm, and he was the one who greeted them.

"Miss Siegal, I'm Sergeant Grays Gordon." The officer, a young man with a head of light brown hair and green eyes, held his hand out. "Thank you very much for coming. I'm glad you're here. My men and I are at our wits' end."

He was an average-looking man, rather plain, with no outstanding features that would have made him stand out of a crowd. Even his eyes, which shone with intelligence, appeared somewhat lackluster.

Catherine shook his hand. "I take it you're in charge of this case, then?"

"Yes," he said.

"What can you tell me about it?"

"Not much, other than that it's unlike anything any of us have ever seen." The group began walking, Catherine taking the lead with Gordon walking alongside her. "The scene is, well, you'd have to see it for yourself to really know how bad it is. The pictures we sent to the LAPD don't do it justice."

"It's worse than what we've seen in the pictures?" Catherine raised a surprised eyebrow.

"Much worse," he said in a grave voice.

The air outside the airport was crisp and cool. Despite the horrible situation that Las Vegas was facing, the day was sunny and cheerful. Several cop cars sat outside, parked in front of the entrance/exit. A number of officers stood guard around the cars and near the entrances. They didn't seem too concerned. Most looked relaxed and were talking amongst each other, seemingly apathetic to the possibility of whoever massacred the train coming to an airport and doing the same thing.

Catherine and her team were directed into one of the larger cop cars. It was a transit police vehicle, basically a large van with an open-spaced trunk that could easily fit a good deal of high-tech equipment inside. It was a boxy vehicle, with a short hood and a heavy cargo/passenger hauling capacity. Just as she had suspected, the inside was filled with computer monitors and radios that were set into a rack built into the van on its left side. A lone bench spanning the back's entire length was on the right.

They were all bade to sit down. Catherine sat in the middle of her group, with Kreya on her right and Andy on her left. Benson sat next to Andy, but he was paying more attention to the equipment than his boisterous partner.

"That's some pretty out-of-date equipment you guys have," he commented with a critical frown.

Benson was the kind of guy who enjoyed using cutting-edge technology. His reasoning was that old, junky pieces of crap couldn't handle the rigorous paces he put their processors through. Catherine didn't know much about computers—she had a basic Apple laptop and that was it—but she trusted his intuition.

"We don't have a whole lot of funds to spend on high-tech equipment." Officer Gordon didn't seem too upset about the insulting comment, though he did look a tad miffed. Unlike her group, who were sitting down on the bench, he was sitting in a bolted-down swivel chair next to the rack of computers, monitors, radios, and various gadgets that Catherine had no clue about what they did. "Las Vegas may be a prosperous city as far as making money goes, but most of that money is lining the pockets of businessmen and senators, not the police."

Which Catherine took to mean corruption in the city was rampant. No surprise there. Sin City wasn't known for the value it placed on the law. There was a reason it had earned that nickname, and it wasn't just because of the red-light district like most people assumed.

And, of course, politics and corrupt businessmen weren't the only reason for that name either.

On their way to the police station, Catherine tried to pick Officer Gordon's brain about the train massacre. It was important to know everything that the Las Vegas police knew going in. That way she would at least have a starting point for their investigation.

Most unfortunately, there wasn't a whole lot that could be told, other than what she already knew from the reports. Someone had boarded the train, massacred everyone on board to the point where all but one person had been literally turned into pulp splattered against the interior, and then left sometime before the train stopped in the train station.

"What about the two suspects?" Catherine asked, leaning forward, her elbows against her knees as she pinned Officer Gordon with an intense look. "Have you found them?"

She was *very* interested in knowing whether those two had been found or not. She hoped they were, because she wanted to have a rather long conversation with them.

"Unfortunately not." Officer Gordon shook his head. "They've disappeared somewhere in the city. I've had men patrolling the streets and asked people to call in should they see them. So far, though, nothing."

"I see."

Catherine didn't let it show, but she was disappointed. While she didn't believe that Christian and Lilith were responsible for what happened on that train, she knew that, regardless of their innocence, they had likely been stuck in the middle of whatever happened during the train ride. Finding them could solve this entire case.

With the airport behind them, the large van soon pulled onto the I-15.

Las Vegas was something of a paradoxical city, possessing a distinct dichotomy not found in most large cities. Unlike Los Angeles, Las Vegas did not have many large, towering skyscrapers. It had a few, to be sure, as all cities of its size did. But, by and large, the vast majority of the buildings within the city limits consisted of casinos and hotels, and hotels with casinos in them. While those buildings were pretty large, with some even reaching ten or fifteen stories in height, they didn't really compare to the thirty to fifty—and in some cases, seventy to one-hundred—story tall skyscrapers in cities like Los Angeles or New York.

The building holding the Las Vegas police department was a study in contrast when compared to the LAPD. Small and squat, made from red brick and possessing a number of cracks and peeling paint, the tiny structure didn't strike much in the way of admiration or reverence. As Catherine and her group exited the van and made their way to the entrance, Andy looked at the slightly run-down building with nostalgia.

"This really brings back memories."

"And here we go again." Benson rolled his eyes. "No one wants to hear your tales about the olden days, old man. Give it up."

Not even bothering to look at Benson, Andy said, "Hmph! Who said I was going to be telling you any stories? Disrespectful brats like you don't deserve being told about all the incredible things I've seen while on the field. Besides, you don't work on the field anyway, being such a damn twig."

"There are more important things than field work." Benson shrugged. "Without me providing you guys with intel, half of the things we've accomplished would have been impossible."

Ego aside, the man had a point. It had, in fact, been Benson who'd discovered the No Life King's location after researching possible abandoned houses within Seal Beach's general borders. Without him, they would have never learned where Damien had been staying.

"Whatever. If it wasn't for me, half of the people on our last mission would have been killed," Andy grumbled.

Another simple truth. It had been Andy's monstrous strength and unique abilities that allowed her men to survive the ghoul assault. It had also been thanks to him that Alpha squad had only lost half of their numbers when the No Life King showed up, though he had not escaped from that battle without injury.

"Why don't you idiots just give it a rest?" Kreya snapped. "In case both of you have forgotten, the only reason you two are even alive right now is thanks to Mr. Crux. Without his aid during the Seal Beach incident, none of us would even be here, so quit trying to stoke your own ego. There's no point to it when neither of you even compare to some of the people who are fighting out there."

Catherine withheld a snort. While she didn't think Kreya had a crush on Christian—not like it would matter if she did—the amount of respect she held for the Executioner—former Executioner, she corrected herself—was second to none.

Kreya had been one of the officers who had watched the clash between Christian and Damien. She had lain witness to the skills the young man possessed. While none of them really knew much about No Life King's—even Andy's information was limited—she knew enough to understand that what he had accomplished should have been impossible. Humans were not supposed to be capable of going toe-to-toe with monsters like that. They just weren't. That he had fought against a creature of immensely superior power head on and won, albeit, with the aid of Lilith near the end, was astonishing.

"Gurk!" Andy held a hand to his chest, acting wounded. "Must you always bring that up? You're always comparing me to that guy. Can't you let sleeping dogs lie for once?"

"No," Kreya answered. "Because if I did, then your overinflated ego would grow even larger."

While Andy pretended to act wounded, Benson scoffed. "Well, I know I wouldn't have died. I wasn't even a part of the assault." Before he could say anything more, a glare from Kreya had his mouth snapping closed. "Shutting up now."

As Catherine let loose with a gusty sigh, tiredly pressing her hand against her forehead, Officer Gordon appeared to be trying to follow their conversation with little success. He did get one thing out of it, however, and he didn't hesitate to turn to Andy. "So, did you work for the Las Vegas police department at one point?"

Andy grinned and nodded. "I did. It was a while ago, however. I doubt anyone I know is still on the force."

"Do you know Commissioner Strailser?"

"Strailser? Hmm… Strailser, Strailser." Andy cupped one massive hand to his chin and rubbed it. A second later his eyes lit up. "I do remember a Strailser! Tiny girl, blonde hair, toughest damn woman I've ever met." He then glanced at Catherine and grinned. "Next to you, of course."

"Of course," Catherine agreed with a roll of her eyes.

"Does she still work with the department?" Andy asked.

Officer Gordon shook his head. "No. She retired last year, though she occasionally comes in to make sure we aren't slacking off."

Andy slapped his knee. "Haha! That sounds like her! I'll have to give her a call and see if she remembers me."

The building's interior was surprisingly clean. The white tiles were fairly new and polished to a shine. Several chairs for people in waiting were set up along the wall, in front of a table with a number of newspapers and magazines. They even had a flatscreen television hanging in one corner of the room. It was playing a sports channel, specifically basketball. The room was mostly empty now, save for someone sitting behind the counter, looking bored. It made a sharp contrast to the outside, which looked old and worn.

"Come on." Officer Gordon gestured for them to follow him. "I'll show you guys to the office that you'll be using while you're here."

Officer Gordon led them through one of several doors. Their feet tapped light, off-beat rhythms on the tiles as they walked. The hallway they were led to was a little cramped, at least for Andy. The oldest among them was forced to stoop down as they walked, and his bulky frame took up much of the hallway.

Entering a wide, long room with a low ceiling, the group strolled through a series of desks and tables. A number of officers were working at these stations, some greeting Officer Gordon as he led them to their designated room, others looking at the newcomers in curiosity. A few didn't pay any attention to them. These people were busy giving their work, be it on a computer screen or a bunch of files sitting on their desk, a hard stare as they tried to complete what they could. Quite a few of these officers looked like they'd been up for days.

The office they were led to was small and longer than it was wide. A rectangular table sat in the center, surrounded by basic, straight-backed chairs. Situated on the table was a very basic, old, and battered projector. A whiteboard sat near the "front" of the room, and hanging from the ceiling above it was a pull-down screen.

"This is where you guys will be able to set up shop, so to speak," Officer Gordon announced. Standing at the front of the office, he turned to face them. "If you have need of anything, be sure to inform either myself or Commissioner Cliara, and we'll see if we can provide it for you. I'll tell you right now, though, our funds are limited. While we've been given a budget increase in order to catch this killer, it's still not much, especially compared to what you're probably used to."

What Officer Gordon was basically telling them was that, due to the city's reputation and the widespread fear and panic caused by a possibly insane killer hiding amongst them, the senate had decided to temporarily raise their budget in order to make up for the various deficiencies that were normally found within the police. They were, in essence, trying to cover up their police department's lack of manpower and equipment by handing them more money than they usually did. It was corrupted politics at its finest.

Catherine hated politics.

"Thank you," Catherine said. "We'll be sure to let you know if we need anything, and also inform you of any findings we make. If possible, would you be able to take us to the train the killings took place in after we get Benson set up here?"

Officer Gordon agreed. "Of course. Just come find me when you're done. I'll be in my office. It's on the other side of the main room. My name is on the door, so you can't miss it."

After Officer Gordon walked out of the door, Catherine closed it behind the man and turned to look at Benson. "You know what to do."

"Right." Benson nodded.

Setting his sleek case on the table, Benson placed his thumbs on the small indents on either side. Said indents also served as thumbprint scanners. There was a light beeping, then a click, before a soft hissing emerged from the case. Lifting the lid revealed several objects. The first was, quite obviously, a laptop. With it came several cords and a USB drive, all set into small indents within the foam padding.

Next to the mobile computer was an L-shaped device with a trigger. It was not a gun. Benson didn't use guns. It was a scanner and scrambling device. Set on the back of the item's "barrel" was a small screen. After picking the device up and turning it on, the screen flickered as it was booted up, and then displayed an option menu. Once he had finished tapping on several options, Benson got to work.

As their computer tech moved around the room, scanner in hand, Catherine turned to Andy, who had taken a seat and was leaning the chair on its last two legs. He looked like a kid. An extremely large, muscular kid who'd been taking steroids for years, but still a child… with a beard.

"Do you think you can track down the suspects?" she asked.

"Maybe…" Andy looked up at the ceiling, his nose wrinkling. "But not unless I manage to pick up their scent. With so many people around, that's going to be difficult. This place isn't like Seal Beach. It's crowded and large. I doubt I'll be able to find them that way."

Well, damn. Catherine had been hoping to rely on Andy's incredible sense of smell to pick them up, but it looked like that wasn't in the cards right now. That meant she'd have to find another way of tracking them down.

"I've got some contacts in the city, though," Andy added upon seeing her disheartened expression. "If they're looking to lay low, they'll have probably traveled to one of the places, where some of my contacts might have seen them."

"We're clear," Benson told them, interrupting anything Catherine might have said. "There are no listening devices in this room."

"Sergeant, do you really think Mr. Crux and Lilith had anything to do with what happened on the train?" asked Kreya once she knew that no one was listening in on them. "I don't know either of them very well, but from what you've told me, Christian at least, isn't the type to do this. And we all know that Lilith isn't capable of it."

"I don't think either of them are responsible," Catherine said. "But I know they were on that train, which means they know what happened. I want to find them, get their statements, and then see where we can go from there."

"I'll visit one of my contacts later today and see if he knows anything," Andy said. "He's confined to a single area, but he always seems to know more than he should."

"Do you want anyone to go with you?" asked Catherine.

"Nah." Andy grinned. "It's best if I go alone for this. He doesn't take well to humans, you see."

"Right." Catherine nodded. "In that case, Kreya, you're with me. While Andy's checking in with his contacts and Benson's getting himself set up, we'll go visit the train that the massacre took place on... and the morgue where they're keeping the only body that survived."

As she got affirmatives from the officers under her, Catherine mentally prepared herself for what lay ahead. She had the distinct feeling that this case would prove to be even more troubling than the one where she, Christian, and Lilith had first met.

Chapter 18

Oasis Comics was, as the name suggested, a specialty store that sold, well, comics. One section of the wall outside of the store was painted in an image that depicted almost every major comic book character known to man. All of the favorites were there. The rest of the building was made of window panes, metal bars painted a dark black, and the wall in back of the store was made of red bricks. The entrance consisted of a standard push door with glass windows that showed a view of the inside.

As one would expect from a store that sold comic books, the walls were lined with shelves, which were in turn lined with comics of all kinds. The islands set up periodically around the store, likewise, had many different comics to choose from. Naturally, they did not sell *just* comics. There were plenty of old cartoon series, anime, manga, and what have you that any nerd worth their weight in gold would have loved to get their hands on. There were even a few items that cosplayers would kill to buy. Some of those items included swords—fake ones—that were made of metal and looked real enough to the unknowing eye.

Christian and Lilith were one of several people inside the store, perusing its vast selection. With the entire city in lockdown, there was little they could do to escape until things calmed down. They'd thought about hitchhiking, but chances were everyone knew of them by now, and trying to hitch a ride out of state would have looked suspicious. That meant they had a lot of free time on their hands and nothing to do.

Oasis Comics was, while not necessarily on the outskirts of the city, far enough away from any heavily populated districts that they felt comfortable staying there for much of the time. That it allowed them to indulge in their guilty pleasure was just a bonus. Really.

"What about this one?" asked Lilith.

"Slayers?" Christian looked rather boyish with the grin he was wearing. "A bit old-school, don't you think? Why not one of the newer series?"

"Hey! This is a great series," Lilith defended her selection. "And it brings back memories. This was the first series I ever read."

Slayers was one of the first light novels ever published. In fact, Slayers was the series that coined the term "light novel." It was a fantasy series about a girl named Lina Inverse, a sorceress of incredible power with a rambunctious personality to match.

"Really?" Christian asked.

Lilith nodded once. "Mmhm. I was eight years old when I read Slayers. I remember, Mom took me to New York, and they were having this really big convention. I begged her to take me to it. It was there that I saw the stand selling these, and I became fascinated by the art-style. Among them, Slayers was the series that piqued my interest the most."

"So it was the artwork that drew you in and not the actual story." Christian chuckled as Lilith puffed up her cheeks. "I see. I guess I have no right to judge, since I didn't get into them until I was much older." He looked at her, his head tilted. "Do you want to buy it?"

Lilith bit her lip before, after a moment's silent contemplation, she put Slayers volume one back down. "No. I mean, yes, but I don't think we should. We're trying to travel light, so we can't afford to have anything we don't need on us, especially if we're going to wind up in more trouble and be forced to abandon our stuff again."

Knowing their luck, that was probably what would happen. Their journey thus far had not been what either of them would have called safe, pleasant, or even mildly therapeutic. Chaotic was more like it.

"Still, we might be able to buy at least one or two…" Christian began.

Lilith stared at Christian, and then looked over at where he was looking. A smile crept on her face as she looked back at him. "Really, Christian? Vampire Hunter D? Weren't you just teasing me for liking an old light novel series?"

"I like the horror aspect." Christian tried not to blush. "And D's life kind of reminds me of my own."

Lilith grinned. "Maybe the vampire hunting part, but the rest? I'll admit, you pulled off that enigmatic persona very well when we first met, but anyone who knows you, and I mean really knows you, knows that you're about as mysterious as Tuxedo Mask is masculine." This time, Christian did blush. "And besides, you're not a *Dhampir.*"

Dhampir were half-breeds born of a vampire father and a human mother. Much like most beings known only in myth, legends, and the entertainment industry, they actually did exist. And just like most stories in which they played a part, dhampirs were outcasts of both societies. Vampires hated them because they were not true, pure-blooded vampires; and humans hated them because they were not fully human. While most dhampir did not share a vampire's weakness to sunlight, crosses, or garlic, they did share in a vampire's unnatural beauty. It was how the Executioners caught most of them.

Most dhampir were taken care of by the Casteless. While they shared some of their vampire parent's traits, including superhuman strength, and lacked their general weaknesses, they also had their own inadequacies. Their strength was only about half that of a normal vampire's, sometimes less. Their eyesight was only as good, maybe a tad better, than a normal human's. While they didn't have the weakness to sunlight or crosses, a normal bullet to the head or heart would kill them just as easily as it did a regular human.

As Christian's face turned an interesting shade of red, Lilith's lilting giggle caused a few people to look their way. Most went back to what they were doing after a time, but a few of them—mostly boys—continued to stare. At least, they did until Christian realized they were staring and sent them a sharp glare filled with the intent to commit bodily harm upon them. Then they looked away, trying in vain to ignore the pair and pretend like they weren't about ready to lose control of their bladders.

"I suppose we could get a volume or two." If Lilith found it odd that she was being the one to try and think logically and keep Christian from splurging, she didn't say anything. "I've never read Vampire Hunter D."

"Horror's not really your thing." Christian nodded, understanding. "Neither are vampires."

"Yeah, but if you like it, maybe I should give it a shot."

She smiled at him, causing him to smile back.

Despite knowing that it probably wasn't a good idea, they decided to buy at least two light novel volumes anyway. One was from the series Christian wanted to read. The other was another classical series called

Chrome Shelled Regios that Lilith thought looked interesting. They went up to the register to pay for their orders, then left the store, with Christian carrying a small bag filled with their purchases.

With some prodding from Lilith, they also decided to stop at a small Mexican restaurant to grab a bite to eat. While standing in front of the cash register, getting their orders taken, Christian found himself frowning at the cashier.

The woman standing behind the register was attractive. Very attractive. Perhaps even unnaturally so. Her olive-colored skin complemented her dark brown, shoulder-length curls and doe-like brown eyes. Ruby red lips that were curled into a smile made her look all the more enticing. Those were the kind of lips most men would fall for. Set above her lips was a straight nose that fit her face perfectly and, much like Lilith, the girl had a body that most supermodels would commit genocide to possess.

And that was the problem. This woman was simply too perfect. Even her face was perfectly symmetrical, with no sign of one eye being larger than the other, or lower than the other. It was almost like…

"Oof!" Christian let out a breath as an elbow smacked his ribs. He looked over at Lilith, who was glaring at him, in shock. "What was that for?"

"I don't know what you're talking about." Lilith gave him a beatific smile. "I just wanted to let you know it was your turn to order."

Christian frowned at the gorgeous blond, but then looked at the menu. "I guess I'll have a, um, fish taco plate."

"Would you like a drink with that?" the woman asked.

"Just a cup of water please."

"And would you like that for here or to go?"

Christian glanced at Lilith, who just huffed and looked away. His frown growing larger, he looked back at the woman. "For here, please."

"Alright, your total comes to $16.23." After being paid, the woman rang it up on the till, then gave him back the change owed to him. "Just sit down anywhere and your order will be right up."

Christian was about to thank the lady, common courtesy and all that, when Lilith grabbed him by the arm and began dragging him outside. "Come on, Christian."

"But what about our drinks?"

"Worry about them later."

They eventually found themselves sitting outside, their table a basic round one made of plastic. Shading them from the sun was a large umbrella. There were a few other people sitting around them, two different families and a young couple. None of them paid him or his partner any attention.

Lilith was frowning at him, her arms crossed under her bust, and Christian was trying to figure out what he had done wrong.

"Are you… upset?" he asked at last.

"No. Of course not. Why would you think that?" Lilith looked away. "I mean, it's not like I caught you staring at another woman."

Christian blinked several times, and then asked, "Lilith, are you jealous?"

"Of course not! Why would I be jealous of some floozy working a minimum wage job where horny men can stare at her boobs all day?"

Frowning for just a moment, Christian decided on his next course of action. He wasn't exactly sure why Lilith would feel jealous of that woman. Yeah, she was pretty, but Lilith was far more beautiful, and it wasn't like he had been looking at the woman because he found her attractive. There was just something off about her that stirred something inside of him, like a distant memory that he could recall but not quite see, as if it was just outside his peripheral vision.

She had also been staring at Lilith, he had noticed.

"You know I'll never love another woman besides you, right?" asked Christian.

"Then why were you staring?" Lilith asked right back.

"Not because I thought she was attractive." Christian rolled his eyes and gave Lilith a look, his mouth flat, eyes showing a strange earnestness that didn't sit well on his face—possibly because the contacts and brown hair just didn't match his facial structure. "You are the woman I love. No one else. And you're far more attractive than her."

Lilith was not convinced. "Again, if that's the case, then why were you staring at her?"

"Because I thought there was something familiar about her," Christian said, frowning thoughtfully. "I don't know what, though. It seems strange. I know I've never seen her before, but I just can't help but feel like there is something about her that I've felt before."

Christian knew he wasn't making much sense, but he couldn't really explain it better than that. There was something about her looks that gave him a strange sense of, not quite nostalgia, but definitely something that stirred up feelings of familiarity. Deja vu, maybe?

Lilith stared at him. She then looked away again, her arms uncrossing. "So you weren't staring at her because you thought she was pretty?"

"No."

"And you weren't comparing her to me?"

"Why would I do that?" Christian was honestly confused. "No one can compare to you."

Lilith relaxed in her chair, visibly slumping. "Sorry. I know you're not the type to look at random women. I don't know what came over me. I just felt so… angry, when I saw you staring at that woman."

"I'm sorry, too," Christian said. "I didn't mean to upset you."

"It's okay." Lilith's voice was soft. She looked over at him, her hair moving around her face, lending a sort of alluring mystique to her. "However, I think I need some reassurance that I'm the only woman you'll ever love."

Christian opened his mouth to tell her that he would never love another woman like he did her, when he finally noticed the look in her eyes. He changed directions. "And what kind of reassurances are we talking about?"

"A kiss."

Christian smiled. "I think I can do that."

Chapter 19

Investigating the train in which the mass killings had happened had been a bust. Aside from a lot of dried blood covering almost every car, a couple bullet holes near the back, and several strange strings that were unusually sharp—which Catherine found out when one cut into her after she attempted to pick it up—there was nothing. They'd left the train nearly empty-handed, with only a few pieces of wire to show for their efforts.

The cadaver located in the morgue would hopefully prove to be much more useful.

Catherine, along with Kreya, Officer Gordon, and two other officers who belonged to the forensics department walked along the granite tiles of the forensics research lab. Located within the Las Vegas emergency hospital's lower levels, the lab was where all the bodies from various crimes, accidents, or natural deaths went to be identified, receive autopsies, or be disposed of via burial.

In most cases, the forensics lab would have been attached to the police office, where a team of forensics agents would be allowed to work closely with their fellow officers. Because of the deficiency in funding for the Las

Vegas police department, they had been forced to make accommodations with closest local hospital.

Well-lit halls filled much of the forensics lab. Junctions and turns and hallways with several doors led to rooms containing examination tables, sinks, and an entire wall of cabinets that stored corpses. Just the knowledge that she was in a place filled with dead bodies disturbed Catherine. She'd seen a number of bodies in her life, and studied numerous violent crime scenes. Even so, that didn't mean she enjoyed being in a place that housed the bodies afterward.

The room they were eventually led to looked like every other examination room. It was bare. The white walls were uncovered, with only one small blacklight screen where x-rays were posted during examinations. A sink and counter covered an entire wall on one side, and the one opposite it had large, metal cabinets where the bodies were stored. A little off to the side was the examination table; it was a thin, metal table with several trays that could store a variety of examination and embalming tools.

Laying on the table was a body. Male. Middle-aged. His scraggly brown hair hung around his face in clumps and his five o'clock shadow was scruffy, but it did a strange job of making his gaunt face look a bit more filled out.

Of course, the head wasn't attached to the body, but rather, laying right beside it, which was disturbing. He was also naked, his thin, twig-like body on display, showing a number of scars. Most looked like slash wounds. Those were large, larger than they would be if he had been cut with a knife, even a machete. A sword, perhaps? Several smaller wounds littered his legs and a bit of his torso. Bullet holes. Twelve in all. Judging by the size and shape, they appeared to be from a standard 9mm pistol.

The two officers, a man and a woman of indeterminate age, walked further into the room. The male went to the body, while his counterpart walked up to the screen where several x-rays had already been pinned.

"So, what can you tell me about this guy?" asked Catherine.

"You mean aside from the fact that someone killed him by cutting his head clean off?" asked the male forensics officer, who looked kind of like the love child of a blimp and a clown, except he wasn't wearing makeup and didn't have a red nose. He picked up a clipboard that had been left on the table next to the body. "Only a bit. His name is Nicholas Cruor. Age, 35. Bloodtype, AB. Height, 6'1". Weight, 155 lbs. That's about all the information we were able to gather after identifying him."

"You weren't able to find out anything else? Occupation? Residence?"

"We were able to find out a little bit," the woman hedged. "We don't know where he lives, or what his occupation is, but we do know that he's a missionary for the Catholic Church. At least, we think he's a missionary for the church."

Catherine raised an eyebrow. "You think?"

"Well…" The man and woman shared a look before turning back to her. "We don't know for sure. I mean, they look a little different, but there's a photo of him with the pope in a magazine I have."

The woman grabbed the clipboard from her male compatriot and flipped through the files until she pulled out a small slip of paper that looked like it had been cut out from a magazine. She gave the slip to Catherine, who took it in her hand and looked at it with a small frown.

"This does look a lot like him," she admitted after a moment of careful observation.

Indeed, the man in the photo looked almost exactly like the man on the table. His hair wasn't as scraggly, he was clean shaven, and he wasn't as thin. This looked like a healthier, more lively version of the man on the table.

Coincidence? Maybe, but then again, maybe not. Christian had been working with the Executioners, a group belonging to the Catholic Church. Now he was on the run. Perhaps this man had been one of those sent to kill him and Lilith? But if that was the case, why kill everyone else on the train, or was he not responsible for those deaths?

She shook her head. There were too many unanswered questions to be certain about anything.

She looked back up at the forensics team. "Have you discovered anything else?"

"Only this," the man said, reaching into a drawer and pulling something out.

Catherine studied the object as he handed it to her, a knife, examining its features with a critical gaze. It looked like a standard army knife, except it was black, almost obsidian. While the front was a straight blade, the back held serrated edges. She ran a finger over it, noting the sharpness. It could easily carve through flesh.

It was while she was staring at the knife that Catherine noticed something else, the small indent on the bottom, which had a tiny hole in it.

"He was holding onto that knife when we found him," the female officer said, a frown marring her dark-skinned face. "We've checked it over and were unable to determine the composition. It doesn't appear to be made from any natural metals in the world, yet the blade is sharper than anything I've ever seen and tougher than diamonds to break."

Absently nodding to herself, Catherine looked at the forensics team. "I'd like to take this knife with me to study it a bit longer, if that's all right?"

"That's fine. We've already studied everything we can about it and couldn't figure it out. Maybe you can find something we missed," the woman said.

"Thanks. In the meantime, would you mind if I had Kreya do her own forensics on the body? I don't doubt your skills, but Kreya knows a bit more about what I'm looking for, so she may be able to find something you wouldn't catch without being aware it exists."

The two officers shared a silent conversation together for all of ten seconds. Eventually, the man of the two nodded his head.

"Very well. I don't see a problem with that. Ms. Kreya," he said, getting the woman's attention. "We'll let you stay here, but let us know when you're done. It takes a keycard to use the elevator. We'll be in our office."

As the two walked out, Catherine turned to Kreya. "How long do you think it'll take to find anything?"

"It depends on whether or not this person has anything worth finding." Kreya shrugged her shoulders. "But don't worry. If there is something abnormal about his body, then I'll definitely find it."

"I'm counting on you."

"Mm."

***

There was an old saying about how some things changed and others remained the same. This quote spoke of the passage of time, how, with time, many things can and will change. Children grew into adults and then became old. Small towns could become large cities. Even the earth would eventually change as tectonic plates shifted the continental landmasses into new formations over the course of several million years. Even the galaxy would eventually change as stars went nova and new planets were born.

Yet there are things that stuck around in spite of the passage of time. Certain stories that never grew old. Feelings that, regardless of the person experiencing them, refused to change. Love. Hate. Empathy. Passion.

The No Tell Motel was one place that seemed not to be a part of the natural time-stream, something that stayed the same in spite of having been around for nearly one-hundred years.

This was not necessarily a good thing.

"I see nothing's changed around here."

Andrew J. Fortis stood in front of the door leading into the motel. The cheap, derelict building looked just as it had fifty years ago when he'd first discovered it. He'd been desperate, searching for a place where he could forget the rest of the world and just disappear. Back then, each day brought with it its own despair. Everything had seemed hopeless to the newly afflicted young man, and he'd been at his wit's end.

He would never say this place helped him, because really, it hadn't. However, it was while he had been staying in this downtrodden, piece of shit dump that only vaguely resembled an inn that he'd realized moping around and trying to pretend he didn't exist wouldn't solve anything. It was also the place where he had learned that, even if time had slowed down for him, it had not stopped. Unlike this place, he was still a part of time's ebb and flow.

Entering the building revealed that the inside looked exactly the way he remembered: disgusting. The lights barely worked, the couch should have been replaced a long time ago, and someone really should have steamed the carpet and scrubbed the damn walls.

Except this place existed outside of time. It would remain unchanged until oblivion came to claim it.

"Well, now…" A soft, wheezing voice choked out a horrendous laugh. "Here's a familiar face… heh heh heh… haven't seen you in awhile, boy. I thought you'd left for good."

"I did leave for good, old man." Andy glared at the poltergeist, arms crossed over his chest. "And don't call me boy. I might not be as old as you, but I've been around for longer than most."

"Heh heh heh." The wheezing chuckle that emerged was like nails scraping against a chalkboard. Andy never did like that laugh. "You're still just a boy to me… *boy.*"

Andy scowled. There were only a few things that really pissed him off. Pricks who thought they were better than him because they were smart (Benson), idiots who disliked him for what he was rather than who he was, and people (or poltergeists) who talked down to him like he was a child who still sucked on his mother teet. All three pissed him off, but that last one in particular made him really mad.

"I'm guessing you came here for a reason, aye? You wouldn't have shown up in my humble motel if you hadn't," the poltergeist continued.

Andy swallowed the harsh words that were on the tip of his tongue (this place? A hotel? Ha!). Instead, he took several deep breaths and visibly calmed down. The poltergeist watched in amusement.

"And I see you learned a thing or too while traveling. You used to be such a hot-headed lad, eh heh heh heh…"

"Shut up, old man! I don't want to hear you patronizing me!" He got enough of that from Benson. He didn't need it from someone else, thank you very much.

The old poltergeist wheezed some more. He leaned against the counter, dark green eyes filled with a hidden malice glinting from beneath a wide-brimmed hat peeked out at Andy. "What can this humble spirit do for you?"

Andy grumbled. Humble his ass. He'd best just get this over with. He didn't want to be around this malicious entity any longer than he had to.

"I'm looking for someone," he began, "two someones, actually, and I was hoping you could help me find them..."

Chapter 20

After leaving Kreya at the forensics lab to find out what she could about the cadaver, Catherine made her way back to the Police Department. There, she found Benson setting up shop. The room, now at a chilling temperature, housed a large monitor connected to a PC. Unlike most store-bought computers, the one Benson was sitting in front of looked like something out of one of those spy movies. It was large and sleek, with a sort of streamlined appearance. There was a long tube filled with flowing, blue liquid running all throughout the computer, like some kind of alien entity attempting to invade a person's body. Benson called them cooling veins.

Apparently, they had something to do with keeping the internal components cool so they didn't overheat, or something like that. Catherine had never cared to know the specifics.

Sitting beside the PC was a laptop.

Why he needed two computers was beyond her.

"I'm all set up here, Catherine." He didn't even look up from his monitor as he spoke. His fingers flew across the keyboard at an insane pace. They were a blur to her eyes.

"Good. I've got Kreya working on discovering what she can from the body." She moved to stand behind Benson and watched as he typed. "Has Andy called in?"

"No. I assume he's still talking to his contacts or whatever."

"I guess I should have expected that."

Truthfully, she had been hoping that Andy would have found something by this point. She knew it was unreasonable—they had only just arrived—but she really wanted to find Christian and Lilith, to get the full story from them as soon as possible. Her gut was telling her that knowing what they knew would be important to solving this case, and she was always one to listen to her gut.

The data on the computer began flowing by at a far faster rate than before. Numbers tumbled down the screen, bright green ones and zeros filled the entire monitor in an ever-changing pattern as they descended from top to bottom like a waterfall. Then the screen blanked, right before it turned back on to reveal several windows that were displaying real-time video feeds from various security cameras located around the city.

"We're in," Benson said unnecessarily. She might not know much about hacking or computers, but she could clearly see that they were indeed inside the various security networks located within the city. "I'll let you know when I find something."

"You do that," she said, then added, "while you're at it, I want you to look up the name Nicholas Cruor."

"Any specific reason?" Benson asked.

"He was the corpse found on the train."

The typing stopped momentarily before starting up again. "Got it. I'll see what I can find on him."

Benson's fingers made a sort of stuttering sound, almost like a camera taking pictures at a really fast speed. Several more windows were pulled up, a couple files started downloading, and the Troogle search engine popped up on the screen.

Catherine watched for another second before turning around. "Good. In the meantime, I think I'm going to get myself a cup of coffee."

"Already? You barely even started working on the job and you're already loading yourself up on caffeine?"

"I suggest keeping the disrespectful tone down, or you may find yourself on latrine duty in the near future," Catherine threatened.

Benson shuddered. "… I'll be good."

Catherine left the room and walked into the main office of the police station. It was only after a few seconds of walking that she realized she didn't know where the coffee machine was. She asked around. It turned out they didn't have one. Apparently, their budget was so low they hadn't been able to afford even a cafeteria. When someone wanted coffee, they either went to the local coffee shop up the street, or the nearest Starbucks.

Catherine hated Starbucks, so she chose the first option.

The air that evening was a little mucky. Much like Los Angeles, Sin City dealt with a lot of pollution. However, unlike the city she worked in, Las Vegas was hot. Really hot. The scorching sun bore down on her and the other denizens of the city, and it was unbearable, like stepping into a furnace. Even the wind seemed to only exacerbate the problem. Catherine was reminded of those times back when she was a little girl where she would use the blow dryer to blow hot air into her face. It wasn't exactly what she would call a pleasant experience.

Most of the people seemed to ignore the heat. The natives. She saw many faces passing her, not even paying the sweat trickling down their skin any mind. Most hardly even noticed that their clothes were sticking to their bodies as they walked along the sidewalk. Catherine guessed that was what happened to people when they became acclimated to something.

After ordering herself a large coffee—she had a feeling she was going to need the caffeine—Catherine found herself thinking about Christian and Lilith. Was the sketch she'd seen of the suspects really them? Did that mean they were still in Las Vegas? And if so, what were they up to? What kind of trouble had they gotten themselves into this time? More importantly, when, or if, she did find them, what would she do?

Catherine felt for the two. She really did. Christian was a young man who'd found himself faced with a serious dilemma and made a choice between doing what was right and what was easy. He'd decided to follow his heart rather than his head, and now he had been branded a traitor by his own organization and was on the run. While she didn't know Lilith as well, she knew that the girl was pure—well, mostly pure. After what she had seen those two get up to in that middle school, she wasn't sure the word "pure" really applied to Lilith anymore. Still, the young woman was quite innocent. If it weren't for the small fact that she wasn't human, the blonde woman would have been just like any other young woman her age.

Which was what made this whole situation so hard to grasp. Neither of those two were the type to slaughter an entire train, especially in such a manner. She just couldn't see it. That was why she needed to find them. She wanted to find out what really happened. Catherine could make an educated guess, and she had even deduced a few things from simple observation and knowledge of the people they were after, but getting confirmation of her theories before acting was important.

And, of course, all of this was dependent on the two suspects actually being Christian and Lilith. She had determined it was them based on the knowledge that the train had come from San Francisco, which she knew those two had been headed for the last time she saw them.

They had been trying to escape from California at the time. Thus, she had taken a leap and deduced that they were the ones who'd been seen leaving the station. The drawings and details given during interviews seemed to confirm their identities. At the same time, she knew that her guesses could be wrong. Those sketches could just be two people who looked similar. It was never good to assume something until you had definite proof.

As she was walking back to the police station, her phone rang.

"This is Catherine," she said into the phone.

"Cathy, it's Andy."

"Andrew, how many times have I told you not to use that name while we're on the job?"

"A few dozen probably, but that's not the point. Listen, I've spoken with one of my contacts, and he says that he saw both of the suspects. It looks like you were right. My contact informed me that one of them was a succubus with blonde hair and blue eyes, and the other was an Executioner with red and green eyes. They spent last night at the No Tell Motel. That place is a dump, but it's the perfect spot for people who want to get a room with no questions asked."

That was good news. In fact, it was the best she'd heard in awhile. Catherine felt her hopes rise.

"That's great. So, do you know where they are now?"

… Silence.

"Andrew?"

"Not right at this moment, no." He sounded apologetic. *"But don't worry too much. I might not know where they are, but I've got their scent. It shouldn't be too difficult for me to track them down. I'll have their location before the end of today."*

Even better news.

"Excellent. Good job. Please keep me posted on your progress, and when you do find them, don't make contact. Just keep tabs on them, track their movements, and wait for me to get there."

"Got it."

Catherine hung up the phone and entered the police station in a much better mood than she had been before. Now she knew that Christian and Lilith were, in fact, somewhere in the city. She just had to find them.

It seemed things were beginning to look up.

Chapter 21

"...The alleged killer responsible for the murder of an entire train traveling from San Francisco is still on the loose. Airports, train stations, and checkpoints leading out of the city are still in lockdown and will remain as such until the one responsible has been caught. Due to this, protestors have sprung up, staying outside of train stations and airports to let their displeasure be known. When asked for his opinion, Officer Gordon had this to say: 'Until the train ride massacre killer is caught, no one will be allowed to leave the city. You can criticize me for this, but catching the person responsible for all those deaths to ensure they cannot kill again is paramount, and protecting the people is more important than whether or not the police department is liked.' We at LV News can only hope that the killer is caught soon. In other news..."

Lilith blew out a breath as she changed the channel to something else, an old Bugs Bunny rerun. Huh. She hadn't even realized that the show was still playing anymore.

Flopping onto her back, Lilith tried not to let herself feel disheartened. It wasn't like she had expected the lockdown to be lifted anytime soon. Only four days had passed since the train filled with blood and body parts had arrived at the train station—relatively little time in the grand scheme of things. That didn't mean she hadn't been hoping for something to change. While there was no widespread panic, the people were feeling uneasy. It had been her hope to see the police cave under the pressure being placed on them by the protestors to reopen the airports and train stations.

It really was unfortunate that life rarely ever gave people what they wanted.

The clicking of a door let her know that Christian was done in the restroom. Using her arms to push herself up, she lifted the upper half of her torso and looked at him. His now brown eyes were glancing at the television, noting what was playing with a sort of absent-mindedness found in people whose minds were elsewhere. Muddy brown hair was parted neatly to the side.

She really didn't like that look. Christian just didn't look as good with combed brown hair and matching eyes. She preferred his messy black locks and heterochromatic eyes. They appealed to her a lot more than the plain look this new hairstyle and eye color held.

"I really wish you didn't have to dye your hair," she couldn't help but comment.

Christian looked amused. "So you've said."

"And I'll say it again, many times if I have to."

"Yes, well, it's not like I have much choice. They know what we look like and they have our hair and eye color. That's why we need to wear a disguise." He gave a helpless shrug. "Anyway, since I'm finished, did you want to reapply your hair dye now?"

At the mention of hair dye, Lilith took a strand of the now auburn-colored locks in her hand. It was now a mixture of red and blonde. Much like she didn't like Christian's hair color, she also didn't like her own. She didn't think she looked good with any color other than blonde. Christian had agreed with her.

"I guess I should," she sighed, standing up before moving to the restroom.

Dying her hair was such a pain, the entire process taking way longer than it should have. What made it worse was that it needed to be done daily. Christian had suggested getting a more permanent solution, but she'd shot him down in a heartbeat. There was no way she was getting her hair permanently ruddy colored, and she certainly wouldn't let his gorgeous hair become ruined by permanent dyes either. Wash-out hair dye was all she'd let either of them use.

When she returned to the bedroom, her hair now a uniform color, Christian was sitting against the headboard of the bed. The television had been turned off, and he was holding a light novel in his hands: Vampire Hunter D, volume 1. He scanned the pages, eyes traveling from left to right, and then back again.

"Reading without me?" asked Lilith, taking small, dainty steps into the room. Her bare feet brushed against the light carpet, scarcely making a sound.

Christian shrugged. "I didn't feel like watching TV."

"It's not like there's anything good on, unless we pay for it." Which they couldn't do since they didn't have a credit card. Why hadn't Tristin thought to give them one of those when handing over that account? It would have made everything so much easier. "And reading is better for you anyways." Lilith climbed onto the bed, crawling toward Christian on her hands and knees until she was right in front of him. Christian lifted his hands above his head and made room for her to sit between his legs, bringing his hands back down until they were resting in her lap. As she nestled against his chest, she finished her thoughts by saying, "though I really don't want to stay inside all day."

From the corner of her eye, she watched Christian bite his lower lip. "I suppose we could go out somewhere… maybe the mall, or something."

The problem with Las Vegas was that, unless you wanted to gamble, get hitched, or watch some adult entertainment, there wasn't a whole lot they could do.

Christian was a very wholesome young man. He didn't drink. He didn't gamble. He also had no need for adult entertainment. Lilith was much the same… mostly. She actually did want to try her hand at gambling, but she was afraid of what Christian would say if she told him that.

"I think I remember seeing something about a really big show of some kind happening later today," Lilith said instead.

"A show?" Christian asked.

"Mm. I think it's happening at the Hollywood Theatre."

Christian was silent for a moment, contemplating. "Do you know the time?"

"Um… sometime in the afternoon?"

"You don't know the time." He deadpanned.

"I wasn't paying too much attention." It had been a commercial. Lilith didn't get any gratification from watching television. Watching a commercial was even worse.

A sigh was given to her in response. "I guess we can head over to the Hollywood Theater after breakfast."

"We don't have to go if you don't want to," Lilith informed him.

"It's got nothing to do with not wanting to go." Christian shrugged. "We really don't have much to do right now. We're pretty much stuck here, so we might as well do something, right?"

"Right." Lilith tilted her head to kiss him on the cheek. "Thanks, Christian."

There were many things that Lilith wanted to do and see but hadn't been able to because of her androphobia. Now that she no longer feared men as she used to, she wanted to go out and do some of those things. There was actually a small list at home, her old home with Maria, that contained all of the things she wanted to do, see, and accomplish in life.

Seeing a big show in Las Vegas was one of those things.

***

Andrew James Fortis had finally managed to track the scent of Christian and Lilith down. It hadn't been easy. It had taken longer than expected as well. Catherine wasn't going to be pleased.

Even with the burnt remains of a pair of panties and a sock, locking down the bouquet of vanilla and musk among the millions of other odors pervading the air had been a wearisome task. If it weren't for the musky scent of arousal, he might not have found them at all.

He was now standing outside of a seven story building called the Fermont Hotel. Nose twitching, he sniffed the air a few more times, ignoring the odd and slightly disturbed stares being directed at him. He wanted to make sure this was the place. There was the scent of linen and various foods. The odor of someone who wore too much cologne and another who probably should start using it. He smelt steel and oil, an odd combination that made his nose twitch. There was also… yes, yes, there it was, the scent of vanilla and a slightly musky smell. The musk was faint but noticeable, and it was centered around this building. He was definitely at the right place.

He checked the time on his watch. 7:34am. He looked back at the hotel. Should he go in? He shook his head. No. Going in could cause problems. He didn't want to be seen. Catherine had asked him to observe them from afar without being noticed. That would be difficult enough due to his size. There was no need to compound the issue by making himself even more visible.

Waiting outside it was, then.

How boring.

***

The hotel cafeteria reminded Lilith of a buffet-style restaurant. It wasn't a 'sit down and take your order' kind of place. They had several tables and a number of booths. In the back of the cafeteria was a long buffet table with a variety of different foods: pancakes, waffles, French toast sticks, eggs, bacon, sausage, oatmeal, hash browns, grits, and a cornucopia of fruits.

Lilith ended up getting some oatmeal plus a bowl of fruit. Her favorites were bananas and strawberries, but she also decided to be a little adventurous and have a couple of boysenberries as well. She looked at Christian's plate, which consisted of scrambled eggs, hash browns, and French toast sticks. Almost all carbs.

Lilith shook her head. She was so envious of his metabolism. Even she, a succubus, would get fat if she ate like him every day.

There weren't very many people eating there that morning, so they ended up getting a booth. They slid onto the red padded seats, sharing one side instead of sitting opposite of each other. For a while, Lilith focused on her food. It wasn't bad. The oatmeal could use some sweetening; it was pretty bland, but at least the fruit was good.

As she popped a boysenberry in her mouth, she looked over at Christian while he ate. Maybe it was her skewed perspective on men after being afraid of them for so long, but she used to imagine that men would be messy eaters with no sense of table manners… which probably explained her surprise at how well-mannered Christian always was when he ate. He never dropped so much as a crumb and always wiped his mouth. It never ceased to surprise her.

She then looked down at the French toast sticks, which he had yet to touch, and got a deliciously wicked idea.

"Hey!"

Grabbing one of the sticks, she grinned at him, took a bite out of it, and then chewed while presenting him with a thoughtful mien.

"Not bad, kind of plain though," she said after swallowing the food.

"I can't believe you just ate some of my French toast," Christian grumbled.

"I only ate half of it. Besides, you can always go and get another."

"Or I can just steal some of your food."

Checkmate.

"Be my guest." She grabbed a strawberry slice and stuck half of it in her mouth. Still grinning, she wiggled it at Christian, who merely stared at her oddly. When, after several seconds had passed, he just continued blinking at her with a dumb look in his eyes, she wiggled it again. "Come on, you wanted to eat some of my food, right?"

And then Christian got it. With a smile on his face, he shook his head at her. "You really have become daring, haven't you?"

Lilith's response was to grin at him. She didn't think she could explain it, but as more and more time passed in Christian's presence, her confidence and temerity continued to climb, as did her need for physical intimacy. Maybe it was a succubus thing.

Leaning down, Christian began to close the distance. Lilith closed her eyes in anticipation, waiting for the moment their lips would connect, for the stars that would explode behind her eyes, and the searing heat of his mouth on hers. She waited. And waited. And waited. And waited. And she even waited some more, until, finally, she felt the strawberry slice slip from her mouth.

No lip on lip action. No stars exploding. No searing heat.

She opened her eyes. Christian was eating the strawberry slice in amused satisfaction. He raised his hand and wiggled his fingers. There was strawberry juice on them.

Lilith pouted at him. "No fair."

"Sorry." He didn't sound very sorry.

"You're mean." Lilith crossed her arms under her chest. Christian's smile widened into a Cheshire cat grin, the expression causing Lilith to look away with a huff.

"Hey, Lilith."

…

"Lilith."

"I'm not talking to you."

"That's too bad. I really wanted to show you something."

Lilith frowned. Was he teasing her? Maybe. He didn't usually do teasing, but he'd started to mess with her a bit, probably in response to her own occasional tempting. Should she respond? It wasn't like she could keep pouting like this forever.

She decided to see what he wanted.

She turned around.

A pair of lips pressed against hers. They were chapped, and slightly rough, but they still felt like heaven against her mouth. Christian's lips. She knew they were his. Well, of course they were his. He was sitting right next to her, but even if she had been in a room of crowded people and blind, she would have known who they belonged to. Her mind had already memorized the feel of his mouth.

And she was thinking way too much. Deciding not to think anymore, Lilith kissed back. She enjoyed the act even more than she had the first time they'd kissed. Maybe it was just her, but she couldn't help but feel like each time they kissed, she could feel him just a little bit more. It was almost like the connection they shared during intercourse but not as intense. Would it become stronger as time went on? She hoped so.

The kiss ended much too soon in her opinion. Christian leaned back, smiling at her and warming her insides.

"So, you like me again, right?" he asked.

"Maybe a little," Lilith admitted reluctantly.

"Just a little?"

"Give me more kisses and that might change."

Christian's response was to kiss her again.

Not too much longer, both had their fill of food and left the hotel. Before they could get too far, Lilith was forced to stop walking when she felt Christian halt in his tracks. A glance in his direction showed him frowning as he looked somewhere to their left. When she looked over there to see what he was looking at, she frowned, seeing nothing out of the ordinary.

She looked back at Christian. "Is something wrong?"

"No," Christian said after a moment, shaking his head. "It's nothing. Come on, let's get going."

A number of people milled about, wiling away their time window shopping or spending their day with friends and family. Noises filled the air, hundreds of different voices all talking at once. The honk of cars and the roar of engines accompanied the masses of people walking to and fro. A little girl holding the hand of her mother was looking in a window, pointing at the large dollhouse on display.

"Mommy! Mommy! I want that!"

The mother looked amused and exasperated at the same time. She must have heard that line before. "If you're really good, maybe Santa will get it for you for Christmas."

"Ohh! But I want it now!"

"I'm sorry, honey, but I can't get it for you now."

As the girl began to whine some more, Lilith turned her head to Christian. She was almost taken aback by the look on his face, that mixture of pain and longing as he stared at the child and her mother.

His own parents had died when he was just a child, she knew, as he'd told her in confidence. Was he wondering about what his life would have been like if his parents hadn't died? Maybe he would have been almost like that girl, arguing with his parents because he wanted a toy that he had seen in the glass display of a store.

"Hey, Christian, what were your parents like?" she asked.

Christian turned away from the scene of the mother dragging her little girl away from the toy store. He looked at Lilith for a few silent seconds.

When he did speak, it was softly, as if his mind were trapped within the annuls of time. "My mother was a very kind, sweet woman, but she also had a bit of a temper. While she would always dote on me, she used to get really fired up whenever my dad did something she thought was stupid. I think she might have also been a feminist activist or something," he added. "She was always going on about how my dad shouldn't treat her like a glass doll because she had breasts, and that she was just as capable as any man."

"Sounds like a strong woman."

"She was. I think she also practiced marksmanship, too. I distinctly remember her saying something about being a good shot. She might have been talking about something else, though. I don't remember ever seeing her carry a gun."

"What about your dad?" Lilith asked.

"My dad?"

Christian squinted his eyes and pressed a hand to his forehead. His eyes flickered before he groaned a bit and rubbed his temples.

Lilith began to grow worried. "Christian?"

"Sorry," he said in response to the worry in her tone. "I was just trying to see what I remember. Truthfully, I don't remember a whole lot about my father. I remember... I remember that he looked really different from most people."

"Different?" Lilith carefully pulled Christian out of the way of someone walking down the street while talking on his cellphone. "Different how?"

"Well..." Christian's face scrunched up some more, making his facial features all wrinkly like a newborn puppy's, except not quite as cute. "He was really tall, like, much taller than most people. And he had sharp teeth. I think, yes, I used to call them shark teeth because they were kind of pointy. He also had red eyes."

"You mean like your left eye?"

"Yes. Only both of his eyes were red. I don't remember much else about him, except for something he said to me before... before I lost him and mother in the fire that consumed my town. He told me to 'always make the right choice.'"

"I'm sorry. I shouldn't have brought it up."

Lilith let go of his hand, but only so she could wrap an arm around his lower back. Christian's soft smile made her body warm up and feel strangely like goo. It also made her feel more than a little hot, but she ignored the tingle between her legs and focused on giving him what comfort she could.

"It's fine. I don't really mind telling you these things."

Hearing this made Lilith smile. "Then would you be willing to tell me a bit about your mother?"

"I don't see why not," Christian responded. He paused, seemingly thinking about what he should tell her. Then he said, "why don't I tell you about the time Mom scolded me for turning her kitchen into the Death Star's trench…"

Lilith paid close attention to Christian as he began his tale. This was a part of him that she didn't know. It was important to remember every detail.

Chapter 22

After ducking behind a corner, Andy pressed his back against the wall and breathed a minor sigh of relief. That had been too close. For a brat barely out of diapers—compared to him, at least—that kid had great instincts. Being able to know when someone was watching and determine their approximate location? It was damn impressive. Granted, Andy could admit that his skills in stealth were rather uninspiring, but even so, it should have still been difficult to feel him out among a gathering of people this large.

Waiting for a couple more seconds—a necessary precaution—he eventually moved. His hulking frame peeking out from behind the wall, Andy watched his two targets as they walked down the street. One of them was a brown-haired man with brown eyes. The other was a woman with auburn hair and green eyes.

Unlike most people, who might have been fooled by those disguises, it was as obvious as day to him that the two people wrapped around each other as they moved through the crowd were the same two people who had fought alongside him, Kreya, and Catherine against the No Life King. His nose never lied.

The two were getting further away from him. He waited just a little longer, and then began walking down the street, following them. Tailing. What an arduous task. Why did Catherine make him do this? She knew he wasn't good at spying, tailing, or anything that involved subtlety. Oh. That's right. His sense of smell was better than a trained police dog's. Damn.

Keeping himself from grumbling, he advanced down the street, the crowd before him parting like the Red Sea, his booted feet hitting the ground with something of a small rumble. He tried to ignore the wide eyes and gawking looks aimed at him. They bothered him, but he was used to it by now.

Tailing two people in broad daylight was harder than it looked. The movies always made this crap look so easy. Several times Andy was forced to turn corners and walk into various stores and restaurants when the kid looked his way. Each time was a close call, and they seemed to be getting closer. Fortune favored him, though, because he didn't need to see them to follow them. He had already picked up their scent, so he decided to follow them from a distance, hoping it would help him avoid detection.

He tailed after the two as they did things that any normal couple on vacation would do. They checked out stores, window shopping and occasionally going inside. They never bought anything, but he sometimes peered in through the window to see the female trying on outfits.

Hours later, he watched as they went to a small bistro and ordered some food. They sat there, eating slowly and talking in soft voices. He didn't know what was being said, but from the smiles on their faces and the way they kept stealing kisses, he reasoned that it was probably couple-speak.

After having their fill of lunch, the two set off again, and he kept tailing after them. He didn't know how much time passed, but per his orders, he continued to watch them. It was a tedious process, and he was bored out of his mind. The two weren't doing anything interesting, just a bunch of lovey-dovey couple stuff. Who knew that a hardened warrior, an Executioner at that, could be such a sap?

Checking the time again, Andy found that it was 7:16pm. Had he really been following these two for nearly ten hours?

The sun was going down. The air was cooling off. A multitude of colors splashed across the sky, red, orange, yellow, purple. They made the buildings look like they were on fire.

It was during this time that the young couple stopped in front of a building. It wasn't a massive building, but it was still large. The architecture made it look similar to those Arabian palaces found in picture books, movies, and cartoons. The roof was mostly flat, but had rounded, dome-like half-spheres in certain areas. Two square towers stood on either side of the dome, each with their own domed roof. The tan walls were rough as limestone, and the whole thing had a middle eastern feel. In the very front of the building was a large sign in glowing neon orange that identified it as the Hollywood Theatre.

So they were going to see a play or something? He supposed it made sense. They were clearly trying to blend in, and what better way to do it than follow the crowd. And what a crowd there was. The place was packed up the wazoo with hundreds of people looking to kill time. If anyone wanted to vanish against the backdrop of humanity, this would have been the best place to do it.

The pair went up to the box office. Andy didn't follow them. Instead he dialed his phone and began making the call to Catherine. He'd done his job. The rest was up to her.

***

The Hollywood Theatre was massive. Truly. Able to seat what had to be at least several hundred people, the stadium-sized theater was a work of wonder. Like most theaters, the seats were tertiary, each row was elevated above the one in front, allowing those further out to see the stage without someone's head blocking their view.

Christian's and Lilith's seats were in row D, near the very back. This suited them fine. They were more interested in the experience as opposed to the show that was going to take place. The two squeezed past several people who'd already taken their seats, a man who looked like he had eaten a few too many cheeseburgers, a young woman with too much makeup and her boyfriend, and a group of middle-aged men who wolf-whistled at Lilith. One of those men actually tried to get a little grabby when Lilith passed him, which resulted in his hand being almost broken when Christian grabbed it and squeezed with all of his considerable strength. That stopped the rest from making anymore comments or even looking in their direction.

Sitting down on the dark red seats, a cup of Coke with two straws in the cup holder between them, the pair settled in and waited for the show to begin. Because it was so loud, they had to sit close together in order to hear each other speak. As if that would bother them. They stayed close, whispering to each other instead of speaking normally. Several kisses may have also been stolen during the interim.

The lights eventually dimmed and the show began. A woman walked onto the stage. Her resplendent hair shimmered with each step she took, turning various colors depending on how the light hit it. Red. Magenta.

Maroon. Orange. Gold. It was constantly shifting every second. Eyes the color of pearls peered out from underneath several bangs, pupil-less but somehow all-seeing. The grace with which she walked was otherworldly. Hips swung with a sensual elegance, the long white dress scintillating in the light. A glance, barely a peek of smooth, milky white thigh would occasionally poke out from the slit in her gown, captivating those in the audience.

Then she began to move, dancing to a rhythm that none could see but all could feel. Small flares of light filled the air around her. Tiny balls of flickering flames danced as she moved, flowing around her hips, her bust, between her legs as she kicked them high into the air. Her hair twirled about her head, the multitude of colors coming out all at once in ever-changing, organic patterns, whipping freely about her face as if each strand was a sentient organism.

Christian narrowed his eyes. He looked over at Lilith, who was captivated by the dance as much as everyone else. Leaning into her ear, he whispered, "that woman isn't human."

Blinking, Lilith snapped out of her trance and looked at Christian. "Really?"

"Mm. Check out her eyes and ears."

Lilith looked at the woman again. The orbs had grown into flaming streaks of light that blazed complicated patterns around her. Some struck each other, creating a shower of sparks that cascaded to the ground, illuminating her dress and the elegance of her figure.

"I can't see her ears," Lilith whispered back, looking through the small binoculars they'd been given near the entrance. "Her eyes are odd, though. Is she blind?"

"No. At least, not in the sense that you're thinking." Christian looked back at the woman. She was staring at him and Lilith. He was sure of it. She was staring and… smiling? Weird. "She's one of the fae."

"A fae? You mean like a fairy?"

"Not the kind you're thinking about," Christian was quick to correct her. "The fae aren't those little pixie-like creatures who sprinkle fairy dust on you to make you fly or anything. There's always been a lot of debate about the fae among the Catholic Church. Some believe they are fallen angels that were caught on the other side of Heaven when God ordered the gates of Heaven shut and remained in the human world instead of going to Hell. Others believe they were cast out of Heaven. Not good enough to belong there, but not evil enough to be sent to Hell, they ended up in the human world."

Christian paused.

"Of course, that's only the debate going around the Catholic Church, not other religions. The truth is that no one really knows where the fae come from, or what they are. What we do know is that they are immortal and cannot be killed. At least, I've never heard of one being killed or dying."

"Have you fought one before?" asked Lilith, her eyes sparkling.

"No." Christian shook his head. "In fact, no Executioner has gone after one of the fae for nearly six-hundred years. The last time the Executioners tried to kill a fae was when one had been discovered living in a lake in Britain. The results were not pleasant. Everyone was killed, and ever since that time, the Executioners have left the fae alone."

"A lake in Britain…" Lilith murmured before her eyes widened. "Do you mean…?"

Christian gave a helpless shrug. "Who can say for sure?"

The dance lasted for nearly an hour. In that time, everyone except Christian and Lilith were stationary, stiller than even the obelisks that surrounded the stage. When the dance was over, the people stood up and gave the woman a standing ovation, clapping and hollering and wolf-whistling to the vision of inhuman beauty, who merely smiled at them before taking her leave from the stage. As she walked behind the curtains, she cast one last glance at Christian and Lilith, and then disappeared with a flap of fabric.

With the show done, the young couple stood up and began following the crowd. Lilith kept her arms around one of his so as to not get separated. Progress was slow, but eventually, they reached the exit and made their way into the guest hall. The crowd thinned out a little, but there was still much pushing and shoving. They continued to move through the crowd, trying to work with the flow rather than against it.

They probably would have made it outside had a large man with skin the color of dusk and eyes just as dark not stepped in front of them. He stared at the two, towering over them and impeding their path.

"Can I help you?" asked Christian, eyes narrowed as he prepared to possibly run. He didn't want to start trouble in the middle of a civilian center.

"Miss Titania wants a word with you two," the dark-skinned man said, his voice a deep, bass rumble.

Christian stiffened. A shiver traveled up his spine. That woman was Titania? *The* Titania? He tried to suppress the thrill of fear that he felt, but he was not wholly successful. There were few beings in this world that he would not touch with a two-hundred foot pole. Titania was one of those beings. What did she want with them?

"Christian?" Lilith whispered worriedly in his ear. "Are you okay?"

"Yes, I'm fine." No, he wasn't. "You said Titania wanted to see us?" He looked at the large man, finally noting the pointier than normal ears. He was a fae as well. Knowing better than to resist, Christian made a hand gesture. "Please lead on."

Much as he would rather not meet with this woman, refusing an invitation from someone like The Titania was not smart, not if what little he knew about the fae was true.

The man nodded. "This way, please."

The two were led through a door, and then many winding and twisting halls. Soft red carpet muffled the sound of their footsteps. All this did was serve to make Christian perfectly aware of the way his heart was trying to beat its way out of his chest. He hated to admit that he was afraid, but that was exactly what he felt as he and Lilith followed the hulking fae.

They eventually reached a small corridor with a single door at the end. Titania was waiting inside. She was laying on a divan, her body draped elegantly across its length. The slit running along her leg was peeled back, revealing the perfect flow of curves that defied the laws of men. She was looking at them, her pale lips smiling pleasantly while her milky white eyes scanned them from head to toe. Much like Lilith, the woman before him was too perfect to be human.

"I've been waiting for you two." Her voice, lilting and soft, sounded almost like there were two people speaking instead of one. "You don't know how long I've been waiting to finally meet you two face to face."

"Um, not to be rude, but who are you exactly?" Lilith asked with a kind of bluntness that Christian was not used to. His eyes went wide as he stared at Lilith. Did she not know who she was talking to?

Despite the somewhat rude tone that Lilith spoke with, Titania smiled, seemingly unbothered. "You need not be worried, dear child. I would not dream of taking your mate. Even if I desired him, he is not someone who can be seduced by me. He'll not stray from your side. I doubt even death would keep him away for long."

Lilith, properly chastised, flushed a deep shade of red.

"As for who I am, my name is Titania. I am one of the Four Queens of Fae, and she who rules over the summer solstice."

And just like that, the red left, replaced by a pale-white. Lilith stared at the woman in abject fear. It seemed she understood the severity of their situation now.

Titania smiled again, her lips arcing with gentle grace. "You needn't fear me, young succubus. I mean you no harm." Her smile widened as she looked at Christian, who had moved to stand protectively in front of Lilith.

"You truly are a knight, aren't you? I confess, I am amazed that you remain as untainted as you are, even from your own darkness."

Christian blinked. "Uh, sorry?"

Titania waved her hand in a dismissive gesture. "Do not worry about that for now. You will eventually have to confront the darkness that resides within you, but it will not be for some time. I wished to speak with you for another reason."

Her face darkened and, for just a fraction of a second, Christian and Lilith felt as if they had stepped into an inferno. No sweat broke from their bodies, yet they felt as if they were being burned. It only lasted for less than a second, but it was enough to make them fear the woman in front of them, who could end their lives with a mere thought.

The fae queen soon calmed down. "Everything in this world has a balance. There can be no good without there being an equal amount of evil. No light without darkness. No love without lust. No temperance without avarice. The world has always held this delicate balance, tilting from one side to the other, but never tilting too far in either direction."

Christian had no idea what she was walking about. This was something that went beyond him. He'd heard that the Fae were cryptic, but he had never truly believed it until now.

"That balance is now on the brink of breaking. Dark forces are gathering, threatening to destroy this delicate equilibrium." She stared at the two, her white eyes penetrating them, leaving them naked and vulnerable as her unseeing gaze went straight through them. When she spoke again, it was slowly, as if she was choosing each word with deliberate intent. "I have foreseen that you two will be the key to restoring the balance."

Christian and Lilith shared a look.

"Look," Christian shifted a bit, uncomfortable underneath Titania's pupil-less gaze, "I don't know what you've foreseen, but all we want to do is get out of the country. We're not looking to restore some great balance to the world. Even if we wanted to help, I doubt we could do much."

"That is where you are wrong," Titania stated with certainty. "You are the young man who slayed Abaddon, a demon of great power and infamy. That is a feat unheard of among mortals. If there is someone who can restore the balance, it would be you."

While Lilith gawked at Christian, he ran a hand through his currently brown hair. "I think you overestimate me. I'm talented, but I'm not invincible. I can't do anything about restoring balance or whatever."

"Can't? Or won't?" When Christian looked away, Titania smiled. "Your desire to protect the one you love is admirable, but you should know, this danger, whether you choose to face it or not, will come after you regardless."

Christian narrowed his eyes. "Then you know what it is?"

Shaking her head, Titania gestured with her hand. "I only know what I am telling you now. I am not all-knowing. I cannot see everything. All I can see is the balance being destroyed, and you and Lilith standing in confrontation with the force that threatens to destroy it." She smiled at him, causing him to look away. "You do not believe me now, but in time, you will."

No one spoke for a while. Christian was lost in thought. There were rumors that the fae were prophetic to some degree. He had not really believed them before, as he did not believe in fate or destiny. However, hearing this woman, this queen of the fae, speak, he was beginning to question whether or not there was some truth to those rumors.

"Now then, I have a gift for the both of you." Titania's legs slid off the divan as she flowed gracefully to her feet. She walked until she was standing just a few feet from the pair. "I am not allowed to interfere in the affairs of mortals, so I cannot offer my aid. However, I can give you my favor, and a small token of that favor, a symbol, if you will."

First, she walked over to Lilith, handing the young woman a set of beautiful crystal earrings that glimmered in fractal patterns as prisms of light bounced inside their pentagonal forms.

"These earrings will offer you some measure of protection. I believe you will find that, in the times to come, they will prove the difference between life and death."

She then turned to Christian, who stared at her with wariness.

"For you, I offer this." She held out a pendant. The crystal, embedded at the end of a silver spiral that grew smaller as it moved toward the chain, reminded him of a teardrop. "When times are desperate, this pendant will grant you the flames which can eradicate entities of darkness. Its use is limited, however, and it will run out of power eventually, so I suggest you use it wisely."

"Uh, thank you," Christian mumbled, accepting the pendant. After a moment or two of staring at it, he decided to slip it inside of his pocket.

"Now then, I have delivered my message, so you may leave. However…" she gave them a beatific smile that was so cheerful it forced her eyes shut. "Should you ever find yourselves in Las Vegas again, do come by. I'll give you a free pass to all my performances."

Chapter 23

"What do you think?" Christian glanced at Lilith, his eyebrow raised. Seeing this, Lilith gestured toward his pocket and her earrings, which she had put on because, well, they were really pretty. "About all this, I mean, what Titania said."

He resisted the urge to run a hand through his hair. "Honestly, I'm trying not to think about it."

It wasn't that he *didn't* want to help. There was a part of him, the part that had dedicated himself so thoroughly to the Executioners' cause, the part that had worked toward a single goal, the protection of humanity, that wanted to help. Yet that part of him, while there, was small compared to the other part. The one that cherished Lilith above everything else and wanted to protect her at all costs, even if it meant abandoning the rest of the world, was far larger than the piece of him that wanted to defend the world's balance.

They stood in the elevator as it took them to their hotel room. After the shocking meeting with Titania, the pair had walked to their temporary residence in silence, each left to their own thoughts. Lilith's words were the first that had been spoken.

"Do you think what she said was true?" Lilith asked.

"It wouldn't matter if it was. I'm not doing something that will risk your life," Christian said.

"But if what she said is true, then won't these dark forces be coming after us anyway?"

"If they do come after us, we will deal with it then." He turned his head to stare into Lilith's eyes. He reached out, clasping her smaller hands within his larger ones. "You are my priority now. Your happiness is all that matters to me, and I won't risk your life on the off-chance that some great evil is going to come after us."

Had Titania come to him months ago, before he met Lilith, and told him those words, he may have accepted. No. He would have definitely accepted. But that was then and this was now. He had new priorities, and they did not involve demon slaying, monster killing, or world saving.

"Christian…"

Lilith's eyes became soft pools of blue. She leaned in toward him, partaking in a kiss. Slender arms wrapped around Christian's neck as Lilith tilted her head, allowing him to more easily access her lips. She pressed herself against him, every slope and curve of her ravishing body conforming to his perfectly, as if they were made for each other. He gripped her hips, eliciting a delightful moan from her parted lips. The lilting sound was muffled, however, by the tongue that bypassed her teeth and began exploring the inside of her mouth.

A ding signified that they had reached a floor. The doors slid open. The two paid no attention to this, or to the woman with the young daughter—the same pair they had seen a little over two hours ago in front of the toy store—staring at the two, one in horror and one in curiosity.

The girl looked at her mom while pointing at the pair.

"Mommy! Mommy! What are they doing?"

The mom was silent for a second, then said, "… I'll tell you when you're older, honey."

The door soon closed and the elevator began moving again. The mother and her child had not gotten on. They eventually reached their floor.

He and Lilith did not break their kiss. Christian's hands slid from her hips to her thighs, which he grasped firmly, lifting her up. Lilith offered no resistance. As her feet left the ground, she encircled her legs around his waist. She hooked her feet together at the heels to keep her from falling. Christian then ambled down the hall toward their door.

Getting the keycard out of his pocket was difficult, as it involved much squirming from Lilith, which did not help him concentrate, but he managed. He even managed to open the door with his foot. It was an impressive feat, to be sure. Christian walked into the room, which was lit. They must have forgotten to turn off the lights.

Christian was just about to carry Lilith to the bed where they would take things up a notch. Before they could get too far, a voice spoke up.

"I really hope you two aren't going to make a habit of this every time we meet. I would rather not see either of you in mid-coitus again."

… Silence. Christian and Lilith stopped kissing, frozen in place. Their heads soon moved with a sort of mechanical slowness, turning toward the source of the oh-so-familiar voice.

Catherine smiled at them from her place on the soft blue chair. One leg was crossed over the other. Her hands rested in her lap.

"Hello Christian, Lilith. It's good to see you two again. I was hoping you could answer some questions for me."

"C-Catherine!? What are you doing here?" Christian asked.

Similar to a thunderbolt striking the earth, Christian felt a jolt travel up his spine, toward the crown of his head, and then back down his spine toward his tailbone. Shock did not begin to cover what he felt at seeing the woman who'd helped him and Lilith get to San Francisco.

"Officially, I am investigating the train massacre that happened four days ago. The Las Vegas police were apparently baffled by the violence of the act, assumed the cause was something outside the scope of what a human could do, and made a request for the LAPD to send their Special Investigations Unit in to help." Catherine looked at the two, her expression deadpan. "Look, I know you two are still in your honeymoon phase, but could you please get off each other? It makes talking to you awkward."

"Huh?"

The perplexed noise came from both Christian and Lilith. Neither realized what the woman was talking about, until they looked at each other. Lilith was still being held up by Christian, his hands underneath her thighs, her legs wrapped around his waist, feet locked at her heels. Slender arms still had a firm hold of his neck.

"Oh." That one came from Lilith. Her face flushed a bit, embarrassed that she had been so caught up in her shock that she had forgotten that she and Christian had been about to do something that should be kept private.

"Uh." Christian looked out of sorts as he also realized what Catherine was talking about.

"Well?" Catherine demanded. "Don't just stand there. Get off each other and sit down. We've got a lot to talk about."

The two did as told, Lilith unhooking her legs and Christian shifting his arms to let her stand on her own two feet. They broke apart, reluctantly, and took several slow, deep breaths to calm themselves down.

As one, they turned back to Catherine.

"You look like you're doing well," Christian tried to start a conversation.

Catherine's inelegant snort seemed to contradict his words. "Are you trying to be kind or condescending?" Before Christian could open his mouth to respond, she sighed and gestured for them to take a seat. "Come on. Sit down. Let's talk."

"Is this an interrogation?" asked Christian, even as he sat down in the chair next to Catherine's. Lilith, after taking a moment to decide on where she wanted to sit—there were no extra chairs—she eventually just plopped down on Christian's lap. The action made Catherine's right eyebrow twitch.

"I'd prefer not to think of it as an interrogation," Catherine said, staring hard at Lilith as the younger woman made herself comfortable. "You're not under arrest, so neither of you are being interrogated. And could you please get off him and sit down like a normal person?"

"No."

"Lilith…"

"No."

Catherine's face turned an almost puffy shade of red. She opened her mouth, no doubt in order to make some attempt at berating Lilith about propriety and how, just because she and Christian were permanently locked in their honeymoon phase, they should at least show a modicum of decency. Something along those lines.

"If it's that big of a deal, Lilith and I can just sit on the bed," Christian said before Catherine could speak. He then hooked an arm under Lilith's legs and another around her shoulder, stood up, and proceeded to the bed. After setting her on the soft comforter, he took a spot right next to her, close enough that their thighs were touching.

Catherine sighed. "I suppose that's better than nothing." With that small matter out of the way, she fixed the two with an unbending look. Whatever she wanted to talk about was serious, and she had no intention of letting either of them get off without telling her everything they knew. "Now, why don't you tell me what happened on that train?"

"Alright," Christian said. It would be good to talk to someone in authority about this. Maybe if they did, Catherine could convince the Las Vegas police department to lift the lockdown. Christian looked over at the young woman by his side and nudged her in the arm. "Lilith?"

She looked at him, understanding what he wanted from just that simple glance.

"Okay," she said, releasing a deep gust of breath. Her body shuddered once, as if reliving the memories of that night on the train. Christian wrapped an arm around her shoulder, and she did not hesitate to lean into him, drawing what comfort she could. When she refocused her attention on Catherine, the expression on her face was a little calmer, a little more confident. "I ran into a man named Nicholas when I was on my way to the restroom…"

***

There. It was done. It had taken a long time, much longer than any other system he'd broken into, but he'd finally managed to hack the security on the Catholic Church's network. But damn. Who knew that the Catholic Church would have a security system like this? Even the Executioners didn't have algorithms like this one did, and they were supposed to be the secret arm of the church itself.

Well, whatever. None of that was of any consequence now. All that mattered was downloading all the data he could before someone sensed the intrusion. After that, he could begin sifting through it to see what sort of dirty little secrets the Catholic Church was hiding that required such tight security. Whatever they had secluded away inside this network must have contained some serious dirt, something that could potentially cause the entire church to unravel at the seams.

Tristin discreetly plugged his USB into the computer. He technically wasn't allowed to download any information dug up on the Executioners' network into a portable hard drive. He would get in some major trouble if someone caught what he was doing, permission from Samantha be damned. Caution. He needed to be cautious here. Prudence would be his greatest ally.

Heh, he felt kind of like one of those ninja that Christian liked reading about so much. Gathering intelligence on a potential threat. The potential for death that would come if he was caught. Was this what every Executioner felt when they were on a mission? This heart-pounding adrenaline? If so, he could almost see why so many Executioners were enthusiastic about their work. It was an addicting, heady feeling.

It was unfortunate that Christian had never enjoyed his work. It was always business with him. That kid was just too straight-laced and up front. Well, he had been before he met Lilith.

"Hehe." Soft giggling erupted from Tristin's throat as he thought about what Christian and Lilith must be doing right now. "They're probably getting up to all kinds of naughty fun right about now."

Knowing succubi the way he did, it would not surprise him in the least if Lilith was using every opportunity she could to connect with him. It was, after all, the purpose for their existence. Connecting with others. Christian probably didn't even know how lucky he was. The bastard.

A very soft ping alerted him to the fact that his downloading was done. Acting with discretion and prudence, he unhooked the USB and slid it into a place where no one would even think to look for it. He then began the process of backing out of the security system and closing all of the backdoors and temporary stasis fields he'd been forced to erect in order to proceed further.

It was during this time, in which he had just finished backing out of the last checkpoint on the cyberspace network, that the doors to the Intelligence Division were blown wide open. Tristin, along with everyone else, turned in shock. Several dozen people, men and women, marched in with automatic rifles in their hands.

Long black jackets that trailed down to their booted feet ruffled and swayed as they strode in, looking prepared for war. Buttons ran diagonally at a slight angle up their jackets, starting from the waist. The material that made up the center was darker and a more matte color. It moved around the shoulders, creating sharp points that looked like soft armored shoulder pads before flowing down the back. A large collar covered the lower half of their faces, masking their lips and noses from view. On the front, stitched over the right breast, was a red cross with rose thorns covering it.

Who were these people? How did they get in? Why hadn't Tristin ever seen them before? These questions and more inundated him. There was definitely something wrong going on here.

The feeling of wrongness became even more pronounced when most of those people surrounded Tristin and pointed their guns at him. Not knowing what else to do, Tristin did what came naturally.

He made an ass of himself.

"Woah, woah!" He raised his hands in a friendly gesture. "Ease up on on the gun pointing, fellas. We're all friends here."

"Tristin Baluf," one of the men said.

This one was different from the others. For one thing, his trench coat was white. For another, it was possessing of a hood. Instead of buttons moving diagonally up one side, it relied on a series of buckles to keep its front together. It was impossible to see his face because of the hood and collar, but the glowing ice blue eyes underneath were more than just a little frightening. This difference in general aesthetics clearly marked him as the leader.

There was something else that caught Tristin's attention, however, something disturbing.

This person isn't human...

"You are hereby placed under arrest for treason against the Catholic Church. Your things will be confiscated, and you will be sent to a detention cell until we can determine your guilt. I suggest you come with us quietly," the man continued.

Well, this wasn't good. These people, whoever they were, suspected him of committing treason—which he had. Hacking into the Catholic Church's security network was definitely an act of treason. He was still surprised, though.

Tristin was sure he'd been careful not to get caught. He'd taken every precaution he could think of, including putting up a number of walls that acted as camouflage and made it appear like there was nothing but negative space there. How they managed to find him was a mystery, one that he would have liked to solve.

It really was too bad that he might not get the chance for a while. He was surrounded, they were pointing guns, and he was under arrest. What to do? What to do? He really didn't want to go with them, but he also wasn't sure he had any way of getting out of this situation unscathed without revealing more than he was comfortable with.

"Well? Are you going to come quietly?" the man asked.

Thinking the situation through for a few more seconds, Tristin eventually sighed and nodded his head.

"Yeah, sure. I'll come with you guys." Not like he could do much else. "Just make sure you don't ruin my computer when you're going through it in search of whatever you're trying to find on it, okay? I really do like that computer."

"Seize him!"

Tristin winced as his arms were forced behind his back and a pair of stun cuffs were put on him. They were a lot like handcuffs, except these would send several dozen volts of electricity through anyone trying to run away. If someone was shocked with them too much, they would become a vegetable. They were rather brutal devices, if he did say so himself.

As he was led out of the Intelligence Division's network chamber, Tristin lamented. Of all the days for Samantha to be out, it just had to be this one.

Life was so unfair sometimes.

***

Catherine sat in the chair she had commandeered in Christian's and Lilith's hotel room, leaning back, her arms and legs crossed, and a tired frown marring her face. She had listened to their tale on what had transpired since they parted ways, and she had only one thing to say about it.

"You two really don't know how to stay out of trouble, do you?" she asked with a demeanor somewhere between exasperated and amused. "If it were anyone else telling me this, I would have never believed them."

She knew she probably shouldn't be entertained by their hardships. Some of the incidents they told her about were horrendous, especially when they mentioned how the one called Nicholas had butchered the entire train, and then tried to assault Lilith. This was something that just didn't happen to normal people.

"But you believe us, right?" asked Lilith.

She had done most of the talking this time. Catherine could tell that it had been hard on the young woman. The stunning former blonde had, at some point during her story, crawled onto Christian's lap, clinging to him for comfort and support. Catherine hadn't had the heart to demand the young woman stop showing so much blatant affection during the telling, so she let things be.

"I don't have much choice," Catherine said, shaking her head back and forth. "You and Christian aren't the kind of people to lie, and I also know that neither of you would have killed an entire train of people. We also don't have anything else to go on. Nicholas Cruor is dead, so we can't ask him, and you two are the only witnesses left alive. Now the only problem is figuring out how to tell the story so it reveals what happened but doesn't divulge your identities."

"Do you have a plan?" asked Christian.

"No, but I'll think of something." Catherine stood up, tossing Christian a cellphone that he caught with his left hand. "I figured you wouldn't have one anymore after everything that's happened. When I've got a solid plan, I'll give you a call. Don't worry, that phone can't be tracked by anyone."

After staring at the cellphone, a thin smartphone in white casing with silver outlines, the young man proceeded to pocket it. He looked up at Catherine as she grabbed her coat off the chair and put it back on. The sleeves rustled as she stuck her arms through them, and then she made sure her collar straightened out.

"I'll leave you two alone now," she told them. "Try and stay out of trouble."

"It's not like we try to get in trouble, you know," Christian grumbled just a bit.

"Considering how much trouble you get into, I find that hard to believe." Catherine didn't give Christian the opportunity for a comeback as she left, closing the door behind her. She had work to do.

Chapter 24

Samantha really hated driving in Los Angeles. It was too congested. The streets had too many other vehicles moving about, the drivers were aggressive and inconsiderate, and some of them were quite stupid as well. Horns honked and engines revved. It was the sound of a chaotic symphony that could only be produced by a large city like this one. And Samantha absolutely despised it.

It had taken almost two hours just to reach her destination, and it took another thirty to find a parking space. All of the street-side parking spots had been taken, forcing her to find a parking garage. When she finally found a place to park her car, the area she happened to park at was a twenty minute walk from her destination. It had also cost her $30.00 just to use the garage.

Needless to say, she was not in the mood when she finally walked into the LAPD office. Looking around, her face set in a stern frown, Samantha walked up to the desk, where a young man sat, typing slowly on a keyboard.

"Excuse me." She coughed into her hand, getting the young man's attention. The boy looked up, taking a gander of her. Samantha grimaced when she saw the way his eyes traveled up and down her body, along with the blush on his face.

Why was it that almost every man she knew was a complete pig? Tristin. This kid. The Executioners that didn't hold to God's teachings—which consisted of about 90% of the Executioners anyway. The only person who wasn't a complete perv was Christian, and he was already… she shook her head.

No. Don't think about him, Samantha. If you think about how he chose to run off with some succubus instead sticking around, it's just going to make you want to cry… or strangle someone.

Where was Tristin when she needed him? He was always good for some therapeutic verbal abuse.

"I would like to speak to the Commissioner," Samantha spoke in her best *"I am superior to you in every way, so you'd better listen to me"* voice. She had a lot of practice making that voice, what, with being the leader of a sect filled with ruffians that the church hired to fight monsters.

"Uh…"

"Well?"

"R-right away, ma'am!"

Under the force of her glare, the young man scrambled to pick up the phone and press the button that would connect him to the man in charge of the LAPD. Samantha waited, arms crossed under her chest, staring down at the glasses-faced boy. She watched the way he eyed her nervously as he put the phone to his ear. His sense of urgency and fear was practically palpable.

"S-sir, there's someone here who wants to see you. No, I, uh, I don't think she has an appointment. A name? Um."

He looked up at her.

"It's Samantha D'arc."

He went back to the phone. "Samantha D'arc, sir. Oh, I, um, I see. Very well. Yes, sir. I'll send her right up." He hung up the phone, and then looked at her. "He said he'll see you now. Commissioner Fletcher's office is on the top floor. Last door on the right."

"Thank you."

Her hair swishing behind her, Samantha made her way into the elevator and up to the top floor. She really wished she could have taken the stairs, as she hated elevators, but this building had far too many floors for that. The ride was slow, but the doors eventually opened with a soft ping. Samantha made her exit, her heels clicking along the floor, until she came to the door that led into the Commissioner's office.

She knocked once.

"It's open!" A gruff voice called out from the other side. With such an invitation, Samantha could hardly refuse. She opened the door and walked in, observing her surroundings as she stopped directly in front of the desk, which a monster of a man sat behind. The large, hulking figure looked up at her, his rough voice rumbling. "I never expected someone like you would come to see me."

"Things change, and I find that I am in need of some... outside assistance." Asking someone for aid, and a person outside of the Executioners at that, was a bitter pill to swallow. Yet swallow it she did, even if doing so made her grimace.

"My assistance?" Commissioner Fletcher raised one of his bulky eye ridges. "That's new. Though we have worked together in the past, you never asked for assistance before. As I recall, even our most recent operation together, I had to practically browbeat you over the head to convince you to accept our aid." Placing his massive hands on the desk, the commissioner leaned forward. "Tell me, why should I help you now? What exactly is it that you even need help with?"

Samantha took a deep breath. "There has been some... suspicious activity within the Catholic Church. The new pope has made several decisions that don't make much sense, and I have been unable to shed any light on them."

"And you need help finding out what's going on in your own organization without evidence leading back to you, is that it?" he asked.

"Not exactly," Samantha hastened to correct the man's assumption. "I doubt there is any information you can dig up on the Catholic Church. They're a global community while the LAPD is stationed in Los Angeles and doesn't have any real authority outside of California."

"Then I'm not sure what you're coming to me for," Commissioner Fletcher confessed.

"Because, while the LAPD doesn't have much authority, they are one of the only forces within the US that are aware of the supernatural and have created their own division in order to deal with them. That is why I wanted to ask if I could have Sergeant Catherine Siegel and a small team from the SIU help me in a matter of great importance."

Commissioner Fletcher was silent for several seconds, his eyes panning to her face, studying her with the look of someone who had been around the block long enough to have a good deal of experience behind his belt. Samantha had seen this look before, on her master, the one who'd trained her in being an Executioner. It was not the kind of expression that could be gained from anything other than learning hard life lessons firsthand.

"You still haven't mentioned what you want the SIU's help with," he said at last.

"That's because I'm not exactly sure what the problem is myself," Samantha admitted reluctantly. "Recently, the pope has made several choices that undermine the Executioners' authority."

Her own division was proof of that. The pope had given the title of Bishop to Vertrou who, ever since he came to office, had been looking over the Executioners' shoulders—and Samantha's in particular. To top it off, the pope had stopped training orphans to become Executioners and had instead hired them from outside. Thanks to these changes, the Executioners' efficiency had dropped. Most of the newer members were no better than common thugs.

"So you don't like that this new pope of yours has been downgrading your forces and undermining your orders, and you want to find some dirt on him. Is that it?"

"That's not it at all." At least, that wasn't the only thing. "Ever since Pope Biesfial came into office, the Executioners have been weakening. Monster attacks have been happening with more frequency than ever before." Which was actually the reason for the SIU's creation. The Executioners had slipped, a cop discovered the existence of the supernatural, and the Supernatural Investigations Unit had been formed. "If it wasn't for one of my best operatives being so good at what he does, death rates in the western hemisphere would have skyrocketed."

And there was another point of contention. Christian was no longer with them. Her best operative, a young man who'd not only fought but defeated a high-class demon, an action that was previously considered impossible, was now on the run. Samantha was beginning to suspect foul play. It made sense. The assignment to slay a succubus, the reason this particular one was targeted. The church knew what would happen, or at least suspected that this would be the outcome.

Christian was an upstanding young man. He'd always been one who walked a straight path, never straying from what he believed was right. During his stint as an Executioner, he had done his duty with exemplary performance, taking out monsters of all kinds, not just vampires and werewolves, but also arachne, bunyips, cerastes, cyclops, gogmagogs, golems, gremlins, grendels, and dozens of other creatures. He never did it out of a sense of hatred or bloodlust, but because he felt it was the right thing to do. Christian always tried to do the right thing, regardless of what anyone else thought.

Which was why his actions had been so perplexing at the beginning. Why run off with a succubus? Had he forgotten his duty? Had he forgotten what succubi did to men? Those were her thoughts at first. She had assumed that he had been besotted by the succubus's Aura of Allure and run off with her.

It was only after Bishop Vertrou had come into her office, bearing a letter from the pope that stated she, and by extension the Executioners, were no longer in charge of dealing with Christian's desertion, that she had begun to suspect otherwise. Why else would the church make her send Christian on that mission if not to bring about this outcome? They knew of his strong moral fiber, and if that succubus was as innocent as reports seemed to claim, then the church knew he would not kill her. Christian was a destroyer of evil, not a cold-blooded murderer.

But of course, all this only brought up more questions. Why did they want to get rid of Christian? What were they hoping to accomplish? She had so many questions and nowhere near enough answers, which was why she had decided to seek outside help.

"I still fail to see where you are going with this," Commissioner Fletcher said. "Why do you need our help? What can the SIU do that your 'best operative' can't?"

"My best operative cannot do anything anymore." Samantha tried hard not to let her anger at losing Christian show. "He was branded a traitor a little over two weeks ago now. A massive manhunt was undertaken by the Executioners to bring him in, but the church, the pope, has commanded us to stand down and claimed they will deal with him."

Samantha clenched her fists while Commissioner Fletcher watched on.

"You have to understand; for the hundreds of years that the Executioners have existed, never has a pope made such attempts at undermining our authority and position. We have always been a part of the church, acting as their right hand and cleansing the world of those who would hurt humanity. However, Pope Biesfial has been pulling away from the Executioners. He's been undermining us and hampering our ability to do our job. We're no longer the force we once were."

"And now my best operative is on the run because the church ordered him to kill someone he should have never been tasked with killing in the first place. It's almost as if they wanted this to happen, like they're trying to weaken the Executioners for some reason." She bit her lip, struggling to keep her composure. "The problem is that I just can't see what that reason might be."

"That is why I am hoping for the SIU's aid," Samantha continued. "I want someone who works outside the Executioners and the church, who can act covertly without the Catholic Church being aware, to keep an eye out for Christian Crux, my operative, and lend him a hand. As the only police force with a foothold in the supernatural world, you're the only ones I can turn to."

"Hmm."

Commissioner Fletcher closed his eyes and hummed, a deep, rough rumble that built up in his throat. His brow ridges furrowed, face set in expressive contemplation. Samantha stood there, waiting for the man to say something with clenched fists.

"I understand where you are coming from," he said at last.

Samantha blinked in surprise. "Then you'll help?"

"Maybe." The commissioner held up a hand to forestall any argument that might erupt. "Before I can even offer my assistance, I need to speak with Catherine first. She is the one in charge of the SIU. However, Catherine is currently out of state, on loan to the Las Vegas police force due to an incident that occurred there a while ago."

That was disappointing news, but it couldn't be helped.

"I see. Do you know when she'll be back?"

"No. It depends on how long the investigation takes. It could be a few days, or a few weeks." Samantha grimaced. How disparaging. To think that the one time she needed help, and they couldn't give it to her. "However, I will send her a report letting her know what is going on here, and that she should get back to you as soon as she is finished."

So, there was nothing she could do but wait. That was not the answer that she'd been hoping for, but it was better than the worst case scenario, which was that she got no offer for aid. With this, there was at least a possibility of receiving some help. Even a tiny sliver of hope was better than nothing.

The sound of her phone ringing caused both her and the commissioner to stare at her pocket. She pulled the sleek mobile device from her purse. She stared at it, then at Commissioner Fletcher. He gestured to the phone, to which she nodded and placed the device against her ear.

"This is Samantha."

"*Samantha! Something bad has happened!*" a voice said from the other end.

"What is it? What's wrong?"

"*It's Tristin! He's been arrested for treason!*"

Samantha's eyes widened. "What!?"

As the woman listened to one of her people babble on the other end, a cold chill clenched at her heart. Like an iron fist, it squeezed, making her feel lightheaded and a tad faint. Tristin? Arrested? Had the church found out that he had been trying to hack into the Catholic Church's database? What about the data he was gathering? What would happen to him now? And more importantly, what should she do about it?

"Do you know where he is being kept?" she asked.

"No."

"Then find out now. I'm on my way back." She hung up the phone, then looked at Commissioner Fletcher. "I apologize, but it seems an emergency requires my attention."

Commissioner Fletcher nodded. "I understand. I'll be sure to inform Catherine that you were asking for her and tell her to give you a call when she comes back."

"Thank you."

Samantha quickly left the LAPD police department building, her mind a whirlwind of emotion.

Could this day possibly get any worse?

***

As Catherine's footsteps faded, Lilith stared at Christian, her lips downturned into a frown. "Why didn't you want me to tell her about our meeting with Titania?"

During their retelling of what had happened to them thus far, Christian had stopped Lilith from saying anything about Titania. Catherine knew nothing of their meeting with the Queen of the Summer Solstice.

"Because there isn't much that can be done about that," Christian answered with a shrug. "I don't even know what she was talking about, so telling Catherine that the balance of the world apparently rests on our shoulders wouldn't have done any good. And I'm not sure she would believe us, either, since I hardly believe it myself."

That made sense, she guessed. "So what do we do now?"

"We put our trust in Catherine and wait. We're all out of options, and right now, she's our only hope."

"And what should we do while we wait?"

Christian thought about that for a moment, then smiled. "Well," he began with exaggerated slowness, "we could always pick up where we left off? I do believe we were right in the middle of something important when Catherine interrupted us."

Lilith smiled. "We were, weren't we?"

With that, the two picked up what they had been doing before Catherine appeared.

It was a good thing that their neighbors were out hitting the casinos, or they would have undoubtedly complained about the noise.

Chapter 25

Samantha stormed into the Executioners' headquarters like a whirlwind. The doors to the entrance were slammed open with a *bang!* that resounded loudly in the small waiting room. Claire, who had been organizing some papers, was so startled by the noise that she let out a loud shriek and threw all the papers into the air, making them scatter across the floor.

"Oh, no!"

As the girl scrambled to grab all the papers that were now fluttering about, Samantha stomped into the room. She made a single sweep of the waiting room before her eyes landed on Claire, who was now on her hands and knees, trying to pick up and organize the papers.

"Claire!" Samantha snapped. Claire shrieked again, throwing the papers she'd been organizing into the air once more.

"S-Samantha!?" The young woman looked at her in shock, staring at Samantha with wide eyes as she stomped over to the downed brunette. Poor Claire shrank back when she saw the burning look in Samantha's eyes.

"Did Bishop Vertrou come in here recently?" Samantha asked.

"Uh, the Bishop?" Claire looked up at the ceiling, her face a reflection of deep contemplation. "Yes, actually. He was, now that I think about it. I wasn't on shift when he came in, but Amanda told me that Bishop Vertrou and several people dressed in strange-looking coats came in a few hours ago. Why do you ask?"

Samantha didn't answer. She was no longer paying attention. Her mind whirling, Samantha stood to her feet, her hair lashing around her like it was caught in a strong breeze as she took off at a fast trot. She went through the door leading to the elevator. When she pressed the button, the thing couldn't come fast enough. When it did come, she rushed in, waited until the elevator reached the next floor, and rushed out. By the time she reached the Intelligence Division's workplace, she was out of breath, huffing and puffing, with anxious sweat dripping down her brow.

She looked about the room, eyes searching, scanning the area. Several division members were there, all of them staring at her in shock. It wasn't often that she came to the Intelligence Division's workplace. She ignored the looks they were giving her and, after performing a cursory glance, she nearly let out the curse that wanted to escape her.

Tristin wasn't there.

Wanting an immediate answer to the questions now raging in her mind, Samantha stormed up to the nearest intelligence agent. The person who found themselves underneath her erroneous glare, a young man with thin arms and legs, and a head that reminded her of a basketball, tried to shrink backwards into his seat.

"Where is Tristin?" asked Samantha. When all the man did was stare at her with wide, frightened eyes, her lips twisted into an expression of displeasure. "Well! Where is he!?"

"H-he was taken away, ma'am." The answer came not from the man who found himself pinned by her paralyzing gaze, but from someone else.

Samantha turned to look at the person who'd spoken. It was an older woman. Crows feet crowded her eyes and laugh lines could be seen around her mouth. Shoulder-length brown hair with streaks of gray sat on her head in a messy bun. Her eyes were the color of the earth, a deep, dark brown. Like all members of the Intelligence Division, she was wearing their standard uniform, a long-sleeved turtleneck shirt, a knee-length skirt, a small shoulder cape, and a 9mm pistol strapped to her thigh.

"Taken?" Samantha narrowed her eyes at the older woman. "By Bishop Vertrou?"

"Yes. The Bishop came in with several dozen men and arrested Tristin on charges of treason."

This time, Samantha could not quite keep in the swear that escaped her mouth. Several members of the Intelligence Division gaped at her crass words, but she didn't pay attention to them, not to their looks, nor to the whispers that were undoubtedly about her. Instead, she whirled about, leaving the division room and stalking up to her office which, upon entering, she moved over to her chair and sat down with a heavy slump.

Nothing seemed to be going her way these days, ever since that mission to take out the succubus girl, in fact. That had been the catalyst for all this: Christian's desertion, Bishop Vertrou barging in and assuming control over the task of bringing her greatest Executioner to justice, and now this latest development along with everything in between that had happened to her. The entire world seemed to be doing its best to try and screw her over.

After burying her face in her hands, Samantha tried to compose herself and think rationally. There had to be something she could do to patch up this situation. This may have been an unprecedented predicament, but that didn't mean it was impossible to fix. She just had to figure out how.

She pressed the button on her intercom that opened a direct line to the front desk and spoke into the speaker. "Claire, I need you to call Amanda and tell her to come in right now."

There was a pause. *"Um, okay. I'll call her."*

"Thank you."

Samantha leaned back in her seat and looked at the ceiling. She was going to fix this mess, no matter the cost. She had to. The life of her best operative and good friend was on the line.

***

Ears twitched as the sound of clinking metal reached them. The pervading scent of blood and sterilizing agent pervaded his nose. Something cold and hard and made of metal was underneath his back. Steel, maybe. A table? He wasn't wearing anything. A cold breeze wafting across his front informed him of this fact. So he was naked? Hmm. Interesting. Someone must have stripped him. The question was: why?

He opened his eyes, only to blink when he found himself staring at his headless body. Now there was an interesting sight. How long had it been since he was last beheaded? Fifty years? One hundred? He hadn't lost his head since the last time he and the other kings tried to take over the human world. How long ago was that?

Frowning a bit, he established a stronger mental connect to his body, which was much harder than it sounded, and made it sit up. Two hands reached out and grabbed his head, lifting it and reattaching it to his neck. There was an uncomfortable moment where he felt his skin stitching itself together. One second passed, then two. He blinked, then tilted his head to the side, testing the strength of his neck. Everything seemed to be in working order.

Excellent. Now to business.

Wanting to know where he was, he turned his head to find out where the clinking noses were coming from. There was a woman standing several feet away, her back turned to him. She was unfamiliar. He didn't know her. Intriguing. The sound he heard, it must be a faucet. So she was washing her hands? No. There was another clinking sound, like metal against metal. She was cleaning something, then. Tools maybe. But what kind of tools?

He had his answer upon surveying the room further. Boring white walls, a table filled with mortician supplies, and one wall with large, steel cabinets. A morgue. So, after that Executioner guy had killed him, he'd been taken to a morgue where they tried dissecting him to see what he was made of.

A grin spread across his face. How exciting.

Standing up without making a sound, he got to his feet and slowly walked over to the woman. Now that he had a closer look at her, he could see that she was pretty hot. Those clothes might have been completely unflattering, but that tight, firm ass and those legs were amazing. He wondered if she was a screamer. It was unfortunate that he didn't have the time to find out.

Upon stopping directly behind the woman, he swiftly acted, reaching around and place a hand over her mouth, fingers clamping around her jaw. He pulled her backwards with a quick jerk, while simultaneously driving a knife-edge hand into her back.

Blood splattered across his hand, wrist, arm, body, and the floor in thick droplets. It leaked down the woman's body and stained her clothes. The woman jerked once, twice, and then went limp. Still grinning, he withdrew his hand from the woman's back, letting the limp body fall to the floor with a dull thud.

In his hand was a no longer beating heart, slightly pinkish, with blood leaking from the ripped arteries. He drew it to his mouth, inhaling the scent with relish. Slowly, as if savoring the moment, he took a large chunk out of the heart, moaning as an intense burst of flavor entered his mouth. It was a little sour, but there was a hint of sweetness. It was too bad he hadn't gotten the chance to make her feel despair. Hearts tasted the best when the person they belonged to died at the height of despair.

After he finished his meal, he looked down at the body of the woman. She was lying on her side. He turned her over with his foot, her left arm flopping uselessly to the floor. He crouched down, straddling her stomach and observing her face, the wide, dull eyes, slack-jawed mouth with blood dribbling down the sides, and black hair that had once been in a strict bun but was now in disarray.

"Hehe. Not as hot as that Lilith, but you're definitely still my type."

It was a shame that he'd been forced to kill her so fast. It was much more fun to make them suffer before killing them. He frowned as he continued to look at the woman. What should he do now? He wasn't one for corpses, but it seemed like a waste to just get rid of it. He was always horniest after just getting killed. Damn, he wished he knew where that Lilith was. She would be able to satisfy him, he was sure of it.

"Well, beggars can't be choosers, I guess."

He quickly began to strip the woman of her clothes, ripping off her police uniform. A low whistle escaped his lips when she was down to just her bra and panties. But damn, was this girl fit! How many women did he know who had abs like that?

A clicking sound alerted him to someone opening the door. He turned his head in time to see a person standing just inside the entrance, staring at him in open horror. White lab coat. Clipboard in hand. A scientist.

Clicking his teeth, he grabbed the nearest scalpel, one of several that lay scattered around the now half-naked woman, and threw it with pinpoint precision. The scalpel easily penetrated the flesh of the man's neck, carnelian liquid spurting out as the man pressed a hand to his throat instinctively. The scientist, wide-eyed and pale-faced, gurgled as he fell backwards, out of the doorway and out of sight.

A scream went up from the hallway beyond.

"Tch!" Standing up, he gave the corpse one last look of longing. "Too bad. I was looking forward to having some fun with you. Oh, well. You win some, you lose some. That's the way it's always been."

Whistling a jaunty tune, Nicholas Cruor walked out of the room, leaving behind a lot of blood and the body of the now deceased Kreya.

***

Catherine wondered if she should have taken the stairs. She had never liked elevators. They were small and uncomfortable, and she often felt claustrophobic whenever she was in one. Plus they were slow. What would take thirty seconds to reach via the stairs often took twice as long on an elevator. She knew that it was just her impatience acting up, but every second wasted standing around was another second she could be using to fix the mess that Christian and Lilith had found themselves in. She owed them, if for no other reason than they'd help take out a powerful and dangerous evil being.

Wanting to be at least somewhat productive, Catherine tried to come up with a plan, a course of action, if you will. Now that the truth was known to her, she should be getting ready to take steps to help ensure that the rest of this mission went smoothly. There was a lot that needed to be done.

First things first, she needed to speak with her team. They were the only ones who could know the truth, the full truth. She trusted them, and they her. Not to mention, if she wanted any of her plans to be successful, she was going to need them in on it. After presenting a plan to them, they would be able to help her rework it into something that would meet her new goals.

Raising her hand, Catherine checked the time on her watch. It was 10:45pm. She grimaced. Had she and those two really been talking for two hours? Though now that she knew what time it was, she realized that she was beginning to feel kind of tired.

It looked like she was going to need some sleep before deciding on a course of action.

As she left the Fermont Hotel, Catherine began walking back to her car. With the sun having gone down, the air outside was a little cooler, though not by much.

She walked into the parking lot and entered her car, a police vehicle that she'd been allowed to use for the duration of her stay in Las Vegas. Starting it up and hearing the engine thrum, Catherine pulled out onto the street. The lanes were mostly clear. Most of the people in the city were probably hitting up the casinos or something. Catherine was able to make it to the police station within twenty minutes.

Entering the station, she felt a slight wave of dizziness and realized that she was not merely tired, but completely exhausted. How long had she stayed up? When was the last time she'd slept? Well, regardless, she would definitely need to get some sleep now.

"Sergeant Catherine," Officer Gordon greeted her as she entered the police station.

"Officer Gordon," Catherine said, blinking. She absently rubbed at her eyes. They were beginning to feel droopy. "I apologize for asking, but I was wondering if you had a cot that I could set up in the office?"

They hadn't been given room and board when they'd been assigned this mission, so unless she wanted to pay for a hotel out of her own pocket—not happening—she needed to get some sleep at the police station.

"Of course. We've got several cots for when some of our men have to work overnight. They're over here in the supply closet," Officer Gordon said.

"Thank you."

Together, the two of them grabbed a couple of cots for her and her team. They then walked into the office, where Benson was still sitting behind his computer, typing away.

"You're back," the young man said, unnecessarily.

"I am," Catherine said as she set up the cots with Officer Gordon. When they were done, the man told her to let him know if she needed anything else before proceeding out of the room. When he was gone, she sat down on the cot and looked at Benson. "Have you found anything yet?"

"Not yet," he murmured, his eyes unblinking as he stared at the monitor like a man possessed. Catherine thought it was freaky how he could just sit there like that. She wouldn't say anything because his help was invaluable, but damn if it didn't creep her out. "I've been monitoring the various networks, but I haven't found anything. You?"

"I had a pleasant conversation with Christian and Lilith. Very illuminating. When the others get in, I'll inform you of what I know. And speaking of..." Catherine frowned as she realized that they were the only ones in the room. "... Where are Andy and Kreya?"

"I imagine Kreya is still at the forensics lab." Catherine nodded. "As for Andy, well, knowing him, he's probably gone out drinking or something."

Catherine felt a vein begin to throb on her forehead. "He'd better not have!"

She pressed a palm against her face, dragging it up and then running it through her hair. Benson must have noticed how tired she was, because he actually turned away from his computer to address her. "Listen, Sarge, why don't you get some shuteye? You're looking exhausted. I'll call you if anything comes up."

Catherine thought about it for a minute before relenting. Right now, it wouldn't have mattered if the whole team was there; she was too tired to think properly anyway.

Laying down on the cot, Catherine raised an arm and put it over her eyes. Just a little rest, she told herself. Once she'd gotten a few hours of sleep, she would be right as rain, or at least, that was her hope.

***

Catherine was startled awake by something vibrating in her pocket. She was so alarmed that she actually ended up falling right off the cot she'd been sleeping on, smacking her head against the floor with a loud *crack!*

"Very graceful, Sarge," Benson said from his place by the table. The young man was still typing away, making Catherine wonder if he'd even gone to sleep yet.

"Shut up, Benson," she groaned, rubbing her head as she sat up. The vibrating continued. It took a second for her to realize what exactly was causing it. When she finally figured it out, she reached into her pocket and pulled out her phone to see who was calling her at 4:35 in the morning.

The title on caller ID said Andy Fortis.

With a soft sigh, she accepted the call, held the phone to her ear, and said, "Andy, do you have any idea what time it is?"

There was a moment of silence. For a second, Catherine thought she had been cut off. Then Andy spoke from the other end. He sounded distressed. *"Sorry for the early call, Cathy. We, well, there's been a situation down at the forensic lab. You should come here, now."*

A problem at the lab? Really?

Catherine sat up straighter. "What kind of problem?"

"The—look it's—I don't want to tell you on the phone. Trust me, it'll be better if you come here and see for yourself."

That sounded ominous. Something was definitely wrong. Should she ask for specifics? She could make the order and Andy would obey, but, no, if he was saying this, then it was because whatever had happened was really bad. Better to see what he was talking about with her own eyes than be told over a phone.

"Alright, Andy, I'll be right there."

"See you soon."

She put the phone back into her pocket and stood up.

"Trouble?" asked Benson.

"Looks like something happened down at the forensics lab," Catherine said, grabbing her jacket and sliding her hands through the sleeves. Next she put on her heels. Fully dressed, Catherine was soon walking out the door. "If possible, I want you to get into the Las Vegas emergency hospital's network and see if you can pull anything up. Having another perspective can never hurt."

"Got it."

The last she saw of Benson was him going back to typing on his computer.

The parking lot was almost empty. She hadn't noticed it when she came in last night. Was it always this desolate? Or were the police at a crime scene? The hospital? Did that mean she was going to be the last one there?

Groaning, Catherine was quick to reenter her cop car, turn it on, and tear out of the parking lot. It was another short drive to reach the hospital, at least fifteen minutes. Thankfully, the streets still only had a few people driving that morning. With how distressed Andy sounded, she didn't want to spend an hour on the road.

By the time she arrived, the officers had already parked their cars out front in the fire lane, proving that she was, in fact, the last one to arrive. Why hadn't Andy called her sooner? Why hadn't Officer Gordon or anyone else said anything to her? As she walked forward, stewing, she noticed that the entire hospital was blocked off with caution tape, and she could see at least a dozen police officers standing by the front door.

Not that she couldn't see why. Reminding her very much of the scene on the train, the entire hospital looked like someone had taken a hose spraying out blood instead of water and let loose. Even though her only glimpse into the hospital was the sliding door entrance, she could see enough. More than enough. Just looking at the red splatters against the windows, the pulped mash of flesh and muscle lying strewn across the floor, made her stomach queasy.

Standing outside of the hospital doors with several other officers was Andy. He looked grim, his mouth set in a stiff line, face creased, and there was something else, something she couldn't quite identify, perhaps because it was such a foreign emotion on his face. Sadness. Loss. Anger. Pain. A conglomerate of emotions, all of them negative, mixed together and creating an expression that gave Catherine an uneasy feeling.

"Andy," she called out, walking over to him. He turned, his face looking, if possible, even grimmer. "What's the situation?"

"It's a massacre, Cathy, just like the train." He turned his head, staring into the window, then turned away just as quickly, his face turning green. "There wasn't a single person left alive. Everybody who'd been in that hospital was killed. Their bodies, well, there's not much of them." He gestured to the hospital doors, as if trying to emphasize his point, which really had no need for emphasizing at all. "As you can see."

Catherine grit her teeth. "How did this happen? Who could've—" her eyes widened as another realization struck her like a bullet to the head. "—Kreya!"

"Gone." Andy shook his head, his large hands clenched into fists. "She was—they suspect she was the first to die. Surprisingly, she's the only whole body they found in the entire hospital, though her heart was ripped out from her back."

"Her back? Ripped out?"

Another grimace. "It'll be better if you see for yourself. I don't think I can really explain it properly."

Catherine was led over to an ambulance that was parked next to the cop cars. The back was open, a stretcher set inside. On the stretcher was a body, one that she would recognize anywhere.

Her pace quickened.

It was definitely Kreya's body. She was lying on her stomach, nude. Bereft of clothes, her lightly tanned skin looked more than a little pale without blood flowing through her body. As Catherine stared at the corpse of one of her colleagues, she could see what Andy meant. There was a large hole located in her back, it looked like something had torn straight through her flesh, shattered her shoulder blade and ripped her heart right out in a single, brutal move. The inside of the mortal wound was somewhat visible. There was dark, oozing liquid seeping around the edges of the fist-sized canal, and she could see the muscle and sinew that lay beyond, strands of fleshy fiber that were an ugly pinkish-purple color.

Catherine clamped a hand to her mouth, both in horror and because the queasiness in her stomach had become a full-blown sickness. She swallowed the bile that threatened to escape her, trying to curtail her desire to vomit. Unable to withstand the sight any longer, and not wanting to see her comrade's corpse, she turned away.

"Do we know what happened?" she asked.

"Not yet," Andy admitted. "One of the reasons why no one contacted you until now was because no one actually knows what happened. We assume whoever did this cut the phone line and locked down the hospital before anyone could leave. They also destroyed the security system, so there's no way for us to access the video recordings. The only thing we know is that the body forensics brought in is missing."

Catherine turned to him. "Missing?"

"Yeah." Andy looked to be at a loss for words, much like Catherine felt. "No one knows what happened to it, but the body was gone when I arrived."

Catherine's hands clenched into fists. She felt like a hole had just opened underneath her feet, and she was falling down a dark pit in which nothing but doubt and incertitude lay in wait.

She took a deep breath, trying to calm her nerves. She needed to think rationally. She needed to come up with a plan. She needed to do something, anything, lest she find herself lamenting everything that had happened that led up to Kreya's death and this new mystery of a disappearing body.

"I'll give Benson a call and inform him of what happened," she said at last. "He should be able to do something, maybe hack into the hospital's mainframe and download the video files remotely."

"It sounds like a long shot," Andy said.

"It's also the only shot we have."

"I suppose that's true." Andy ran a hand through his hair, his shoulders slumping. He looked tired, Catherine realized. He probably hadn't gone to sleep yet. There were bags under his eyes and his face was looking a little gaunt.

"Why don't you go back to the station and get some rest?" she suggested softly.

"Can't," Andy grunted, "I need to stay here with—" he cut himself off, but she understood. Catherine saw his eyes divert to the motionless form of Kreya. The hard-as-nails woman and Andy had never seen eye-to-eye, but they were two of the only non-human officers in her force, so they tended to look out for each other.

Well, Andy tried to look out for Kreya, despite the woman thinking he was being a chauvinistic pig because of his old-fashioned views.

"Alright," she conceded. "I'll be heading out then. I need to inform some people of this new development. If what I suspect is true, they may be in danger."

"You're talking about—" once more cutting himself off, he looked about the area to see if anyone was spying on them. No one was within hearing distance, and the closest person near them was a paramedic standing near the front of the vehicle. "—You're talking about Christian and Lilith, right?"

Catherine nodded. "Yes. I'm going to bring them to the police station, as I suspect whoever did this may be after them."

"I gotcha. Okay then." Andy straightened up. "I'm gonna take care of Kreya. The least I can do is see to it that she's treated with respect and dignity."

"In that case, I'll see you later."

"Right."

As she walked away, a small frown crossed Catherine's face. She already had a hunch on what happened, given her conversation with Christian and Lilith, but she really didn't want to believe her own theory. Before jumping to conclusions, it would be best to speak with someone who had more experience with the scene before her, someone who would be able to offer some valuable insight.

And currently, there were only two people she knew who could do that.

Chapter 26

Andy watched Catherine leave, his left hand reaching to the back of his head, where he began to scratch at his neck—it was prickling something fierce; the smell of blood sometimes did that—with a look of awkward remorse. He couldn't even begin to imagine what his sergeant must have been going through. He was hurt, but Catherine took anything that went wrong personally.

Catherine Siegel was a woman who liked to do things herself. She never foisted her work onto anyone else, and she always tried to take on the heavy tasks without help. That she was leaving him in charge of looking after Kreya and heading up the rest of the investigation, when she knew he wasn't much for detective work, must have meant this situation was really getting to her.

A look back at the body of Kreya caused his face to twist into an unpleasant expression. He could see why this would be an issue for her. Catherine took her responsibilities very seriously. To her, the protection of each member of the SIU was a part of that responsibility. She probably knew that protecting everyone wasn't possible, but to lose a member of a team she'd handpicked herself only a few days after their investigation began was a severe blow.

Speaking from personal experience, he didn't know why she would think that way. An event like this was unprecedented. No one could account for a situation that they had never seen before.

Catherine wouldn't think that way, though.

"Excuse me," a voice said.

Blinking himself out of his thoughts, Andy turned around. A thin man with brown hair tucked under a cap and a gaunt face stood behind him. The paramedics outfit signified him as the emergency vehicle's driver.

"Can I help you?" asked Andy.

"I was just wondering what you would like me to do with, eh, well, your friend," he began, looking uncomfortable. "I mean, did you want her taken to the next hospital or something?"

Andy frowned. "Don't worry about that. I'll be handling Kreya."

"Ah, well, I can't just let you deal with the body. There are protocols that I need to follow when it comes to things like this, you know." The man squirmed under Andy's stare.

"Look," Andy began, his voice as patient as could be given the circumstances, "I don't really care for your protocols or whatever. That's my friend lying on that stretcher, and I'm not gonna let some creep I don't even know take her body somewhere. You got that?"

"G-got it!" The man squeaked. "Ah, in that case, I'll just, um, let you get to it then. Heh. Heh heh."

"Since you're going to leave this to me, you can leave now."

The man couldn't get away from the emergency vehicle fast enough, and with him gone, Andy was able to walk over to Kreya's body. He looked over the young woman's figure, taking note of how pale her skin now looked. She wasn't quite ghostly white, but the tan she'd been sporting from being out in the sun so much was now gone.

Andy shifted his attention to the gaping hole in her back. Just seeing that wound made his blood boil. If he ever caught who did this, they were going to suffer.

Grabbing a small medical sheet from a cabinet in the vehicle, Andy carefully laid it over Kreya's body. As he did this, the prickling hairs on the back of his neck became more pronounced, causing a chill to run down his spine.

It was the only warning he had before something viciously tore into his shoulder.

Blood splashed against the walls of the paramedic vehicle.

***

While she was driving down the street, Catherine brought out her cellphone and quickly flipped through the list of numbers before reaching the one that belonged to the phone she'd given to Christian. Pressing the call button and holding the phone to her ear, she waited until someone answered. A frown marred her features when, after ringing several times, the phone went into voicemail. "tsking," she called again, twice, in fact, before someone finally picked up.

"H-hello?" came the tired yawn on the other end. It was Christian. He sounded like he'd been just about to fall asleep.

Catherine shook her head. She didn't want to know why he sounded so exhausted. She really didn't.

"Christian, I need you and Lilith to meet me outside the Fermont Hotel right now. A new situation has developed."

"What kind of situation?" asked Christian. The sound of rustling could be heard from the other end. She sincerely hoped that noise was the kind that came from two people getting dressed.

"The kind that involves an entire hospital of people being massacred in the same way the train you were on was," she answered.

"W-what!?"

"Look, I'll explain everything when I see you. Just come outside the Fermont Hotel. I'll be in the LVPD vehicle outside."

"... Right. Okay. We'll see you then."

Catherine hung up the phone and focused on driving to the hotel. She flipped the switch on her patrol lights, turning them on. The sound of sirens filled the air as her car picked up speed. She drove down the lane far faster than was safe or legal, other cars moving out of the way for her. Those that didn't move quickly enough, she swerved around like a psychotic stunt driver. It was insane driving, reckless even, but Catherine didn't care. She was in a hurry.

When she reached the Fermont Hotel, Christian and Lilith were already standing out front. They were dressed, thankfully, Christian in his black jeans, black shirt, and orange hoodie, and Lilith in a pair of blue jean pants, a formfitting white t-shirt, and a pair of gladiator strap sandals. The guitar case that she had given them over a week ago in California was at their side.

Pulling up, the tires screeching as the car skidded to a halt, Catherine rolled down the window nearest them and gave both a demanding glare.

"Get in!"

They promptly complied.

As soon as they were in the back of the vehicle, Catherine drove off, the tires squealing as she floored the gas and sped away at a speed that was in no way safe. Neither Lilith nor Christian were buckled in yet, and both were sent sailing across the backseat, Christian hitting the door while Lilith landed on his chest, causing the young man to let out a loud "oof!" as all the air was expelled from his lungs.

"By the Almighty, Catherine! What's the rush!?"

"The rush is that I've got an entire hospital full of dead people, including one of my subordinates, and you two could very well be next on that list if my hunch is correct. Now shut up, sit down, and buckle up!"

The two, completely baffled by her snappish reply, could do nothing more than what she commanded of them. They strapped themselves in and held on for dear life as Catherine made like the fast and the furious, only even faster and ten times more furious.

By the time they arrived at the station, Lilith was green in the face and Christian looked more than a little ill himself. Catherine did not give them any time to get their bearings as she got out of the car. They were forced to exit as well, quickly—Christian barely managed to grab his guitar case, as she picked up the pace, her long legs carrying her across the parking lot with powerful strides.

"So, will you tell us what happened now?" asked Christian as he moved to catch up. Lilith was tagging behind him, her hand firmly clutching at his.

"We don't know everything that happened," Catherine quickly started to explain the situation, even as she pushed the door to the police station open. "However, some time in the past several hours, the entire Las Vegas emergency hospital was massacred. Everyone who was there at the time is now dead. The manner in which they were killed is exactly the same as the slaughter on the train."

While Lilith nearly stumbled at the mention of the train ride to Las Vegas, Christian was frowning, his eyes narrowed in thought. They entered the police station. Christian and Lilith followed behind her.

"And there's something else you guys should know," Catherine spoke again. She looked at the two out of the corner of her eye. "The body of Nicholas Cruor, the man that you killed, wasn't at the hospital, which is where we left it."

Christian's body nearly went rigid, a remarkable feat considering he was walking. "What do you mean by that?"

"I mean just what I said. Nicholas Cruor's body was taken to the forensics lab inside of the Las Vegas hospital. I had one of my own members, Kreya Fairbanks, studying the body to see if she could find anything the Las Vegas Police's forensics team might have missed. Now Kreya is dead and the body is missing."

Biting his lower lip, Christian struggled to come up with a viable explanation that would shed some light on this new information. "There are only two possibilities I can think of to explain what happened. Either Nicholas wasn't working alone, and he had someone waiting in the shadows to dispose of the body and everyone who saw him in case he failed…"

"Or?" Catherine asked.

"Or," he breathed deeply, "he isn't human."

Silence met his proclamation. Catherine actually stopped in front of the door that she had led them to and turned to face him. Lilith, while not appearing shocked by the news, trembled as though her worst fears had been confirmed.

Christian continued. "My best guess is that he's some kind of demon. There are a number of demonic entities who are immortal in some form or another. Surviving having their head chopped off would be simple for them."

Demons were some of the most varied among all known non-human entities. There were hundreds of different types of demons, maybe even thousands. Their powers varied as much as their species. The reason for this was because most demons were actually born human.

There were two ways that a human could become a demon. The first was simple. Humans died. After they died, they were judged. Those deemed sinners were sent to one of the nine circles of Hell based on the sins they had committed. There, they suffered, and in their suffering, their bodies became a physical manifestation of their sins. The more powerful the sin, the more powerful the demon.

The second way was for a living human to become a demon. Arcane rituals existed in which humans could give up their humanity in exchange for power, thus turning into a demon. Another way for them to become demons was for their sins to be so great that a demon on the same level as Abaddon felt their sins like ripples on a pond and reached out to them, enticing them into becoming that which was no longer human.

"I know of at least seven demons who are said to be immortal and capable of regenerating from any wound," Christian continued. "Asmodeus, Belphagor, Beelzebub, Leviathan, Lucifer, Mammon, and Satan. They are the Seven Demon Kings who are said to rule over the nine circles of hell."

"You're kidding, right?" asked Catherine.

"I am not."

"You're telling me that the demons from the bible are all real?" Catherine asked.

"Of course they're real," Christian said. "How do you think we know that the bible is true? We know that the bible is true because the demons listed in it are real. There are recorded documents from a group of Executioners who fought against one of the Seven Kings of Hell within our archives."

Catherine wanted to shake her head and deny everything that Christian had told her, but even though she wanted to, she wouldn't. That would have been irresponsible.

"What can you tell me about them?" she asked.

"I don't know a whole lot about the Seven," Christian admitted, his audience listening on in rapt attention. "Very little is actually known about them other than their names. However, it is said that these are the seven most powerful demons known to man, and that each one is capable of destroying an entire country."

Beside him, Lilith's shaking intensified. Her fear was almost palpable. Christian noticed this, or maybe he felt it. Catherine wasn't sure. He turned to the young blonde and pulled her to his chest. As his arms wrapped around her, Lilith let out a slow, shuddering breath, and relaxed in his embrace.

Catherine found herself feeling slightly sorry and slightly envious of the young woman. A succubus Lilith may have been, but it was clear to her that all this was beyond Lilith's ability to deal with. Despite her origins, she was just a normal girl who wanted normal things in life.

The envy came because she had Christian. Catherine did not have any desire for the man. He was attractive, to be sure, but he wasn't her type. She preferred bright and sunny personalities over his enigmatic and brooding ones.

Then again, maybe Lilith just saw a side of him that she didn't get to see. Who could say for sure?

Getting back to the topic at hand, Catherine penetrated the young man with her piercing gaze. "So you're telling me that we may have one of the Seven Kings of Hell coming after us?"

With Lilith still in his arms, Christian tilted his head, his raven hair swaying ever so slightly and his eyes narrowing in thought. He licked his lips, wetting them. "I don't know. Possibly. I don't know much about the Seven Kings of Hell, though I do know that they cannot pass the gates of hell and enter the human world. At least, their physical forms cannot pass through. There is supposedly some kind of barrier surrounding the gates leading to Hell that keep the Seven Kings from leaving. However, while their bodies cannot leave Hell, their spirits can."

"How does that work?" Catherine asked, brows furrowed and a small frown creasing her lips.

"Possession," was the answer she received. "Their spirit forms leave Hell, passing through the gates. The gates, as I understand them, are not meant to hold weaker demons, and when one of the Seven Kings are in spirit form, they are substantially weakened. This allows them to slip through. Once in the human world, they can then move on to possess a person whose biggest sin matches the one with which they're personified by."

The Seven Kings were an unusual bunch. Each king was the personification of one of the seven deadly sins. Wrath. Avarice. Sloth. Pride. Lust. Envy. Gluttony. The seven most deadly sins one could commit. Each sin held great power, power which demons could feed upon. It was for this reason that the Seven Kings had taken one of those sins into themselves in order to increase their own already substantial power.

"Do you think that's what's going on here?" asked Catherine. "Maybe this human was possessed by one of the Seven Kings of Hell?"

In response to her words, Christian's face twisted, morphing into a self-reluctant grimace. "It's possible, though I'm hoping it's something else. I really don't want to go up against one of the Kings of Hell, even one weakened from possessing a human. They're considered the strongest among demonkind for a reason. Even if they have less than a tenth of their true strength, they'd still be more than a match for any human. What's more, without knowing which one of the seven kings we're up against, defeating them is going to be impossible."

At the small interval of silence brought on by Christian's words, Lilith, her face still buried in his chest, finally spoke up. "Why is that?"

Christian answered, his brow furrowing as he drudged up long unused knowledge. "According to the ones who taught me demonology when I was training to be an Executioner, the Seven Kings of Hell each have exactly one weak point, an Achilles heel, if you will, that, when hit, will kill the body they inhabit and send them back to Hell."

"Then it's only temporary?" asked Catherine, raising an eyebrow.

"Of course. You can't kill a demon like that. The Seven Kings of Hell are immortal in every sense of the word." Christian paused, tilted his head, and then shook it. "Though it's not like anyone's ever fought one of them in their true form to find out if they can be killed."

"So, to defeat one of them, we need to find their weak point?" Catherine continued.

"Yes."

"And how do you find out where their weak point is?"

"I don't know." Christian gave a helpless shrug. "There has only been one time in the entire history of the Executioners where someone fought and defeated one of the Seven Kings, Lucifer, if I remember correctly. According to the tomes that existed back then, Lucifer's weakness was the Solar Plexus. However, Lucifer's is the only one that we know about."

"So, to sum things up, you're basically saying that unless we can find out who we're fighting against, and then determine where their weak point is, we're screwed?" Catherine said after a long, drawn-out pause.

She was not pleased with this information. Not that anyone would blame her. The situation was volatile enough without have to worry about facing off against one of the seven most powerful demons in existence.

"That's only if we're fighting against one of the Seven Kings, though," Christian opined, his assurances said more to ease the girl in his arms than because he actually believed his own words. Catherine could see what he was doing clear as day, and she assumed Lilith did too. Yet the reassurance and physical contact still appeared to work wonders on easing the young woman's mind. "We might be fighting against something else. I'm not sure what other creatures there are that possess immortality, especially ones that can disguise themselves as human, but there's a lot about this world and the many creatures in it that I still don't know about."

His words rang true enough. Even after a thousand years of existing, the Executioners were finding new monsters all the time, or rather, they were only now discovering them. Either way, within the past year, there had been several different monsters that had been added to the classifications list. Christian told Catherine that he suspected there were many more that no one had discovered yet.

"And do you think what we're up against is one of these unknown creatures?" asked Catherine.

"I don't know." Christian sighed, his eyes closing. "We could be, though I'm not sure if that's any better. I would personally prefer it if we were up against one of the Seven Kings of Hell. At least then I would be able to put a name to my enemy."

"Well, hopefully, we'll be able to find out what we're up against soon."

With that, Catherine stopped dithering and opened the door. She entered quickly and took a sweep of the room as Christian and Lilith trailed in after her. Benson was still there, just as she'd hoped. He was typing away at his computer, his fingers moving across the keyboard. They were moving so fast that his fingers sounded like the beating of a hummingbird's wings.

"Benson," Catherine said without much ceremony and quickly got right to the point. "Have you been able to recover any of the hospital's security videos?"

"Just two," Benson told her. "The security surveillance room was destroyed not longer after that Cruor guy went on his rampage. I suspect it was the first thing he hit after locking the hospital down."

"What? Rampage?" Lilith asked.

Catherine had also caught his words. "What do you mean? Cruor is dead."

Benson shook his head. "Just come here and watch the video."

Catherine, Christian, and Lilith walked up until they were standing behind Benson. The somewhat nerdy-looking man looked up, finally realizing that his boss wasn't alone and had brought some company. He gazed at Christian for a moment, and then looked at Lilith.

…

"Ouch!" Benson's eyes went back to Christian, glaring, his hands holding the top of his head where the younger man had smacked him good. "What the hell was that for!?"

"You were staring."

"So? She's hot!"

"She's also with me. Stare at her like that, and I'll hit you so hard your head will cave in."

"God, the hell is your problem, man—Yeowch!"

"Don't use the Lord's name in vain either."

"What are you? Some kind of religious freak or something—Ack!"

"Or something," Christian commented, absently shaking out the hand he'd been using to smack Benson with. "Your subordinate's got quite the mouth on him." He regarded Catherine with a raised eyebrow. "Don't they teach discipline in the police department?"

Catherine sent him an uncaring look. "They do, but unlike the Catholic Church, swearing isn't something we discourage."

"I had hoped you would, but then, I suppose I can't blame you. All of the newer Executioners are pretty foul as well." Christian offered them a self-depreciating smile. "Of the nearly fifty-thousand members we have, only the members of the XIII, and a few whose faith in God was strong, didn't swear. The rest, well…" he shook his head, "they aren't even Catholic."

"So there are people working for the Catholic Church who don't follow the religion themselves?" asked Catherine, frowning. That didn't make any sense. Why have someone work for a religious organization if they didn't share that religion's beliefs?

"The Executioners is a separate branch from the church, not exactly a part of the church, but not separated from it either. I suppose you could say we're like the dark side of the church. We do what they cannot."

"But why have people who aren't Catholic work for you?" Catherine pressed.

Christian ran a hand through his hair. "Desperation, mostly. We don't really have much choice in who we recruit these days. They were orders from the pope, who told us that with the amount of monster attacks growing each year, we can no longer afford to be selective about who we accept into the Executioners' ranks. You have to understand, there aren't that many people out there who have what it takes to be an Executioner, and even less of those people are Catholic."

Slowly, as though coming around to the idea like a snail, Catherine nodded. "I can see where you're coming from. You're probably right in that not everyone can do what you do."

"Exactly."

"Not to break up this fascinating conversation," Benson interrupted, his tone dry. "But I've pulled up those video files you wanted, Catherine. So, if you two could just stop talking and pay attention, that would be nice."

His words were met with two glares, but those looks of aversion were soon diverted toward the monitor and changed to an intense focus. There, on the screen, was a video of the forensics examination room. They watched as the body on the table, the one belonging to Nicholas Cruor, came to life. They saw it grab its own head and set it back onto its shoulders. They watched as the flesh on its neck seemed to stretch and turn into some kind of ooze-like liquid before the severed head was once more connected to the body.

They watched as it got up. Watched as it moved across the room. Watched as it killed Kreya by stabbing her through the back with its hand, ripping out her heart. The group was even given the gruesome sight of the man gorging himself on the organ.

Lilith, unable to bear the sight, buried her face in Christian's chest, her body heaving as if she were about to lose her lunch. Meanwhile, both Christian and Catherine remained stoic, though the female Sergeant was gritting her teeth with barely suppressed emotion as she glared at the monitor.

When the video ended, Christian was the person who spoke first. "At least now we know a little more about what we're dealing with. Nicholas Cruor is definitely not human. I am also almost positive that we are dealing with one of the Seven Kings of Hell."

The time of the video was 11:53pm, which meant it had happened sometime after Catherine had been talking to Christian and Lilith. A glance at the clock now revealed it to only be 7:08am, meaning very little time had actually passed.

Catherine rubbed at her eyes, feeling the way they wanted to droop. She had been up all day yesterday, and she had stayed awake well into the night and this morning. Tired. She was so tired.

Chancing a look at the two lovebirds, she saw that both of them looked tired as well. Christian masked it well, but she could see the slight sag in his shoulders and the small bags under his eyes. Lilith, on the other hand, looked dead on her feet. Her half-lidded eyes had large bags underneath them, like a rim of black eyeliner that had gotten smudged, and her shoulders were slumped. Catherine was sure that the poor girl would have been swaying in place were it not for Christian holding her around the waist, allowing her to lean into him. She almost looked as tired as Catherine felt.

They were probably having sex well into the morning.

She was not jealous. She wasn't.

"Would you like to use a cot?" asked Catherine, gesturing to the four cots she'd set out for her team last night.

"Uh, no. Thank you, but I'm fine," Lilith said, but she was interrupted by Christian, who shook his head.

"You're not fine," he countered, giving her a mild look. "You're exhausted." Lilith opened her mouth to say something, but he silenced her by gently placing a finger against her lips. "Don't try and say otherwise. Everyone can see how tired you are, especially me." He smiled down at her. "You don't need to try and act tough for me. I know you're not some little girl who can't do anything for herself, but just because you're capable doesn't mean you should run yourself into the ground either. Got it?"

Lilith was blinking at him, her eyes staring into his with the kind of intensity someone had only when they were searching the depths of another person's soul. After nearly a full minute of staring, Lilith eventually nodded, her hands going up to clasp the one that Christian had placed near her mouth.

"Okay," she said, kissing his finger. Catherine rolled her eyes. These two acted so couple-y with each other, it was disgusting.

She was also seriously not jealous.

Before anything else could happen, a loud sound blared from outside the station. It was a sort of shrieking, yowling sound, like a car alarm, only ten times louder and a hundred times more obnoxious.

"What's that?" asked Lilith.

"That sounds like an emergency response vehicle," Catherine murmured, confused.

Christian cocked his head to one side, his eyes tapering into a slight, concentrated glare. "Whatever it is, it's getting louder."

Everyone remained silent, listening to the sound of the siren blaring. It was definitely getting louder. Each second that passed, the volume seemed to rise, turning what had once been a blaring siren into a loud, keening wail that echoed off the walls.

Lights appeared in the window on the eastern side of the room. Catherine only had enough time to widen her eyes as the wall directly in front of Benson exploded inwards. A shower of rubble flew through the air as an emergency response vehicle plowed through the wall with the force of several thousand tons. Benson, who did not have the reflexes or physical conditioning of a standard police officer, could not get out of the way in time.

His body was pelted by rubble, one large brick smashing his face in, while the others impacted him with bone-shattering force. Then the vehicle ran straight into him. Benson stood no chance. The speed the large vehicle was moving at combined with its weight ensured that when it hit the intelligence analyst, it didn't just kill him; it tore his body apart.

Large chunks of what had once been a body were thrown through the air. Blood splashed everywhere, striking the vehicle and covering the ground. Catherine, Christian, and Lilith could only stare on in horror as someone who'd been right next to them suddenly became a literal stain of blood and raw chunks of meat.

Lilith lost whatever was left of her dinner. She bent over, hurling several chunks of food and liquid from her mouth. Christian and Catherine were too experienced to follow suit. They prepared for the worst.

The door to the vehicle opened and out walked a man. After recovering from losing her dinner, Lilith froze in shock, while Catherine whipped out her gleaming silver Desert Eagle Mk XIX Hand-Cannon. At the same time, Christian moved swiftly in front of Lilith and kicked open the guitar case. Another kick sent his two swords hurtling through the air, straps and all. Like something out of a video game, he swayed his body, allowing the straps to fall exactly as he wanted them to, and then proceeded to tighten them around his torso. He did the same thing to his guns, holsters and all. Once he was finished, Gabriel and Phanuel were whipped out of their holsters and pointed straight at the grinning, gaunt face of Nicholas Cruor.

"Hello everybody. I hope you're all ready to die today."

No one in the destroyed office moved. No one blinked. Hardly anyone even dared to breathe.

Except for him.

Nicholas took in a deep breath, a disturbingly cheerful smile on his sunken, deranged features. He looked at the three people inside of the room.

He passed over Christian after a second's worth of observation, as if the young man wasn't worth his time before moving on to Catherine. His gaze lingered on her a bit, his look appreciative.

"Not bad. Not bad at all." He grinned at her, causing the SIU Sergeant to shudder in disgust. There was something wrong with that grin. It was more than just deranged and lustful. Only a special kind of sicko could smile like that after committing the acts this monster had. "You and me will definitely be having some fun later."

As Catherine's grip on her gun tightened, Nicholas's gaze landed on Lilith. His eyes lit up.

"Well, hello there, babe. Did you miss me?"

Lilith began to shake. Her breathing became quick, harsh, hyperventilating pants. Blue eyes grew wide, pupils dilated in fear, and her body broke out into a cold sweat.

Christian saw this and decided that enough was enough. With loud, thunderclap-like bursts, he pulled the triggers on Phanuel and Gabriel, unloading a full salvo into the man before them. Nicholas did absolutely nothing to move this time. He took the bullets head on.

His body jerked this way and that as each bullet smacked into him, penetrating his flesh. A round tore through his shoulder, jerking it back as blood spurted out of the wound like a faucet. Another hole appeared in his left calf. The sound of bones splintering was overpowered by the twin roars of Gabriel and Phanuel. More and more small wounds appeared, causing Nicholas's clothes to become stained crimson.

Each clip had exactly fifteen rounds, and Christian was a damn good shot. All thirty bullets struck their target with pinpoint precision. A shot to the kneecap, the shoulder, the jugular. Each bullet hit something vital. Several were headshots.

Even after Christian's guns were spent, emitting a *click-click* that let him know there were no more bullets, he continued glaring at the body of Nicholas. A body that was now bent backwards at an awkward angle, with blood pouring out of multiple wounds and a leg whose femur had been splintered by a bullet. He watched, and he waited, wondering if he should reload his guns. There were only six clips left. That meant three for each gun. He didn't want to use them all at once if he could help it.

But then, just as he was thinking that maybe he'd won, a loud, hissing sound came from the body that had just been pumped full of lead. Catherine, Christian, and Lilith were all forced to watch, horrified, as the bullets were pushed out of the skin and the flesh knit itself together, smoke wafting off the wounds as they were sealed shut.

Nicholas's torso came back up, straightening to reveal a grinning face with bloodshot eyes that were overflowing with a twisted kind of lust. No longer brown, they gleamed brightly, two glowing orbs the color of a blood-red dawn. The twig-like man cracked his neck once, then twice, with a sickening crunch that caused Christian's stomach to feel more than a little queasy.

"Mm mm mm." A strange chuckle emerged from Nicholas's throat. His mouth was closed, muffling it. There was a smile on his face, bright and cheerful and filled with sadistic glee and the intent to cause harm. "Did you enjoy that? Did it make you hot and bothered? Seeing my body get penetrated by dozens of your balls? I hope you did." His smile widened into a face-splitting grin. "Because I am going to have so much fun ripping the flesh off your bones and penetrating your body with my own steel."

Christian did not swear, but he wanted to. By the Almighty did he want to let loose with something foul and vulgar. This man, Nicholas, was most definitely not human. Neither was he a vampire or a werewolf. They wouldn't have died from getting shot with normal bullets either, but they would have taken much longer to recover, too. He was, most certainly, a demon of great power.

"Your name?" Christian demanded, his eyes narrowing. "Your real one. What is it?"

Nicholas smiled. "Now why would I tell you my name?"

Christian holstered his guns and unsheathed his blades. He stepped directly in front of Lilith, shielding her as he raised the gleaming silver and black swords, pointing them at the being before him. "Because I want to know the name of the demon I'm going to kill."

"Ho?" Nicholas's eyes seeped with amusement, glittering like a thousand daggers in the moonlight. "So confident, are you? I like that. I like that very much. It'll make killing you all the better. Very well, my name is Asmodeus," the demon said, performing a very formal bow at the waist. When he straightened back up, Christian and the others got a glimpse of two small, almost unnoticeable horns sticking out of the creature's forehead. "A pleasure to meet you."

This time, Christian did curse. Of all the Seven Kings of Hell they could have faced off against, it just had to be the one who was the personification of lust. Was this some kind of karmic justice or something? Or was Murphy just trying to screw with him?

Christian tried to recall everything he knew about the being standing before them. Asmodeus, like the other Seven Kings of Hell except for Satan, was originally an angel that had joined Lucifer's rebellion and was eventually cast out. There were many stories told about him, but the one

Christian knew the best was from the deuterocanonical Book of Tobit, and the legends concerning the construction of the Temple of Solomon.

He was also the one who turned humans with intense sexual desires into demons, twisting the lust they felt into something depraved, perverting them in ways few things could.

There were no records of anyone having knowledge of Asmodeus's weakness. There had been rumors that, around six hundred years ago, an army of Executioners had fought against him, but nothing had ever been confirmed. The army that had gone out to battle never returned.

This is really not good.

Catherine seemed to understand how much trouble they were in as well. Holding her gun in both hands, she fired off a round. The Desert Eagle in her grip had some serious recoil. As the shot was fired, both her arms were launched upwards to point at the ceiling.

It also packed some serious firepower. The bullet, a well-placed shot to the torso, tore right through Asmodeus's body like it was made of wet paper. Blood, bone, muscle, and what looked almost like liquidized organs flew all over the room, splashing against the floor, ceiling, and walls with powerful, wet, slapping sounds.

Asmodeus stared down at the hole on the left side of his torso. It was large and gaping, with blood leaking out of it like a river, pouring in thick, gushing rivulets down his body. The edges of the skin were frayed, too, as if the bullet had not just torn through the skin but shredded it apart while setting the edges on fire.

Five more rounds, sounding out like the blasts of a cannon, echoed within the room. Each shot tore another hole through Asmodeus, whose body began getting yanked around like a ragdoll. More carmine fluids mixed in with the purplish ooze of what had once been muscles and organs. By the time Catherine had finished unloading her shots, the demon looked like swiss cheese.

Asmodeus looked at the holes in his body, and then fell backwards onto the rubble and blood-strewn floor.

"Ouch…"

Recognizing this as their chance to escape, Christian grabbed Lilith's hand and took off toward the door. "Come on! Let's get out of here before he awakens!"

"Awakens?" Catherine looked wide-eyed at Christian, only to realize that he was no longer paying attention to her and was moving farther away at a rapid pace. She ran to catch up. "Wait! Christian! Dammit! What do you mean awaken? Are you telling me that didn't kill him?"

"Of course not!" Christian shouted back, his hand tightening on Lilith's, helping her keep pace even as she stumbled. "Don't you remember what I told you? The only way to kill that thing is to find its weak point!"

The door that led outside the station was in front of them. Christian did not stop running as he pulled Gabriel from its holster and reloaded it before firing twice. The bullets struck the door handle and the area around it, destroying the locking mechanism inside. With the lock gone, the door slowly opened.

Christian slammed into it with his shoulder, a loud *bang!* going off as the door was busted off its hinges. He didn't let it slow him down as he half-dragged Lilith along behind him. The blonde woman was keeping up as best she could, but her fear and lack of athletic ability was hindering her.

"But couldn't I have hit his weak point?" Catherine and Christian were running side by side now. Their feet thundered against the pavement. Catherine's car was just a few feet from them. Just a little further now. Just a little further.

A loud explosion, not the kind that came from a bomb or high-yield explosive, but from a powerful physical mass reducing another physical mass into rubble, echoed behind them. Christian turned his head, just in time to see Asmodeus standing in what had at one point been a wall.

The wall was no longer there.

And Asmodeus no longer looked like the man they remembered.

His body, now ash gray and with several hundred cracks spreading across it like a spiderweb, no longer resembled a human. His upper body was human enough, with a human-shaped torso and a humanish shaped head. He was bald, had no ears, and arrayed around his head like a crown were nearly a dozen horns. While his torso and head looked somewhat like those of a homo-sapien, the rest of his body did not. Large, bony protrusions jutted out of his elbows. His hands were only possessing of three fingers, all of which were reminiscent of talons. His legs were like the hind-legs of a goat, and his feet had more hoof-like characteristics, though they were also clawed. Behind his body, flickering in and out of their vision was a long, spaded, tri-tipped tail.

Catherine, in her shock at seeing something so obviously inhuman, almost stopped, but a shout from Christian kept her moving toward the car.

"Don't stop! Not even for a second!" He spun, tossing Lilith into the other woman. They both stumbled, but managed to remain upright thanks to Catherine's physically fit body and quick reactions. "Take her and get in the car!"

"Christian?" Lilith said in shock.

"What about you?" asked Catherine.

"I'll be right behind you two! Move!"

Not wasting a second, Christian spun around again. Gabriel and Phanuel were in his hands and fully loaded minus the two bullets he'd used before. He unloaded both clips into the demon, however, there was little to no effect. Asmodeus didn't even move. He just let the bullets ping off his skin, not even penetrating the hard, outer shell anymore.

"Hahaha! You're gonna hafta to do better than that, Former Executioner!" Asmodeus cackled.

Christian gritted his teeth as he reloaded his guns and unloaded another salvo into the demonic entity. Behind him, Catherine had just shoved a struggling Lilith into the car, shut and locked the door on her side, and then got in as well. Seeing this, Christian holstered Phanuel and pulled a small flashbang from his pocket. It was a good thing he always kept one of these on hand now.

Without waiting for any kind of signal, he chucked the grenade right at Asmodeus. The fierce-looking demon snorted when he saw the tiny cylinder hurtle his way. Swatting at it with contempt, he was unprepared for the flash of light that exploded into existence almost right in his face.

Seeing his work done and not wanting to get left behind, Christian jumped into the car on the other side just as Catherine hit the gas and sped out of the police station, the alarms and sirens blaring.

"Christian!" Lilith cried out in alarm when the young man slumped against the seat. "Are you alright?"

"Yes." Christian leaned his head back, letting Lilith look over him like a concerned spouse. "Just feeling a little down, I guess. I can't believe we're facing Asmodeus. This entire situation just got a thousand times worse."

"You don't say," Catherine's voice was dry, but the worry she felt rang clear in her tone. She was nervous. Anxiety was written on her face clear as day, from the way her eyes flickered to the rearview mirror, as if expecting Asmodeus to appear at any second. She gripped the steering wheel hard enough that all the blood had rushed out of her fingers, turning her normally pale hands ghostly white.

They moved down the street at a blistering pace, never stopping for anything be it traffic or pedestrians. Most people were smart to get out of the way, but a few, those who were petrified by the sight and unable to move, Catherine swerved around with reckless abandon. Street lights, cars, people, and buildings all passed them by in a blur of light and color.

"What do we do now, Christian?" Catherine asked, her voice hard. Christian, hearing what amounted to a command in her voice—and reminding him of a certain blonde-haired Executioner commander—tried to think of what their next course of action should be.

He came up blank.

"I-I don't know," Christian admitted. He rubbed at his face with both hands. They were shaking, he realized. Jitters of fear. He was frightened. Him, Christian, a member of the XIII and the one who had fought Abaddon the Destroyer in one-on-one combat and came out on top, was scared.

A deep sense of disgust worked its way into the pit of his stomach. He should not be feeling this way. He couldn't afford to feel fear. When people were afraid, they made mistakes, they let their fear cloud their judgment. It could, if given the opportunity, consume their every waking thought. Fear was man's greatest enemy. How could he even fight against something when he was too afraid to do anything?

"C-Christian?"

Lilith's voice. Christian looked up, staring into Lilith's eyes, which had gone wide. Her mouth was open, pink lips parted in a tiny "o" that made her look rather fetching. The look was somewhat marred, however, by the emotion in her eyes. Shock. Concern. Uncertainty. Fear. Emotions too many to name, all rolled up inside and boiling just beneath her irises.

"Are… are you okay?" she asked, her voice halting, hesitant. She was afraid.

"I…"

Christian could feel something unraveling inside of him. He felt like he was drowning, submerged in a sea of despair and hopelessness. There was no way they could fight that demon and expect to win. This was not some minor vampire or werewolf. Even No Life King's and demons on the threat level of Abaddon were nothing compared to this monster. How could they fight something that couldn't die? How could they hope to win if they didn't even know its weakness?

"I can't…"

Why was everything getting so unfocused? His vision, he couldn't see. Images were blurring together, an amalgamation of shapes and colors bending and writhing to an unnatural and haunting melody which he could not hear. His ears were ringing, loud, obnoxious sounds that blared inside of his mind, bouncing around his skull with increasing volume and frequency.

Was this the end? Dying ignobly against a demon whose very presence caused him such fear? Christian wasn't sure that he cared much if he died, but would that be enough to repent for his sins? What about Lilith? She didn't deserve to die, but how could he protect her from a monster that was capable of razing countries to the ground?

In that moment, Christian felt small, an infinitesimal speck whose purpose in life meant less than nothing. His life had no meaning. It didn't matter if he died here. Would it change anything? Of course it wouldn't.

The world would still move when he was gone. Life would continue, and no one but a select few would ever know of his passing.

He closed his eyes and gnashed his teeth. Behind his eyelids he could see it, that grinning visage, a mask of lust containing in it the desire to bathe in the blood of the pure. Those crown-like horns, spiking around that balding head, sharp and pointed. They were probably sharp enough to kill a man. And those eyes. Christian's head spun as those eyes penetrated his mind, invasive and overwhelming, glowing an unholy crimson. They were looking at him! God, they were looking at him! Why!? Why!? Why!? Why!? Wh—

"It'll be okay," a voice said.

Christian blinked. His mind snapped back to reality. He realized that his head was resting against someone's chest. Lilith. She was cradling his head to her bosom, her hands stroking his hair in a gentle and loving fashion. Her heart was beating steadily in her chest, the soothing rhythm somehow making his body relax and his mind grow calm. She planted a kiss on the crown of his head, and an unusual, incredible warmth spread from the spot where her lips touched to the rest of his body, encompassing him in a warm glow.

He looked up at her. Lilith's face was strangely placid, calm even. How could she be so calm? They were about to die. There was no way that two humans and a succubus could take on one of Hell's kings.

"Lilith?"

"Everything will be alright," she said, and somehow, Christian could not help but believe her. "I have faith in you, in us. We have too much to live for to die here," she smiled at him, "right?"

"Right." Christian returned the smile. "Thank you."

"Anytime."

"I really hate to break this touching scene up," Catherine interrupted, shouting at them. "But we've got company!"

At that exact moment, a shadow fell over them. Two heads looked out the window and up to see Asmodeus flying above them, in broad daylight. He had no wings, but that hardly seemed to hamper the immortal being's flight capabilities.

Didn't this demon have any common sense? There were thousands of people moving down this road! What was—

"Christian," Lilith stole his attention again, "what's wrong with everyone? Why aren't they panicking?"

Christian looked out the window as they continued driving. Lilith was right. No one was running away, no one was screaming, no one looked like they even knew what was happening right next to them. The only thing people were reacting to was the car they were in, which flew down the road fast enough to leave everyone wide-eyed.

Comprehension smacked him between the eyes.

"It looks like they might be trapped within an illusion. Asmodeus probably put this up in haste. Otherwise he would have created a parallel dimension and used it to separate us from the rest of the world. No one can see Asmodeus but us."

"That's all well and good to know," Catherine shouted, "but it doesn't help us."

"I know that!" Christian snapped. "And I'm trying to come up with something! This isn't easy, you know? I've never fought against one of the Seven Kings of Hell, so just give me a second!"

"We don't have a second! He's gaining on us!"

A glance outside revealed the truth in Catherine's words. Asmodeus was descending toward the car at a rapid pace. He would be on them in seconds.

Gritting his teeth, Christian reloaded his guns again. He didn't know why he was doing this. Regular bullets were useless. But then, what other choice did he have?

"I'll see what I can do. Just try and get him off our tail!"

"What do you think I've been trying to do?!"

Christian ignored Catherine's snark and kicked out the back window. The piece of thick glass went flying, hitting the street and cracking, chips flicking off.

With the way now clear, Christian took aim with his guns. Asmodeus was almost on top of them. Ten meters. A pair of eyes, one green and the other red, narrowed as they stared down barrels of gleaming silver and obsidian. Five meters. Slow, calming breaths did an admirable job of clearing the mind, at least insomuch as was possible in the given circumstances. One meter. His lips peeling back, Christian took careful aim, and then pulled both triggers.

A single bullet ejected from each gun, soaring through the air at high speeds. Asmodeus didn't even try swerving out of the way. It was doubtful he could, but even so, why should he? Normal bullets had no effect on him.

Those were probably his thoughts until the two small metal projectiles hit his eyes, penetrating the thin flesh of his eyeballs and breaking through the cornea, anterior chamber, iris, and the lens. Asmodeus yowled, his hands clawing at his now bleeding eyes, his body swerving in his flight.

Distracted and unable to control where he was going, Asmodeus smacked right into a moving semi-truck in the other lane. The truck's entire hood crumpled in on itself before, with startling suddenness, the engine ignited and the entire vehicle flared up in a massive explosion.

The truck must have been carrying something that was highly volatile. The explosive blast was far more powerful than what it should have been. The shockwave blew away everything near it, pedestrians, lamp posts, and cars were tossed aside with the force of a wrathful god. Even Catherine's car, which was several dozen yards away, was sent skidding off course and out of control.

Reacting on instinct and the desire to protect Lilith, Christian grabbed the screaming young woman and curled his body around her. The car twisted sideways, then flipped over and rolled along the street. Neither of them was wearing a seatbelt so the two were forced to endure having themselves thrown about the back of the car. Christian's shoulder slammed into the metal bars separating the back from the front, and a searing pain coursing through his body like fire let him know that his shoulder had been dislocated.

Newton's First Law of Motion claims that when viewed an inertial reference frame, an object either remains at rest or continues to move at a constant velocity, unless acted upon by an outside force.

The LVPD cruiser that Catherine, Christian, and Lilith were in continued following Newton's first law, rolling and tumbling along the ground, until it was struck by an outside force large enough to halt its motion: a large brick wall. The momentum at which the car moved combined with its weight and the speed it struck the wall at caused its entire right side to crumple inwards. Christian heard a loud, sharp cry from Lilith, and then everything came to a halt as his world went black.

Chapter 27

Sobs. That was the first thing Christian heard as he came to. Someone was crying. They sounded familiar, but for some reason, he just couldn't recall where he remembered hearing that voice.

Pain came next. His body ached in ways he'd never thought possible, and considering he'd nearly died several times in his life, that was saying something.

Something wet dripped onto his forehead. It smelled acrid and rank. Gasoline, or what he assumed was gasoline.

Opening his eyes, Christian stared at the floor and seat of a car. He needed a moment to realize what this meant. He was lying on the roof of Catherine's police car, which meant the car must have tipped upside down.

Another sob reached his ears. He turned toward the source. There was a beautiful young woman with blonde hair and blue eyes that were rimmed with red and had tears staining her cheeks. He recognized her. Lilith. Her face was set in a pained grimace. He soon saw why. Her left leg was bent at an awkward angle, in a way that no human leg was meant to go. It was also stuck between the front seat and the crushed side of the car.

"Lilith," Christian's voice came out as a low, pained groan. His head was throbbing something fierce. There was a dull ringing in his ears, causing the throb to increase with each passing second.

"Christian," Lilith managed to get out through her sobs. "It hurts."

"It'll be okay," he tried to reassure her. "I'm going to get you free. Just… just hold on for a second."

Christian did his best to maneuver himself until he was pointing toward Lilith feet-first. It was difficult, to be sure. The car was much smaller now that half of it was crushed, but he managed, planting his feet on the ceiling as he stood hunched over next to her.

Unsheathing Raphael, which was miraculously still strapped to his back along with Michael, Christian cut through both the chair and mangled metal that was keeping Lilith pinned. When she was free, he sheathed his sword and held out his hands. Lilith took them, allowing him to pull/drag her to him. As soon as she was close, he wrapped an arm around her, keeping her near.

"We need to get out of here," he told her. "I need to check your injury. It looks bad."

Lilith nodded, not saying anything. Deciding not to waste anymore time with words, as they weren't needed, Christian started to drag both of them out of the car.

The task was tough, made all the tougher by his own wounds. Cuts littered his body from where shattered glass had bit into him. There was a particular large shard impaling his right thigh. He didn't think it had hit an artery, but it was bleeding a lot, staining his pants and making it hard to concentrate.

They were able to get outside by crawling through the window. Christian had to sweep aside several sharp glass fragments that had managed to stay stuck to the window, lest they be cut further, but after that, the two of them were out in the open. Christian set Lilith on the blacktop and knelt down.

"Let me see your leg," Christian said, pulling the glass shard out of his leg with a grunt. Blood spurted from the wound, but he ignored it in favor of his companion. Lilith sat up, hands holding onto the leg, her teeth grit as she tried to keep from whimpering in pain. Christian looked it over, not touching it. "How much does it hurt?"

"A lot," Lilith answered, the words whistling through her clenched teeth. "It hurts so much, Christian…"

"Your knee is broken." Christian carefully placed a hand over it, just barely touching the bent knee. It was swollen now, swollen and red, looking almost like a balloon. Lilith hissed when his hand ghosted over it. "I imagine the knee cap might actually be shattered. We're going to have to get you to a hospital soon."

"I thought… we couldn't… go to… a hospital," she rasped, the pain beginning to get to her. The adrenaline running through her system was likely gone now, spent, and with it, all of the previously dulled pain she felt was being magnified.

"We don't have much choice." He shook his head. "This isn't something that will heal with time unless we get it properly set. I'm sure Catherine can vouch for us and ensure our safety."

"Catherine… where… where is she?"

Eyes widening, Christian scampered over to the car again. He looked in the front. Catherine wasn't there. Almost ready to panic, he looked around to see if he could spot her, finding her eventually when he looked in front of the car. She was several feet away, lying on her side. Christian hurried over to her.

"Catherine?" he asked, getting no response. "Catherine!" Still no response. He placed a hand on her shoulder and moved her until she was lying on her back.

A wince came to him when he saw the damage that had been done to her. Sharp lacerations from glass shards littered much of her body, including her face, arms, legs, and chest. She was breathing, which was good, but she wasn't responding to any outside stimuli, not even when he shook her and shouted her name.

Christian tried to pick her up, so that he could carry her over to Lilith. He tried, but he couldn't. He could lift her in his arms, but his leg couldn't support both her weight and his. The only thing he could do was grab her by the arms and drag her toward Lilith, and even then, the act exhausted him.

He lay Catherine down next to Lilith, then dropped onto his bottom. Sucking in deep gulps of air, Christian used this moment to catch his breath.

Lilith's pained whimpers grew louder.

"It really hurts, doesn't it?" asked Christian, turning to face her. Lilith seemed to have run out of tears, but her teeth were still clenched, and her face was grimacing in an expression of agony.

Lilith nodded.

"Is there anything I can do?"

There really wasn't. Christian wasn't a doctor, nor did he have any experience with healing other than basic first aid. That would not help them here. But, still, he couldn't leave her like that. He wanted—no, he *needed* to do something to help ease her pain.

"K… kiss…" she spoke through her rasping pants. "Kiss… me…"

Christian blinked in confusion. Out of all the things she could have asked of him, he hadn't expected this one. He probably should have, but he didn't think she would be asking for a kiss while they were in such a precarious and potentially lethal situation.

He still wasn't going to deny her.

Crawling over to her, Christian leaned in and pressed his lips to hers. Something seemed to happen during the kiss. As far as locking lips went, this one didn't start off any different than usual. It was merely a pressing of the lips. But, after a moment had passed and Lilith had tilted her head to grant him better access to her mouth, something unusual happened.

The first sign of this change was from within Christian. He could feel something; he didn't know what, but it was almost like there was a second presence located in the center of his chest. This spectral existence was familiar, though he didn't recognize it. With the unusual presence came a sense of companionship, of love and lust, of faithfulness and devotion, of an undying flame, passion, and warmth that spread throughout his body and set him on fire. Yet the fire did not burn him, merely warmed him up, numbing the pain that he was in.

The second sign came from Lilith. For someone who was suffering a serious injury that, if not treated, could result in the leg needing to be amputated at the calf, she was getting way too into it. Her mouth was open wide, her small tongue pushing and pulling against his. Saliva was dripping down her chin and she was completely heedless of that fact.

By the time the kiss had ended, both of them looked confused as they realized something. Lilith was still sitting down, but her leg was now looking a bit better. It wasn't as swollen. The redness that had pervaded the skin was mostly gone. The leg was also no longer bent at an impossible angle. Now it just looked like a regular fracture.

Christian was straddling Lilith's thighs. That was a little strange, as he did not remember moving, but what was stranger were that his own injuries felt a little better. He was still bleeding, but it was not as bad as before. The many dozens of cuts still littered his arms, legs, back, and chest, but they were smaller now, as if they had healed.

"Christian?" Lilith said, her voice not bothering to mask her wonder. "What is this? What's going on?"

"Let's… let's not think about this right now," Christian said, shaking his head. Too much was happening at the moment, and there was too much they needed to do. Piling this new mystery on top of everything else wasn't something they could afford. "Let's just focus on the task at hand. We need to get out of here. You still need to go to a hospital, and Catherine does, too. We should probably call for an ambulance."

"Do you even still have your phone?" asked Lilith, causing Christian to search his pockets. He found the phone, but he wouldn't be able to use it. It was broken, smashed beyond repair, its circuitry sticking out of its body like guts on a zombie.

"Maybe Catherine will have her phone," he offered.

"Maybe." Lilith sounded skeptical. He didn't blame her.

Before he could begin crawling over to Catherine, the conflagration that was the semi-truck exploded with energy. Potent and powerful, a large maelstrom of vile red energy detonated with more power than even the original blast had. The fire was dispersed with a violent gust of wind that was strong enough to knock anybody still in the area off their feet. Not sure what else to do, Christian hunkered down over Lilith while grabbing onto Catherine to keep her from being blown away.

When the hurricane-like winds died down, Christian looked up to see what had caused such a wild unleashing of energy.

What he saw made his eyes widen in horror.

"That was a good shot, boy," Asmodeus said as he stood in the center of the writhing flames. For once, he was not grinning. His eyes were healed, but there was blood dripping down his face. **"It seems I really did underestimate you. It won't happen again."**

Chapter 28

Asmodeus stood before a horrified Christian and Lilith in all his glory. His hairless body was as pristine as ever. There wasn't a scratch to be found. Even his eyes had healed completely and now looked the same dusky crimson that Christian remembered.

So much for that being his weak point.

"You're quite the little fighter, boy," he said, his voice an ugly and deep snarl that oozed with dark intentions. His tongue clicked as he talked, as if the language of humans was foreign to his palate. **"I can see now why that old bishop said I should proceed with caution when I fight you. You truly do deserve that title your companions gifted you, and I understand why Abaddon lost."**

Old Bishop? Was this demon talking about Vertrou? But how did he know that man? Were they…? But no. That couldn't be. Bishop Vertrou was a greedy man without an ounce of compassion, but he was still a man of God.

Wasn't he?

"No more games, child." Asmodeus narrowed his eyes, his brow-less eye ridges furrowing. **"You've given me enough trouble. I'm going to make you suffer."** His eyes turned toward Lilith, who became petrified under his gaze. **"I think killing her in front of you will suffice as punishment."**

"Like hell you will!" Christian snarled.

Feeling a strength that he didn't have before, he stood up and unsheathed his swords. Normal bullets didn't work so his guns were out of the question. That meant swords were all he could use here. Would they be enough to injure this fiend? They were made of Orichalcum, true, but he'd never used them against a demon of this caliber. Could they cut through that thick hide?

He supposed there was only one way to find out.

"Christian?" a voice said.

Looking behind him, Christian found Lilith staring at him with an uncomprehending gaze. He offered her a smile.

"I won't let him touch you."

After a second of looking at him, she smiled in return.

"I know."

"Ugh." Asmodeus grimaced. **"Would you cut that out? All this love floating in the air is killing my mood."**

Ridding himself of all hesitation, Christian marched forward, sweaty locks of raven hair slapping against his face. He moved several yards away from Lilith, still in front of her, protecting her from the monster's gaze, but far enough that any backlash from the coming battle would not do her harm.

"Why don't you come over here and make me stop?" Christian said, his eyes narrowed and his lips peeled back to reveal pearly-white teeth.

Asmodeus glared at him. Sharp teeth like razors bared themselves in a monstrous snarl. Malevolence irradiated from the inhuman entity, manifesting itself as a thick, dark red haze that covered the demon's body, wreathing it in ethereal flames. A hissing sound, sibilant and deadly, materialized in Christian's ears. It was the ground, he realized. The pavement was being burned away, melting into a viscous ooze that pooled about the thing's claw-hoofed feet.

A stare-off, like something from a classical western gunfight, lasted for several seconds that seemed to stretch on endlessly. Asmodeus shifted his feet in preparation to charge. Christian changed his stance into his *Fake Opening Style*, arms held loosely at his sides, knees slightly bent, his guard full of holes.

The battle did not begin with a mutual agreement between two opposing forces. This wasn't a cartoon in which a cool breeze would pick up, blowing leaves between the two heated enemies and kickstarting their battle. Things like fair play and equal opportunity never happened in real battles, where one's life was on the line.

Instead, the fight started when Asmodeus kicked a glob of molten cement at Christian's head. The red-hot globule sphere of searing liquid cement moved fast, speeding toward him at a pace that no human should have been able to follow.

It missed.

Moving like he had predicted the attack, Christian rolled forward. He ignored the burning in his shoulder as he hit the road, continuing forward until he leapt back to his feet. By the time he came up, Asmodeus had already closed the distance between them. The powerful demon king's three claw-like fingers shot forward, aimed at the opening that Christian presented to him.

It missed.

Raphael came in and intercepted the attack. A loud *clang!* rang out as blade met claw. A shockwave was unleashed from the two weapons meeting. Asmodeus was unaffected, but Christian was. He stumbled to the left, but quickly turned that stumble into a roll as his demonic foe tried to take advantage of another opening, this time at his back.

It was blocked.

Bringing Michael up to his back, Christian allowed the claw to strike the flat of the blade. The force of the demon's thrust pushed Christian forward. He moved with the momentum rather than against it, rolling along the ground. As he came up to his feet, he swung Raphael in an arcing slash that struck Asmodeus's left leg.

Nothing happened. No cut. No damage. Just a loud screech as if the appendage was made of mithril.

Another claw came in to rip Christian's face off, but he moved again, leaping several yards back. Asmodeus laughed as he charged forward, his claw-hoofed feet gouging out chunks of pavement. Christian judged the time it would take Asmodeus to reach him, and then reacted faster than the speed of thought.

Asmodeus's claws came in to rip out Christian's throat, but by that point in time, he was already ducking. The attack missed entirely, as did the brutal gust of cutting winds that came after.

Following his evasive maneuver, Christian moved into a shoulder roll that took him underneath the demon's legs. He came up behind Asmodeus before thrusting Raphael forward to impale the demon through the back. The attack bounced off, causing Christian to curse as he threw himself backwards.

Asmodeus whirled about, his left arm sailing forward in a parabolic arc. Where the arm passed, an explosive blast of searing winds erupted from his palm. The wind missed Christian, who fell backwards into a roll, allowing the wind to pass over his head. After the damaging attack passed him by, he leapt back to his feet and charged forward, his arms at his sides, hands gripping his swords.

Rather than seem annoyed by his miss, Asmodeus was almost ecstatic. **"Yes! Yes! This is it! Fight! Struggle! Use all the power you have to try and survive! It'll only make killing you all the sweeter! Yes! Yes! Yes!"**

Propelling himself forward with enough kinetic energy that the ground exploded beneath his feet, the ancient and immortal being reached Christian in record-breaking time, beginning a coordinated assault that took him by surprise.

Claws and arms blurred, and Christian found himself on the defensive. He fell back, shuffling along the ground with a fleet-footed swiftness that just barely allowed him to keep ahead of his enemy. His blades were held at angles, not outright blocking the blows that attacked his many openings, but instead letting them glide off the blades to pass harmlessly around him. It worked, if barely. The power of each strike packed an incredible punch. While Christian managed to minimize the damage, he was still sent stumbling every time a clawed hand came his way.

Asmodeus smashed into Raphael as Christian held it at a forty-five degree tilt. While the diamond-hard appendage slid off the blade, a large burst of power erupted from the hand, sending a burst of hot winds that caused Christian to nearly fall onto his backside.

Another attack came in, from the left this time. Michael was there to intercept it, the blade angled down instead of up as Christian raised it over his head. It took Asmodeus's fist, and the angle it was held at caused the hand to grind off the blade with a screech. The kinetic force of the attack still sent Christian sprawling, but he avoided the blast of cutting winds by falling to his right.

An explosion struck the ground, the searing winds slamming into the road with monstrous force. Black chunks of pavement were lifted into the air and hurled in all directions as if they had been swept up in a great gale. Christian gritted his teeth as he wove between the fragments, splitting in half those he could not dodge. Several cuts opened on his skin as smaller rocks struck him, stinging and distracting him.

All the while Asmodeus was groaning in delirium. **"Yes! Oh, yes! This is so good! Keep it up! More! Give me more!"**

Christian cringed. This demon was actually taking sexual pleasure from their battle. In all his years serving as an Executioner, he'd never seen something so strange, so disturbing.

"Come on, boy! Keep fighting! Keep struggling! Oh! Oh, fuck yes! That's it! That's it!"

Teeth clenched in fierce determination, Christian continued to cross blades with the King of Hell. He moved more swiftly than he had ever moved before. He pushed his muscles harder than he ever thought possible. His mind raced as he was inundated with information from all of his sensory perceptions, allowing him to predict which opening his enemy would strike at next.

A swift, thrusting claw aimed at the opening in his left torso was avoided when Raphael intercepted the strike and let it glide off the blade's edge in a hiss of sparks. Christian spun around, flowing with the leftover power from the attack, moving left. He lashed out with Michael, aiming at Asmodeus's eyes, the only part of him that he knew could be penetrated.

And Asmodeus knew it, too, for his left arm came up. There was a loud clang followed by a shriek as Orichalcum met the impenetrable hide of a forearm that was four times thicker than Christian's wrist. The blade bounced off. Christian stumbled, but he turned his stagger into a backwards roll. This decision allowed him to avoid Asmodeus's followup, a swift and brutal heel stomp that left a large crater in the road. As dust kicked up and debris flew in all directions from the vicious attack, Christian, back on his feet, slid into his stance with ease of practice.

Flying out of the dust was the raging Asmodeus, his loud shouts of ecstasy and lust accompanied by a deranged, slasher's smile. He closed the distance in less time than it took to say "hell" and unleashed a brutal series of claw swipes and thrusts. Christian dodged most of them, and when he couldn't dodge them, he let his two swords negate the damage with carefully aimed parries and used the residual buildup of kinetic energy to lash out with his own attacks. They didn't do anything, merely bounced off Asmodeus's skin, but it was better than just dodging and waiting for himself to slip.

"Yes, yes, yes, yes, yes! Fucking hell yes!"

As the battle raged on, something became clear to Christian. Asmodeus was playing with him. His blows were swift and powerful, but not as powerful as he would have expected from a King of Hell, even one forced into a human body. What's more, the ancient demon wasn't even breathing heavily, or he was, but it wasn't from exertion.

Christian tried to keep from grimacing as Asmodeus licked his lips. It was a sensual move, one overflowing with lustful urges and salacious intentions. It was also disgusting. Christian could feel his stomach rebelling as he was struck with just how turned on this demon was getting from the battle.

Dodging another series of blows, Christian tucked himself into yet another shoulder roll, and then he was moving past the demon. He leapt to his feet. He made several quick steps, and then twirled around, about facing as Asmodeus charged him. His adversary's monstrous visage was a rictus of snarling teeth as he raised his left hand and tried to swat Christian away.

Christian backpedaled. The hand blew past him with the sounds of rushing wind. For a second, he thought he'd managed to avoid the blow. That second soon passed and Christian's eyes widened when a devastatingly powerful gust of cutting winds smacked into him with enough strength to send him hurtling backwards like a bullet train as it sped along the tracks. Dozens of tiny cuts and nicks appeared all over his skin, tearing his clothes to shreds.

He heard shouting, but he didn't know who it was coming from. It could have been him. It could have even been the rushing wind howling in his ears like a thousand tormented souls.

His back soon hit the ground. What little was left of his shirt was ripped off his flesh, leaving his skin to take the brunt of the damage as he skidded along the rough pavement. Searing pain lanced up his back, biting and stinging as the road tore away several layers of skin.

He tumbled to a halt several yards from where he had been previously, now lying on his back. Something thick and wet spread out underneath him, clinging to his body. Blood, most likely. His back was burning and his aching spine made him wonder if a horde of angry trolls hadn't stampeded over him.

Footsteps echoed along the road, getting closer. Christian struggled to get up. He moved, slowly, pushing himself up, his triceps straining, blood running down his arms, his back groaning in protest. He gnashed his teeth together, moving, pushing, fighting to get up.

Asmodeus was walking toward him with a slow, steady gait, unrushed and unhurried. The powerful demon looked like he was taking a simple stroll. That confident walk, which bordered on arrogance, that deranged grin containing a lust for blood, death, and violence, hidden behind a veil of cocky self-assurance, it really pissed him off.

"You have done surprisingly well for yourself, but it's all over now," Asmodeus gloated. It was something all demons did. If there was one thing Christian knew about demons in general, it was that every single one of them was incredibly arrogant. He'd never met a demon who didn't like to lord their superiority over him when they thought they'd won. It was how he'd beaten Abaddon. **"Do you see now, the difference in our power? You, a mere human, cannot hope to stand against a superior being like myself. Now, be a good boy and sit there while I slowly peel your skin from your bones and savor your screams of agony as I devour you one strip of flesh at a time."**

Christian wrinkled his nose in disgust as the demon began to pant. All this talk of ripping and eating flesh was turning it on. Well, Asmodeus was the demon of lust, so it would only make sense. It still creeped him out, though.

"This fight is not over." Christian wobbled a bit, but he regained his fighting stance. He refused to go down, not when dying meant Lilith would suffer. "Don't think you've won just because you got one good shot in."

"Ho? Still willing to fight me? How…" Asmodeus shivered, licking his lips with a strange sensuality that made Christian want to hurl, "… **delightful!"**

The battle began again, but this time there was a clear difference between the two. Asmodeus's strikes were coming in faster and they struck with more power, or maybe Christian was just getting weaker. There was only so much physical abuse the human body could withstand.

At some point, the body will reach its limit, and once that happens it will begin to wear out, to tire. Movements become slow. Strength ebbs and wanes, eventually disappearing as all the energy in the body is spent.

A harsh strike from a clawed hand sent Christian stumbling backwards as Raphael flew from his grasp. The sharp blade landed several feet away, point down in the road. The attack left Christian's entire left flank exposed, which Asmodeus took advantage of by plunging his hand forward. His movements were so fast that Christian didn't even have time to shout.

The world went white. There was a loud scream. Christian realized it was coming from him. Searing pain hit him next, a feeling of fire consuming his shoulder. Wetness leaked down his shoulder and arm, and Christian blinked several times as a strange numbness came over the limb. He looked down to see a hand shoved straight through his shoulder, ichor flowing freely from the wound.

"Christian!!!"

More screaming. Someone was calling his name, but he couldn't figure out who. All he knew was the pain in his shoulder. All he could feel was the searing heat as acid dripped in his veins. All he could hear was a loud ringing that pounded his ears and made his head throb.

He looked at the arm attached to the hand that was stabbing his shoulder. Thick and muscular, the wrist was nearly four times larger than his own. Veins bulged around the muscles, pulsing in time with the heartbeat that was pumping blood through them.

Asmodeus smiled at him, making Christian's skin crawl. He wondered if this feeling of violation was what Lilith felt every time a man looked at her. If so, he could understand why she disliked it so much. It was not pleasant.

A second later, agony ripped through Christian's chest as three sharp, deadly claws raked across his skin. Blood, thick and glistening crimson in the waning hours of the day, poured down his skin in copious amounts. Christian tried to struggle, but the grip on his shoulder was ironclad.

Blood splashed against the ground, viscous, wet raindrops that hit the road as another wound opened in Christian's torso. Despite biting his lip, Christian's mouth opened and a scream tore its way out of his throat.

"Christian!!"

"That's it! Scream for me! Scream! Scream! Scream! Let me hear that sweet melody!"

More and more wounds opened up on his skin. Each cut stung. Each cut made him shout in agony.

"Christian! Christian!" Lilith screamed.

"Hahahahaha! Oh, yeah! This is the feeling I'm looking for! So good! It's so good!"

Christian's vision began to blur. His mind and body were becoming numb. He could feel his strength ebbing away. Limbs of lead weighed him down. His body hung limply in Asmodeus's grasp, all the while the demon tearing his flesh apart laughed.

"Kyahahahaha! This is exactly what I want! Don't disappoint me now, boy!"

The world was turning, spinning faster and faster. Christian felt dizzy, sick. Why wouldn't everything stop gyrating? Christian's head lolled back, his eyes fluttering as darkness encroached upon him. His eyes slowly closed.

"CHRISTIAN!!"

"What the hell is this!?"

Pain shot through him like a lance as he was dropped onto his tailbone. His eyes shot wide open, a hiss escaping his lips.

He looked up, his blurry vision sharpening quickly. Asmodeus was standing before him, his figure towering over him like a monolithic statue. The demon struggled, lashing out and fighting against… nothing? Christian blinked, then looked harder. Asmodeus was struggling, his arms straining as he fought against nothing. There was nothing there. Christian tried to figure out what was happening, but as he continued to watch the demon fight against what seemed like invisible bindings, he kept drawing a blank.

As he continued to stare, his left eye began to sting. He felt something warm and wet trail down his cheek. He ignored that in favor of what his vision was showing him. He closed his green eye and focused on the demon with his red one.

Are those… vines?

Indeed, they were. Innumerable vines were sprouting from the ground, grabbing onto Asmodeus, wrapping around him, coiling like serpents. The demon would rip one off only for several more to take its place.

What is this?

There were a lot of strange things in this world, things that were unexplainable, that didn't make sense. Christian had long ago learned to accept that and not let it bother him. Even so, what he saw right then baffled him. He had no idea what was going on.

Christian focused harder. All color seemed to bleed away. Everything became monochrome, nothing more than shades of gray, except for one point, which burned a dark red. A small circle on Asmodeus near his lower abdominals. No, it was his back. It only looked like the spot was on his stomach because he was facing Christian, but somehow, Christian knew that the spot was actually on his back.

What was that? What was going on?

"T-this is…" An angry snarl escaped Asmodeus's lips as he turned around to glare at Lilith. Christian also looked. Lilith was kneeling, her hands pressed against the road, fingers splayed, shoulders heaving, and her blue eyes glowing with power. **"Y-you! Damn you, succubus! When I get out of this, I'm going to tear your heart out and use your corpse as my fucktoy! You hear me! When I get out of this, you're fucking dead!"**

Christian heard the words and gnashed his teeth together. Anger surged inside of him, a tidal wave of molten hot lava that burned everything away except for his desire to kill the thing in front of him.

Asmodeus turned around, stalking toward Lilith, taking one step at a time. Vines sprouted up everywhere to wrap around him. The demon's power surged. The vines would shrivel and burn, and then more would sprout and coil around him, holding the King of Hell back.

"He wants to kill her…"

This demon wanted to kill Lilith.

"Are you going to let him take her from you?"

"No," Christian's voice came out as a harsh whisper. He wouldn't let this monster take Lilith from him. Lilith was his!

"Then you know what you have to do, right? You have to kill him. End his life. Then he won't be able to take Lilith away from you."

That's right. If Asmodeus died, then he couldn't take Lilith. She would remain his.

"Kill him…"

His left eye burned as though it was being poked with a branding iron.

"Kill him."

More blood seeped from his eye and trailed down his face.

"Kill him!"

Surging to his feet, Christian grabbed Michael by the hilt and rushed forward. He charged across the space between him and the struggling Asmodeus, who was managing to walk toward Lilith against the strange vines that were binding him. Beyond the King of Hell, Lilith began to wilt. Her arms gave out, and she fell face-first onto the road. The vines that were wrapped around Asmodeus disappeared, and the demon let out a triumphant shout.

That shout, so filled with the surety of victory, soon turned into a harsh and grating scream of agony as Christian plunged Michael right into the tiny red dot he'd seen on the demon's back. The volume of the pain-filled yowling increased. Asmodeus glowed a bright, vibrant red. Cracks started appearing on his body, lighting up like molten lava inside of a volcano.

No warning came when the explosion was unleashed. One second, Asmodeus was screaming in outrage, pain, and fear. The next his body combusted, violently. All of the energy that had been stored inside of the human vessel was unleashed with more power behind it than a bomb going off.

Christian, who was standing right behind the demon as Asmodeus exploded, was thrown backwards, his body seared with so much pain that the world went black.

When he came to, he was lying on his back. He didn't feel any pain. He was sure that wasn't a good thing.

A woman was standing over him. He didn't know who she was, though she looked familiar. Olive skin. Dark brown hair and large eyes of the same color. Full lips and a straight nose that fit her face perfectly. He knew her from somewhere. Where did he know her from again? He couldn't remember… why?

He looked at the woman again, darkness flirting with his vision. He felt something grab at him. Several somethings. Hands. Soft, delicate, female hands. Who was touching him?

A moment of weightlessness came over him, except for where the hands were grabbing him. He was being lifted. The hands set him on something. It wasn't soft, but it was softer than the road. What was it? Why was his body beginning to sway?

The woman was still there. Her head bobbed up and down, or was that from the swaying? He couldn't tell. The dusk-filled sky soon turned to a dull, uniform gray. The swaying stopped, and he felt something hard against his back.

A sound next to him made Christian turn his head. He blinked as Lilith was set beside him. Her eyes were closed. Christian felt panic rise within him. Was she dead? Please don't let her be dead.

He tried to open his mouth, to say something, but no words came out. Why couldn't he speak?

"Do not worry," a voice said. Christian turned his head again, reluctantly, to see the olive-skinned woman. She was smiling at him, her expression tender and full of compassion. "You and your mate are safe now. The woman you two are with is also safe, as is the werewolf." Woman? What woman? Who was a werewolf? "Now, why don't you get some sleep?"

Christian opened his mouth to tell her that he was not going to sleep. How could he sleep when Lilith was lying next to him, possibly injured, or worse, dead? He couldn't sleep. Not now. He had to make sure she was alright.

A hand covered his eyes, and for some reason, he felt tired. The idea of going to sleep didn't sound so bad anymore. Yes. Maybe he should take a nap. Just a little one. Lilith wouldn't mind, surely.

His vision went dark and his mind became silent. Christian slept peacefully for the first time in days.

***

Samantha stood in front of Sebastian, a member of the Executioners' Science Division and someone who's sanity she questioned every time they spoke.

Rubbing her forehead, Samantha sent Sebastian an irritated glare. "Look, all I want to know is if you and the Science Division can create a device that can hack into any security network."

Pushing his glasses up the bridge of his nose, Sebastian replied, "and I'm telling you that's impossible. Unless you want something that explodes, I'm afraid we can't help you."

It was almost impossible to deal with the Science Division. They were insane at the best of times and monstrous at the worst of times. Out of all the divisions, they were the worst. There were more deaths in the Science Division than any other division in the Executioners, which was impressive since they never left the lab.

"I should have known talking to you wouldn't help me," Samantha grumbled.

Sebastian swept his blond hair away from his face. "Indeed, you should have."

"Oh, shut up."

Before Sebastian could respond, if he had such an intent, the entire laboratory shook. Samantha bent her knees to retain her balance, but few scientists had her reflexes. Many of them fell to the ground. Several of their experimental devices also tumbled to the ground.

Samantha winced as a number of loud explosions went off. A few of the scientists were next to the devices that exploded, and so they were consumed by flames. It was fortunate that they kept fire extinguishers around. Even as she watched, several scientists scrambled to their feet, grabbed an extinguisher, and put out the fire covering their comrades.

She shook her head. She didn't know what was worse: that several people had caught fire, or that she was so used to this she didn't even care anymore.

The loud blaring of a siren alerted her to more danger.

"What is going on?" demanded Samantha.

"I believe that is the intruder alarm," Sebastian said, once more pushing his glasses up his nose.

"I know what that is!" Samantha snapped. "I meant how is it possible that we have intruders?"

"I don't know." Sebastian's lab coat fluttered as he shrugged.

This man is useless.

Samantha would have groaned, but at that moment, several hundred magic circles appeared in mid-air. Each circle glowed a bright red. Inside of the circles was an arcane language that Samantha couldn't read. However, while she didn't know what the language said, she at least recognized it.

After all, Abbadon the Destroyer's body had been covered in writing just like it.

"These are demonic spells!" Samantha's eyes widened.

"This isn't good," Sebastian muttered.

Even as he spoke, the magic circles suddenly changed. The language disappeared as an image appeared within the circle, a scene of fire, lava, and several hundred demons. Samantha felt a sense of horror come over her as she realized what these magic circles were. Portals. They were portals that led to Hell, but how were there so many? Why were they appearing in their headquarters? The Executioners' headquarters was supposed to be protected against this kind of intrusion!

Regardless of how it was happening, it didn't change the fact that it *was* happening, and Samantha was not so rusty that she wouldn't respond to such a threat. She reached for the sword strapped to her waist and unsheathed it. Like Christian's twin blades and guns, this sword was made from Orichalcum. It would work well against demons. As several demonic monstrosities marched out from the portal, Samantha narrowed her eyes and prepared for battle.

It was going to be a long day.

Afterword

I actually meant to make this story more complete, but sadly, I found myself unable to do that. The reason is because this particular story extends far beyond what's acceptable in length for a single novel. I'm sorry for the disappointing ending and hope everyone who reads this can forgive me.

Onto more pleasant matters. The Executioner series, that is, Succubus and Escape, is my single yearly-published series. I publish this one yearly for a number of reasons. First: I currently have four major series that I am working on. A Most unlikely Hero, American Kitsune, Arcadia's Ignoble Knight, and this. You know, I just noticed that every series except this one begins with A. Weird, huh? Anyway, unlike my other stories, which are basically Americanized versions harem light novels that use anime tropes and fan service, this one is a western urban fantasy series. It's not a story that I'm used to doing. That means it takes longer for me to write, edit, and publish it. I want to do a good job.

The Executioner is a series that I began writing after reading The Dresden Files by Jim Butcher. I wanted to try my hands at an urban fantasy series. This was the end result.

I don't delude myself into thinking my story is even close to Jim Butcher's, but I hope you all found it entertaining.

There's not a whole lot to say in this afterword, so I'd like to give some thanks before leaving you all.

Thank you Mom, Dad, Chuck, and Donna for supporting me in my writing.

Thank you Amber and Tyler for trusting me to babysit my niece.

Thank you Dominique Goodall for editing this story.

Thank you Lawrence Mann for being an amazing illustrator and making my covers.

And thank you readers. I hope you enjoyed this story. Once again, please forgive me for leaving you on that cliffhanger. I'm rather ashamed of myself for that.

Have you been turned on to Brandon Varnell's light novels yet?
Wait. That sounded kind of wrong.

If you enjoyed this story, then be sure to check out American Kitsune... it's Brandon Varnell's debut light novel series.

Don't forget these other awsome light novels!

Arcadia's Ignoble Knight
Volumes 1-2

A Most Unlikely Hero
Volumes 1-2

Follow me at www.varnell-brandon.com!
Or:  @AmericanKitsune  @BrandonBVarnell

 Brandon Varnell  Brandon Varnell

 brandonbvarnell bvarnell1101.tumblr.com/